DOVE BOOKS

presents

absolute disaster
fiction from los angeles

edited by
Lee Montgomery

A Santa Monica Review Anthology

Copyright © 1996 by Santa Monica Review

Santa Monica College
1900 Pico Boulevard
Santa Monica, CA 90405

ISBN 0-7871-1052-3

Printed in The United States of America

Dove Books
8955 Beverly Blvd.
Los Angeles, CA 90048

Distributed by Penguin USA

Text Design by Wendy Knight and Bill Lancaster

First Printing: December, 1996

10   9   8   7   6   5   4   3   2   1

¹di•sas•tər\de'z│aste(r), │aas-, │ais-, │as *also* de's│; -'s- *is less frequent in "disastrous" than in "disaster", probably because three identical sounds (here, S-sounds) within as many syllables cause a stronger tendency to dissimilation than do two*\ *n -s often attrib* [MF & OIt; MF *desastre,* fr. OIt *disastro, fr.* dis- ¹dis (fr. L) + *astro* star, fr. L *astrum,* fr. Gk *astron*—more at STAR] **1** *obs* **a :** an unpropitious or baleful aspect of a planet or star **b :** PORTENT **:** malevolent influence of a heavenly body **2 a :** a sudden calamitous event producing great material damage, loss, and distress <a flood ~ > <a mine ~ > <such a war would be the final and supreme ~ to the world— Archibald MacLeish> **b :** a sudden or great misfortune **:** CALAMITY <the loss of his wife was the culminating ~ of the trip> c **:** a complete failure **:** FIASCO <only his skillful direction saved the play from being an unqualified ~>

Contents

Acknowledgments

Many people contributed to the making of this anthology. Very early on in the process there was the support of Dr. Piedad Robertson, Frank Jerome, Jim Krusoe, and Rocky Young at Santa Monica College and Michael Viner, Deborah Raffin, Doug Field, Chris Hemesath, and Mary Aarons at Dove Books. There is also art guru Brian Keenan of Clifford Selbert Design in Santa Monica who designed and created the cover of this book for dinner and a few lousy beers. Wendy Knight, Bill Lancaster, and Robin Clewell typeset the monster amidst myriad computer disasters. Carol Muske Dukes took on the task of the introduction twice because of a computer failure that ate the original. Carrie Osper read submissions and offered ideas. Jean Rains, Thomas Greenberg, Thomas Byrnes, Julia Seltz, Marielle Horton, Joshua Tompkins, and Julie Kleinman read and reread stories to avert typography disasters. And of course, there are the writers whose fine works grace these pages.

Introduction

You write your Manhattan story and you put in your taxis, your junkies, Kafka at Zabar's, Soho galleries, Shakespeare in the Park, drag queen ophelias, Broadway, clubs, heavy irony, the schmaltzy skyline. Then you try your L.A. story: Hollywood sign, freeways, the Marlborough man smirking death-like down on Sunset, contemplative smogs of sulfur dioxide and Paco Rabanne, daffy palms, studio turn-around, gangs, D-girls, no rain, no irony . . . but something's wrong. L.A. doesn't *hold still* the way New York does. L.A. is moving.

It's moving, of course, all the time, round-the-clock in cars on its lethally interconnected empire of freeways. It's moving in the sky, in helicopters, jets, Goodyear blimps bearing one-liners out over the basin. Its weather is moving, jumpy as context in video-cam reportage. As Joan Didion observed a while back, the weather of Los Angeles is not resort-like, it is *apocalyptic.* We have fires, floods, Med-fly plagues, tidal waves, strange low-pressure cells, fog, lost satellites and insistent UFOs. And don't forget, the earth is moving. Los Angeles is constantly inching, crawling, hauling itself toward the Outer Rim: a city with a colossal case of the *creeps.*

You might say all of these stories have the creeps. They glance back over their shoulders, in rear-view mirrors, hand-held compacts. We are so used to disasters here that we expect disaster, we write it into or stories like firey *backdrop* ("Appease the Natives" by Peter Craig) or Lawrence Thornton's unnerving operatic disaster, like Harlan Ellison's ghastly, contemporary Billy the Kid (William Bonney) cruising the freeway in his death-mobile, a blood-red diabolically-equipped Mercury GT. We are, in a sense, "pre-disastered," so that anything that happens to our characters, catastrophe-wise, has a distinct aura of deja vu, anti-climax, post-mortem. In regard to the latter, we have "Tongue" ("Love is a tricky business") by Jenny Cornuelle and Benjamin Weissman's "The Present": politely (or not so politely) toying with post-death (as in *dead*) loved ones, tales of necrophilia and necromancy or plain old stubborn refusal to acknowledge that final unappealable sentence.

Michelle Latiolais subverts (and "involutes") our sense of disaster by unraveling exposition, description—reducing it to an oddly vulnerable extreme in "legal" language—letting us take a long nearly-unwilling look at the subject, like freeway accident-gawkers. "Crying," a story by Jerry Renek, raises accident-gawking to a level of semi-dignity: a fascination with car crashes forms the primary bond in a relationship. Amy Gerstler revamps our sense of expectation, ("Minute by minute we conquer things and continue") as Jim Krusoe's character, a walking disaster, turns the tables on fate.

Some, as in Krusoe's story, thrive on disaster, some understand its random, ongoing appearance in Los Angeles better than others. In "All Along the Watchtower," a tale of gangs in South Central, Jervey Tervalon records the grim riffs on a once-innocuous lifestyle that random violence invites.

All those outdoor gatherings, something one would expect in Southern California, an afternoon with family and friends in one of the many neighborhood parks, became a big gamble.

We are moving fast here in L. A. and disaster moves with us, always just a step ahead or behind, in the car, in a park, at home, in the garden, in the hot tub (forgive me, where it is absolutely *obligatory* that disasters happen! I think Raymond Chandler would agree, the sybaritic invites Big Trouble, Nathaneal West would sure deep-six his least-invigorating characters in that hot chemical-blue water). Here, our characters envision Los Angeles' "arrow of time" (a term in physics) as reversed: we forget the future even as we move through it, heading forward into the past (now the future). An earthquake, for example, can call up memories of what will be—just as the brave and mercurial stories in this collection tell us that we are moving away from that sunny California-dream future that seemed (at one time) assured. We are moving into rupture, memory; we are remembering the worst of it even as we imagine it. We have our earthquake kits and our first-stage alert masks—we have this remarkable anthology as aesthetic First Aid—we are inching closer to that wild temporal edge, our hour come round at last.

As Carolyn See says in "Light Ages:"

> *There will be those who say it never happened, that we squeaked through. Believe them if you can.*

—Carol Muske Dukes
Los Angeles, 1996

DISASTERS IN LOVE

Hell's afloat in lovers' tears
—Dorothy Parker

SANDRA TSING LOH

Raiding The Larder

There is something about sweaty nineteen and twenty year-old men in gyms—playing basketball, volleyball, whatever.

Their torsos have just started to thicken into real man's torsos, formerly loose t-shirts tightening across barrel chests. They're having to figure out the facial hair situation. And yet, amid all these changes, their legs remain skinny and coltish, bowlegged sometimes, covered—incredibly—with fuzz, with big springy tennis shoes on the ends.

They can jump high and handle the ball, but they're a little awkward about changing directions quickly. They tend to crash into things—other men, nets, bleachers. They're healthy physical specimens, exploding with energy, but untamed, awkward, careening around, with an undependable sense of coordination. It's an age where they don't yet understand how to control their center of mass.

Laura, Joan and I, after our little regime of jogging, light weights and the obstacle course, used to stay around the Caltech gym on Saturdays to watch the men. In a way, it was embarrassing to be there. We were three women who should have moved on after college—moved to a different city at least, something. But nothing definite had ever gelled, and here we were with our weekends wide open.

On the weekends the gym and field were rife with undergraduates from the university—on the North field there was soccer, softball, and sometimes an ultimate frisbee game. Inside the gym, there was basketball and volleyball. A few random fencers would occasionally be flailing about in the corner, or maybe a pair of wrestlers, or the karate people. Out by the pool were the swimmers.

Laura had always liked swimmers. As an undergraduate here, she had done stats for the water polo team and that had given her easy access to them. A year after graduation, she married one. Although Paul was now an engineer at

Hughes, wearing extra-large shirts and struggling with a weight problem, he too had once been one of these young muscle-bound men who walked slowly and deliberately around the pool, regulating their breathing after a few quick laps, goggles pushed up, alabaster skin dripping in the sunlight, hair drying into little spikes, carelessly bulging Speedos.

We'd leave Laura alone in the afternoons, when she would sit by the pool and watch the swimmers for hours and hours.

Soccer and other land-oriented sports were more to Joan's taste. She used to play on a women's soccer team before her company transferred her to California, so she knew something about the game. There was one guy she always wanted to watch, a skinny European with exceptional ball-handling skills. Joan was always particularly partial to technique. With just one foot, he could keep the ball up in the air for hours. In addition, he had fantastic legs—there were sinews visible not only on the fronts but on the backs of his thighs, for which he earned exceedingly high marks, and his calves had all kinds of intriguing tendons in them.

Apparently, he had a t-shirt that said "Danish Dynamite" on it. That clinched it for Joan. It was too perfect. "Danish Dynamite," she would chuckle, lifting her eyebrows and giving me a knowing nod.

My post was inside the gym. I was more into indoor sports, volleyball especially. The one I always watched would be Number 29 (on the back of one of his shirts), who would be there every weekend, rain or shine. He was 6 feet, 2 inches, nineteen years old, with a mop of curly brown hair, a retainer, and was always crashing into the net.

He was clumsy, but there was a kind of intensity to him. Long after everyone quit, Number 29 would still be there, throwing the ball up into the air for himself, hitting it, chasing it, and then repeating the process from the other side of the court. He would do this, by himself, for twenty, thirty minutes. Toss, hit, sprint, toss, hit, sprint. The sweat would make his curly hair flatten against his head. His breath would come in gasps. His jaw would clench. His feet, the ball crashing against the ground, in a harsh, uneven rhythm.

And yet he would continue, his body twisting in agony. Toss, hit, sprint. Toss, hit, sprint. Toss, hit, sprint.

***

Active, aggressive seduction is not one of my natural talents. The charms I have to offer a man are of the solid, comfortable, non-threatening kind. What I am is a twenty-eight-year-old vaguely attractive English graduate student, marooned somewhere in the third year of my dissertation, maybe a 6 or 7 on a scale of O to 10 in terms of looks. Eight-minus on a particularly good day. My car, though it is an unwashed somewhat beat-up '79 Toyota Corolla, runs. As I said, there are various personal idiosyncracies, delights and surprises to me—slim ankles, a short period, a take-you-by-surprise off-beat sense of humor—but of course nothing that would hit a man in the face at first glance.

In short, I am not one of those rare women blessed with an immediately winning hand, one of those women who walk into a room, hair moussed to staggering proportions, and the men drop dead all around. I am of the persevering kind, of the school that availability and being a good listener will prevail.

On a purely statistical level, however, there was no reason for me, in what was theoretically the full sensual bloom of my womanhood, not to charge forth unchecked into the undergraduate dorms. Caltech had only recently converted from being an all-male institution, leaving a ratio of 7 to 1, men to women. Since it was a technical institute, most of the students were sciency and socially inexperienced. Meaning most of the freshmen and sophomores were yearning to be deflowered, if only for purposes of male initiation.

And here I was, an articulate, literate humanities major from another university, offering gourmet cooking, superior cultural tastes, Bill Blass sheets, patient and tireless oral sex. This would be too good to be true for some unwashed sophomore with Star Trek posters on his peeling dorm wall. Plus, I had plenty of free time on my hands. Plenty. As long as I kept a low profile (checking my box in the English office at five-thirty in the afternoon when everyone except the secretaries had gone home, holding office hours at times variant to those told the students, little things like that) USC would pay my stipend regardless of whether I turned in something this year or the next year or the next or the next or the next.

Ultimately, then, the Caltech campus could be looked at as a vast sexual smorgasboard. There were stories upon stories about it. You had only to walk onto the quad on a Friday afternoon, put your lunch tray down, and the young men would come running. Not all of them would be desirable of course—you'd have to weed out a few of the more depressing ones, the ones too much into Tolkien, the ones wearing capes and knickers in the eighty-eight degree heat—but most assuredly something decent would turn up.

Joan in her heyday had had a lot of success with undergraduates. Nothing lasted more than three months, but at least she had gotten them into her house, alone. It was possible. Basically, she had always used the direct approach: you hung around campus, discovered their habitual haunts—the gym, the coffeehouse, the bookstore—engaged them in conversation, let nature take over.

In addition, owning a car was an invaluable tool for an older woman running amuck on a college campus. "You would be surprised how many of them don't drive," Joan pointed out helpfully. One look at the bike rack in front of the gym seemed to corroborate this. And once they got into your car, even if it was only a lift to the grocery store, a kind of trust would ensue. They would begin to open up almost immediately.

I tried to imagine the kind of life a guy like Number 29 must be leading now, the kinds of things that would be on his mind. It had been six or seven years since my own grotesque undergraduate career. I tried vainly to recall what it had been like, what undergraduates thought about, the kinds of concerns they had. Dirty kitchenettes with the caked-on scrambled eggs of legions of freshmen was something intimately connected with the collegiate experience, I knew. You could not pick up a fork without something being stuck between the tines. It was as if no one had ever heard of hot water or steel wool. And who could forget those ugly couches studded with large suede buttons? Falling asleep in who knows whose beanbag chair to deafening Pink Floyd music, drool stuck to one side of one's face, was another thing about college.

And then, there were the parties, the infamous college parties. Caltech apparently had an enormous all-campus one every November, and I could well imagine what it was like. Apparently it was a sloppy public celebration where each student house had a theme and a band, there were kegs of beer everywhere, and alumni returned by the hordes to savage the area. Bizarre hats, obscene skits with life-size inflatable dolls figuring prominently in them, tire tracks gouged into lawns, and people's hands down the halter tops of their neighbors would be the norms here.

Would I feel at ease drinking cup after cup of rancid rum punch and falling all over complete strangers? Gyrating and pumping my arms to overloud, badly-mixed live rock bands that had clearly been hired at a discount? To go for broke, to say mad and suggestive things, to lose a shoe even?

★★★

As it turned out, I was to lose more than a shoe. Two weeks before Interhouse, I had an accident, for which I was eventually—after a struggle—awarded a cast. Coming off one of the low hurdles in the obstacle course one Saturday afternoon, I came down on my foot wrong. I lay in the grass for a moment, my eyes closed tightly.

Joan and Laura helped me hop back to the gym, and onto one of the cots in the training room. All I could think of was the low throb in my left foot. I leaned my head back against the wall, clenched my fists into balls, and asked myself, "Why, why, why? Why me?"

The trainer, a young short-haired woman, matter-of-factly removed my shoe and sock and began to feel around in the ankle area. She would press my toes back briefly and say, "Does that hurt?" When I shook my head no she would say, "Good." This went on and on. The expression on her face was calm, bored even. In five or ten minutes, it became depressingly clear that since no shards of bone were actually forcing their way out of my skin, like wreckage shorn from some Western European frigate, no one was going to call the paramedics.

I was awarded a bag of ice and a rather ancient-looking ace bandage to wrap around my leg in whatever style I wished. That was it. The trainer hurried off to some disaster on the soccer field. I was left with a lone football player with a large, beefy white chest, who looked out glazed-eyed from his perch in the small, steel-walled whirlpool bath in the corner.

My mood was further soured by Joan, who eventually rejoined me in the training room after jogging around the field once or twice. Though appropriately sympathetic and indignant about the ankle, her refusal to accompany me to infamous annual Interhouse was absolute.

"I'm thirty years old," she said flatly, looking away, as if it was hopeless, as if the concept was beyond me. "I have to move on. You know what I mean?"

I was shocked. This approach to the issue was completely unexpected. Usually, all it took was one person's momentum and we were off, off to the gym, off to 2-for-1 night in the disgusting yet pheromone-filled back courtyard at Burger Continental, off to seek out attractive, available men who were yet from Caltech and therefore guaranteed safe, intelligent, career-oriented just like us and somehow a better bet than other strangers off the street.

"Move on? Move on to what? Christ, it's just one Saturday night out of your life to go and have a good time. What the hell are you talking about?"

Joan turned away for a moment, nodding "hi" to the guy whose head poked out of the whirlpool, who nodded dully back. Her mouth sagged in weariness and some irritation. "Oh come on," she said. "You know what I mean."

"No, I don't. I honestly don't. I just thought it would be a fun thing to do. I've heard a lot about Interhouse. I've always wanted to go. I mean, why not just do it?"

"I just don't have time for that kind of thing anymore. I just don't have the energy for it."

"For what? What are you talking about? You got something better to do that weekend? The ballet perhaps?"

That was a bit of a sore spot. We both knew how bored Joan was of the ballet, of using expensive cultural pursuits as a substitute for "dancing the buttocks jig."

Even as I stared at her, however, I knew why, I knew exactly why Joan was being this way. She had not escaped the compelling symbolism of her thirtieth birthday, and had been moving in that certain inevitable direction ever since. A recent bout of successes in therapy had led her to be more discriminating with her men, to the point of not having had sex in a year and a half.

This from a woman who used to trek after a young man solely on the basis of an alluring jump-shot. This from a woman who, number eleven on a co-ed summer softball team, would inadvertantly spill gin-and-tonics down the front of her bathing suit and collapse giggling somewhere in right field. This from a woman who, in her undergraduate days, had gone through the entire frisbee team in under a month.

"Joan, what's happened to you?" I breathed. We had moved out onto the field; we sprawled out in the sun, ice melting over my ankle, watching the shirtless soccer players shout at each other and run up and down the field. There was a light breeze and wads of puffy clouds were smeared across the late afternoon sky. For a moment, I could imagine that no matter what else happened in the world, this field and these people would always be here, there would always be a shirtless, anonymous group of men running up and down the sun-dappled grass.

"I just don't want to do it anymore. I don't want to have crushes here and there. It's not cute anymore. I'm thirty. It's an ugly pattern. I want to get married. I want to be loved for myself. I want things to work out right," Joan droned, as if it were all hopeless.

The zoning flags fluttered lightly in the wind, and one player, Danish Dynamite very likely, broke away from the rest and sped towards the goal. Looking quickly over his shoulder, he made a sudden decision and shot the ball towards the net. The goalie, his entire body extended, dove sideways to the ball, just managing to deflect it away from the goal. The sun shone and the men cheered in excitement, slapping each other on the backs and arms, happy simply to be alive.

"I make thirty-five thousand dollars a year and I still have particleboard bookshelves in my house." Joan's voice washed over me, like the gentle hum of the washing machine on a Sunday afternoon.

"I still have bricks under the coffeetable. My mattress still sits on the floor. Why do I live in this wreckage? When will I ever get my life together? When will I stop wasting money? It's an ugly pattern. I've got to break out of this."

I closed my eyes and lay back in the sun, wondering what it would be like to have Number 29, the nineteen-year-old volleyball player, in bed. To deal with the retainer, to feel the fuzz on the lower part of his belly, to have him squirm around awkwardly, his body shaking in panic and yet in excitement. I would be the first. You never forget the first. More than that—I could tell him great stories and we could drink wine on the balcony, he in awe of it all. Life, large interesting Life. He would just be awakening to it all.

"I'm still paying off student loans. I'm not saving any money. At this point in my life, I should be saving money. My credit cards are charged to the breaking point. This is it now. My salary isn't suddenly going to double. My life isn't radically going to change. This is my career now. I have to cope with the situation as it is now. I'm not going to graduate from this somehow into a world of endless possibility. This is my life now. This is it. This is it."

I imagined him on top, lights off, unwilling, embarrassed, and yet continuing, his body twisting, suddenly drooping, unable to control himself. The sweat would make his curly hair flatten against his head. His breath would come in gasps. This was the real thing now, not something elegant and practiced, not something done by bored people who had done it a hundred times before, but something raw, something that truly winded you, something truly difficult.

★★★

Two days later, and the swelling in my ankle still hadn't gone down. Grimly, I visited my own doctor, who fortunately had no objections to putting me in a fiberglass walking cast for ten days. Ten days! It was essentially two weeks, since the appointment to get it off actually fell on a Friday. I phoned USC to cancel all my student appointments, resigning myself full-time to the arduous grueling duties of rehabilitation therapy, which meant many hours using the weights and whirlpool at the gym. More time at the gym. More time at the gym. I pictured my students, backpacks sagging in disbelief as they stood openmouthed before my office door, abandoned, uncorrected papers clutched in their hands.

★★★

I thought about what Joan said and decided she had a point about being thirty, or almost thirty. It was true that I was no longer nineteen, and could no longer run my life that way. I came up with two new maxims: 1) Life is too short to spend hours having meaningless conversations about films, nobody making the smallest fucking move. 2) If you want something, go for it. Long unspoken courtships, elaborate maneuverings where you just happen to be at the same place at the same time due to ingenious scheduling, indirectness in general are out. When you are nineteen it is one thing. When crow's feet are starting to happen around your eyes, it is another.

Hanging out at the gym six days a week, being a presence, was not enough. Hoping that it would all come together at the mad drunken revels of Interhouse, assuming I could even find him, was also a cop-out. I had to make a move. In the gym. On sacred ground. On home turf.

I had long since stopped talking to Joan about these things. "Let me make my own mistakes," I told her finally. She was driving me mad with her even-temperedness. I had let slip something about asking this guy Number 29 if he wanted to take a shower and she had come down on me immediately, trying to analyze me rather than helping find out if he was a sophomore, a senior, or what. Therapy had ruined even the most simple pleasures between us.

"I've seen you play," was what I finally said to him. Amid all the indecision and hysteria, I suddenly cornered him one day as he stooped over the drinking fountain. We were face to face before I even knew what I was doing. It happened very quickly. "You play well. Do you play on the team here?"

He straightened up abruptly, wiping his mouth on one drenched sleeve. "Oh!" he replied, in surprise. He actually had a zit or two, when confronted at close quarters. The corners of his mouth went down when he smiled instead of up. He looked quite different. He was really sweaty. It was frightening, not exactly what I had expected.

"I just—I just see you here a lot. . . I mean, you play really well, you should know that. . ." I was floundering. This was not good. I had no idea where to go from here. How old are you anyway, I wanted to ask. "I think volleyball's such a—such a great sport. To watch, I mean." Guffawing lamely, I indicated my foot, clad attractively in its fiberglass cast. He might as well know right away that I was posing no threat to him in terms of athletic ability, that I wasn't one of those threatening kinds of women. . .

He ducked his head awkwardly two or three times, as if digesting a delicious if somewhat difficult morsel of food. For a moment, he looked at me with a shy, almost coy glance—however, it only lasted a second and it may have been completely my imagination. He looked away. "Thanks."

He had let the ball drop. He was terrified. I was terrified. I took a deep breath, hating myself. "Warm day, isn't it? The smog is terrible. I sometimes don't know why I still live in Pasadena. I don't even work here."

He didn't reply, didn't offer assistance of any kind. It verged on rudeness. Here I was opening my soul to him and he didn't so much as bat an eyelash. And yet—amazingly enough—he didn't move away. He simply stood there, one hip jutted out, gazing down at the floor. It was as if he had no interest at all in pursuing this conversation, but that I was somehow, through means of some elaborate mechanical device, holding him there transfixed.

I tried a new tack. "I'm Barbara. What's your name?"

"Jeff," he said reluctantly, as if that was unimportant. Suddenly he looked up. "I'm not really that good, you know. There are guys here who are a lot better than me. You should watch them."

I froze. It was as if I had been struck in the face. Was this young guy, zits and all, telling me to get off his back, to fuck off? Was he sneering at my attempts to make stupid conversation because I was too wimpy to get to the point? I approach him with charm and flattery, and I get. . . this?

"I mean. . . " he looked pained, as if realizing he had blown it. In a way he had. My ego was not to be toyed with. My whole persona was ready to collapse as it was. But then he did an amazing thing. He half reached out his hand towards me, as if explaining something. It was an awkward, tentative, oddly touching gesture. "I mean, if you want to see real volleyball. It's just that I—I haven't been playing for very long."

I looked out the door at the playing field, my wrath souring in my throat. This was treacherous. This was dangerous. He had never dealt with courtship rituals before. He didn't know the rules. He didn't know how to bow out of something gracefully.

Out on the field today were members of the Indian contingent from Caltech, in their white hats and pants, playing cricket. Friends and family, also in white hats, sat off to the side and played the drums and chanted for their favorite team. That's how life is, that's how they pass the summers, there, in Calcutta.

"How long have you been playing volleyball?" I felt strapped here in Pasadena, helpless, resentful without quite knowing why.

"Almost a year. Actually, I started in the summer."

I mechanically moved another pawn two squares forward. Another logical and yet unbrilliant move. "You're terrific for only having played a year!" Too much enthusiasm, too much.

"Well, I've played on the beach before, just a little bit at home."

"Oh really? I heard that's really good for you, builds up your leg muscles." Where had I heard that? In the training room, somewhere? Did that even make sense?

"Maybe. It really doesn't help you much for indoors, though."

I had insulted him. I was insinuating that, with all that experience on the beach, he should be better. I attempted to recant.

"You mean that it's a different game? Sure, I know what you mean."

"No, it's the same game, it's just that it's different. The timing is different. It's hard to explain. Forget it."

He looked out the door, angry. Not at me, but just in general, beaten by the limits of language. He knew what he meant. He knew what it meant to leap up into the air to hit the ball and have it not quite there where you expect it. To be hovering in the air for that split second before pounding it straight down—and then somehow having it not quite work out, the wind, something unforeseen taking the ball off course. . .

"No, Jeff," I had no idea how to convince him, to convince him that this was something worth articulating, that I was willing to wait for half an hour until he found words to express it, that I would help him, that it was that important. "I know what you mean. I do. Really. Timing is everything."

"Yeah. Well. Anyway." It was hopeless. He was drifting away into monosyllables again.

And so it went on, our awkward conversation, stopping and starting like a stick-shift in the wrong gear. And yet, the whole contraption went forward. He stood his ground and I stood mine, each of us dreading every minute, every pause, but still thrashing it out of necessity. I didn't know exactly what it all meant to him, whether I was the first woman who had ever approached him of her own accord, whether back at his undergraduate dorm his talking to me for ten minutes would earn him some mysterious kind of coup. Yet somehow I sensed a fighting spirit there, not encouragement necessarily, not attraction, no special interest, but someone putting out a damned good effort to hang in there and keep the ball rolling.

I wanted desperately to tell him something, and yet I didn't know how. I didn't know how to put it in a way that would make sense to him. The passage I wanted translated was:

Jeff, you are safe with me. Everything will be fine. I will take care of everything. I have Bill Blass sheets on my bed and make a great Chicken Dijon. This is the best offer you are going to get in your entire Caltech undergraduate career. Believe me, I know, I've seen the wreckage made of other electrical engineers' lives who also thought they could make it through life without women. Don't make that fatal mistake. I'm offering you an escape. I have large batik pillows in my living room rather than ordinary furniture. It's funky and bohemian.

The force of gravity alone will make it easy for you to collapse drunkenly on the floor, amenable to being swiftly undressed, and you will lose your virginity easily and pleasantly, you'll see how easy it is, and you will have one thing less to worry about in your troubled young life.

"You need a lift back to your dorm?" is what came out, and immediately I knew the tone was wrong, too casual, too incidental. It was wrong, all wrong, a calculated error, a strategic blunder.

Because he immediately crumbled, the strain of it all finally getting the best of him. He mumbled something unintelligible, swayed dizzily for a moment, and then disappeared into the men's locker room forever. That was it.

★★★

This is Joan's postscript to the story. She had discovered the answer from her new therapist. She explained it all to me as she flexed her leg with a ten-pound ankle weight:

"There is an ancient story told by some Indian tribe near the Pacific about a house full of vaginas that all have teeth. The young hero comes along and tames all the vaginas by ritualistically removing the teeth and therefore ending up with a house full of friendly vaginas, gumless variety. This same tribe has all kinds of complex, penis-focused initiation rites for young men. The idea is to come to terms with the essential differentness of woman. First there is a routine circumcision, not only a mild form of castration, but a demonstration that men too can bleed and can therefore menstruate. A few months later comes a ritual slitting up the urethra which symbolically gives them a vagina of their own."

A large, muscular guy came in to bench-press. Joan nodded "hi" at him in passing. He stared at her.

"In the Western world, unfortunately, we don't have such rituals. Great confusion is the result. You see, Barbara, he wasn't simply seeing you and your '79 Toyota Corolla, offering him a simple ride to his dorm. He was instead confronted with an enormous vagina, with teeth in it probably. So you see it was nothing personal."

That was the little fable that haunted me for a long time after that. That image, of an enormous vagina sitting in the bleachers, yawning open like a venus fly-trap, was the one that would return to me everytime some sweating young man made a particularly good slam-dunk.

JULIA SELTZ

How To Marry a Republican

On election day in 1972, I remember crying when my father wouldn't let me put a "McGovern'72" sticker on the chrome bumper of his Volkswagon.

It was the first Presidential election I can recall, and at the age of thirteen, I was more passionate about being a Democrat than riding horses or killing boys.

I don't know how it goes now, but when I was in Jr. High School, every kid got on the stump for their favorite candidate. I was rabid for McGovern and got into daily screaming matches with *really* young Republicans. Nixon was the Devil. Elephants were the enemy.

When Tricky-Dick won, I became hysterical and vowed to move to Massachusetts, the only state that voted Democratic. As fate would have it, I did wind up in Boston and years after that when I moved to Los Angeles, I got a job working on a movie about Nixon.

Most of my fellas have been left-wingers and I've never really been in the market for a Republican, but inadvertantly, I've discovered how to wag the Elephant's tail, even if by accident.

My first Republican was Stuart. We met through mutual friends in Boston whose social lives crossed the circles of art and commerce.

Stuart lived on Beacon Hill and had never dated a wild, artsy type. Republicans love danger and I suppose my black leather jacket/high hair/ patchouli number must have started a riot in those Brooks Brothers boxers.

I thought he was smart and sexy for awhile, but it wasn't long before our dinner conversations changed from, "I want to rip your panties off with my teeth . . . grrrr," to,

"I see myself in ten years married into a fine family and to a beautiful gal, who's clean as a whistle and looks like Claudia Schiffer. I'll be like a young JFK (politically adjusted, of course), spending our summers at the family island, surrounded by my beautiful, blond children dressed in Tommy Hilfiger, throwing the football around with the clan on holidays...and all of us enjoying the fruits of my glorious career that will have something to do with great sums of money."

Cancel Camelot! It was that and the birthday presents he gave to me: a *Nantucket Bucket* (some wicker item with a subtle whale and lace motif) and a gift certificate to Laura Ashley, that sent me packing for the more familiar ground of junkie bike-couriers, boozy poker games and about a hundred hair-do's.

This lifestyle lasted for years until I wrote a screenplay, moved to Los Angeles, and, again by accident, snared another member of the Grand Old Party.

Now, if *you're* in the mood for a Republican boyfriend, listen up. Republicans can be useful at times, so it's important to always have one on deck. Never let distance become a deterring factor...I threw this love-lasso all the way from Los Angeles to D.C.

Preparation

1. Write a screenplay that includes the following:
   A. blowjobs
   B. Saabs
   C. preppies
   D. revenge

Allow one year and a half to pass during which you perform the slave duties expected of the assistant to anyone in the entertainment industry.

2. After surviving the employment horrors of working on various low-budget horror, cop, and soft-porn thrillers, receive phone call from girlfriend who lives in Colorado who says, "Remember that play you wrote a while back, well, I gave it to my best friend who's an Attorney slash Movie Producer slash Real Estate guy slash Republican from Washington D.C. ... he usually does action stuff, but he thinks maybe it's time for another female movie and

he's looking for material."

Allow two weeks to pass.

3. Receive a fax at current place of employment, you lovingly refer to as the *Director Barn,* (read: car commercial production company) that says, "He likes it...He wants to meet you and discuss p r o d u c t i o n." Allow yourself the luxury of feeling that maybe dreams *do* come true. Leave thousands of copies of fax lying around office in order to incite curiosity among the car directors.

4. Spend next week spitting out acceptable second draft to send to Republican.

5. Look in all directories available for his film credits and discover that although he's not a huge contender, he has made two movies shown in wide release. One you actually liked.

6. Next, without your knowledge, have Girlfriend in Colorado describe you in a flattering manner, "She's a damn, raven-haired beauty!" "Tall as the hills!" "Slim, Jim!" "Legs as long as a river, and then some!" "Makes me laugh like a stinky hyena!" *and* "She's real creative."

7. Girlfriend must then set up a weekend meeting between you and the Republican in Denver where she and her husband will be present.

8. Before the meeting, Girlfriend must liken Republican to the Pope of Single Men during sixty-five minute phone call, (your penny):

Height:	6'4"
Education:	Yale, B.A.
	University of Virginia
	School of Law

Occupation(s)	A. Movie Producer
	B. Real Estate Mogul
	C. Attorney
	D. Some Marketing
	thing you don't get.
Number of residences:	Four
Locations:	Beach Shack, Malibu
	Bachelor Pad, Georgetown
	Condo, Upper West Side
	Chalet, Alta
Vehicles:	Jaguar (Los Angeles)
	Mustang (D.C.)

Character descriptions from Girlfriend: "The most amazing man...on earth! He makes the cowboys cry, he's so damn handsome! Curly, light brown hair with hints of gold and diamonds and NO HAIR LOSS! It's in his genes. Has more money than he knows what to do with! Only dates single women!"

9. After assessing the previous information, realize that he has fulfilled the minimum requirements as a "suitor worth his salt," according to your mother.

10. Based on the previous realization, immediately, and most certainly distrust him. This will be a key element in setting your allure.

When the moment of travel arrives, the following itinerary should set the mood for a good Republican love fest.

DAY ONE
Travel and Initial Social Meetings

1. Simple airport outfit should consist of jeans, white tee and linen jacket. Sporty half-boots from London for footwear.

2. Arrive at LAX Airport Parking early only to sit for 45 minutes in bus that should whisk you to departure gate in under ten.

3. Miss United 424 to Denver by seconds and throw a screaming fit that includes profanity, pratfall and staged tears.

4. Have Customer Service bump you into first class VIP on next flight out to Denver. Readjust make-up on board. Note how far a good tantrum will take you.

5. Land in Denver, lose your mind over how strange and inefficient the new airport is and be surprised at lack of cowboys.

6. Because Republican's flight does not arrive for five more hours enjoy lunch with Girlfriend at local restaurant that serves buffalo meat. Appropriate topics of discussion during luncheon can include the following:

> Lack of love life (yours)
> General distrust of entertainment industry
> Her child's transition from diapers to toilet
> HIV tests
> The riots, floods, fires and earthquakes in L.A.

Finish Buffalo Burger and try not to think of how the white man ran this wooly species into extinction.

Dinner

1. Make sure Girlfriend cooks dinner at her home for your first evening together. If you're nervous, get on the phone and announce you're calling your "s e r v i c e" (even if it is a ten-year-old Panasonic answering machine), No messages? . . . not a problem . . . just listen to the dial tone and execute dramatic handwriting skills.

2. Republican should first appear right before the wine is poured. At first sighting of Mr. G.O.P., take note of low voice and intense eye movement. During dinner with Girlfriend and her husband, continue with airport outfit and try to drink moderately.

3. Make sure to *bellow* the following over steak and fries, "I'm creative, smart and everything I do, I do *well.*" Do not let the reaction of utter silence and slack jaws issued from the group at the table intimidate you in any way. Two more glasses of wine will not matter at this point; go ahead and relax.

4. Appear outwardly skeptical (raised eyebrows...open mouth) as you listen to all monologues that Republican puts forth on movie deals, sex in the cinema and how cool the new Republican congress is.
    A. Be *amazed* by how fast he speaks.
    B. *Furrow brow in disbelief* when he says, "I just wanted to meet the woman who could write such a script."
    C. Avoid *choking on food* when he reveals that he was Pat Buchanan's first campaign manager.

DAY TWO
The Script Meeting

1. While dressing for the script meeting, recall how your friend, Mr. Assistant to the Literary Agent said, "Who the fuck flies a perfect stranger to Butt-eater Colorado for a script meeting to discuss *P R O D U C T I O N?* Nobody talks production until after the first kiss. Get him to sign something, you schmuck!"

2. Select a transparent dress to cover your body stocking...placement of nude-colored Band-Aids over nipples will tell any republican that you're no show-off.

3. Anoint pulse points with a secret good-luck-witch mixture of patchouli oil and Guerlain's Vetiver.

4. Pray to God for about 1.5 minutes that he will offer some sort of money for your script.

5. Arrive at breakfast after he does and allow yourself to be seen in silhouette as much as possible. Good Luck! ! !

6. Small talk before the meeting may include:
> A. Tiny stories about how he, the Republican, is the last of his friends to fall prey to marriage.
> B. Ideas of what his wedding will be like, including his choice of music (Ray Charles), and in exactly which ear of his bride (left), that he will croon Ray's songs.
> C. Discussion of your half-breed religious background.
> D. During the car ride to swanky production office conference room rented just for the occasion of discussing your screenplay, avoid feelings that arise when you stare at the back of the Republican's neck (the little golden curly hairs that are shimmering like diamonds).

The Actual Meeting

1. During the meeting attended by Republican, Girlfriend and Husband, be prepared to follow your notes but drop plans immediately when he hands out 50 or 60-page agenda. Like the lion in the jungle, understand that the Republican rules any conference room. Get the feeling you're just a snack for Simba.

2. Allow him to explain why he's in the movie biz: *To make*

money...exclusively. Take note that this statement is accompanied by the physical reactions of dilated pupils and the pressing together of hands at fingertips.

Private reactions as follows:
    A. *Marvel* at the rate at which he speaks.
    B. *Glow* when he says your concept is a "sexy pitch."
    C. *Realize* this is a person who could sell sand to the Saudis or smog to the citizens of Pasadena.
    D. *Try not to shift uneasily* when he looks into your eyes with all 210 pounds of Yale Heat.

3. At lunch, complain about painful tricep injury incurred by pratfall at airport. If he offers, allow Republican to massage said injury and disregard the combined feelings of lust and embarrassment.

4. During a break in the meeting, try not to strain neck muscles while eavesdropping on three phone calls made by Republican. Highlights of overheard conversations will include words like:
"international goals,"
"twelve to twenty million," and
"pussy."

5. Resume meeting.

6. Have sinking feeling in stomach when Republican mentions, "Although I like a good *female* project, your script has poor marketing potential; i.e., target audience is *female.* "
Wonder WHAT THE HELL DOES THAT MEAN?
Despite the idiocy of that "female target audience" thing, you may, however, allow yourself to enjoy the following comments:
    A. "It's high time for another relationship film,"
    and
    B. "It's got good late-summer potential."

7. Allow him to discuss the timetable of his current production, a testosterone/pyro/muscle fest which will star yet another unknown mental midget with a foreign accent and is currently prepping in the convenient location of Malaysia.

8. Nod in agreement when you hear the word "option" and the numbers "between one dollar and five thousand dollars."

9. Fall into doom ravine when he says time may prevent his ability to offer option until six months from the present.

10. Before meeting concludes, get a funny feeling that you have either almost sold your concept (not your screenplay), or that you have just spent eight hours in a conference room with a person who has no intention of ever becoming involved with your life's work.

11. Wonder why you're in Denver.

Après Meeting

1. After meeting, return to Girlfriend's home in Suburban Denver for pleasant barbecue with Husband and Baby.

2. Feel the awkwardness of being single and childless as Girlfriend and Husband dote like junkies on their beautiful baby.

3. Feel flu-like symptoms in stomach when Republican sits next to you on porch swing and asks you if you ever plan to have kids.

4. At that point, change subject and move on to beach ball activity in back-yard. Allow Republican to chase you around.

5. To set the right mood, imagine yourself as the star of low-end fragrance

commercial because of sheer, flowing dress factor. Picture Republican gently grabbing your waist as you try to nab beach ball. All actions should be in slow motion and enhanced with visual effects.

6. Realize that the air is thin up in the mountains and cease sports activity due to lack of oxygen. Ponder later if waist-grabbing gesture was act of flirtation on part of Republican.

7. Remove any doubt in your mind regarding flirt-factor when he issues a lewd innuendo that has something to do with his lower body.

8. Enjoy dinner, until Girlfriend and Husband launch into 45-minute graphic description of childbirth, fueled by eager questions from Republican.

9. Excuse self from table when topic becomes the elimination of afterbirth and attempt to do dishes in kitchen.

10. Get lost in thoughts until Republican hugs you from behind and says, "Oh, I didn't think you could get so domestic." Chant to yourself, "Be nice, Be nice, Be nice," until the thought of castrating him subsides.

11. Retire with group to living room for *digestifs* and fall asleep on couch while seated next to Republican.

12. Awake to the sound of the group laughing one hour later and find that your head is on Republican's lap and his arm is around your shoulders.

13. Arise, say, "Wow-what-a-day-I'm-bushed-Goodnight," and beat it to bed. Have intense dream about making love to every single part of his Grand Old Party and then gassing him with mace.

DAY THREE
Sightseeing

Now that script meeting segment of trip to Denver is over, allow hosts to treat you to a wonderful day of sightseeing.

1. Wear casual jumper and tennis shoes for comfort during tours.

2. Have lunch at counter-culture bistro, your choice, and feel bile well up inside when the topics of politics and abortion arise. A nice eyeball-roll-into-socket moment would be appropriate.

3. Prepare to beat the hell out of Republican when he issues the predicted right-wing manifestos regarding preceding topics. After listening to what he has to say,
> Bite tongue in amazement.
> If he has managed somehow to make the preceding dicta sound acceptable, you know you've got a real whopper on your hands.

4. Before winding up at local carnival, lower jaw to sternum upon hearing Republican issue,
> "I can tell just how a woman will be in bed by how she gives a massage."

5. Although your location is back seat of Girlfriend's car, worry if your reaction to previous massage-statement (a combined feeling of shock and embarrassment), is noticed as your cheeks bloom into a world-class blush.

6. Allow Republican to continue with,
> "The way to my heart is through massage...I will marry the woman who can truly give me a good massage."

7. Wonder if these probably inappropriate statements were meant for your

benefit. When the car stops, exit and counter with,
> "Look, I'm frigid...I haven't had sex since 1985, so shutup."
> Walk apart from group and feel like you don't fit in.

8. Decide that moping would be rude and quickly rejoin Girlfriend, Husband, Baby and Republican.

9. Use the chant: "Be nice, Be nice, Be nice," for motivation.

10. After assessing danger-factor of various rides at carnival, decline the invitation of Republican to join him for a spin on the "Strangler."

11. Do accept his invitation to beat the hell out of rubber reptiles for a buck-a-whack.
> A. *Surprise yourself* when your first shot lands a prize.
> B. *Get happy* when you land the second one and-
> C. *Squeal like a pig* when you get the third.

12. Win three stuffed animals that are probably frogs. Relish the fact that Republican has not even scored *o n c e* .

13. Decide to have a good time at carnival and accept second invitation for a ride on "Strangler."

14. Scream with wild abandon and hope that Republican does not equate such vocal release with your potential boudoir opera. Feel close to orgasm and wish that you had a "Strangler" at home for personal use.

15. After the fun, take his arm as an escort and wonder what's going on. Try and disregard feelings of affection for Republican.

16. Fail.

The Last Supper

1. Return to Girlfriend's home and prepare for big evening out on the town.

2. Wear super-vixen tiny dress with killer heels. Make hair big and wear favorite Chanel red lip-outfit.

3. When Girlfriend, Husband and Baby are out of the room, notice very acceptable dinner outfit of Republican. Nod to yourself that he is indeed handsome, and try to forget that Pat Buchanan thing.

4. Proceed to corner him and say with big voice, "Are you trying to seduce me?...because if you are, you're just so forward...so overt. It's tacky. Why are you doing this?"

5. Furrow brow when he says, "I don't ever go after anything that I don't really, really want."

6. Blush till the *cows come home* and appear startled when Girlfriend and Husband enter room.

7. Have great time at fancy Denver restaurant. Insist on ordering wine for the table.
    A. Listen to Republican's movie stories.
    B. Listen to Girlfriend's old-boyfriend stories.
    C. Listen to Husband's stories of eccentric family members.
    D. Laugh. A lot.

8. Towards end of dinner, try and play footsie with Republican, but cease attempt when unable to determine difference between his chair and his trousers.

9. Think truly sinful thoughts about what it would be like to unbutton his

dinner outfit.

10. Then, in order to restore your image as a geek, knock water glass into his lap.

11. Upon exiting restaurant, hiss at woman who gives you evil-eye when she observes the absence of material covering your legs.

12. Walk to downtown bar with group.

13. During after-dinner drinks, ask Republican what's on his mind. Feel something like a fever when he says, "I've been thinking about this woman who wrote this script and how it would feel to get my arms around her."

14. Again, recall friend's advice . . . "Get him to sign something, you schmuck!"

15. At this point, lose resolve. *Completely.*

16. During ride home, try to maintain conversation with Girlfriend and Husband while attempting subtle hand massage on Republican in back seat of car. As you move up his thigh, marvel at Republican's ability to speak in an even timbre about international news events.

The Prize

1. After arriving home, decline the invitation from Girlfriend and Husband to watch *The Little Mermaid.*
2. Suggest to Republican that he take a walk with you outside. After perfunctory small talk and the feigning of decorum, allow the Great White Shark to take his prey. Hope that the neighbors are not awakened by the feeding frenzy.

DAY FOUR
Travel and Reflection

1. Be the last to arise for breakfast. Wear airplane outfit from Day One.

2. Pass by Republican at breakfast nook and say "Good Morning." Share about thirty milliseconds of acknowledgement before Baby throws combination of waffles and carrot slop between you.

3. Enjoy excellent breakfast with Girlfriend and family. Realize that you have eaten more food in the last three days than you have in months.

4. At his request, give Republican photograph of you taken by Husband. Feel confused.

5. After mini photo-op for record of great weekend in Denver, walk out to car with Girlfriend for relaxing drive to airport. Say thanks and good-bye to all.

6. Walk up to Republican, give hug and peck on lips. Burn in your mind the last gesture he makes in your behalf: the blowing of a kiss as you haul out of the driveway.

7. Make sure to dodge all inquisitions made by Girlfriend during ride to airport and thank her for a great weekend.

8. Reflect on weekend events during flight home to Los Angeles. Try not to feel bad about giving in to his charms and what effect this may have on any future sale of screenplay/concept.

Decisions

1. Upon return to Los Angeles, receive dirty message on answering machine from Republican requesting your presence, nude, on a ski lift in Alta.

2. After setting up a lawyer friend to represent your interests regarding the possible purchase of your work, return to Republican days later. Leave message with his service inquiring about your script.

3. Wait two days, and sign for Fed-Ex which contains one first class ticket to Park City for the following weekend and a "Talbots" catalog affixed with a red-white-and-blue Post-It that reads, "Pick out something *sexy*."

4. Try the slow-breathing-into-paper-bag technique to maintain balance during the daytime, and low doses of Xanax in the evening to clear the image of you and the Republican, both dressed as Dina Merrill in her heyday, skiing down a snowy mountain.

5. Return to former lifestyle, which now includes much older bike couriers, boozy poker games and prolific movie openings.

6. Shelve your screenplay. Read lots of magazines until you come across an article in some entertainment rag about "The New Sharks." Locate your former Republican among the man eaters and feel relief not to be involved with his most recent endeavor: the media representation of a man whose penis was removed by his angry wife.

Final Notes

Sex is OK with an Elephant, but keep the G.O.P. away from good girls with writing skills.

ALLYSON SHAW

Patsy is New in Town

The Earth moves.

The minute she moved there she stopped shaving herself, stopped cutting her hair and nails. She saw this, however subconsciously, as the physical accumulation of a past. Everywhere there was a postcard horizon in this town, something to roll the credits over in a sit-com. It was on one hill she met a boy, unbathed, a patina of his own cells making him gray and salty. He was a bike messenger.

They met at 3:04 p.m. during an earthquake. He was thrown off his bike by the tremors—and she straddled the street, grabbing a lightpost. *It never feels as you imagine it,* she thinks. *You think it will just be rumbles, but it is much deeper, a kind of churning as if the ground is a huge sea serpent you are riding.* His bike was transplanted to the middle of the road and he lay at her shaking feet.

Some buildings will cave in weeks afterward, as if they had gone brittle. She'll run her fingers over his scabs days later, counting the colors in their thickness, gingerly. He would look annoyed at her as she did this, thinking she was starting to love him. But really she loved his distressed body, the long lean muscles, how his skin seemed to never get totally clean, never heal.

He wouldn't talk much, but when he did, he talked to her about Russian history, his quasi-hobby. The Bolsheviks during the revolution held particular interest to him, and he believed that they had been the future model for revolution until Stalin made promises he couldn't keep. None of this revealed very much about him, and she tried to look at his ideas in some sort of allegorical fashion. This proved to be fruitless and he disappeared from her life as elegantly as he arrived, simply by ceasing to return her phone calls. Never the less, he had become a bench mark of this new place.

When she first met him, he was on the ground in front of her, wearing men's cutoff pants with longjohns underneath, high tops and a motorcycle jacket with "Crass" and "The Clash: Know Your Rights" fading on its cracked and graying leather.

She wore her navy shoes circa 1939, the highest heels she has, with a Navy dress that now fits with a high waist because she shrank it. The yellowing label says "Forever Young," circa 1951. Over the dress she wears a tight blue sweater, all the buttons replaced, mismatching. She bends down over the messenger, afraid to touch him. She has a sense that something propels her forward, down to him, to say just the right thing.

"Are you o.k.?"

Vintage Clothing

Her clothes smelled like someone else, or worse, someone in a different state, an old woman maybe or a dead woman. The underarms of her dresses had been discolored by another woman's sweat, and the smell of the bleeding pattern has had time to mustify. Her clothes wait in her closet for her, like Gepetto's toys, all of them making an attic smell. This, and the fact that she chose all of them so painstakingly, made her a melancholy girl.

Camelot

Before she had decided to leave her mother's house, her mother had given her a box of old negligees with the cloying smell of White Shoulders. They did not fit either of them. They may have fit Patsy at thirteen, but she would have had no use for them then. Even now, Pasty wonders how one uses these things, the peach chiffon, spaghetti straps, rose appliqués. But she kept them, even brought them with her to this new place, as a reminder of the impossible past thinness of her mother. As she packed, her mother complained of her own disappearing bone structure while eating dinner. Both of them ate mostly buttered noodles and cookies. They had just taken one of their "sugar naps" when Patsy picked up the box of negligees from the closet and smelled them, thought of her mother sleeping in them barefoot, then waking up to a specific morning: the morning JFK was assassinated. Her experience of this day was one of the few stories her mother told in great detail. Patsy turned to the full-length mirror and held the lingerie to herself. She remembers the story her mother tells of the assassination: "Camelot was over, it was like time stood still, everyone was crying. Wherever you went, people cried. And on TV Jackie was wearing that stupid pink suit, this horrible melon pink. It was covered with his brains, and she tried to put them back in his head." Patsy looks at her pasty face and wishes no one would be blamed for a color they've chosen to wear.

Lost and Found

She works part-time in the public library, where she folds origami monkeys at the desk. On weekdays, before school gets out and the kids flood in, it's mostly retirees in the weekly reading group, all of them voracious readers who call her "hon." Or there are transients who hover by the heating vent next to the Civil Service Exam Books. And there's the man, the Thursday man, who looks at her with hatred as he loads a table with books on Emily Dickinson. He wears Chinos and Hush Puppies, white shirts with stiff, wide collars worn tieless, circa 1976. Once, after closing, she was cleaning off his table and found a snapshot of a little girl in underwear, sitting on a ratty mustard-yellow sofa, laughing. Her nipples were like little buttons. Her hair was stringy, and her underpants had pink mice on them. Patsy's stomach knotted. She threw it in the Lost and Found, along with a mitten and an umbrella.

The History Lesson

One night, before he left her, the messenger had her lay on the bed for a really long time, just waiting, naked, while he paced around thinking, then he stopped and got some whiskey out from under the bed. She heard the faucet run.

I kept my eyes closed as he pulled my head up by my chin and put the glass to my lips. I pretended that I couldn't move—that he had just rescued me from a pile of rubble or a burning at the stake. I let the whiskey run down my chin without wiping it off. I heard him walk behind me where I felt him spread my legs. He didn't do anything for a long time then. I kept my eyes closed and flexed my muscles inside, trying to make something out of emptiness. He put his fingers over my vulva, put his thumb in my vagina. I came as soon as he touched me. Red washed over me, like a bull must see red and charge it and then it lifts to something else— sky, sand. Then he put something in my ass slowly, and things got dark and constricted around the bottom half of me, around his hands. He was laughing, and that turned into darkness, too, into part of my body that I was losing at the time.

He didn't touch her after that. He poured himself a drink and sat at the foot of the bed, his back to her. She lay there fathomed, and began to cry in a very strange way, as if her eyes were faucets, turned on cold, just pouring. She grabbed her sweater from the floor. *Think of something to say*, she thought to herself, *quickly*.

"The other day I was working and the Thursday Man came in, you know, the Dickinson freak, well—he left a photo on the table. A photo of a little girl in her underwear." Her face was sticky from tears. "I just put it in the lost and found box, in the open box, because I didn't want to hold it anymore, you know? I should've thrown it out but I thought, she's smiling—she lives somewhere, is out there and this happened to her—something—I don't know." Feeling the salty mucous run into her mouth, she thought she should keep talking about anything.

He fills a glass with water, says, "Drink this, keep drinking. If you preoccupy your body it won't have time to be sad."

She gulps it down, wishing it were true.

The USA Cafe

After he was gone, she would often go to the USA Cafe just to have the old woman there serve her a bowl of soup and bread. That woman has an apron just like the kind a woman would wear in the Midwest, in 1945, while hanging clothes on a clothesline. Once, while she was eating at the large window that faced the street, Patsy failed to notice a destitute man staring at her. The old woman came running out from behind the counter, making sharp "tsk" noises, a wet towel raised above her head. He ran. She looked at Patsy wide-eyed, patted her own chest and said, "He looks at you down there."

Often Patsy wonders if she will speak to her mother again. It's been over a year now, and they are both very stubborn.

Super Blue

When her grandmother died four thousand miles away, Patsy and her mother did not have enough money to fly to the funeral. They had to go two years later to see the spot where the ashes had been sprinkled. Once there, she and her mother stood over a blank patch of grass, next to the headstone of her great-uncle. Neither one looked at the other. Then suddenly, her mother started to choke, refusing to cry. She looked away to the car and started walking in silence. Patsy followed and said maybe they should save up and get a marker, maybe a stone angel. Her mother looked at her from the driver's seat and snapped, "She won't know the difference."

That night they drove to a drugstore where her mother bought "Super Blue" bleach, and they went back to the hotel room. Her mother put her fingers in Patsy's hair, bleaching her blonde. Pasty looked in the mirror and saw both of them pushing their lips out, out of habit, making movie mouths in the mirror.

Women Have Been Shot

She set out the newspapers in the morning on the wooden sticks in the rack, hanging them like wet hose. On the cover of one there is a picture of a woman, a nurse, taken while she was still alive. She smiles stiffly at the camera, her eyes bright and embarrassed in front of the lens. Others were also shot at the clinic, but their photos are not shown. There's another photo of a woman, a "bystander" who regularly picketed the clinic. Her mascara's running and she's pushing a crucifix into the picture frame, and in back of her there's a thin man with a little girl under his one arm and in the other he holds a placard with a photo on it, showing what looks like a baby's head on a fork.

This morning she checked for the photo of the little girl in the Lost and Found and it was gone. Every now and then it passes through her, the memory of it and she feels a twinge of pain, which she doesn't even know the cause of right away, the image of the girl surfacing much later.

Meeting Harvey

She met Harvey on her Wednesday shift. He was a regular, one of the few that were her age. She enjoyed framing him with her thumbs and forefingers, especially when he was in proximity to Miss Schweppe, the branch librarian. Miss Schweppe wore polyester double-knit sets and sensible shoes, her gray hair severe in a bowl cut, grazing her hooked nose like a cartoon Ringo Starr.

Harvey looked just like John Lennon— round glasses and scraggly blonde hair.

He would stare at her chest as she held his books under the red bar of light. *How to Clean and Cook the Perfect Fish, Gourmet Guide to Game* and *A Beginners Guide to Dissection.*

"I'm a painter." He said, "I p...p...p..paint this stuff."

"Mm..." She nodded vaguely, noticing a man stumble violently through the door. He is shiny with dirt. "That's interesting," she said distractedly, thinking about the drunk man who just came in, and how she might have to clean up after him. That was the beginning of Patsy and Harvey's three-week romance.

Harvey loved her breasts. He stuttered when he spoke, especially when he was nervous. This fascinated her, so she let him pursue her. They went to movies together, mostly at the art house cinema on the corner of her block. "Y....y....y...you j...j....j...just love me, d...d...don't you, Patsy?" He would joke sarcastically. She never let him up to her place, and he was getting discouraged. "You know, I thought you weren't that way, that you weren't so—I...I...I d...d..d..don't know— repressed."

She suddenly saw herself as a slovenly woman leaning on a doorjamb with a half-empty bottle in her hand, bouffant tipping into her eyes. She said, "So before you thought I was.....?"

"J...J...Just forget it."

She felt a pang of guilt and suggested they go get a beer. She wanted to buy time, to consider her options. Outside the bar cats were fucking and she could hear them. Someone once told her that male cats have barbs on their penises. *That's ruined everything.* She kind of wanted him before, his bleach smell, a chloriney musk mixed with a whiff of mildew. *A distinctly bachelor smell,* she thinks. He had almost hairless arms with really soft skin, like a girl's.

He leaned down to kiss her suddenly, in an awkwardly determined way. She said, "Oh, Rhett," into his mouth as he did it and it came out meaner than she had intended. He pulled away from her and she saw her lipstick, bright red and perfumey, all over his mouth.

Stealing Books

The next day at work she walked into the break room and heard Miss

Schweppe talking about her, saying to the Children's Librarian, "I think Patsy's mildly retarded. Maybe her mother drank. She is so slow at shelving," Patsy cleared her throat loudly and walked to the desk where she stood numbly fingering the returns.

That night, before locking up, I stole several books on origami and a book on the circus, where there's a picture of a girl with feathers on her ass, hanging from her teeth.

Drag Queens and Film Noir

That night she lay on her bed with her hair in rollers after drawing on her brows à la Joan Crawford. Once she was walking down a hill at four in the morning after drinking at Jorge's Latin Palace, when a beautiful woman passed, her legs very muscley, heels pushing the calves up. Her face was a mask, her wig a bit crooked. She smiled at her and said, "You sleep tight, sweetie." Her voice was deep and hoarse, like a man's but tenderized, and smelling of gin. *I must take this as a sign, as my guardian angel who has appeared to me momentarily.*

But tonight she will go to her favorite film noir, where the aging boxer, still young but useless, sits on his bed beautifully in a white undershirt and high-belted pants, head in hands. He knows he will be hunted down, betrayed by the brunette, even as his enemies order eggs. This she loves. She hooks her girdle. It elongates her, contains her.

When she left her mother's house last, the poodle growled at her, and her mother said, "She knows you are abandoning her. She knows." Her mother diapered that dog because it was incontinent. And while she diapered it she would talk to it to restore its dignity. "What a pretty girl you are, yes, you are. Such a pretty."

Patsy recognized it as the voice reserved for pets and babies, a voice to which she had no access.

She imagines herself pregnant, remembering a *Mademoiselle* article, *Men like symmetrical women. Not too pretty, but regular. This is the mark of good genes.* It showed a composite face, a combination of 50 different faces, jumbled by a computer to make an average of all the others. Lab testing showed this face to be most popular to men. Patsy pulls her underarm hair and daydreams that she is on a gurney in the middle of a medical classroom, and a young intern wearing rubber gloves measures her vagina with his fingers. His eyebrows meet in the middle in concern. Then she jumpcuts to her mother, knitting beside her in a hospital bed. She imagines herself in a negligee with caribou feather trim, sitting in a small puddle of her own blood, sighing. Then her mother puts her knitting down, gets up and touches her daughter's forehead, sighing, too, saying, "What a beautiful baby it might have been."

AIMEE BENDER

Fugue

1. Dinnertime

I sit across the table from my husband. It is dinnertime. I made steak and green beans and homestyle potatoes and even clipped two red roses from the bush in the backyard; they stand in a vase between us which is clear so I can watch the stems drift in the water as he speaks.

He puts his elbows on the table. He opens his mouth while he chews. He gesticulates with his fork, prongs out.

Me, I nod and nod. He tells me all about work. The memos are misspelled, he tells me. That new secretary can barely speak. I listen and chew with my mouth closed. The potato, no longer hot, breaks under my teeth, melts across my tongue, my upper lip seals to my bottom lip, and everything is private inside my mouth—loud and powerful and mine. A whole world of noise going on in there that he can't even hear. Reaching forward, he spears a big piece of potato with his fork. He lifts it up, takes it in, bites down. I watch the food disappearing in his mouth and it's my food and I bought it and I made it and I have to will my hands to keep still because I think I want to rescue it. I want to rescue my food, thrust an arm across the tablecloth, spill the drifting roses, dodge his molars, avoid his tongue, and seize it back, bring it all out, drag it down into the dish, until there is just a mush of alive potato between us, his stomach empty, my mouth still closed.

2.

Inside the pill factory, the muttering worker was switching things around.

"I'll put the yellow pills in here," he said to himself, mutter mutter, "and the white ones in here." He took the bottles to the child-sealing machine and went home.

Two weeks later, outside in the world, people with prescriptions fell down dead. The muttering worker read about it in the paper, felt a surge of importance, and decided it was time to move on. He called the pill factory office and told them he quit. They asked why. He said allergies. They said: allergies to what? And he said Allergies to the telephone and hung up.

This was the fourth job he'd grown tired of in a month. Two weeks before he'd gotten a gig teaching English to immigrants. He'd taught them the wrong things. He'd said: pussy means woman and asshole means friend. During the week, one female student got propositioned. Two men were beaten up. They stomped into their classroom, bruised and confused, but their misleading muttering teacher was long gone—already shaking the hand of the pill factory boss, in fact, his eyes flicking with interest on the vats of colored ovals and the power hidden beneath their shells.

But, now it was time to change again. The muttering man put on a tie and looked at himself in the mirror. This always made him spit. He projected it out, pleh, littering his face. The muttering man had been an ugly child. He had been an ugly teenager. Now he was an ugly adult. He found this pattern very annoying.

This time, he applied for a secretarial job. Decided he needed to do something calm and quiet for a while, like memos. Here he met his match: loud man.

Loud man wore a necklace, talked very loud and was very honest. He looked everyone square in the eye and said: Let me tell you what I honestly think and then did just that.

Muttering man hated him for several reasons, one being that loud man was his boss, another being that loud man was loud and the third and final and most awful being that loud man was good-looking. Really good-looking.

Muttering man went to loud man's house with a gun.

"Hello," he muttered, "I'm here to steal from you."

Loud man didn't quite hear him right. "You're here to what? Speak up."

"Steal," said muttering man as loud as he could which was not loud at all, "I want to steal things. Like some jewelry. Like your mirror. Like your wife."

Loud man was angry, flushed a becoming pink and said many things, including, "Let me tell you what I honestly think."

"Please," muttered muttering man, "tell away."

"I think you're my employee!" said loud man in a huge voice, "and I Think You're Fired!"

Muttering man fired the gun and hit loud man in the knee. Loud man yelled and sat on the floor. Muttering man squared his shoulders and took what he asked for.

First, he told the trembling wife to wait at the door. He tried to catch a glimpse of her face, to see what kind of woman such a good-looking fellow would nab, but he couldn't see much underneath her overhanging hair.

Next, he told loud man to remove his gold necklace which he happily slipped over his own ugly head.

"I've never had a necklace," he muttered, pleased.

Finally, he walked up and down the halls looking for the perfect mirror to snatch. He passed several boring oval ones but when he turned the corner and walked into the master bedroom, he found exactly what he was looking for. Hanging on the wall, just opposite the large bed, was a huge rectangular mirror in a lavish silver frame. Mumbling under his breath in delight, muttering man gently lifted it off its hook. This mirror had been reflecting loud good-looking man for years and so had turned soft and complacent, and was likely to be kind to even muttering man's harsh features. He took a quick peek at his necklaced self and fought down the blast of hope.

With some difficulty, he angled the huge mirror under his arm and shoved the wife into the passenger seat of the car, leaving loud man howling in the house. Muttering man started the engine and took off down the street. He glanced sideways at the wife, examining her profile, searching for beauty. She was okay-looking. She didn't look like a movie star or anything. She looked sort of like four different people he'd met before. She stared straight ahead. After fifteen minutes, he dumped her off at the side of the road because she didn't talk and muttering man wasn't good with silent people. Plus, he wanted to be alone with the mirror.

"Bye," he said to her, "sorry."

She watched him through the window with large eyes. "That necklace is giving you a rash," she said. "It's made of nickel."

He itched the back of his neck. Before he pulled away, he threw her a couple of cigarettes and a pack of matches from the glove compartment. She gave a little wave. Muttering man ignored her and pushed down on the gas. Less than ten miles later, he slowed and pulled to the side of the road. He lifted the mirror onto his lap. Running his fingers in and over the silvery nubs, he fully explored the outside before he dared to look in. He could sense the blob of his face sitting inside the frame, unfocused and patient, waiting to be seen.

3. Visitor at Haggie and Mona's

"Mona," said Haggie, "I'm tired."

Mona was stretching her leg up to the edge of the living room couch. "You're always tired," she said. She put her chin on her knee.

Haggie settled deeper into the green chair, the softest chair ever made. "Hand me that pillow, will you?"

"No." She reached forward and held her foot.

Haggie sighed. He could feel the start of that warm feeling inside his mouth, the feeling that he could catch sleep if he was quiet enough. He felt hyper-aware of his tongue, how awkwardly it fit.

Leaning down, Mona spoke to her knee. "You'll just doze off and you sleep way too much," she said. "You practically just woke up."

"I know," he said, dragging a hand down his face, "you're absolutely right. Now hand me that pillow so I can take a nap and think about that."

"Haggie," said Mona, switching legs, "come on."

Mona was Haggie's one remaining friend. The rest had gone to other cities and lost his phone number. Haggie sat around all day, living off money in the bank from a car crash court settlement, while Mona trotted off each morning to work for a temp company. She typed something like a million words per minute. She was *always* offered the job at the place she temped, but she always said no. She liked the wanting far more than the getting, and, of course, was the same with men. She had this little box in her room containing already two disengaged engagement rings. She'd told the men: Sorry, I can't keep this, but oddly enough, they each had wanted her to. She seemed to attract very generous men. As a memento of me, they said, little knowing there was another such souvenir residing in a box on her dresser.

Haggie tugged on his tongue. It felt mushy and grainy and when he pinched it hard, he felt nothing.

"Are you doing anything tonight?" she asked, chin on her other knee.

"Me?" he garbled, still holding onto his tongue, "tonight?" Mona swung her leg down, and gripping the side of the couch like a barre, began a set of pliés.

He released his fingers and swallowed. "Tonight?" he said, clearly this time, "nothing. Those bowling friends of yours are having a party but I said no. They asked if you wanted to go but I said you didn't. Do you?" He paused. Mona didn't answer. "They all want you, you know."

"Really?" Mona, in mid-plié, dimpled up, pleased. "Which ones? All? Really? What exactly did they say?"

Haggie scratched his head. He didn't even know if it was true, he just liked to see Mona leap for things.

Mona bent down and touched her head to her knees. "I have a date anyway," she said, voice muted.

Haggie let his body slump into the chair. He hated it when Mona went out—the house felt dead without her. "Hey," he said, "please. The pillow?" He pointed again to the couch, just a few feet out of his reach. His blood felt weighted, each corpuscle dragging its own tiny wheelbarrow of rocks.

"Haggie." Mona shook out her legs and looked at him. "Go outside."

"Blech," he said to the ceiling, "I hate outside."

She walked over and stroked his hair. "Do something good," she said, "Haggie. Do something."

He leaned briefly into her hand. She smelled like vanilla and laundry detergent. "I really would," Haggie said, "you know, really. If I could only get out of this damn chair."

Mona touched his cheek. She stood next to him for a moment, then gave a little sigh and disappeared into her bedroom. Haggie turned his head and watched her doorway for awhile, eventually closing his eyes. After forty-five minutes, Mona emerged, shiny, in a brown dress. Haggie was drifting off.

"Hag," she said. "Wait, wake up, I have a question." She twirled around. "High heels or not?" Haggie shook his head awake, looked at her and tried to focus.

"No," he said after a minute, voice gravelly, rubbing an eye, "you're too peppy already. Wear boots," he said. "Weigh yourself down a little."

She stuck out her tongue at him but vanished into her bedroom again and came out in two minutes wearing lace-up brown boots.

"Lovely," Haggie said.

There was a knock at the door.

"There he is," said Haggie, "Monsieur Pronto."

Mona looked at her watch. "No," she said, "I'm picking him up. Are you expecting anyone?"

He laughed. "My illicit lover," he said. He sank deeper into the chair. "Maybe we're getting mugged. Didn't I tell you? We should get bars on our windows."

The knock interrupted again: *rap rap rap.*

Mona went to the door. She peeped in the peephole. "It's a woman. Who is it?" she called.

A muffled voice came through.

Mona looked at Haggie. "Should I let her in?"

"Is she cute?" he asked.

Mona rolled her eyes. "I don't know," she said, "her hair is covering her face." She opened the door.

"Hello," said Mona, "how can I help you?"

The woman tugged off her wedding ring. "Please," she said, holding it forward, "please, will you take this in exchange for a place to stay?"

Haggie burst out laughing.

Mona shook her head. "Oh no," she said, "I can't keep that." The woman's hand was trembling as she held the ring forward, and the edge of her dress was charred black.

"Haggie," Mona said, "shut up. Stop laughing. She wants to stay here."

"Fine," he called from the chair, eyes closing. "But tell this one to keep the ring."

Mona opened the door wider. "Please," she said, "come on in, you look so tired." She took the woman by the elbow and guided her into the living room. "Haggie," she said, "get out of the chair, Hag, can't you see this woman has been through something terrible and is about to collapse?"

Haggie sat there for a second. "But the sofa," he said, pointing ineffectually.

Mona glared at him. "Haggie." The woman's legs started to curve beneath her. Haggie put one hand on each arm of the chair and hoisted himself up, wobbling a bit on his feet.

"Where are you from?" Mona asked, leaning down to relace the top of her right boot.

The woman closed her eyes. "Sinai," she said. Haggie sat on the floor.

"What did she say?" Mona whispered, relacing the left boot for the hell of it, "did she say cyanide?"

He looked up and noticed the woman was already asleep.

"Faster than me, even," he said with respect.

"Do you think she's a poisoner?" Mona hissed.

Haggie laughed.

"Sssh," said Mona, "she's sleeping."

"Her dress is burnt," he said.

"I know," said Mona, "she smells like smoke, too. Campfire smoke or something." She stood up. "Listen, Hag, I've got to go. Are you okay? Should I stay? What if she poisons you?"

Haggie made an attempt at a scared face but he couldn't get himself to do it. He felt too tired. "Go, Mona," he said. He laid his head back on the arm of the sofa.

Mona paused. "Do you think she's sick?"

"She's just tired." His voice was fading. "She just needs some sleep." The sofa arm dug into his neck. "I can't believe she wanted to give you her ring."

Mona smiled and checked herself one last time in the mirror. As soon as the front door closed and the *clop-clop* of her tightly-laced boots faded away, Haggie tried to doze off, but the floor was hard beneath him and the air felt clotted and thick without Mona stirring it up, and he couldn't find the familiar relief of that slow descending weight.

Heaving himself up, he sat on the couch. He almost twitched, craving the comfort of his chair. The woman snored lightly now. She had flushed skin and her eyelashes made simple black arcs on her cheeks.

"Hello lady," said Haggie, "wake up and talk to me." She kept sleeping, sending out her breath to the air and pulling it back in. Private.

It made him feel worse to be awake when there was someone else there that was asleep. The house seemed twice as big and twice as lonely. Dragging himself up, Haggie lumbered over to the bathroom. He wondered: was it possible to die simply from an absence of tempo? Sure, Mona was ruled by some kind of frenetic march, but there was no doubt that *something* was moving her inside— Haggie's internal rhythms were so slow that he wondered if they counted as rhythms at all.

Inside the bathroom, he opened up the medicine cabinet above the sink; sometimes Mona kept sleeping pills in there that she used when she was too wound up. Which was often. Holding the mirrored door, Haggie took down the tiny redbrown bottle. He read the label. *Do not exceed two in six hours.* Haggie spilled them out on his hand; they shimmered like miniature moons. I'm bigger than she is, besides, he thought. He took nine, his lucky number, and washed them down with a handful of water from the tap. That should do something, he thought. Because I don't have my chair. And I'm tired, he thought again. I'm very tired and I want to sleep. He sat down on the floor of the bathroom and waited for a strange feeling to overtake him. The woman in his chair stopped snoring and the house filled with darkness and quiet.

4.

When he had finished exploring every knob and bump in the frame, he took in a breath and got ready to face the mirror straight on. He fiddled with the itchy gold necklace. This time would be different, in this fancy man's mirror, this good-looking man's looking-glass. He crossed his fingers inside the chain and let his eyes shift in and focus.

5. At the Side of the Road

That night, I sleep in a bush. I don't sleep very well there, but I never do, I've never been a good sleeper. I can't ever get comfortable. So it's okay; the dirt on my cheek is okay, doesn't make any difference to me. A pillow is no better.

I dream about my husband. I am dreaming that he is going to the refrigerator to fix himself a sandwich, my food, my bread, my self— digested then gone— and that's when the shot rings out and that's when I'm off, in the race, I'm off. He grabs his knee, and I'm out the door. I'm a racer, I'm so fast. In my dream, I run a lap around the world and some people in another country build a monument around my footprint.

When I wake up, I want to walk for a long time, I think I could walk forever and never get tired. I take one of the cigarettes that man left me and smoke it, it's been a long time since I did that, and when I stub it out in the bush, it catches on something and the bush starts to burn. Just near the bottom, but it is burning, the bush is on fire. The air is dry, sure, but it was one tiny cigarette and so I am shocked and I look at the bush burn and then I think: maybe this is something spiritual. Here, by the side of the road, just me without any money, just me wanting a new place to go, this is the time for something spiritual to happen, this is my right timing. I wait for God to speak to me.

The flames snap and hiss.

A couple drivers pass by and slow: Want a Ride? but I shake my head, no, and it's not because I'm worried about rapists, I'm not. Something is about to happen here—something big. I'm going to hear what this bush has to say to me and then I'm going to walk forever by myself since I never have and because it's a better quiet outside than it is in a car and because all I took was one puff and I set something on fire. Me. The bush keeps crackling. I wonder, what will it tell me? What is it that I need to hear? Lean in closer and listen with my whole being. I can't tell what it's saying. I can't find any words, just that fire sound, the sound of cracking and bursting. I start to feel a bit panicked—what if it speaks in a different language? What would I do then? The warmth of the flames flushes my face.

I speak English, I whisper to the bush as a reminder. Talk to me. I'm listening.

6. Same ugly man.

7. Back at Haggie and Mona's

At one in the morning, a key turned in the lock and Mona tiptoed into the living room. She could see the shape of the woman still there, lungs lifting and releasing. She felt a surge of pride that the runaway was alive and had stayed, and eased herself down on the couch across from the woman and unlaced her boots.

It had been a great date. He'd been one of those men who kissed hard, trying to merge their faces. Hand at the back of her head. It was quite urgent kissing for a first date but she liked that. She left the boots by the couch, tiptoed into the bathroom and flipped on the light and there was Haggie lying on the floor, legs tucked into his chest.

"Haggie," she said, stopping still, "what's going on?"

He craned his head and looked up at her with enormous eyes.

"I committed suicide," he said. "But it didn't work."

"What?" Mona squatted on the floor.

"I mean," he said, "I just wanted to sleep and sleep, sleep and sleep, so I took nine pills, nine dangerous white pills, those pills you use to sleep sometimes? I took them hours ago. Hours and hours ago. Nine of them. I'm sure of it. And I feel fine."

She stared at him. "Did you puke?"

"No," he said, "I didn't even puke."

"Haggie," she said, "are you okay?" She reached forward and felt his forehead. "You're not feverish," she said. She sat down next to him. "Are you okay?"

"I think so," he said.

She stared at him still. He stared back. Standing up, Mona pulled the bottle down from the medicine cabinet and read the label. She looked down at him and shook her head. "Nine?" she asked, and he nodded. She kept shaking her head, placing the bottle back on the shelf and closing the door. Then she squatted down next to him again and touched his hair. Her voice was quiet. "I'm worried about you," she said.

"I know." He reached up an arm to grasp the counter. "Me too." He pulled himself up. "But still, it's all so strange."

Mona grasped his elbow. "Do you need help walking?"

"No." He shook his head. "That's the thing. I don't."

He walked into the living room and stood against the back of the stiff sofa, facing the big window that looked out onto their small backyard. Mona followed him in.

"She's still here," she whispered, pointing.

"Did you have a good date?" Haggie looked at the woman sleeping. Her entire face was relaxed. He thought she looked beautiful.

"Yeah," she said, "it was really nice. He liked the boots." Haggie smiled. "Are you going to sleep?"

"I guess not yet," he said, "I'm feeling pretty awake right now. I think I'll just stay in here."

"Okay." She touched his shoulder. "You're sure you're okay?"

He nodded. "I'm good," he said. "Good night Mona. Sleep well."

Mona picked up her boots and pattered into her bedroom. The woman shifted in the chair. Haggie went over to her and gently rolled the chair forward until they both were in front of the window. He looked at their reflections silhouetted in the glass. She still smelled like smoke and it smelled good. He remembered Mona: what if she poisons you? and smiled. He sat on the arm of the couch and watched their undetailed shapes in the glass. Once Mona went to the bathroom. Other than that, it was perfectly still. After several hours, sunlight began to seep into the backyard, slowly opening out the flatness of the glass and revealing the grass and one tree. A dew-covered white plastic chair. An empty wooden bird feeder. He watched as their silhouettes faded from the window and dissipated into the morning.

8.

He started to cry, same ugly man, always: that tidal wave of disappointment. Transformation impossible. He pulled the itchy fake gold necklace off and threw it at the glass where it made an unsatisfying clink; he let out a small, ineffective spit which didn't land on the mirror at all but instead arced down and splatted onto the fancy silver frame. The muttering man started to rub the spit into the frame, but as he did, the saliva seemed to remove a bit of the silver. What? he said out loud. He leaned forward. He rubbed more. Silver paint lifted off, thin and papery. Beneath it was scarred wood. The muttering man licked his finger and rubbed again. The paint continued to peel off. Darkened silver, iridescent black, collected under his fingernails, on the tops of his fingertips. Ignoring his face, he hunched down and kept rubbing. What do you know, he said, mutter mutter, well who would've thought it was a fake frame too. He rubbed the entire frame until his hands were black and it was no longer silver at all, but just a rectangle of flawed bumpy brown wood.

Turning the mirror around, he opened up the hooks and removed the glass from the back. Then he hung the frame around his neck. "Will you look at my new necklace," he said out loud, to the empty street. "This one doesn't itch at all."

9. Mine

I sit with the bush for a long time but it says nothing to me. It continues to burn, still mainly near the bottom. I listen harder and harder, feeling a certain despair build, wondering if it will ever reach out and talk, if ever I will understand the message meant for me, but then, just as I'm listening as hard as I possibly can, it hits me, pow, like that: of course. It is saying nothing. It's a listening bush. It wants me to talk. My burning bush would be different, my burning bush would be like me.

So I clear my throat and I tell it things, I talk to that bush. I don't think I've ever said so many sentences in a row before, but I talk for at least an hour about myself—about me and my husband and my mother and my allergies, and sometimes I don't know what to say and then I just describe what I see. The street is gray and paved. The ground is dry here. The sky is cloudless.

It's wonderful. It's wonderful to talk like that. After a while, I'm exhausted and I think I've said enough. I feel great but my throat is dry and I need some water, so, thanking it over and over, I leave the burning bush by the side of the road for somebody else. And I start to walk.

It's hours later when hunger and fatigue hit, and I find myself in front of one house, the only house on the block without bars on its windows. That's the one I knock at. And that's the one that answers. It's a nice place. It is quiet inside. Just as I'm dozing off, ready to really sleep for the first time in a long time, I think about my husband and where he is, what he's doing. I like to think he's limping around the house, shouting my name, sitting on the bed and looking where the mirror was and staring at the grain of the wood. I like to think he opens the refrigerator and sees me inside.

But truthfully? Let me tell you what I honestly think. I think, maybe he hasn't even noticed that I'm gone.

But. I have.

DISASTERS IN DEATH AND DYING

And the fever called the "living"
is conquered at last!
—Edgar Allan Poe

JENNY CORNUELLE

Tongue

From the start I hated the old man. My husband always made excuses for his father, but he was a prick and it just made it worse that my husband stood up for him. My father-in-law, Jed (those were his initials not his name, his first name was Jerome, I think) was the type of guy who asks a woman's opinion just to make fun of the little lady's reasoning.

And I hated his tongue. Years ago he had had part of his jaw removed, a tumor or something, so his tongue fell out of his mouth and he drooled like an old dog. When he noticed that his tongue was hanging he would reel it in with lots of slaps and slobber.

My husband, Dick, didn't want to leave his father alone, so we all lived, three peas in a pod, in Jed's house (which by the way was in the middle of nowhere, thirty miles from the nearest town and a hundred from anything that could be even humorously called a city). I wasn't allowed to alter a thing. Jed's wife or I guess I shoud say Dick's mother had decorated it herself and even the aqua tassels on the shiny chammy curtains in the breakfast nook were sacred. Can you imagine spending your days surrounded by pea green polyester? Take my word for it, it gets to you. I woke up every morning and stared straight into the button eyes of a needlepoint pheasant and I wondered what I did in a previous life to deserve this torment.

"Blood is thicker than water."

That's what Dick would say when I suggested that the old man might be more comfortable in a home. A few months ago I heard it once too many times. The three of us were celebrating our second wedding anniversary and as I stared at Jed's chin, counting the drops of drool, I decided it was time to drown the son-of-a-bitch.

My husband is or was a mystery to his father. Jed was a retired fireman; his son was a sensitivity consultant; he taught tolerance in the workplace. His main client was the navy, his basic job was making "how to" videos teaching sailors that gay-bashing is inappropriate behavior and that men who can't get it up are just "phallically impaired." His father just didn't think his son worked, and frankly, on this one point I was on his side. I've worked every peon job you can name but at least I had dignity, I mean, at least it was a job. I did something. When I was a receptionist I had pages of yellow slips at the end of the day; when I cleaned houses at five, I had a vacuum cleaner full of other people's dirt. You need to have something to show for your time. What does my husband have at the end of a work day? Only the hope that these no-nonsense Neanderthal navy types are a smidgen more sensitive.

But sensitivity is not my expertise. When I was in kindergarten the other girls' imaginary friends were child-size bunnies or cute bears—mine was a larger-than-life gila monster. His scales felt soft like the fur of one of Armstead Covington's expensive stuffed animals. ("My father buys them special in New York," she would always throw in my face.)

My mom always said: "My Jenny, she's from another planet. She knows trouble like the sound of her own name."

My mother thought my promiscuous behavior was a cry for help. Being an over-zealous born-again she was shocked by my need for sex, so she had me committed when I was sixteen. Don't feel sorry for me, the facility I was in had a great library and I had a lot of time on my hands for reading. Luckily we lived in Pennsylvania where all the quality people are in the pen. In fact, there was a movement there a few years ago to change the license plates to read THE STATE OF MULTIPLE PERSONALITIES, but I think it didn't fit—too many letters or something.

Anyway I was born for exciting times. I was born running—got to stay in front of the pack—not a leader exactly but if I wanted to be leader I could. My sheer energy and unnatural speed have always got me through the day. I don't understand the value of control and I *know* my husband's control in and out of bed pissed me off and his father's tongue had drooled once too often on my tuna casserole. The vision of a world with no one snapping their fingers in my face and telling me to stop and think for a second about what I had just said gave me courage. Why think before you leap if leaping is what you want to do?

One Tuesday, my husband left on a five day business trip to Washington—

the new administration was requiring all consultants to learn the Democratic
definition of sensitivity. Dick was nervous. He was sure there would be
cutbacks and that registered Republicans would be the first to go. I pointed
out that he was Jewish and that was a point in his favor. That night would be
the night. I excused myself and went to my room to prepare. I was excited as
if I was getting all fixed up for a party. Everything in my bedroom seemed to
now be printed in bold; I moved around at lightning speed, and every once in
a while I heard myself giggle with anticipation. Oh boy, by midnight Jed
would be dead.

When I emerged from my bedroom I was surprised to find the dining room
table set for two. The candles at the center of the table were already lit.

"Dinner will be on the table in a jiffy. Would you like a glass of wine?"

I was stunned but not suspicious. Jed was courting me, his son's wife. Life
does take curious turns.

"Sure."

"Sit down. I'll bring your plate."

Over coffee he began to make his move.

"You make me crazy."

"I know."

"No, that's not it. I tried to hate you, but I want you—really want you."

"I don't think your son would understand."

"I want . . . ."

"Let's not talk. I'll meet you in the tub. Bring the candles."

The only tub was on the first floor, so after barely moving the cold tap and
turning the hot full I ran upstairs and stripped and shimmied into my cashmere
robe and in my right pocket put the handcuffs that an old friend I had met in
the pen gave me as a joke at my bachelorette party. Before rushing back
downstairs I checked the mirror: the bulge was not noticeable but I saw my
cheeks were rosy. This would be fun.

Jed was already in the bath and had brought the candles in from the table.
The tub was built-in; on three sides there was a bench. Jed's head rested on
one of those blow-up rubber pillows with suction cups on the back that look
like giant clams. I opened my robe and straddled him from behind, but I didn't
get in. I was already clean. My pubic hair mixed with his white hair. His head

turned and his tongue licked my inner thigh.

"I have a surprise for you."

I took my sash and wrapped it around his eyes. It went around three times. Slowly I cuffed one wrist; then the other. He was smiling.

"I've read about this stuff."

"Mmmmm," was all I could say.

"You're not trying to kill an old man, are you?"

"Sure as hell am."

And then with all my might I shoved his head under the water. I smiled as I watched as the water stilled.

II.

Love is a tricky business. I don't believe love is part of human nature, not for a minute. I mate, but not for life. A couple of weeks ago I saw the new Dracula movie and I walked out of the theater thinking: "BULLSHIT." Nobody with that kind of sex appeal would carry a torch beyond the grave for some pale babe who in my opinion was unattractively thin.

My own relationships last two, three years at the outside, then I'm out of there. I like to be the one who leaves, being left doesn't look like fun. Besides I hate being bored. I read somewhere that in China courtship takes place on horseback. They play Catch the Maiden mounted on the fastest horses they can beg, borrow or steal. The basic game plan is the men chase the rider of their choice and if he succeeds in catching her he is rewarded a kiss before the maid goes after him with her riding crop, I suppose to see what her guy is made of, who knows? Got to hand it the Asians, they sure have a handle on the kissing-cousin relationship between love and hate.

My husband didn't understand about Jed. I told him that I discovered Jed's dead body in the tub and panicked. With my history of emotional problems I was sure I would be blamed. I told him I had buried his father's body under the house. Dick was stunned by my stupidity. At this point, he said, if he reported it, the police would surely suspect foul play; but I was sure that Dick was the suspicious one. For days he had trouble looking me in the eye and my presence, he told me more than once, made him sick to his stomach. He couldn't stand to be in the same room with me. Five minutes tops—then he would bolt as if I smelled like old vomit.

In my opinion he was overreacting. His dad went out happy, for Christ's sake, but of course in Dick's defense he really didn't know that because I thought it best not to tell him that his father had made a pass at me. But the point was simple: your dad is dead; I'm sorry, but it's time to move on, time to let the living live.

At the end of the second week of silent treatment I was developing an inferiority complex. I mean, enough is enough. Yell at me, hit me, cry, just don't mutter and shake your head.

By the time the third week arrived my nerves were shot. During the day I was stuck in the house. Dick took one car to work and locked the other one and took both keys, saying I had proven what he had long known: I was not to be trusted. We live far into the mountains and there is nothing but meadows in walking distance and it was snowing with a wind-chill that put the temperature in the negative numbers. Did I say I hate being cold?

The licking started this morning right after Dick left for work. Dick had been working hard on a big project. By the end of the week he had to present his opinion on the effect of transparently packaged products on sailors' morale. I had read his notes because he, of course, wouldn't talk to me. Apparently Coke now is made in a clear liquid and comes in a clear container and it was supposed to make its drinkers feel healthier and happier. What will they think of next? About ten I noticed a lapping sound like pond water in a breeze. By noon the sound was louder, like a dog drinking from a toilet. I checked all the bathrooms. Nothing. By three the sound became piercing and I knew what it was. It was a wet lingering lick—*his*.

I tried to steady my pulse. Dick would be coming home in a few hours but I was having trouble blocking the image of his dad. I kept reliving the three hours it took me to roll him down the stairs, pull him into the crawl space, dig a hole and with no ceremony bury the S.O.B.

I turned the stereo on max and grabbed one of Dick's books, *The Beauty Myth* and tried to make a dent in the introduction, but I could still hear it. So I found a collection of Poe's short stories and tried to scare myself back into reality but I could still hear it like a gigantic bitch was bathing her litter of twenty with quick licks. By about four I was in a panic.

When I realized I was drooling just like the old man I took a shovel and knife down to the basement and began to dig him up. Recovering the body wasn't a big deal; I had done a shabby job burying him. The grave was shallow—I mean, parts of the pink polka-dot sheet I'd wrapped him in were visible to the naked eye.

When my husband found me he was horrified. I had lost all track of time and hadn't noticed it was close to six. I had his father's tongue in my hand and was about to cut it into a thousand pieces when I felt I was not alone. My husband was at the doorway staring at me like I was a monster.

"Give me that."

He tore the tongue from my hand and knelt next to the body and tried to put it back on.

"Have you no shame?"

I guess that's what did it. Too many people have asked me that question, and frankly, if you want to know the truth: no, don't even know the meaning of the word.

So I walked to Jed's toolbox (Dick was not what you would call "handy") and grabbed the biggest hammer in the top tray. When I returned Dick was telling his dad in a boy's voice how sorry he was. He didn't even notice me come up behind him. I move like a cat, everyone says so. I think I hit him five or six times in the head. Dick's head sounded so hollow I burst out laughing. I had expected an amplified nutcracking noise but instead it was a thud like a fat person's footsteps on uncarpeted stairs. Then I went upstairs to pack a knapsack. I don't stay where I'm not wanted.

Now as I walk toward the interstate the only human sound I hear is my own breathing. I turn around and the flames are a real heart-stopper. The house looks beautiful all lit up. The fire crackles and snaps its red tongues in the moon's face and suddenly I remembered the agony of Girl Scout overnights, how I used to be teased around the campfire when the counselors were off smoking. The other girls would sing: "Sometimes I feel like a fatherless child." I would pretend I didn't care that I didn't even know what my dad looked like but later in my tent I lay awake trying to picture where my father was and I swore that one day I would find him and give him a piece of my mind. Maybe the time has come to look him up.

I got the idea to torch the place when I went to collect Jed's savings. Jed didn't trust banks so he kept his pension in old paint cans in the tool shed. I thought he must be hording *Playboys* or a bottle of something potent—so, one afternoon when the old man was napping, I searched the shack and found his cash. I was careful to leave the disorder exactly as I had found it. I knew someday I might need Jed's nest egg and if he knew I knew his hiding place he would move it and then it would take time to find it again.

Anyway, as I stuffed the bundles of crisp bills into my bag I happened to notice that next to the cans there was an inordinate amount of paint thinner and it struck me that fire conceals as it cleanses.

The first thing I'm going to do is take a vacation. I definitely need a rest from men. What did Emily Dickinson say, select your own society and slam the door on the rest of the shits? I know I'm taking liberties with her text but the gist is there and I for one have always taken old Emily's advice to heart and God knows now I have reason to hope she was right when she wrote that not even love can raise the dead.

It's odd but I'm calm, in fact I'm more relaxed than I've been in years. I am free again and all is right with the world. I know sooner or later I'll have to find a replacement for Dick but for now I'm happy flying solo. Alone with cash to burn: how totally tits, as my sister used to say when an outfit or a man struck her as perfect. And what is truly wonderful is when I close my eyes I hear nothing, as if the world I now hike through is a videotape and the sound has been turned off. The world of men is muted—not a gulp or a mumble, not a lick, a swallow, or a nibble—all mouths paralyzed, all tongues temporarily disabled, and all the children who cry alone, now sleep and dream of a different life.

T. CORAGHESSAN BOYLE

The Sinking House

When Monty's last breath caught somewhere in the back of his throat with a sound like the tired wheeze of an old screen door, the first thing she did was turn on the water. She leaned over him a minute to make sure, then she wiped her hands on her dress and shuffled into the kitchen. Her fingers trembled as she jerked at the lever and felt the water surge against the porcelain. Steam rose in her face; a glitter of liquid leapt for the drain. Croak, that's what they called it. Now she knew why. She left the faucet running in the kitchen and crossed the gloomy expanse of the living room, swung down the hallway to the guest bedroom, and turned on both taps in the bathroom there. It was almost as an afterthought that she decided to fill the tub too.

For a long while she sat in the leather armchair in the living room. The sound of running water—pure, baptismal, as uncomplicated as the murmur of a brook in Vermont or a toilet at the Waldorf—soothed her. It trickled and trilled, burbling from either side of the house and driving down the terrible silence that crouched in the bedroom over the lifeless form of her husband.

The afternoon was gone and the sun plunging into the canopy of the big eucalyptus behind the Finkelsteins' when she finally pushed herself up from the chair. Head down, arms moving stiffly at her sides, she scuffed out the back door, crossed the patio, and bent to turn on the sprinklers. They sputtered and spat—not enough pressure, that much she understood—but finally came to life in halfhearted umbrellas of mist. She left the hose trickling in the rose garden, then went back into the house, passed through the living room, the kitchen, the master bedroom—not even a glance for Monty, no: she wouldn't look at him, not yet—and on into the master bath. The taps were weak, barely a trickle, but she left them on anyway, then flushed the toilet and pinned down the float with the brick Monty had used as a doorstop. And then finally, so weary she could barely lift her arms, she leaned into the stall and flipped on the shower.

★★★

Two weeks after the ambulance came for the old man next door, Meg Terwilliger was doing her stretching exercises on the prayer rug in the sunroom, a menthol cigarette glowing in the ashtray on the floor beside her, the new CD by Sandee and the Sharks thumping out of the big speakers in the corners. Meg was twenty-three, with the fine bones and haunted eyes of a poster child. She wore her black hair cut close at the temples, long in front, and she used a sheeny black eyeshadow to bring out the hunger in her eyes. In half an hour she'd have to pick up Tiffany at nursery school, drop off the dog at the veterinarian's, take Sonny's shirts to the cleaner's, buy a pound and a half of thresher shark, cilantro, and flour tortillas at the market, and start the burritos for supper. But now, she was stretching.

She took a deep drag on the cigarette, tugged at her right foot, and brought it up snug against her buttocks. After a moment she released it and drew back her left foot in its place. One palm flat on the floor, her head bobbing vaguely to the beat of the music, she did half a dozen repetitions, then paused to relight her cigarette. It wasn't until she turned over to do her straight-leg lifts that she noticed the dampness in the rug.

Puzzled, she rose to her knees and reached behind her to rub at the twin wet spots on the seat of her sweats. She lifted the corner of the rug, suspecting the dog, but there was no odor of urine. Looking closer, she saw that the concrete floor was a shade darker beneath the rug, as if it were bleeding moisture as it sometimes did in the winter. But this wasn't winter, this was high summer in Los Angeles and it hadn't rained for months. Cursing Sonny—he'd promised her ceramic tile and though she'd run all over town to get the best price on a nice Italian floral pattern, he still hadn't found the time to go look at it—she shot back the sliding door and stepped into the yard to investigate.

Immediately, she felt the Bermuda grass squelch beneath the soles of her aerobic shoes. She hadn't taken three strides—the sun in her face, Queenie yapping frantically from the fenced-in pool area—and her feet were wet. Had Sonny left the hose running? Or Tiffany? She slogged across the lawn, the pastel Reeboks spattered with wet, and checked the hose. It was innocently coiled on its tender, the tap firmly shut. Queenie's yapping went up an octave. The heat—it must have been ninety-five, a hundred—made her feel faint. She gazed up into the cloudless sky, then bent to check each of the sprinklers in succession.

She was poking around in the welter of bushes along the fence, looking for an errant sprinkler, when she thought of the old lady next door—Muriel, wasn't that her name? What with her husband dying and all, maybe she'd left the hose running and forgotten all about it. Meg rose on her tiptoes to peer over the redwood fence that separated her yard from the neighbors' and found herself looking into a glistening, sunstruck garden, with banks of impatiens, bird of paradise, oleander, and loquat, roses in half a dozen shades. The sprinklers were on and the hose was running. For a long moment Meg stood there, mesmerized by the play of light through the drifting fans of water; she was wondering what it would be like to be old, thinking of how it would be if Sonny died and Tiffany were grown up and gone. She'd probably forget to turn off the sprinklers too.

The moment passed. The heat was deadening, the dog hysterical. Meg knew she would have to do something about the sodden yard and wet floor in the sunroom, but she dreaded facing the old woman. What would she say— I'm sorry your husband died but could you turn off the sprinklers? She was thinking maybe she'd phone—or wait till Sonny got home and let him handle it—when she stepped back from the fence and sank to her ankles in mud.

★★★

When the doorbell rang, Muriel was staring absently at the cover of an old *National Geographic* which lay beneath a patina of dust on the coffee table. The cover photo showed the beige and yellow sands of some distant desert, rippled to the horizon with corrugations that might have been waves on a barren sea. Monty was dead and buried. She wasn't eating much. Or sleeping much either. The sympathy cards sat unopened on the table in the kitchen, where the tap overflowed the sink and water plunged to the floor with a pertinacity that was like a redemption. When it was quiet—in the early morning or late at night—she could distinguish the separate taps, each with its own voice and rhythm, as they dripped and trickled from the far corners of the house. In those suspended hours she could make out the comforting gurgle of the toilet in the guest room, the musical wash of the tub as water cascaded over the lip of its porcelain dam, the quickening rush of the stream in the hallway as it shot like a miniature Niagara down the chasm of the floor vent . . . she could hear the drip in the master bedroom, the distant hiss of a shower, and the sweet eternal sizzle of the sprinklers on the back lawn.

But now she heard the doorbell.

Wearily, gritting her teeth against the pain in her lower legs and the damp lingering ache of her feet, she pushed herself up from the chair and sloshed her way to the door. The carpet was black with water, soaked through like a sponge—and in a tidy corner of her mind she regretted it—but most of the run-off was finding its way to the heating vents and the gaps in the corners where Monty had miscalculated the angle of the baseboard. She heard it dripping somewhere beneath the house and for a moment pictured the water lying dark and still in a shadowy lagoon that held the leaking ship of the house poised on its trembling surface. The doorbell sounded again. "All right, all right," she muttered, "I'm coming."

A girl with dark circles round her eyes stood on the doorstep. She looked vaguely familiar, and for a moment Muriel thought she recognized her from a TV program about a streetwalker who rises up to kill her pimp and liberate all the other leatherclad, black-eyed streetwalkers of the neighborhood, but then the girl spoke and Muriel realized her mistake. "Hi," the girl said, and Muriel saw that her shoes were black with mud, "I'm your neighbor? Meg Terwilliger?"

Muriel was listening to the bathroom sink. She said nothing. The girl looked down at her muddy shoes. "I, uh, just wanted to tell you that we're, uh—Sonny and I, I mean—he's my husband?—we're sorry about your trouble and all, but I wondered if you knew your sprinklers were on out back?"

Muriel attempted a smile—surely a smile was appropriate at this juncture, wasn't it?—but managed only to lift her upper lip back from her teeth in a sort of wince or grimace.

The girl was noticing the rug now, and Muriel's sodden slippers. She looked baffled, perhaps even a little frightened. And young. So young. Muriel had had a young friend once, a girl from the community college who used to come to the house before Monty got sick. She had a tape recorder, and she would ask them questions about their childhood, about the days when the San Fernando Valley was dirt roads and orange groves. Oral history, she called it. "It's all right," Muriel said, trying to reassure her.

"I just—is it a plumbing problem?" the girl said, backing away from the door. "Sonny . . . " she said, but didn't finish the thought. She ducked her head and retreated down the steps, but when she reached the walk she wheeled around. "I mean you really ought to see about the sprinklers," she blurted, "the whole place is soaked, my sunroom and everything—"

"It's all right," Muriel repeated, and then the girl was gone and she shut the door.

★★★

"She's nuts, she is. Really. I mean she's out of her gourd."

Meg was searing chunks of thresher shark in a pan with green chilies, sweet red pepper, onion, and cilantro. Sonny, who was twenty-eight and so intoxicated by real estate he had to forego the morning paper till he got home at night, was slumped in the breakfast nook with a vodka tonic and the sports pages. His white-blond hair was cut fashionably, in what might once have been called a flattop, though it was thinning, and his open appealing face, with its boyish look, had begun to show signs of wear, particularly around the eyes, where years of escrow had taken their toll. Tiffany was in her room, playing quietly with a pair of six-inch dolls that had cost sixty-five dollars each.

"Who?" Sonny murmured, tugging unconsciously at the gold chain he wore around his neck.

"Muriel. The old lady next door. Haven't you heard a thing I've been saying?" With an angry snap of her wrist, Meg cut the heat beneath the saucepan and clapped a lid over it. "The floor in the sunroom is flooded, for god's sake," she said, stalking across the kitchen in her bare feet till she stood poised over him. "The rug is ruined. Or almost is. And the yard—"

Sonny slapped the paper down on the table. "All right! Just let me relax a minute, will you?"

She put on her pleading look. It was a look compounded of pouty lips, tousled hair, and those inevitable eyes, and it always had its effect on him. "One minute," she murmured. "That's all it'll take. I just want you to see the backyard."

She took him by the hand and led him through the living room to the sunroom, where he stood a moment contemplating the damp spot on the concrete floor. She was surprised herself at how the spot had grown—it was three times what it had been that afternoon, and it seemed to have sprouted wings and legs—like an enormous Rorschach. She pictured a butterfly. Or no, a hovering crow or bat. She wondered what Muriel would have made of it.

Outside, she let out a little yelp of disgust—all the earthworms in the yard had crawled up on the step to die. And the lawn wasn't merely spongy now, it was soaked through, puddled like a swamp. "Jesus Christ," Sonny muttered, sinking in his wing-tips. He cakewalked across the yard to where the fence had begun to sag, the post leaning drunkenly, the slats bowed. "Will you look at this?" he shouted over his shoulder. Squeamish about the worms, Meg stood at the door to the sunroom. "The goddam fence is falling down!"

He stood there a moment, water seeping into his shoes, a look of stupefaction on his face. Meg recognized the look. It stole over his features in moments of extremity, as when he tore open the phone bill to discover mysterious twenty-dollar calls to Billings, Montana, and Greenleaf, Mississippi, or when his buyer called on the day escrow was to close to tell him he'd assaulted the seller and wondered if Sonny had five hundred dollars for bail. These occasions always took him by surprise. He was shocked anew each time the crisply surveyed, neatly kept world he so cherished rose up to confront him with all its essential sloppiness, irrationality, and bad business sense. Meg watched the look of disbelief turn to one of injured rage. She followed him through the house, up the walk, and into Muriel's yard, where he stalked up to the front door and pounded like the Gestapo.

There was no response.

"Son of a bitch," he spat, turning to glare over his shoulder at her as if it were her fault or something. From inside they could hear the drama of running water, a drip and gurgle, a sough and hiss. Sonny turned back to the door, hammering his fist against it till Meg swore she could see the panels jump.

It frightened her, this sudden rage. Sure, there was a problem here and she was glad he was taking care of it, but did he have to get violent, did he have to get crazy? "You don't have to beat her door down," she called, focusing on the swell of his shoulder and the hammer of his fist as it rose and fell in savage rhythm. "Sonny, come on. It's only water, for god's sake."

"Only?" he snarled, spinning round to face her. "You saw the fence—next thing you know the foundation'll shift on us. The whole damn house—" He never finished. The look on her face told him that Muriel had opened the door.

Muriel was wearing the same faded blue housecoat she'd had on earlier, and the same wet slippers. Short, heavyset, so big in front it seemed as if she were about to topple over, she clung to the doorframe and peered up at Sonny out of a stony face. Meg watched as Sonny jerked round to confront her and then stopped cold when he got a look at the interior of the house. The plaster walls were stained now, drinking up the wet in long jagged fingers that clawed toward the ceiling, and a dribble of coffee-colored liquid began to seep across the doorstep and puddle at Sonny's feet. The sound of rushing water was unmistakable, even from where Meg was standing. "Yes?" Muriel said, the voice withered in her throat. "Can I help you?"

It took Sonny a minute—Meg could see it in his eyes: this was more than he could handle, willful destruction of a domicile, every tap in the place on full, the floors warped, plaster ruined—but then he recovered himself. "The water," he said. "You—our fence—mean you can't, you've got to stop this."

The old woman drew herself up, clutching the belt of her housedress till her knuckles bulged with the tension. She looked first at Meg, still planted in the corner of the yard, and then turned to Sonny. "Water?" she said. "What water?"

★★★

The young man at the door reminded her, in a way, of Monty. Something about the eyes or the set of the ears—or maybe it was the crisp high cut of the sideburns . . . Of course, most young men reminded her of Monty. The Monty of fifty years ago, that is. The Monty who'd opened up the world to her over the shift lever of his Model-A Ford, not the crabbed and abrasive old man who called her bonehead and dildo and cuffed her like a dog. Monty. When the stroke brought him down, she was almost glad. She saw him pinned beneath his tubes in the hospital and something stirred in her; she brought him home and changed his bedpan, peered into the vaults of his eyes, fed him Gerber's like the baby she'd never had, and she knew it was over. Fifty years. No more drunken rages, no more pans flung against the wall, never again his sour flesh pressed to hers. She was on top now.

The second young man—he was a Mexican, short, stocky, with a mustache so thin it could have been penciled on and wicked little red-flecked eyes—also reminded her of Monty. Not so much in the way he looked as in the way he held himself, the way he swaggered and puffed out his chest. And the uniform too, of course. Monty had worn a uniform during the war.

"Mrs. Burgess?" the Mexican asked.

Muriel stood at the open door. It was dusk, the heat cut as if there were a thermostat in the sky. She'd been sitting in the dark. The electricity had gone out on her—something to do with the water and the wires. She nodded her head in response to the policeman's question.

"We've had a complaint," he said.

Little piggy eyes. A complaint. *We've had a complaint.* He wasn't fooling her, not for a minute. She knew what they wanted, the police, the girl next door, and the boy she was married to—they wanted to bring Monty back. Prop him up against the bedframe, stick his legs back under him, put the bellow back in his voice. Oh, no, they weren't fooling her.

She followed the policeman around the darkened house as he went from faucet to faucet, sink to tub to shower. He firmly twisted each of the taps closed and drained the basins, then crossed the patio to kill the sprinklers and the hose too. "Are you all right?" he kept asking. "Are you all right?"

She had to hold her chin in her palm to keep her lips from trembling. "If you mean am I in possession of my faculties, yes, I am, thank you. I am all right."

They were back at the front door now. He leaned nonchalantly against the doorframe and dropped his voice to a confidential whisper. "So what's this with the water then?"

She wouldn't answer him. She knew her rights. What business was it of his, or anybody's, what she did with her own taps and her own sprinklers? She could pay the water bill. Had paid it, in fact. Eleven hundred dollars' worth. She watched his eyes and shrugged.

"Next of kin?" he asked. "Daughter? Son? Anybody we can call?"

Now her lips held. She shook her head.

He gave it a moment, then let out a sigh. "Okay," he said speaking slowly and with exaggerated emphasis, as if he were talking to a child, "I'm going now. You leave the water alone—wash your face, brush your teeth, do the dishes. But no more of this." He swaggered back from her, fingering his belt, his holster, the dead weight of his nightstick. "One more complaint and we'll have to take you into custody for your own good. You're endangering yourself and the neighbors too. Understand."

Smile, she told herself, smile. "Oh, yes," she said softly. "Yes, I understand."

He held her eyes a moment, threatening her—just like Monty used to do, just like Monty—and then he was gone.

She stood there on the doorstep a long while, the night deepening around her. She listened to the cowbirds, the wild parakeets that nested in the Murtaughs' palm, the whoosh of traffic from the distant freeway. After a while, she sat on the step. Behind her, the house was silent: no faucet dripped, no sprinkler hissed, no toilet gurgled. It was horrible. Insupportable. In the pit of that dry silence she could hear him, Monty, treading the buckled floors, pouring himself another vodka, cursing her in a voice like sandpaper.

She couldn't go back in there. Not tonight. The place was deadly, contaminated, sick as the grave—after all was said and done, it just wasn't clean enough. If the rest of it was a mystery—oral history, fifty years of Monty, the girl with the blackened eyes—that much she understood.

★★★

Meg was watering the cane plant in the living room when the police cruiser came for the old lady next door. The police had been there the night before and Sonny had stood out front with his arms folded while the officer shut down Muriel's taps and sprinklers. "I guess that's that," he said, coming up the walk in the oversized Hawaiian shirt she'd given him for Father's Day. But in the morning, the sprinklers were on again and Sonny called the local substation three times before he left for work. She's crazy, he'd hollered into the phone, irresponsible, a threat to herself and the community. He had a four-year-old daughter to worry about, for christ's sake. A dog. A wife. His fence was falling down. Did they have any idea what that amount of water was going to do to the substrata beneath the house?

Now the police were back. The patrol car stretched across the window and slid silently into the driveway next door. Meg set down the watering can. She was wearing her Fila sweats and a new pair of Nikes and her hair was tied back in a red scarf. She'd dropped Tiffany off at nursery school, but she had the watering and her stretching exercises to do and a pasta salad to make before she picked up Queenie at the vet's. Still, she went directly to the front door and then out onto the walk.

The police—it took her a minute to realize that the shorter of the two was a woman—were on Muriel's front porch, looking stiff and uncertain in their razor-creased uniforms. The man knocked first—once, twice, three times. Nothing happened. Then the woman knocked. Still nothing. Meg folded her arms and waited. After a minute, the man went around to the side gate and let himself into the yard. Meg heard the sprinklers die with a wheeze, and then the officer was back, his shoes heavy with mud.

Again he thumped at the door, much more violently now and Meg thought of Sonny. "Open up," the woman called in a breathy contralto she tried unsuccessfully to deepen, "police."

It was then that Meg saw her, Muriel, at the bay window on the near side of the door. "Look," she shouted before she knew what she was saying, "she's there, there in the window!"

The male officer—he had a mustache and pale, fine hair like Sonny's—leaned out over the railing and gestured impatiently at the figure behind the window. "Police," he growled. "Open the door." Muriel never moved. "All right," he grunted, cursing under his breath, "all right," and he put his shoulder to the door. There was nothing to it. The frame splintered, water dribbled out, and both officers disappeared into the house.

Meg waited. She had things to do, yes, but she waited anyway, bending to pull the odd dandelion the gardener had missed, trying to look busy. The police were in there an awful long time—twenty minutes, half an hour—and then the woman appeared in the doorway with Muriel.

Muriel seemed heavier than ever, her face pouchy, arms swollen. She was wearing white sandals on her old splayed feet, a shapeless print dress, and a white straw hat that looked as if it had been dug out of a box in the attic. The woman had her by the arm; the man loomed behind her with a suitcase. Down the steps and up the walk, she never turned her head. But then, just as the policewoman was helping her into the backseat of the patrol car, Muriel swung round as if to take one last look at her house. But it wasn't the house she was looking at: it was Meg.

★★★

The morning gave way to the heat of afternoon. Meg finished the watering, made the pasta salad—bow-tie twists, fresh salmon, black olives, and pine nuts—ran her errands, picked up Tiffany, and put her down for a nap. Somehow, though, she just couldn't get Muriel out of her head. The old lady had stared at her for five seconds maybe, and then the policewoman was coaxing her into the car. Meg had felt like sinking into the ground. But then she realized that Muriel's look wasn't vengeful at all—it was just sad. It was a look that said this is what it comes to. Fifty years and this is what it comes to.

The backyard was an inferno, the sun poised directly overhead. Queenie, defleaed, shampooed, and with her toenails clipped, was stretched out asleep in the shade beside the pool. It was quiet. Even the birds were still. Meg took off her Nikes and walked barefoot through the sopping grass to the fence, or what was left of it. The post had buckled overnight, canting the whole business into Muriel's yard. Meg never hesitated. She sprang up onto the plane of the slats and dropped to the grass on the other side.

Her feet sank in the mud, the earth like pudding, like chocolate pudding, and as she lifted her feet to move toward the house the tracks she left behind her slowly filled with water. The patio was an island. She crossed it, dodging potted plants and wicker furniture, and tried the back door; finding it locked, she moved to the window, shaded her face with her hands, and peered in. The sight made her catch her breath. The plaster was crumbling, wallpaper peeling, the rug and floors ruined: she knew it was bad, but this was crazy, this was suicide.

Grief, that's what it was. Or was it? And then she was thinking of Sonny again—what if he was dead and she was old like Muriel? She wouldn't be so fat, of course, but maybe like one of those thin and elegant old ladies in Palm Springs, the ones who'd done their stretching all their lives. Or what if she wasn't an old lady at all—the thought swooped down on her like a bird out of the sky—what if Sonny was in a car wreck or something? It could happen.

She stood there gazing in on the mess through her own wavering reflection. One moment she saw the wreckage of the old lady's life, the next the fine mouth and expressive eyes everyone commented on. After a while, she turned away from the window and looked out on the yard as Muriel must have seen it. There were the roses, gorged with water and flowering madly, the impatiens, rigid as sticks, oleander drowning in their own yellowed leaves—and there, poking innocuously from the bushes at the far corner of the patio, was the steel wand that controlled the sprinklers. Handle, neck, prongs: it was just like theirs.

And then it came to her. She'd turn them on—the sprinklers—just for a minute, to see what it felt like. She wouldn't leave them on long—it could threaten the whole foundation of her house.

That much she understood.

BENJAMIN WEISSMAN

The Present

My son thinks just because his mother is dead that we should bury her, before we've tried everything. She is dead, that much is true; but what isn't a hundred percent is whether all other avenues have been fully explored. The world is a slippery place; it's dirty and confusing. Death might seem like some kind of one way street, but who says you can't float back, when the traffic is light.

In one sense I understand my son trying to get his mother into the earth before she rots. But disgrace is not always avoidable, especially when it comes to the preservation of life. The boy's got the right idea: put dead people in the earth, and through that procedure, hold that spiritual creature dear and tight, or they us. The relationship develops unexpectedly through absence. A constant buzz ensues; the ground you walk on is a perpetual reminder. In your sleep new situations are played out. Everyone knows how a ghost, or a gang of them, can stand on your bed and disrupt your sleep. They flush the toilet, try on your clothes, tickle your cock. Once a ghost gets used to her new-found form she develops peculiarly normal qualities. She whines a lot, and gets strangely insecure. She begs for attention, and after she's gotten it, of course, she pretends you don't exist.

What we don't put down into the earth we burn up. People worship ashes, or at least savor the small gloomy urn. I'm aware of the laws and customs of our society. The problem is, we as people can't lay down our own dead. A citizen is not allowed to bury his own, personally and privately. The most painful moment in my life has to be made public, and costs me more money than seems right. People who live in this area make arrangements with the incorporated father-and-sons team in town. An Irish family. Callahan. A pack of drinkers and roughnecks. They bury everyone. A monopoly on the dead. In one sense my son is saving me a lot of money. $1568.90 to be exact. I don't like the idea of anyone other than myself stripping my wife naked, sponging her clean, dressing her in something pretty, and pulling a smile back on her face. We can dig our own hole and ease her down ourselves; but if we're caught I'll go to jail. They might even think I killed her since a real doctor has yet to examine her. Hospitals treat patients like worthless furniture. I'm a Christian Scientist. Matter is the unreal and temporal, it's mortal error. My wife died all by herself, in a chair. Spirit is immortal truth. My big concern is loving her. That's what she needs right now, my concentration. Calling on a doctor isn't something we do. Love always has and always will meet our needs. Someone's measuring spoonfuls of salt into my poked-out eyeball.

I once killed a man for digging a hole. A stranger. I was drunk. I saw him digging. It got me angry. I can't explain it. The hole was wrong, stupid looking, and it was a very hot day. Why should anybody be digging? While I was in jail I thought of all the times I've wanted to kill someone, at least once every day. I'm always blowing my stack. Temper's an odd little toy. At that crucial moment, right before you do anything, and then once you've decided to go ahead and do it, killing is an honest reaction. You're pissed and the other guy needs to be creamed. But I tell myself no, don't kill every day, don't kill everyone who upsets you, don't throw pitchforks at the faces of strangers who look at you with insinuating eyebrows. When I was my son's age I thought of killing my parents all the time. Amazingly enough I didn't and they didn't push me down the garbage disposal, either. They could've; I was their little one. All I did was eat. My indigestion alone turned their lifestyle into a sour drama. So now I say to myself, you are a fortunate man; think of how terrible it would be if I were a day-to-day killer, a drug addict of blood? It would bore me. It would be like weighing diamonds full time, or being a professional smoocher of bikini models, or a vagina doctor to the stars. Imagine getting used to that? Excuse me, Ms. Gina Lola Osayno, could you spread your awesome hairlessness a bit wider, I'm having trouble reaching your inner sanctum. And then she says, doctor, is my cunt still pretty, an unnamed leading man is coming over tonight to put out my smoldering inner heat. She looks at me like that man might be me, and I say, unable to hold back a yawn, and bored by the same trivial questions, yes, I say, yes Tina, I mean Gina, your vulva is arresting. But killing once, and learning from it, will turn a man around. And it's wisdom that sets the tone.

All I keep thinking about is the expression, thou shall not inter until life has been attempted to be restored through all the subtle, vague, and often abstract means of osmosis. It echoes through my head like the lyrics to a song I like, that I think is speaking to me personally, but after a hundred efforts of listening still don't fully understand. Osmosis: not as complicated as one might suspect. A mixture of the physical and the spiritual. People die of cancer from standing beside smokers; others are poisoned through a hand-shake. The same can be said in reverse. A dead person can be rejuvenated if they are placed properly beside a vibrant, utterly living, human being—and that thriving entity is yours truly, speaking now.

The moment my wife died my son took an interest in geology. He turned to digging. Right now he's in the yard digging harmless little holes. He knows that a deep narrow rectangle will set me off. The shape of a grave, the squaring off of the human body, not much different than a large bathtub, it's impossible to overcome.

The deeper a man drives his shovel the more he sees how the earth looks, how it changes. We need to know that, men do. I sit here with my son in mind and I speak for our species, the male subdivision. Here is a rock: dry, coarse, with tiny granules covering the surface. I flip the rock over and it's caked with dark wet earth, the first layer. There are worms crawling about performing an unknown task. Let's not go into that. Jab a shovel down and you come up with more damp earth. Somehow the earth is moist all by itself. Inner rivers. The soil of the earth is worth comparing to the soul in a man's body. The earth is comprehensible even if the book my son's reading makes no sense to me, whereas the soul inside us is a total mystery. I see the earth as a big body, an old one, something everyone calls Mother. She grows things all the time, and yet, remains round; to keep us honest she throws a lightning bolt and a hurricane our way, an earthquake. Still round, a floating ball. My body burps up all kinds of surprises that I observe in the same way, with curiosity and fear.

My son smears dark earth on the wall opposite the fireplace. He uses his fingers, and a sock he no longer intends to wear. A first I was disappointed with the picture. I expected something beautiful or realistic like a house, a tree, with people beside it, a dog. All he made were layers. He used water to thin it down. When I got angry at the picture he told me what it was and I got embarrassed. Stupid me. He was drawing the levels of the earth itself. All the joints and cracks, the interesting ripples and strange crumbling things. I look at this brown mess, that could be seen as an offense to decent living conditions, and I think, the world is basically brown: whiskey, beans, steak, hash, my clothes, hair, eyes, and when I am regular an encouraging number two.

I point at random to a paragraph on an open page of my son's textbook on the kitchen table. "The new minerals that develop during chemical metamorphism are, as a result of directed pressure, dominantly flat, tabular, or elongated bladelike forms. The common minerals that have these shapes are muscovite, biotite, chlorite, talc (a hydrous magnesium silicate), and bladed variety of hornblende." The technical world is an excruciating place. You want to know more and all you're left with is a hostile vocabulary beating you on the head.

I just bathed my dead wife in Epson salts to get the final impurities out. The burping drain reminded me of her own booming burps and made me think that she was already back with us. I let her drip dry in the tub for ten minutes before toweling her off. I carry her into the room, gently drop her on one side of the bed (clean blue sheets, like the sky), and leap over her onto the other side. I strip. I lay down next to her. I feel like we're two glazed spiral logs cooling on the rack. This procedure isn't totally out of character. When she was alive I used to make love to her when she was sound asleep. I told her this one afternoon and she said fine, just don't try and stick you-know-what in my mouth.

I roll my wife on top of me. Her eyes are closed. She's gained weight. I wrap my arms around her; kiss her, no tongue, a simple peck. I tuck her face into my neck and breathe the life inside me back into Meredith. You're such a wonderful woman. Wake up sweetheart, I say, make me look silly. I push her off of me and roll on top; kiss her again. Come on back, I say, here I am, wishing you were here, no place like home.

CHARLIE HAUCK

Bust

Francis Gaffney had no talent for goodbyes. If he visited you, and decided to take his leave, the most you would get from him was an "excuse me," as if he were ducking into the rest room or going out to check the mailbox. Fifteen or twenty minutes later, you'd realize he was gone for good.

Young Gaffney, a former candidate for the priesthood, was currently on leave from St. Tristan's College in Erie, Pennsylvania, where he taught media studies. He had been in Los Angeles several months as an official representative of the Vatican's Office of the Congregation of Saints, in Rome. He had been hired by the Catholic Church to write a report on the late Missy Abbot, the beloved star of *The Missy Abbot Show*, a half-hour situation comedy that had been a cornerstone of the CBS Friday night line-up in the early eighties. There was talk of making her a saint.

Missy Abbot died an untimely, and many said a heroic, death from pancreatic cancer. Since then, a few of her more pious fans had claimed Missy performed miracles on their behalf. John Cardinal Powers, the excitable prelate in charge of the Archdiocese of Los Angeles, warmed quickly to the idea of a television star becoming a saint. He lobbied the Vatican to begin the long and arduous process of canonization on Missy's behalf. The cause was also endorsed by the chaplain and the nuns out at the Shrine of the Virgin of Malibu, where Missy had spent her final days. But the most emphatic, although secret, backing came from Hal Barron, the head of Beverlywood Productions, who owned the syndication rights to *The Missy Abbot Show*. Hal thought that having the star of your show declared a saint would do wonders for foreign sales.

Willow Winowski, a bright young woman who had wasted her formative years on boys and recreational drugs, was assigned by Beverlywood Productions to assist Francis Gaffney in his research on the life of Missy Abbot. Willow, during the hours she spent viewing all one-hundred and thirty episodes of *The Missy Abbot Show* with Francis, made the mistake of falling in love with him. The lanky ex-seminarian was a fine enough fellow to be in love with, from many points of view. His inexperience with women only made him the more fresh and attractive to Willow. But Francis was embarrassed by Willow's lack of an education, and her non-Catholicity. So while he would spend long hours with her in bed, making love, he tended not to step out with her in public places. Willow complained that it was like being involved with a married man.

Willow Winowski was fully aware of, and frequently annoyed by, Francis Gaffney's habit of disappearing without a good-bye. Willow understood that her lover would soon be going back home to Erie. She could envision him just leaving, without saying a word. So one mid-December afternoon, she pressed young Gaffney for specific information about his departure. He had no interest in discussing it.

"It's too soon to even think about that," he said.

"Francis! You're pressing my nutty button," said Willow.

"Why worry about it?"

"Because I want to prepare myself."

She pursued the topic. Finally, Francis allowed that the spring quarter at St. Tristan's started "in February." He did not mention that in the zippered side pocket of his Italian-made toiletries kit of matte black kid leather there was an airline ticket that would return him to Erie on January eighteenth.

In reflective moments, Francis berated himself for this unforthright conduct. But like most people, from the pious to the profane, he had no talent for dwelling on his shortcomings.

To compensate somewhat for this little show of rogue male behavior, Francis grew more relaxed about appearing in public with Willow. An invitation to attend the unveiling of a bust of Missy Abbot tested this new leniency. The event, to take place at the Shrine of the Virgin of Malibu two days after Christmas, could connect the young scholar directly to Willow in the eyes of all sorts of Catholic dignitaries, and perhaps even Cardinal Powers himself. Willow, however, would not be dissuaded. She pointed out that, as his assistant, she had received an invitation of her own. She would be attending in any event. Francis relented and agreed to take her with him.

"This bust sort of came out of nowhere, didn't it?" he asked on the drive up the Pacific Coast Highway. He found that trip generally disappointing; mostly, you see the backs of houses that face the ocean, as if you're on a train rolling through an inner city. Days of rain had left the ocean a beautiful green which, as Los Angeles natives knew, was caused by the polluted overflow of municipal sewers. The sun came down through the clouds like the beams of divine light on children's holy cards. Mists rose from the Santa Monica Mountains like vapors from a volcano. "I hadn't heard anything about a bust. Has it been in the works for a long time?" said Francis.

"I don't know," said Willow.

"And Anton Nagy. How did they get Anton Nagy to do a bust of Missy Abbot? Who could afford it?"

"Hal Barron, probably," said Willow.

"Really?" asked Francis.

"You're not supposed to know that," said Willow. "His connection is strictly secret. Hey, look, a rainbow." A splendid rainbow arched over the Santa Monica Bay and stretched inland.

"It looks like it goes right down into the Malibu Colony, doesn't it?" said Francis.

"Then there's gold at the end of that rainbow, all right," said Willow. "Those are five to ten million dollar houses."

The bust of Missy Abbot, covered in white drapery, rested on a square column in a patch of crown vetch several yards from the main entrance to the chapel at the Shrine of the Virgin of Malibu. It looked out over the roiling and waste-filled Pacific. Overhead, a Japanese maple tree provided it shelter; even now, in late December, the tree was heavy with leaves of lush reds and yellows. They seemed prepared to remain until spring, when fresh green buds would force them to the ground.

Attendees gathered on the gravel walk that circled the bust and came, at its furthest reaches, uncomfortably close to the edge of the steep bluff. They conversed among ourselves in polite tones as they awaited the arrival of John Cardinal Powers. They scanned the lane that twisted uphill from the Pacific Coast Highway, prepared to catch the first glimpse of the black Buick Park Avenue that would announce the imminence of the prelate. They were surprised, then, by the sound of a rotor blade chopping through wet air. They looked upward, where a small white helicopter churned through the pewter skies. The heads of the faithful followed the gradual descent of the helicopter like a tier of tennis fans watching a shot in slow motion replay. Father Thomas "Boomer" Dowd, the shrine chaplain, ran to greet His Eminence as the craft alit in the parking lot. The rotor blades fanned the air violently enough to press Father Dowd's cassock flat against his legs. The blades rested and the cardinal emerged splendid in flowing red, wearing a pea green headset, which he removed and presented to Boomer Dowd, who replaced it in the cockpit. He started toward the assembly in strides impressive enough to give his pudgy escort difficulty in keeping pace. The cardinal approached the assembled guests and said, "Okay, let's get the cows to Abeline."

The ceremony was brief. Boomer introduced the sculptor, who acknowledged applause but declined to speak. Cardinal Powers said a few words and read the prayer of intercession to Missy Abbot. Then fell to His Eminence the honor of physically unveiling the bust. He whipped off the white satin with quick drama, like a magician revealing a bowl of goldfish. The wind off the ocean swallowed the polite applause. Missy was done in bronze, in the lost wax method, with metal overlapping on itself to give the whole bust a craggy look. The effect was "impressionistic" enough to convince the naive that this was high art. From a certain distance, she looked like W. H. Auden. She stood facing the bay, "head thrown back, throat to the stars," as Euripides writes of the maenads, like a masthead for the shrine.

A light lunch ("a collation" the sisters called it in their invitation) was served in the refectory, finger sandwiches and pastries and coffee. Francis, who tried not to appear overly linked to Willow, receded into the crowd, hoping Willow wouldn't notice where he'd gone.

"Mister Gaffney..."

Francis turned and was astonished to find himself the object of Cardinal Powers's attention.

"You're leaving us when?"

"On January eighteenth, Your Eminence."

"So soon. I'd like a report from you before you go."

"Actually, Your Eminence, I won't be finishing the *positio* until well into the summer." The *positio* was the official title for the paper Francis would write on Missy Abbot.

"No, just a personal report. An indication of your findings."

"Of course, Your Eminence."

"Let's do it now. After this. I have a confirmation in Highland Park. You can ride with me."

"In the helicopter?"

Willow approached but stood away at a respectful distance, so Francis would not be obliged to introduce her.

"The safest way to fly," said the cardinal.

"I'm afraid I'd be extremely nervous, Your Eminence. And ill, too, probably."

"Drink in new experiences, Gaffney."

"Your Eminence, I'm beginning to perspire right now, just contemplating it."

"It would be very convenient for me, Gaffney, especially since you're leaving town on January eighteenth. Say a prayer to Saint Joseph of Cupertino, the patron saint of air travelers."

A prayer to Saint Jude, the patron saint of lost causes, would be more in order.

Boomer Dowd tugged at the cardinal, urging him to greet an important guest. Francis turned to make his escape, only to encounter the flared nostrils and glaring eyes of Willow Winowski.

"You're leaving Los Angeles on January eighteenth?"

"I just worked out the details. I haven't had a chance to talk to you about it yet."

"Worked out the details when? We had dinner together last night, we slept together. When did you work out the details?"

"Is this the best time to discuss this?"

"You weren't going to tell me, were you? When were you going to tell me?"

"Everybody! Everybody!" called out Boomer Dowd, banging on the side of the coffee urn with a spoon. "Cardinal Powers is leaving. He'd like to give us his blessing."

All turned toward the cardinal. The more pious fell to one knee. Francis joined them, but only because he was finding it difficult to remain erect. Confrontations terrified him, and Willow, at this moment, was as terrible as an army with banners, as the Song of Solomon has it. As Cardinal Powers signed the cross and hummed his blessing across the room, Francis shook as if from a fever.

The crowd rose. Francis turned to Willow and said, "I can explain, but I can't talk now. I promised to go with the cardinal."

He ran across the unevenly-tiled refectory floor toward the blur of red that was leaving the room. Better the terror of a helicopter flight than the blasting wrath of Willow Winowski. And there was an additional advantage in choosing the helicopter: with luck, he might be killed.

That leg of the journey over the waters of the Santa Monica Bay was the worst of it for Francis.

"Relax," ordered the cardinal. "Deep breaths, and relax."

"I worry about sharks," said Francis.

"Nothing to worry about. If we crash, you'll be dead on impact with the water." The cardinal lit a Tiparillo. "These aren't so bad," he explained. "I don't inhale."

Francis tried looking down at his feet, but that made things worse. The floor was part of the plastic bubble that formed the cockpit. He saw green-blue water, flecked white by the wind and only yards away, racing between his insoles.

"Damn it, you're distracting me. Relax!" said the cardinal.

Francis mustered his courage to the best of his abilities. The cardinal cut inland just past the Santa Monica pier. Francis found the linear grids of the streets and the hard angles of the office buildings more comforting than the hidden terrors of the ocean.

"So what do you think of our Missy?" asked Cardinal Powers as they chopped over Santa Monica High School. Much of *Rebel Without a Cause* was filmed there, Francis knew. Further east, at Santa Monica Community College, James Dean and Dustin Hoffman had attended classes together. "Do you think we have a saint on our hands?"

"Of course, that's not part of my purpose, to determine something like that, Your Eminence."

"But your guess?"

"I'd be uncomfortable venturing an opinion. I'm afraid it might compromise—" Francis sucked in his breath as the cardinal dipped the craft abruptly downward, without any apparent reason. "Would compromise my work in the eyes of the Congregation of Saints. If I seemed to be promoting a point of view."

"But unofficially, between us."

"I don't know what I could say at this point that would be appropriate."

The cardinal dipped the helicopter once more, and Francis brought both hands to his mouth, afraid he might vomit. The cardinal looked straight ahead, as if he were glaring at the sky itself, the Tiparillo clenched in his teeth. It occurred to Francis that Cardinal Powers was punishing him for his reticence. Torturing him, in a way. A contemporary Inquisition. It was impossible to be certain, but Francis decided to invent something interesting enough about Missy Abbot to forfend another sudden dip.

"Actually, there's quite a bit in her personal diaries that I would say is very original, in her description of her relationship to God."

"There you go," said Cardinal Powers. "Like what?"

"Like what?" Francis had no idea. Missy's diaries were, in fact, riddled with pietistic banalities. "Well... she writes very eloquently on the spiritual value of the natural world. She discusses how God created the universe, and then Jesus created the beauty of it, for man. The beauty of the world was Christ's loving touch reaching out to us through physical matter. Missy maintains that the love of this beauty is almost like a sacrament."

"Wonderful stuff!" said Cardinal Powers.

It should be, thought Francis. He was, after all, quoting from the spiritual diaries of Simone Weil, on whom he had once written a thesis.

"More," ordered Cardinal Powers.

"More? Uh... Missy writes that generosity and compassion are inseparable, and they both have their models in creation and in the passion of Christ... she says that the existence of evil in the world, far from disproving the reality of God, is the very thing that reveals Him in His truth... she had an interesting thought about loving our neighbor, that it should be a completely anonymous, and therefore a completely universal, love."

Francis delighted the cardinal-pilot with these plagiarisms until the helicopter flew over Koreatown, bypassed the city center, and veered toward Dodger Stadium.

"This is very good," said the cardinal. "You have things to work with."

They came to a sward of green on the border of Elysian Park, and the cardinal began to hover. Below, two police cars waited, lights flashing.

"As a reward for your courage," said Cardinal Powers, "I'm going to rid you of your fear of helicopters."

"How?"

"By demonstrating how amazingly safe they are. What other aircraft could land without incident if it were this far from the ground, and lost its power? None."

"I don't think I understand, Your Eminence."

"Watch. I'm cutting the engine."

"No!" yelled Francis. The cardinal cast him the look of bemused contempt that the expert saves for the greenhorn. The engine of the helicopter was suddenly silent. Francis threw his hands over his mouth again as he felt the machine begin to drop through the air.

"Air catches the rotor blades," explained the cardinal. "Swirls them in the reverse direction. We descend in perfect safety."

The cardinal was greeted by policemen, a pastor, and a delegation of Catholic laymen, most of them Latinos. Francis emerged from the helicopter like a stillborn from the womb. The cardinal shook Francis' hand and said, "My prayers are with you for the successful continuation of your work." The prelate was then escorted to a yellow Lincoln Town Car, the police sirens kicked in and a small motorcade darted off down Avenue 43. Francis found himself alone, disoriented, and without transportation, in a not very safe part of town.

JOHN PETERSON

Water, Blood, Leaves

He was contemplating three potential epigraphs in the late evening.
—It's a problem, he said. They're all so good.

4

Quand mes amis sont borgnes, je les regarde de profil.
(When my friends are one-eyed, I look at their side face.)

289

Les poètes sont plus inspires par les images que par la présence même des objets.
(Poets are even more inspired by the images of objects than by the presence of the objects themselves.)

286

Rien de ce qui le transporte pas n'est poésie. La lyre est un instrument aile.
(Nothing which does not transport is poetry. The lyre is a winged instrument.)
—from *Pensées de Joubert*

Not long before I was married, I went with my brother for a hike in the hills just above the ocean. Rambla Pacifico. Malibu. There was wind that day, and gray clouds. *No. Forget those first two lines. Because we just walked from the car to the first rock (old images—wind and rain).* Both my dogs were still alive then. Robert had brought a girl. *(Robert is dead now, electrocuted nude in his backyard after swimming in the pool then plugging in a floodlight.)* We looked out through the canyon and saw the water. *Robert had said, "Let's imagine this is Hawaii. There's a reef right there. And waves coming in."* I thought I could feel a few drops hit my face. Probably coming from the clouds, all gray. *But I didn't see any waves, and Robert had taken some mushrooms, so he was getting off on it. I told him that I wasn't going to do the make believe thing.*

Robert was leaning in close next to that girl and he laughed at me. Out of nowhere he said, "I think that whole school scene is just something blown in off the ocean, *man.* You're just lookin' at those pictures the blind man sees." *That's what I'm trying to figure on here, because he was feeling real good with the quiet little girl there and he didn't mean anything. He was trying to be my friend. He was just babbling because I was about to graduate college and all I had to do was fly back for one more semester and it would all be over. Then he started talking about the waves again. "I'm right there, I'm right there," he said. And he was squatting like he was surfing and he stuck his lips out like a monkey. And his hair was all smashed down white. So that's why this whole story is so hard to write. So stupid. Here I am trying to deal with Joubert but there's that stupid scene with stupid language and with Robert and that girl and* I don't know where the dogs were.

But Robert just switched channels for a second. He was flying and I looked at his profile while he was watching the ocean telling me about that "whole scene." And Robert's whole image of life was just a cold apparition blurring the background anyway, because water does that. He couldn't see me. *But how could I say these things in a story like this? All that big talk in a stupid story about Robert and that little blonde. Just sitting there, tripping on mushrooms while me I thought* we were all going to get rained on and then I'd have to drive them back *in the Volkswagen, and the dogs all wet and smelling and those two flying, all crunched up in the back. But* It never did rain that day . . . *and Harvard is a blur. Shit, how does this thing end? you go to sleep.*

I've got the bed to myself.

II.

Nell'ora che comincia i tristi lai la rondinalla presso all mattina forse a memória de' suo' primi guai, e che la mente nostra, peregrina più dalla carne e men da' pensier presa, all sue vision quasi è divina,

(At the hour near morning, when the swallow begins her plaintive songs, in remembrance, perhaps, of her ancient woes, and when our mind, more a pilgrim from the flesh and less held by thoughts, is in

its visions almost prophetic,)

—No, he said. Scratch that. Don't use it. This one's better.

We have a continual experience of our immortality in the divination of our dreams, and these would not be possible unless something in us were immortal.

-Dante

I awoke at nine this morning and remembered Mrs. Nestler had taken the children to school.

Sun broke partly through the clouds this morning,
and a wind brushed the back of a Siamese
who stalked one of the red tile roofs
where someone was standing outside of
a house just like ours.

Of course, birds were singing as they do every morning, and I thought the patio should be swept clean, but I always watch that cat (sometimes at night I wake and hear its voice because it sounds like a baby crying). Then, a question crossed my mind. Why would a cat on a clear morning be different from the wind? Or leaves from next door cross the boundary and land on our patio? Is the patio ours? It looks just like theirs. And why would the birds in those trees sing above these images as if these images were not separate? I cannot separate them. Their children are friends with my children. My children are at St. Martin's, the priest is in the rectory. Robert's funeral was in that church. Sunset Boulevard is like a river that has taken everyone to that church, and I believe it is dangerous for me to be sitting inside my head thinking as if things are not separate.

Instead of going down to sweep the leaves, I listened to the birds, their voices in the room. Across, the street, beyond the narrow vacant lot, a small cloud broke.

Rain may trace a sunny meadow
while you stay dry in that same field.
When the clouds are broken the sky is scattered

and drops fall just there near the trees.
And trees too trace a jagged line,
juxtaposed green against the white clouds
around the rim of the dry meadow.

*It's a bad poem, but a poem nonetheless and the narrow lot became a meadow. It
seems as if* The neighborhood acts as a waking image for me. Like blue sky
fresh as rain. The image of rain and blue sky is sudden because the sky is more
often brown here, and even though I cannot touch the sky or feel the rain, by
looking at them I change. I watched the rain from a hundred yards away;
while my face and hands stayed dry, the drops fell on a sunny morning. These
images will not grow old because the sky is more often brown. (I realize I once
said they were old images, but now I am in love with them because I
remember that the sky is so often brown. During a fire, it is worse. The place
where I sat with Robert and his girl and looked at the waves—Rambla
Pacifico—has had its brush burned away from fire twice since I was last there.
The brush returned. I have not seen Robert for many years.)

I see the clock show eleven and my wife drives up in the truck, then parks.
A poem before she gets here:

I, the window, her eyes, the street puddles
blue after the rain and the wind shifting.
Her robe rushing outside like beige silk,
ugly against the grass and oleander.

Gone all night and working like mad
she comes home caught up and satisfied
with a job well done. The business runs smoothly
while I'm worried about Rachel and Tommy
come home early because today, First Friday
is half-day and it might rain again.

She opened the door to the study.
—Hi, she said. Get anything done?

—A few lines, just now.

—I'm going to bed. You?

—Gotta pick up the kids.

—Oh, she said. Don't forget the patio. The bougainvillea stains.

—All right.

III.

**There, in front, are pictures. Don't look. Where pictures block
vision, vision blocks pictures. We write with pictures that
cannot be seen by blind people. Blind pictures block vision. (In
blindness, pictures block vision.)**

—My Own

And when she goes to sleep during the day like that she must dream. She
might dream she's an old man. She might lie on her back as him, her head
propped by a mound of pine needles, ears filled with wind rushed like a wave
through the forest. He might wake from a sea gull's voice and see his dogs,
each with one eye opened, noses at his feet.

All three would pop up, tails wagging. They'd run down a little trail, down
the slope bouncing easily, letting the incline pull their bodies while their legs
kept up.

He'd shout, "Yeah! Hey!" like a cowboy. "Come on! Come on!" But the
dogs would only trot faster, never run, because they're with him and he's old.

But before they know it, he turns off the path and stoops through a clump
of pines to the side. They turn and catch the scent. He huffs and stays ahead.
He veers to his left now, just parallel to the trail. He runs with his knees bent,
scampering boy-like past the trunks, beneath the boughs. Again he turns left
and the dogs are coming. He breaks out of the trees, runs upright, heaving,
and the dogs get caught up in his legs so he falls, and it's soft because they're on
the beach now. The sand.

She would then wake and tell me her dream, finishing in her own way:

"Then they pounced on me," she'd say, "soft paws pushed on my chest.
And one jumped and did a little circle chasing his tail. And they both cried like
puppies do, in their throats, whining, but they were embarrassed to really cry

because I was there. Their master."

"Then I was in the water," she'd say. "The dogs were still there. The salt stung my legs and underarms. I shaved them before I went to bed. Isn't that silly? But there was wind, and gray clouds. It felt so strange in the ocean. We should go to the ocean," she would say. "We should go to Malibu and throw ourselves into the ocean at the place where the mountain crossed the highway during the rain. Oh, and there's more, I forgot."

"There was a school yard near the ocean. A child and teacher stood in the school yard." And then she would tell me how she was, "all-of-a-sudden the child." (And then I would think to myself that the only way she could have gotten to the shore from the ocean was via water-drop transport. Water on wind. And then I'd smile and almost start laughing.)

"This is silly," she would say. "Don't laugh at me. Where are Rachel and Tom?"

—Go on, go on. I'm not laughing at you. They're outside.

Then she would be distracted and I would have to finish writing her dream:

The teacher leaned far over the child so that he, the child, could see only the silhouette of his teacher's chin, nose, and eyelashes. The boy enjoyed the sensation of being covered. He felt the skin below her neck touch his forehead and lips. His teacher's arms were warm and wrapped tightly around his small frame. He did not know it, but this was very much like the feeling he would have later in life when engaged in sex.

"I had a fingernail bite my bare foot in the night," he would say to the teacher. "When I rode my bike to school kids whooped and threw burrs at my cuffs. When I rounded a corner I leaned. I *leaned*. Then I felt the spot on the bottom of my foot inside my shoe. The place where I stepped on the fingernail."

The other children were playing in the yard, a dirt yard, with weeds and dirt mounds to hide and play behind. The wind was blowing, raising dust and pushing water from the ocean, off the tops of waves, onto the school yard. There seemed a storm about to break.

"Let's walk over here."

"No, I think I saw a dog."

"A dog?"

"I saw one."

"Well, lean in closer. But dogs won't hurt."

The teacher allowed her students to play in the front of the storm in the school yard by the ocean. She held one frightened student. The little boy was covered by his teacher. The other children played in the dirt yard. They hid behind dirt mounds, and their black leather shoes became dusty.

—Honey, did you bring my robe in? she said. You're busy, aren't you?

She had poked her head in the study door. Her hair was mussed and her eyes puffed and saggy.

—No. Not so much. Shall I?

She entered the room, and he watched her nude body, taut and smooth across her breasts and down along her belly, cross the room to the window. There were sleep lines on her back. She yelled suddenly:

—Damn! It fell into the leaves. It's all stained now!

He began to gather up his papers, and he looked to see her shadow leave the room. It left the room, but he sensed she was still there. Someone was there with him. And then he thought he should sweep the leaves, but he knew they would be wet, and he did not want to electrocute anyone. And he realized the ocean would look different if he saw it now. Water, have you always been so different? he said. And then he thought about the three epigraphs some more, remembering their sad music and odd messages bleeding into the night and into the morning.

DISASTERS
IN CARS

Nobody with a good car needs to be justified.
—Flannery O'Connor

HARLAN ELLISON

Along The Scenic Route

The blood-red Mercury with the twin-mounted 7.6 mm Spandaus cut George off as he was shifting lanes. The Merc cut out sharply, three cars behind George, and the driver decked it. The boom of his gas-turbine engine got through George's baffling system without difficulty, like a fist in the ear. The Merc sprayed JP-4 gook and water in a wide fan from its jet nozzle and cut back in, a matter of inches in front of George's Chevy Piranha.

George slapped the selector control on the dash, lighting YOU STUPID BASTARD, WHAT DO YOU THINK YOU'RE DOING and I HOPE YOU CRASH & BURN, YOU SON OF A BITCH. Jessica moaned softly with uncontrolled fear, but George could not hear her: he was screaming obscenities.

George kicked it into Overplunge and depressed the selector button extending the rotating buzzsaws. Dallas razors, they were called, in the repair shoppes. But the crimson Merc pulled away doing an easy 115.

"I'll get you, you beaver-sucker!" he howled.

The Piranha jumped, surged forward. But the Merc was already two dozen car-lengths down the Freeway. Adrenaline pumped through George's system. Beside him, Jessica put a hand on his arm. "Oh, forget it, George; it's just some young snot," she said. Always conciliatory.

"My masculinity's threatened," he murmured, and hunched over the wheel. Jessica looked toward heaven, wishing a bolt of lightning had come from that location many months past, striking Dr. Yasimir directly in his Freud, long before George could have picked up psychiatric justifications for his awful temper.

"Get me Collision Control!" George snarled at her.

Jessica shrugged, as if to say *here we go again,* and dialed CC on the peek. The smiling face of a fusco, the Freeway Sector Control Operator, blurred green and yellow, then came into sharp focus. "Your request, sir?"

"Clearance for duel, Highway 101, northbound."

"Your license number, sir?"

"XUPD 88321," George said. He was scanning the Freeway, keeping the blood-red Mercury in sight, obstinately refusing to stud on the tracking sights.

"Your proposed opponent, sir?"

"Red Mercury GT. '88 model."

"License, sir."

"Just a second." George pressed the stud for the instant replay and the last ten miles rewound on the Sony Backtracker. He ran it forward again till he caught the instant the Merc had passed him, froze the frame, and got the number. "MFCS 90909."

"One moment, sir."

George fretted behind the wheel. "*Now* what the hell's holding her up? Whenever you want service, they've got problems. But boy, when it comes tax time—"

The fusco came back and smiled. "I've checked our master Sector grid, sir, and I find authorization may be permitted, but I am required by law to inform you that your proposed opponent is more heavily armed than yourself."

George licked his lips. "What's he running?"

"Our records indicate 7.6 mm Spandau equipment, bulletproof screens and coded optionals."

George sat silently. His speed dropped. The tachometer fluttered, settled.

"Let him go, George," Jessica said. "You know he'd take you."

Two blotches of anger spread on George's cheeks. "Oh, yeah!?!" He howled at the fusco, "Get me a confirm on that Mercury, Fusco!"

She blurred off, and George decked the Piranha: it leaped forward. Jessica sighed with resignation and pulled the drawer out from beneath her bucket. She unfolded the g-suit and began stretching into it. She said nothing, but continued to shake her head.

"We'll *see!*" George said.

"Oh, George, when will you ever grow up?"

He did not answer, but his nostrils flared with barely restrained anger.

The fusco smeared back and said, "Opponent confirms, sir. Freeway Underwriters have already cross-filed you as mutual beneficiaries. Please observe standard traffic regulations, and good luck, sir."

She vanished, and George set the Piranha on sleepwalker as he donned his own g-suit. He overrode the sleeper and was back on manual in moments.

"Now, you stuffer, *now* let's see!" 100. 110. 120.

He was gaining rapidly on the Merc now. As the Chevy hit 120, the mastercomp flashed red and suggested crossover. George punched the selector and the telescoping arms of the buzzsaws retracted into the axles, even as the buzzsaws stopped whirling. In a moment—drawn back in, now merely fancy decorations in the hubcaps. The wheels retracted into the underbody of the Chevy and the air-cushion took over. Now the Chevy skimmed along, two inches above the roadbed of the Freeway.

Ahead, George could see the Merc also crossing over to air-cushion. 120. 135. 150.

"George, this is crazy!" Jessica said, her face in that characteristic shrike expression. "You're no hot-rodder, George. You're a family man, and this is the family car!"

George chuckled nastily. "I've had it with these fuzzfaces. Last year . . . you remember last year? . . . you remember when that punk stuffer ran us into the abutment? I swore I'd never put up with that kind of thing again. Why'd'you think I had all the optionals installed?"

Jessica opened the tambour doors of the glove compartment and slid out the service tray. She unplugged the jar of anti-flash salve and began spreading it on her face and hands. "I *knew* I shouldn't have let you put that laser thing in this car!" George chuckled again. Fuzzfaces, punks, rodders!

George felt the Piranha surge forward, the big reliable Stirling engine recycling the hot air for more and more efficient thrust. Unlike the Merc's inefficient kerosene system, there was no exhaust emission from the nuclear power plant, the external combustion engine almost noiseless, the big radiator tailfin in the rear dissipating the tremendous heat, stabilizing the car as it swooshed along, two inches off the roadbed.

George knew he would catch the blood-red Mercury. Then one smartass punk was going to learn he couldn't flout law and order by running decent citizens off the Freeways!

"Get me my gun," George said.

Jessica shook her head with exasperation, reached under George's bucket, pulled out his drawer and handed him the bulky .45 automatic in its breakaway upside-down shoulder rig. George studded in the sleeper, worked his arms into the rig, tested the oiled leather of the holster, and when he was satisfied, returned the Piranha to manual.

"Oh, God," Jessica said, "John Dillinger rides again."

"Listen!" George shouted, getting more furious with each stupidity she offered. "If you can't be of some help to me, just shut your damned mouth. I'd put you out and come back for you, but I'm in a duel . . . can you understand that? I'm in a duel!" She murmured a yes, George, and fell silent.

There was a transmission queep from the transceiver. George studded it on. No picture. Just vocal. It had to be the driver of the Mercury, up ahead of them. Beaming directly at one another's antennae, using a tightbeam directional, they could keep in touch: it was a standard trick used by rods to rattle their opponents.

"Hey, Boze, you not really gonna custer me, are you? Back'm, Boze. No bad trips, true. The kid'll drop back, hang a couple of biggies on ya, just to teach ya a little lesson, letcha swimaway." The voice of the driver was hard, mirthless, the ugly sound of a driver used to being challenged.

"Listen, you young snot," George said, grating his words, trying to sound more menacing than he felt, "I'm going to teach *you* the lesson!"

The Merc's driver laughed raucously.

"Boze, you *de*-mote me, true!"

"And stop calling me a bozo, you lousy little degenerate!"

"Ooooo-weeee, got me a thrasher this time out. Okay, Boze, you be custer an' I'll play arrow. Good shells, baby Boze!"

The finalizing queep sounded, and George gripped the wheel with hands that went knuckle-white. The Merc suddenly shot away from him. He had been steadily gaining, but now as though it had been springloaded, the Mercury burst forward, spraying gook and water on both sides of the forty-foot lanes they were using. "Cut in his afterburner," George snarled. The driver of the Mercury had injected water into the exhaust for added thrust through the jet nozzle. The boom of the Merc's big, noisy engine hit him, and George studded in the rear-mounted propellers to give him more speed. 175.

185. 195.

He was crawling up the line toward the Merc. Gaining, gaining. Jessica pulled out her drawer and unfolded her crash-suit. It went on over the g-suit, and she let George know what she thought of his turning their Sunday Drive into a kamikaze duel.

He told her to stuff it, and did a sleeper, donned his own crash-suit, applied flash salve, and lowered the bangup helmet onto his head.

Back on manual he crawled, crawled, till he was only fifty yards behind the Mercury, the gas-turbine vehicle sharp in his tinted windshield. "Put on your goggles . . . I'm going to show that punk who's a bozo . . ."

He pressed the stud to open the laser louvers. The needle-nosed glass tube peered out from its bay in the Chevy's hood. George read the power drain on his dash. The MHD power generator used to drive the laser was charging. He remembered what the salesman at Chick Williams Chevrolet had told him, pridefully, about the laser gun, when George had inquired about the optional.

Dynamite feature, Mr. Jackson. Absolutely sensational. Works off a magneto hydro dynamic power generator. Latest thing in defense armament. You know, to achieve sufficient potency from a CO_2 laser, you'd need a glass tube a mile long. Well, sir, we both know that's impractical, to say the least, so the project engineers at Chevy's big Bombay plant developed the "stack" method. Glass rods baffled with mirrors—360 feet of stack, the length of a football field . . . plus end-zones. Use it three ways. Punch a hole right through their tires at any speed under a hundred and twenty. If they're running a GT, you can put that hole right into the kerosene fuel tank, blow them off the road. Or, if they're running a Stirling, just heat the radiator. When the radiator gets hotter than the engine, the whole works shuts down. Dynamite. Also . . . and this is with proper CC authorization, you can go straight for the old jugular. Use the beam on the driver. Makes a neat hole. Dynamite!

"I'll take it," George murmured.

"What did you say?" Jessica asked.

"Nothing."

"George, you're a family man, not a rodder!"

"Stuff it!"

Then he was sorry he'd said it. She meant well. It was simply that . . . well, a man had to work hard to keep his balls. He looked sidewise at her. Wearing the Armadillo crash-suit, with its overlapping discs of ceramic material, she looked like a ferryflight pilot. The bangup hat hid her face. He wanted to apologize, but the moment had arrived. He locked the laser on the Merc, depressed the fire stud, and a beam of blinding light flashed from the hood of the Piranha. With the Merc on air-cushion, he had gone straight for the fuel tank.

But the Merc suddenly wasn't in front of him. Even as he had fired, the driver had sheered left into the next forty-foot-wide lane, and cut speed drastically. The Merc dropped back past them as the Pirahna swooshed ahead.

"He's on my back!" George shouted.

The next moment Spandau slugs tore at the hide of the Chevy. George slapped the studs, and the bulletproof screens went up. But not before pingholes had appeared in the beryllium hide of the Chevy, exposing the boron fiber filaments that gave the car its lightweight maneuverability. "Stuffer!" George breathed, terribly frightened. The driver was on his back, could ride him into the ground.

He swerved, dropping flaps and skimming the Piranha back and forth in wide arcs, across the two lanes. The Merc hung on. The Spandaus chattered heavily. The screens would hold, but what else was the driver running? What were the "coded optionals" the CC fusco had mentioned?

"Now see what you've gotten us into!"

"Jess, shut up, shut up!"

The transceiver queeped. He studded it on, still swerving. This time the driver of the Merc was sending via microwave video. The face blurred in.

He was a young boy. In his teens. Acne.

"Punk! Stinking punk!" George screamed, trying to swerve, drop back, accelerate. Nothing. The blood-red Merc hung on his tailfin, pounding at him. If one of those bullets struck the radiator tailfin, ricocheted, pierced to the engine, got through the lead shielding around the reactor. Jessica was crying, huddled inside her Armadillo.

He was silently glad she was in the g-suit. He would try something illegal in a moment.

"Hey, Boze. What's your slit look like? If she's creamy'n'nice I might letcha drop her at the next getty, and come back for her later. With your insurance, baby, and my pickle, I can keep her creamy'n'nice."

"Fuzzfaced punk! I'll see you dead first!"

"You're a real thrasher, old dad. Wish you well, but it's soon over. Say bye-bye to the nice rodder. You gonna die, old dad!"

George was shrieking inarticulately.

The boy laughed wildly. He was up on something. Ferro-coke, perhaps. Or D4. Or merryloo. His eyes glistened blue and young and deadly as a snake.

"Just wanted you to know the name of your piledriver, old dad. *You* can call me Billy . . ."

And he was gone. The Merc slipped forward, closer, and George had only a moment to realize that this Billy could not possibly have the money to equip his car with a laser, and that was a godsend. But the Spandaus were hacking away at the bulletproof screens. They weren't meant for extended punishment like this. Damn that Detroit iron!

He had to make the illegal move *now*.

Thank God for the g-suits. A tight turn, across the lanes, in direct contravention of the authorization. And in a tight turn, without the g-suits, doing—he checked the speedometer and tach—250 mph, the blood slams up against one side of the body. The g-suits would squeeze the side of the body where the blood tried to pool up. They would live. If . . .

He spun the wheel hard, slamming down on the accelerator. The Merc slewed sidewise and caught the turn. He never had a chance. He pulled out of the illegal turn, and their positions were the same. But the Merc had dropped back several car-lengths. Then from the transceiver there was a queep and he did not even stud in as the Police Copter overhead tightbeamed him in an authoritative voice:

"XUPD 88321. Warning! You will be in contravention of your dueling authorization if you try another maneuver of that sort! You are warned to keep to your lanes and the standard rules of road courtesy!"

Then it was queeped, and George felt the universe settling like silt over him. He was being killed by the system.

He'd have to eject. The seat would save him and Jessica. He tried to tell her, but she had fainted.

How did I get into this? he pleaded with himself. *Dear God, I swear if you get me out of this alive I'll never never never go mad like this again. Please God.*

Then the Merc was up on him again, pulling up *alongside!*

The window went down on the passenger side of the Mercury, and George whipped a glance across to see Billy with his lips skinned back from his teeth under the windblast and acceleration, aiming a .45 at him. Barely thinking, George studded the bumpers.

The super-conducting magnetic bumpers took hold, sucked Billy into his magnetic field, and they collided with a crash that shook the .45 out of the rodder's hand. In the instant of collision, George realized he had made his chance, and dropped back. In a moment he was riding the Merc's tail again.

Naked barbarism took hold. He wanted to kill now. Not crash the other, not wound the other, not stop the other—*kill the other!* Messages to God were forgotten.

He locked-in the laser and aimed for the windshield bubble. His sights caught the rear of the bubble, fastened to the outline of Billy's head, and George fired.

As the bolt of light struck the bubble, a black spot appeared, and remained for the seconds the laser touched. When the light cut off the black spot vanished. George cursed, screamed, cried, in fear and helplessness.

The Merc was equipped with a frequency-sensitive laserproof windshield. Chemicals in the windshield would "go black," opaque at certain frequencies, momentarily, anywhere a laser light touched them. He should have known. A duelist like this Billy, trained in weaponry, equipped for whatever might chance down a Freeway. Another coded optional. George found he was crying, piteously, within the cavern of his bangup hat.

Then the Merc was swerving again, executing a roll and dip that George could not understand, could not predict. Then the Merc dropped speed suddenly, and George found himself almost running up the jet nozzle of the blood-red vehicle.

He spun out and around, and Billy was behind him once more, closing in for the kill. He sent the propellers to full spin and reached for eternity. 270. 280. 290.

Then he heard the sizzling, and jerked his head around to see the back wall of the car rippling. *Oh my God,* he thought, in terror, *he can't afford a laser, but he's got an inductor beam!*

The beam was setting up strong local eddy currents in the beryllium hide of the Chevy. He'd rip a hole in the skin, the air would whip through, the car would go out of control.

George knew he was dead.

And Jessica.

And all because of this punk, this rodder fuzzface!

The Merc closed in confidently.

George thought wildly. There was no time for anything but the blind plunging panic of random thought. The speedometer and the tach agreed. They were doing 300 mph.

Riding on air-cushions.

The thought slipped through his panic.

It was the only possibility. He ripped off his bangup hat, and fumbled Jessica's loose. He hugged them in his lap with his free hand, and managed to stud down the window on the driver's side. Instantly, a blast of wind and accelerated air skinned back his lips, plastered his cheeks hollowly, made a death's head of Jessica's features. He fought to keep the Chevy stable, gyro'd.

Then, holding the bangup hats by their straps, he forced them around the edge of the window where the force of his speed jammed them against the side of the Chevy. Then he let go. And studded up the window. And braked sharply.

The bulky bangup hats dropped away, hit the roadbed, rolled directly into the path of the Merc. They disappeared underneath the blood-red car, and instantly the vehicle hit the Freeway. George swerved out of the way, dropping speed quickly.

The Merc hit with a crash, bounced, hit again, bounced and hit, bounced and hit. As it went past the Piranha, George saw Billy caroming off the insides of the car.

He watched the vehicle skid, wheelless, for a quarter of a mile down the Freeway before it caught the inner breakwall of the Jersey Barrier, shot high in the air, and came down turning over. It landed on the bubble, which burst, and exploded in a flash of fire and smoke that rocked the Chevy.

At three hundred miles per hour, two inches above the Freeway, riding on air, anything that broke up the air bubble would be a lethal weapon. He had won the duel. That Billy was dead.

George pulled in at the next getty, and sat in the lot. Jessica came around finally. He was slumped over the wheel, shaking, unable to speak.

She looked over at him, then reached out a trembling hand to touch his shoulder. He jumped at the infinitesimal pressure, felt though the g- and crash-suits. She started to speak, but the peek queeped, and she studded it on.

"Sector Control, sir." The fusco smiled.

He did not look up.

"Congratulations, sir. Despite one possible infraction, your duel has been logged as legal and binding. You'll be pleased to know that the occupant of the car you challenged was rated number one in the entire Central and Western Freeway circuits. Now that Mr. Bonney has been finalized, we are entering your name on the dueling records. Underwriters have asked us to inform you that a check will be in the mails to you within twenty-four hours.

"Again, sir, congratulations."

The peek went dead, and George tried to focus on the parking lot of the neon-and-silver getty. It had been a terrible experience. He never wanted to use a car that way again. It had been some other George, certainly not him.

"I'm a family man," he repeated Jessica's words. "And this is just a family car . . . I . . ."

She was smiling gently at him. Then they were in each other's arms, and he was crying, and she was saying that's all right, George, you had to do it, it's all right.

And the peek queeped.

She studded it on and the face of the fusco smiled back at her. "Congratulations, sir, you'll be pleased to know that Sector Control already has fifteen duel challenges for you.

"Mr. Ronnie Lee Hauptman of Dallas has asked for first challenge, and is, at this moment, speeding toward you with an ETA of 6:15 this evening. In the event Mr. Hauptman does not survive, you have waiting challenges from Mr. Fred Bull of Chatsworth, California . . . Mr. Leo Fowler of Philadelphia . . . Mr. Emil Zalenko of . . ."

George did not hear the list. He was trying desperately, with clubbed fingers, to extricate himself from the strangling folds of g- and crash-suits. But he knew it was no good. He would have to fight.

In the world of the Freeway, there was no place for a walking man.

JERRY RENEK

Crying

I've seen three motorcycle riders turned to dark pavement, riders without helmets, one in shorts. Yet each time I missed that flash of transformation from rider to street. And they didn't get to me, not like cars, which are different. Frances, who would not be called Fran, is not why motorcycle accidents don't do it for me. On freeways and curvy roads, I think about them no more than anyone. With Frances and me there could have been anything else between us. It wasn't though; it was car accidents.

However, much farther back, when I was nine my mother took me to Dana Point, to what she called "the best secret cave in California." In those days *the best* was how she convinced me we had to go to so many places: "the best San Andreas fault line view," "the best waffles," "the best military weapons storage," "the best Japanese garden." Today *the best* meant walking three miles of broken coastline.

Because these tidal waters were still well protected there was no public lot. She parked in the Marine Studies Institute's lot and we went inside the gift shop so she could buy beach postcards. I asked her if any of them were going to Dad. "No, babe," she said. "I'm mailing them to you." My father had been moved out for two weeks and had not phoned as far as I knew.

We walked north on the beach, which became rock as the distance between the cliffs and the shore narrowed, and Mom told me, "There's this sheer cliff all the way in both directions. To get in the secret cave from the north, we'd need a sturdy raft and big oars. Water's unstable. Even if we can time the waves pretty close, we can't judge depth, and it'll shift just as we have an estimation, and we'll be smashed." She clapped once. "Woosh," she said. "Crash."

We worked our way around slick boulders and through glassy tide pools speckled and splotched with anemone, crab, abalone, an infrequent sea cucumber, and red, orange and purple starfish, some no bigger than nickels, one the size of a hubcap. Mom set a medium-sized red starfish on a pink anemone, and we watched the starfish curl its arms around the anemone's flower body.

The thirty-foot tunnel was low and narrow enough that Mom kept her head down and walked leading with her shoulder. Because I was young and small I ran through without scraping myself. Mom called ahead to me, "Don't touch the sides. There's bugs and crabs."

The cave was a twenty-foot-high half-bowl cut into the cliff, as if a colossal clam shell had been pulled from place. The ocean rolled to the mouth of the cave and had created a gravel beach. I remember my disappointment at the sight. I'd anticipated an authentic cave, deep, cool, underground, with phosphorescent fish in the springs and ghostly multi-legged life slinking into other secrets. *The best.*

Mom said, "This is the only private beach left in the world. Keep it a secret." In this place no one knew about, though not really a cave, my disappointment diminished a degree.

Early on in our time together, Frances flat out called me *transitional.* She'd been split from Ellis for a couple months when we took our first weekend alone at a friend's cabin in Big Bear. As I considered carrying her across the doorstep, she said in a not entirely joking tone, "You know you're transitional. You must understand this . . . this you and I." So I was the rebound, the practice run, the warm-up, the leap; antithesis of her former love, yet a substitute, and, to credit her, she was being straightforward about it.

I lifted and carried her inside the cabin anyway. Into the bedroom I carried her, and said, "You remember the way that red Datsun looked all smashed into the signal pole?"

The red Datsun was the second. Our first happened, coincidentally, on Highway One, north of Malibu. Who knows what Frances and I were arguing about when a blue Nova heading south swerved, caromed off the guard rail— saving it from a two-hundred-foot plunge—cut across to our side of the highway shortly in front of us, bounced up the embankment, and dug in on a level site tire-deep in dry weeds.

I stopped the car, and Frances and I rushed up the hill. The driver, a woman, probably thirty, looked very old just then. Her forehead had butted the steering wheel, rushing blood to her wide eyes, ringing them in red, like she'd painted them while drunk. She said, "I'm going home from work." Her upper lip quivered, and she wouldn't take her hands off the wheel; she'd not stopped driving home.

"I don't know what hit me," she said.

What she'd hit was nothing. From what I remembered, she had a blowout, there was a puff of white, steam. If her car had lost control two seconds later or if I had been a hundred feet farther ahead—for not stopping completely at a stop sign in Malibu fifteen minutes earlier—she would have caromed off the rail into Frances and me.

The woman said, "Do you know? Do you know? Who cut me off? I'm going home from work."

Cars stopped and people jogged up the embankment, looking to Frances or me for management. We were first on the scene, thus in control. Others yelled from their open windows: *She okay? Do you need an ambulance? What happened? What happened?*

When the brush caught fire, Frances and I took the woman's arms and helped her uneasily down the slope. I wondered when she would start crying.

"It's going to take me a long time to get home, isn't it?"

Frances said, "You'll be home for supper, dear. We promise. Don't we?"

"*Before* supper," I said.

We seated her in my passenger seat and released her to the custody of someone claiming to be a nurse practitioner. A teenage boy with a surfboard walked by, saw no bodies, and said, "Cool crash."

Frances and I watched the hill catch and the fire come toward us. We held hands, all our hands, in a bundle. The woman's Nova shivered behind curtains of heat. The front tires lost their air and the car kneeled. If the fire trucks had not come, the flames might have burned our toes. We would have let it happen.

Not much further back, during our earliest nights together, we sat in one of our cars in bar parking lots, listening to the classical station, kissing of course, and speaking imprecisely about a near-future together.

I'd say, "What would we name our kids?"

"Kids? Manny, Moe, Jack, Jill..."

"Crosby, Stills, Nash, *Jung* and Freud."

This accident with the woman brought back those parking lot nights.

★★★

Mom rolled up my pant legs, then she rolled up her own and we walked into the gravel-bottomed water together. The first couple wave sets were clean foot-high swells. These waves rolled into the cave. Farther out in the water the gravel became again a rock bottom.

I went toward the cliff wall, where I saw a space I wanted to climb. The footholds looked sound, and higher up I saw where I could lift myself to a flat section of cliff jutting out. So I got a hand hold, pulled up while cranking my legs in the water and, after four attempts, lifted myself to this first goal, my feet barely above the swells.

Mom reached through the water and brought up an orange starfish larger than her hand. She flipped it in her palm and closed her eyes. A set of miniature waves came, rocking her as each passed, as if going inside and through her body. She laughed.

"Did you know starfish tickle?" she said.

One Saturday expedition, Frances driving, I told her the story of a young husband and wife I'd read about in a college Bio-Psyc text. They had been in a car crash together and taken the *exact* same head injuries, despite the obvious structural differences between the driver and passenger sides of the car's dashboard. The couple lived normal lives afterward, except every few months the husband had seizures and if the wife was nearby, she too would seize.

"It's romantic," I said. "Devotion. Absolute."

"Yeah? You sound like Ellis. He said everything was romantic. He had *no* idea."

"Everything? Even something like this?"

"Especially. Whenever couples do weird acts together, Instant Romance."

"For instance."

"For instance, we bumped into each other in the middle of the night in a dark hall. He said it wasn't an accident. He said it was our souls trying to come together. He was joking, but deep down…"

"Did he kiss your bruised head?"

"Anyway," she said. "What if the seizure wife goes into a seizure first?"

"Didn't happen like that," I said. "Not in the book. I bet he starts gagging and when she tries to shove a wallet in his mouth she catches his bad electricity, and they both seize into each other's arms. Seizures are electric, you know."

"You really sound like Ellis."

"Ellis is a romantic chimp."

She jerked the steering wheel, as if I needed reminding about the ease of a high-speed spin-out or a head-on.

The one accident that did it for us—the one that sent us scrambling for each other—happened at the mainland end of the Coronado Island Bridge in San Diego. My friend Chuck, Frances and I were going to the island's beach, the three of us. As we passed the fire trucks and ambulances, we saw a middle-aged man laid flat behind his car. The trunk to his car was open. What I remember specifically is the car with the open trunk, a low, slow-drifting trail of smoke, like a rain cloud, and on the ground the man wearing light blue socks and a Hawaiian shirt with gorillas peeking from behind palm trees.

"He's dead," Frances said, bored, like she'd come upon this scene every day for a week.

"Damn straight, Frances," Chuck said.

"He'd be covered with one of those shiny silver blankets," I said.

"It's a hundred today," Frances said. "The pavement's got to be a hundred-fifty. They're not going to leave him there to fry like an egg if he's not dead."

"Frances," Chuck said. "Beautiful image. Thanks, really. Thanks. An egg. I'll remember it now."

"It's how I see it," Frances said.

Chuck was *my* friend, not Frances'. I had invited him to San Diego, and I wanted him gone right then as much as Frances did. I wanted to be alone with her, to get started what I figured was going to happen with us.

At the highest point of Coronado Bridge's arc there are signs that say, "We care about you," and beneath these signs are phones with direct connections to hotlines. After seeing the man and crossing the bridge I thought I should make a joke about the man and these signs, and then Chuck said, "I bet he's just taking a nap." Frances laughed rudely. I laughed in bilateral support.

Chuck said, "We should take him a pillow."

What I remember about the next couple hours is this: on Coronado Island, at the beach, I found one tanned leather shoe of the style I wanted—comfortable, practical, with rubber soles guaranteed to protect my feet if I ever unknowingly walked through a puddle of acid.

Frances said a fraternity boy got drunk and swam out to sea and accidentally banged his head on a buoy, his shoe made it back to shore and he didn't, and probably wouldn't for months. "Fish won't eat the bloated corpse of a frat boy," she said. So Chuck buried the shoe in the sand, whistling *Taps* with blues riffs.

I was already planning what Frances and I would do when rid of Chuck. Frances' mood had shifted because of the man on the bridge. This was a big one for us. I had to keep breathing.

When Frances, Chuck and I swam I didn't let my head go below the surface, no matter the size of the wave, and so I took head-on assaults by the waves. For those few hours on the beach I forgot about the man on the bridge, and this seems obvious I would forget, and that is why I now remember the shoe with the same clarity as that man.

With the starfish in her hand, Mom said, "This next wave is going to come up to that rock, the one with the red thing on it," or, "This one won't get past here." She got it right every time. But she finally guessed wrong and the wave surprised me. Though standing upright on the flat rock I'd climbed to, the water came up to my knees. It knocked Mom over but she managed to keep her head dry.

She said, "You get wet?" She'd lost her starfish, and she seemed to be looking for it on her clothes.

"Got my toes wet," I said. My fingers dug into the cliff wall.

She saw the next wave coming in. "Get down," she said. "Quick." She shuffled toward me as fast as she could on the unsteady bottom. "Jump."

But I was spooked and wouldn't jump. The wave came to my ankles and kicked Mom down and to the beach. For a second she disappeared in white foam, then she stood, wiping wet hair from her eyes and mouth. From my perch I saw the last two waves from the set coming in.

"*Mom*. Should I jump?"

"No," she said. "Hold on."

The first one wrenched my legs from under me, and as I went in Mom called my name like she was calling me in to wash my hands for dinner. Exactly like that.

Frances said she needed to "get away from people who didn't seem affected by the sight of the dead man." We'd just dropped off Chuck and I was driving her car. She thought he'd handled the situation poorly, making jokes. But what could he have known of our situation? Car crashes meant something else to Chuck.

It took me fifteen years to return to the cave, but fifteen years later, a result of a car accident, this best secret cave is where I had to take Frances, who was merely a six-month lover. I would have taken her to the cave if she'd said nothing.

"I know a place," I said.

"Where?"

"It's a secret."

"Come on, *Ellis.*"

"Don't do that."

"Ellis, what's the secret?"

"Can't tell."

When she said his name again, I punched the gas and drove eighty-five, dodging cars and trucks until she apologized. We'd come to making threats behind the wheel.

A while later we pulled into a parking lot that had been the open field when Mom took me. In my trunk I kept a flannel duck-print sleeping bag for situations like this, though I'd had it in the trunk two years, never used. Frances carried it, and I carried two fresh deli subs. Sixty miles south of Los Angeles the tail end of smog invented a scarlet and orange striped sunset. Though we had a hike we stopped on the beach to watch the sun scorch the undersides of clouds like, I wished, some surprise fireworks show I'd staged for Frances.

Mom called my name. I banged my head as I fell off the perch, and as I went below the surface I became disoriented in the hazy water. I had been an ocean swimmer for almost two years and knew how to handle myself in the rough tumble of a wave. If I became disoriented, didn't know up from sideways, I knew not to fight the currents, I should remain calm, hands near my face for protection until the water mellowed or until I floated to the surface. I knew the stories about people swimming parallel to the surface until they lost consciousness and floated right up. But my bumped head rattled me, causing a panic. When I opened my eyes I saw my hand pass by. I paddled. My face butted into the sand, and I blew out all of my air. But then I had it. I planted my feet and stood in three feet of water, spitting sand. The receding wave tugged at me, splaying up my legs.

Mom came at me, grabbed my shirt, and dragged me to the rear of the cave, where she crouched over me as if protecting me from mortar fire. The last wave in the set came in, almost reaching our toes.

The walk to the cave is not miles, not what I remembered from my first trip. A small devastation. I'd told Frances it was a worthwhile long hike. I'd explained quests to her. The walk probably wasn't more than half a mile. It took us fifteen minutes. I assume I remembered a long hike because of long pauses in the tide pools. Still, with the sun finally gone, I might have missed the tunnel in the confusing rock shadows if we had not come to the end of shore line and had nowhere else to go.

Frances said, "What if someone's in there?"

So I wondered about my cave, about it being not so unreachable. "This place is secret. It's the *best.*"

I knew she would say his name, and she did.

I led her by the hand through the tunnel, and said, "Watch out for the sides. There's bugs and crabs." The tunnel was black, only a dim moonlight at the end to guide us. Because the tide was up high at the mouth of the tunnel we had to jump through shallow water as a wave went out. Toward the dark rear of the cave we unrolled the sleeping bag.

I said, "I remember the walk being so far. But this isn't so bad. At least we're breaking the law by sleeping in a no-camping area. That's a quest."

Frances didn't seem to be listening to me. She sat on the sleeping bag, hunched over her knees, and stared at the ocean. When I sat beside her she lay back.

With the sound of water into rock, I didn't hear her crying, and then I had to listen for a while to be certain the crying was her and not some harbor seal lonely on a buoy. She cried for the man on the bridge.

"Who was that man?" she said.

This set me off. I lay beside her as I started. I had not cried for anything in so long, since Dad left, which was, I know, different. My repressed weak blurts were clumsy and false. Frances seemed better at crying, so I squeezed close to her, where I matched my sobs to hers until I felt capable enough to roll onto my back and let go. Our echoes whirled in and out with the waves. And I thought I probably wasn't doing it right; it wasn't coming from the stomach. It felt like crying, but it could have been anything else.

Minutes later Frances said, "If the tide comes up any higher we won't be able to get out of here without swimming."

I said, "We can't swim out. There's rocks out there. Maybe sharks."

"Well, what?" she said.

"Tide won't come up any higher."

"This where I trust you?"

"It truly is."

"I feel exactly like we're the couple in your bio-psyc book."

She wiped my nose with her sleeve, and as she slid onto me I'd nearly finished crying. But we took a long time to get started anyway.

More waves came quickly and seemed endless. I cried. I cried in Mom's arms for the longest time, my cheek into her wet, sandy shirt. I cried because my head throbbed and I cried because I was scared from the near-drowning. And when Mom cried I cried because of that. I didn't know mine from hers, if there indeed could have been separation. When she lost her breath I lost mine. When she went into choking spasms I did the same. Every time I turned my focus from Mom I heard waves. There could have been hundreds. I kept crying, thinking about those waves and what they had nearly done to Mom and me.

She touched my head, the swelling bruise there. "Are you okay, babe?"

"It hurts," I said.

"Course it does. Are you okay though?"

"I bumped it hard. It's okay."

"No...*Okay*?"

She went on with her sobbing while mine faded.

I said, "Maybe I got a concussion." She laughed, which is what I hoped would happen. It's what I was trying to get good at doing. So I said, "Or maybe I got a broken neck." She laughed again. I didn't ask her what was the matter, as I had asked in the last few weeks since Dad moved out, because I figured she was crying the same way she had been crying about or because of Dad.

"I wasn't talking about your head, silly," she said. "But I hope you don't have a broken neck."

Being transitional meant for Frances she had liberty to visit Ellis on some weekends, which she claimed were friendly visits. In our fifth week together she said, "We were together three and a half years. You get close. You have to be close friends to stay together so long." A beat later she said, "You'd get along with him. I should introduce the two of you. It amazes me how similar you two are."

"*Similar.* I wouldn't mind meeting him."

"I swear it's true, the two of you..." Then she said, "I should tell him about you."

At the end of one of those visits, Ellis drove her to my apartment. I stood on the balcony above them, watching them talk inside the car with the engine still running. Ellis waved to me. He didn't look like what I'd imagined. I probably expected him to be a pass receiver-type, a lunk; what every man expects of his love's formers. But he had long hair and grinned like an idiot and he puffed out his lips while he listened to Frances talk and he gestured with his hands the way Frances sometimes did, and he looked like someone who'd not be my archenemy under most circumstances.

Frances rolled down the window, leaned half her body out, and told me to come down and say hello. I wondered what she was doing, why she thought Ellis and I should meet, shake hands, say, "Nice to finally meet you." So I stayed on the balcony, watching, expecting them to kiss like old pals, a peck, hoping that is how they would kiss.

When I awoke the next morning the tide was out, and Frances was in it, her pants rolled up not far enough to keep them dry. She gestured to the beach, where we'd slept, and there, within a hop and a leap of our sleeping bag, were two blackened fire pits, twenty or so beer cans, potato chip bags, trash and trash.

She said, "Private beach," using the same tone she'd used to say *He's dead*. So I am not sure if she meant I had betrayed her, or if she had commented on my fantasy of this secluded place.

I said, "I haven't been here in fifteen, eighteen, twenty years."

"That's obvious."

I got us our deli sandwiches and went into the water, pants not rolled. She took her sandwich and tore off baby shark bite-size chunks, tossing them into the whitewash. Each lump floated out, briefly north, then caught the next set and crashed back into the cliff wall.

She said, "Anyone ever get killed here?"

"Who?" I reached into the water and turned over rocks, starfish hunting.

"Looks like a good surf spot. Surfers, maybe? For instance."

"It's actually not a good surf spot here. But I haven't heard about anyone."

"That's too bad."

"I almost did, once."

"You didn't though."

In the ankle-deep water Frances confessed she had been sleeping with Ellis on some, not all, of their visits. I'd suspected this, though I had not asked for the confession.

"Three years together," she said. "It's still something I miss with him. It's different, like you and I are different. Look at us. Jesus. But this thing with Ellis, it's not like all sexual. It's . . . emotional." She was not going to cry.

I stared down into the water. "There's no starfish," I said.

"So?"

"They tickle. When you hold them in your hand they reach out their hundred little suction cups and tickle you."

"But," she said, "they don't mean to tickle you."

I heaved my sandwich past the break of the waves and went back in to sit on the sleeping bag. I wanted to cry again, I tried, but this was as different as a moved-out father, or banging my head on a rock, or seeing a stranger in a Hawaiian shirt turned to pavement, and it would take some practice for me to get out the big sobs.

I said, "It is a sexual thing. That's what sex is." I wanted her to cry. With Ellis she had time, three years, something Emotional. With me, she had car accidents, tragedies, panic, a different way to the same conclusion. Hard experience.

While Mom and I walked back to the car, she told me, "Out here, each wave looks like all the others. I should have told you this an hour ago. In the water you can see the differences rising upon you. You have to be in the water. You judge what a wave's size is before it's formed; the more pull, the bigger the wave. You will know everything about a wave if you look at it and feel. Remember that. I wasn't feeling it today. And now it's happened to you. You'll remember it forever." She stopped walking for a second and gave me a kiss on the forehead. "While we're at it, also remember surfers might tell you that after a set of tiny swells it's usually a good sign a colossal set of waves is due. But other times everything means nothing and nothing is no clue for sure, and the more you throw out a stupid hypothesis the more you'll be exactly wrong. Surfers won't tell you anything certain any more since the waves are crowded. Turf shit. They don't want their secrets out. They want their waves left alone. It's better to watch what they do than do what they say. Surfers are like all insiders. Remember that."

This is what I had with Mom.

We found a San Diego paper on our way out. Back at Frances' apartment she read aloud from the article about the man on Coronado Bridge. She'd guessed right about him being dead. His car had broken down on the bridge, and when he went to his trunk for tools a Cadillac came up too fast to stop. I didn't remember a second car, a Cadillac, though it could have been hidden behind the paramedic van.

She said, "I remember the Cadillac. What were *you* looking at?"

"At the dead man," I said, "in a Hawaiian shirt with a gorilla, his blue socks, his open trunk, and a low, slow-drifting trail of smoke, like a rain cloud." An egg on the pavement.

A week after my near-drowning I heard Mom talking into the phone in a higher-pitched voice she used with Dad, and I went into the other room to listen. She heard me pick up the phone.

"Get off the line."

"Dad, it's me."

Dad said something, but Mom screamed over his voice, "Get the hell off the line!"

"Dad? When are you—"

"Off," Mom yelled.

Dad said, "You should hang up."

★★★

Not even a month after the man on the bridge, Frances was driving us back from lunch. She had spent the weekend with Ellis, and I was brooding in an obvious way. I took off my seatbelt so I could rest my head in her lap and hold her thigh.

She said, "Sit up."

"Why?"

"Makes me nervous. Your head could go through the steering wheel."

With my thumb and forefinger I measured the space in the steering wheel. I held this measurement to my face. Indeed, my head could have gone through the wheel.

"If I'm your problem, you can't do that," she said. "For your own good."

I sat up and locked myself back into the seatbelt. We stayed quiet, like rubbernecks watching firemen use the jaws of life.

She dropped me off, and when I went around to her side for the kiss she told me, through a half-closed window, "I'm going back with Ellis I think. Don't make a big deal about it. We'll talk later." It was that fast and surprising, like, of course, a crash.

"You can't do it like this. Open the window."

"I'm going."

"Will you run me over if I hold on to the door?"

"Yes."

So I wasn't transitional, I was something else. And I took my car that very night to Trabuco Canyon, driving as fast as I could through the difficult curves, experimenting with what I had learned with Frances. I knew I could cut into the headlights of an oncoming car and it would be quick and fiery, so I tried to catch a look at the drivers and passengers of every car I let pass, flicking my highbeams to get them to turn their heads. I saw two marines in a front seat and two blonde women in the back; I saw someone who could have been my cousin and her husband (they lived nearby), both of them giving me the finger; I saw a man with a beard. So many faces I could have crumpled. Then I spooked myself, because I almost did it. I thought, "Don't think. Turn." The first road I came to, I pulled off.

The most foolish thing I ever did was call Frances to tell her about this ride. That ended it for us. She said after a very long pause, "I can't deal. This is the very end."

It wasn't the very end for Mom and Dad. Dad moved into a condominium not far away from Mom and I, so he was always close to us.

On one of the first official father-son weekends I spent with him, he took me to Dana Point. Because a hurricane in Mexico had caused exceptionally high surf, we could not walk up the beach.

Dad said, "There's a secret cave not far away. I wanted you to see it." Then he said, "I used to surf near here. Too dangerous for me now. I'm an old man."

"Thirty-one's old?"

He laughed. "Old. But I still like to watch them out there."

Last summer, not so far back, I took a trip to visit my parents in Las Vegas, where they have lived for seven years. Their houses are a block apart and they are contented together like that. This is as close as they will be forever. Chuck went with me because I cannot stand being alone with them. So far from the ocean, I like to think, my parents and I are reduced to small talk, something none of us are good at doing. Chuck is a serious talent with small talk. I've heard him do fifteen minutes on the space shuttle.

We stayed at Mom's house. Dad walks there for breakfast every morning. When Chuck and I came down for breakfast, the two of them would be seated shoulder to shoulder, playing backgammon and reading the same section of the newspaper.

Chuck and I spent the hot days at the Tropicana's pool, where Mom said they had "the best drinks and ladies." The four of us spent nights at downtown casinos, Mom and Dad on side-by-side nickel poker machines.

On the trip home Chuck slept in the passenger seat, snoring. I did not let him drive because I'd become relaxed only while driving, in command of crashing or not.

When the traffic slowed I focused a half-mile ahead to the accident on the dirt shoulder. The car had rolled, probably several times, and had come to a stop between two Joshua trees. Shattered bike racks still clutched like a spider to the car's top. Two bikes were broken apart, their parts scattered and glittering for a hundred feet. I woke Chuck to show him the accident. I wanted him to guess how one car had crashed by itself.

"Blowout?" I said.

Chuck said, "Coyote in the road, I bet. Or it could've been a tumbleweed."

The police had not yet arrived, and cars had stopped and people with sweat on their backs stood at the driver's door, the side facing us. A man yanked off his green shirt and pressed it to the driver's head as either a pillow or a sponge. No one tended to the passenger nor went to that side of the car.

Chuck had to say it: "Other one must be ugly dead."

I rolled down my window and yelled, "You need an ambulance?" No one answered.

Later, after driving several silent moments, Chuck said, "Why'd you wake me up?"

"I wanted you to see it."

What I wanted to tell him is this:

No matter how it sounds I was a car-crash man. With someone else, I might have been a natural-disaster man or a puncture-wound man or a poisoning man, even a splinter-under-a-fingernail man. With Frances, I was a car-crash man. Because of her I still adore them in that certain way. Car crashes are unlike motorcycle accidents. Car crashes are tragic, tidy events. For a good one, the ruin is contained within, except for the bits of windshield and taillight that are never swept clear. The man on the bridge wasn't necessarily a good one. But if I think about Frances, who never met my parents in Las Vegas, I like to think I'm the same as boxing fanatics or Sunday and Monday football fans.

Chuck said, "Now I can't sleep. This picture's in my head. You remember that man we saw with Frances? The fried egg?"

When I got home from Vegas I called her, and she didn't seem disappointed to hear from me. We hadn't talked since she called to tell me she'd left Ellis for good. Since then she had taken up new residence with a new guy, someone I "would not get along with, not at all." I knew him exactly: he probably had recipes for Chinese and Mexican food in a box above his oven.

We talked about our lives for a while. I lied about a good job. I exaggerated my stability, using "contented" more than once. Then Frances told me she had in the past week driven over Coronado Bridge.

"What is it about that bridge?" she said. "It's weird I think of you when I go on the bridge."

"I sometimes think about it. And you."

She said, "Some *guy* had just jumped. And all these cops were standing by one of those 'We care about you' signs. They had their elbows on the rails and were leaning over the side, staring down. What were they doing up there? I don't know what good it was doing. Don't you think they should've been at the other end, down in the water, not giving depressed people any ideas?"

I tried to guess what she might have told the new guy about Coronado Bridge. Did she tell him she'd seen a dead man in a Hawaiian shirt and it made her sad for a day? Or did she get quiet and let the moment pass. But I believe I know what they did after they saw the jumper. Frances told the new guy to drive fast to the other end of the bridge. They then stood on the new guy's car and tried to see the body being fished out.

This is what they would have together, because it works.

"Yes," I said about the cops being up there, because her question was not rhetorical; she did want to know if the cops should have been down in boats.

I knew and had known, finally, that if I were still connected with her we would be addicted—not just attracted—to car accidents. If that was all we had, we'd need an abundance. It seemed possible I might steal cars, involve myself in hit-and-runs, and drop my stolen cars in convenience store parking lots, where Frances would be waiting with the getaway vehicle. Then together we'd cruise past the broken glass and taillights that never get entirely swept up.

LAWRENCE THORNTON

from *The White Coyote*

Late that afternoon a few dozen Mexicans already stood on the embankment above the levee, though because of the distance you had to take the fact that the tiny shapes were people on faith. The INS truck Harry was riding in with Wilson had to travel another two hundred yards before the dark forms started looking like men and women. When they were large as a thumbnail, Harry picked up Wilson's binoculars and watched a man separate from one group like a drop of water that had finally accumulated enough mass and weight to pull free. Some women appeared on the horizon, increasing the numbers that would swell by the hundreds until nightfall when they'd approximate the size of a small village.

Harry had come across similar gatherings in Thailand, Angola, Bosnia and half a dozen other places he had worked in over the years. But here in San Diego there were no snipers with high-powered rifles hiding in burned-out buildings or massed troops waiting on this side of the river—only a fence, squads of INS patrolmen like Wilson, and some unhappy suburbanites intent upon lining up their cars that night and shining headlights across the river to send a message to governments on both sides that they were sick and tired of being invaded. The demonstration, combined with an overdue debt to an old friend on a Los Angeles paper, had been enough incentive for Harry to accept the last-minute request to cover the event as a stringer. It had meant interrupting his vacation but Harry responded to the allure of trouble as naturally as birds migrate along invisible pathways in the air. He was already homing in on his stock-in-trade, the panoramic shot of ruptured social systems that long ago had made him famous at the agency.

He had no idea how many times he'd photographed such scenes, though the situation here felt different from anything he'd noticed in camps and backwater towns that had doubled as processing centers. To start with, there were no old people. The lip of the embankment was an exclusive domain, a dust-blown El Dorado for the young. There was no sign of the lethargy people wore like masks in refugee camps. Instead, the men and women and boys barely in their teens were just waiting. Whether they stood or sat or lay on the ground napping like one man in a sleeveless undershirt, impervious to the afternoon chill, the collective impression was of motion temporarily delayed and not, as was the case in other places, the exhaustion of arrival. While some were gathered together, many stood apart, hands in pockets or folded in laps, feet balanced on the levee, bodies slouched over crossed arms, silent and separate and alert to what was going on across the river. The camp people traveled with everything they owned, but the Mexicans Harry was watching, scanning left to right and back again, had nothing but the clothes on their backs. They wore jeans and khakis and tee-shirts and flimsy jackets and gathered skirts as if they'd come here with no time to prepare, had simply gotten up from a meal somewhere and walked out of house or hut and headed for the border. Then he got it. The families and loners were together without cohesion. Their purpose was dispersion, not community or sanctuary. Whenever he'd seen people massed at borders before there had been a distinct air of mutual reliance, a desire for the comfort of numbers, group identity. Casual as the Mexicans looked, they were compressed like a coiled spring, waiting to move down the face of the levee when they'd be on their own again, separate entities hurrying across the border toward the darkness on the American side. That tension was what he wanted to get on film.

Wilson didn't share Harry's excitement. He was obviously bored and not too happy that he'd been coerced into providing a tour of the area. The guy could probably navigate the network of dirt roads in his sleep. Harry thought he must hate doing the same thing day and night without a prayer of making a dent in the numbers. But at the moment Wilson was busy negotiating the road which had been turned into a washboard by a recent storm spawned by El Niño. When he'd crossed the place where a colleague had broken an axle a few days earlier, he turned his eyes back to the river and reported to Harry that what he was seeing was normal for that time of day. The old pro telling the rookie about the ways of the world, Harry thought. The tendency to stop seeing when you look at things too much was exactly what he had to fight against in his work. He guessed that as far as Wilson was concerned, the border was nothing more than sluggish water, concrete, fences. Harry was interested in what it meant. He thought about how he and Wilson and the green INS truck must look to the people on the other side, projecting himself into their minds so he'd have an edge later when they started running and it was time to take pictures. One thing was clear; Wilson's border and his had nothing in common with the Mexicans'. To the two of them it was a line on a map, a place of business. In the eyes of the people across the river it was an idea, a doorway to opportunity. Its meaning depended on where you stood, what you had, what you wanted.

The welded steel fence ran like a rust-colored snake along the American side.

"Looks good," Wilson said, "but it doesn't work. They crawl over it like tomcats. Some make a buck digging holes underneath for the ones too lazy to climb. Mostly Mexicans. The rest are OTMs, 'Other than Mexican'. We round them up, sort them out. Mexicans get shuttled back on a bus. OTMs we fly to Central America. Sometimes they come back. The Mexicans always do, even the same night. They've got no respect for the law."

As they cruised the evil-looking strip of wasteland Wilson talked about the nightly battles in what he called the war zone. There'd been no skirmishes yet, wouldn't be until sunset, but scars of conflict were visible everywhere. All along the boundary trails beaten into the ground snaked away from the river branching like ganglia into The States. The area reminded him of grainy pictures of World War I battlefields, an impression heightened by skull and crossbone signs posted on the riverbank warning of contamination in Spanish and English:

"¡PELEGRO!"

"DANGER!"

When they reached a place where the river smelled like an open sewer Harry rolled up his window and Wilson smiled.

"Raw sewage and fecal dust. Better get used to it."

He drove on a minute before glancing at Harry.

"You must not have anything better to do."

"It's a favor," Harry said. "I was on vacation when a friend asked me to cover it because his guy was sick."

"Where from?"

"London."

"No shit?"

Harry got his Leica out of the bag and took a few shots of the levee.

"You get off on this?"

"You could say that."

"Must be a drag sometimes," Wilson said, "like everything else."

"Photographers are like surfers, waiting for the big one. When it comes you have to get there first because once a picture's printed that scene isn't news anymore. Everything else is an imitation."

"Shoot the curl?"

"You got it," Harry said. "Right on the button."

Wilson had exposed the way Harry understood the world. He had thought of his work in these terms ever since Australia. He had stopped at a beach where twenty-foot breakers humped up like moving walls a quarter mile from shore. The curl closed over half a dozen surfers like a handful of transparent fingers. They miraculously appeared again, wreathed by foam and angling across the face of the wave as if they could ride forever. It happened at a time when love and his profession were pulling him in two directions and the waves suddenly offered him a solution. He committed to his work then and there, took a vow that cost him his wife of two years. The choice had put him in more lonely hotel rooms than he could count if he were ever perverse enough to try. And even though he knew that so long as the waves kept coming the world would be new every morning, that wasn't always enough to kill the loneliness. He had women friends, one in London in particular, but she wasn't Marianne, never could be.

He took a picture of four people walking single file on a bridge of tires laid across the shallow water. Wilson said they bought the plastic bags for their shoes from entrepreneurs on the other side of the river.

"Buck a pop. They throw in the rubber bands for free."

The family stopped as Wilson pulled over to the side of the road near the embankment. Harry took another shot before they turned around and headed back to the Mexican side.

"This part's easy. It gets real nasty up ahead where most of them cross.

They throw rocks and bottles. It's not like what you hear. The papers talk about us abusing them but these guys are dangerous. Look."

He rolled up his sleeve, exposing a scar that ran the length of his forearm. The holes where the stitches had been looked like a zipper.

"Fucker knifed me one night on Monument Road. I was pumping blood like a stuck pig." He nodded toward some men waiting by the fence. "They'll go over at Smuggler's Gulch tonight."

"Home free?"

"No way," Wilson said, shaking his head. "Big time banditos hang out in the chaparral. Robbers, rapists, con-men of one kind or another. Sometimes they cross with the rest of them. Wouldn't be surprised if there were some with that group we just passed. The rest of 'em, the good ones, they save their pesos, sell everything but the clothes on their backs—chickens, donkeys, maybe even a house if they own one. Then they get robbed, or worse. When they get by the banditos, they still have to cross the freeways. Cars scarf 'em up like PacMans."

Wilson turned around in a clearing where a bulldozer was uprooting brush.

"The idea is to get rid of places where they can hide. You want to see anything else?"

Harry glanced at his watch. It was a little after four.

"That's plenty," he said.

The information he'd gleaned from Wilson was helpful as background, the substructure of the night's events, but Harry dealt in the way things looked and he wanted to get down to the site of the demonstration.

After Wilson let him out at INS headquarters Harry drove back in the old BMW Bavaria he kept in Los Angeles. A few protesters had arrived and were tailgating, helping themselves to sandwiches and beer from a Ford flatbed parked with other cars in a line that was as straight as a platoon fallen in for reveille. Across the river some Mexicans were gathered around an impromptu taco stand set up on the flats next to a table piled high with tennis shoes. Wilson had told him about the shoe-selling entrepreneurs. Harry brought them close with the zoom lens, focusing on half a dozen men discarding work boots, old wing-tips and go-aheads in a cardboard box and handing over money for the sneakers that would speed them across the border. Above their heads smoke rose from a split oil drum where meat was grilling. He let the camera down on its strap and watched the smoke ascend toward a ragged front that had been sliding in all day from the Pacific. The forecast called for rain by morning, but he wasn't sure it would hold off that long.

He took a few pictures of people eating and buying shoes, feeling his way into the situation he still wasn't prepared for. When the assignment had been offered to him two days ago he had gotten on the phone and hurriedly arranged for the INS tour and a meeting with the protest leader, an ex-Marine colonel named Quinn he'd seen yesterday at his house in Encinitas. Quinn and a dozen neighbors had complained that nobody was interested in their side of the story. Their demonstration was part of a long-term strategy. If they persisted, maybe the government would finally do something about the wetbacks who ran down their streets, cut through their backyards, even ate their garbage. Quinn pointed to the canyon below. Two men were carrying a large slab of plywood through the brush. On the near side of the shack they were heading toward a man relieving himself. Quinn told him to take a good look, adding that he hadn't retired there to watch spics shit in the bushes. A neighbor said it was disgusting and asked Harry how he'd feel if his kids had to see that kind of thing while they were eating breakfast.

Within the hour the rest of the protesters had arrived, raising a plume of dust against the pearl-colored sky. A car with the San Diego Union logo on its doors pulled up and two women got out, the taller one with the cameras nodding to him as her companion headed off to an INS truck, notebook in hand. By the time Quinn appeared a few minutes later in a black Cadillac whose license frame bore the motto, "Semper Fi," half a dozen more journalists had shown up, along with a TV crew. Harry was glad to see the TV people; their presence legitimized the protest as a major event. If he got back to his hotel in time for the late news, he might be able to crib some of what he'd see for the story he had to write.

Quinn quickly took charge of his troops, moving along the line giving orders, shaping them up. He wore khakis bloused in boots and a Marine Corps sweater. Harry smiled, though he knew he had to take Quinn seriously. After all, he was the impression point, the lightning rod, the one who was going to make it happen. Harry kept his eye on him, waiting for him to do something interesting. When Quinn pointed at the Mexicans over the hood of a Chevy Power Wagon as if he were about to lead a charge, Harry snapped three quick shots. Then he sidestepped down the levee for a low-angle of the shacks spilling over the Tijuana hills. Climbing up, he saw Wilson cornered by three blue-haired women who were giving him hell. Wilson looked at him imploringly, but Harry stayed where he was and shot the group against the background of a huge light pole.

He was congratulating himself on the composition when a shout went up along the line. The Mexicans had started edging toward the river, moving like a field of grain bending to wind. Then the mass started breaking up, individuals sliding, running, skidding sideways down the slope, coming to life in dissolution. There was something raw and elemental about the assault. Screwing the zoom lens out to maximum power, he focused on a teenage boy, squeezed off a shot, then another as the boy profiled on his way down, back arched for balance like a bullfighter. Good, he told himself. Memorable. A definite keeper. As he scanned the people cascading down the levee he looked for interesting groupings, quickly aimed at a wedge to the left, already knowing how it would look in the contact sheets—a distorted rectangle filled with anxious faces of men, teenage boys, young women with flowing black hair.

Some men were already climbing the embankment on the American side. He took a close-up of a protester in a jogging suit holding a poster proclaiming WETBACKS GO HOME! and yelling at three Mexicans in flimsy jackets as they scrambled over the fence. A Border Patrolman appeared out of nowhere and grabbed at their feet, pulling one down as the others struggled over the top. Through a gap in the fence Harry saw them drop to the ground and scatter. Two women went over in the same place a minute later. An INS truck screamed along the dirt road toward the one on the right but the chaparral was too dense for the truck to follow.

Another group was charging up the levee when Quinn shouted "Now!" and with precision rivaling a high-kicking chorus line headlights snapped on, creating a brow of light above the river, a thick luminous line that turned the runners white. One of Quinn's people set off a multi-voiced car alarm that filled the air with siren sounds, shrill trilling, a pulsating squawk. Others leaned on their horns or yelled in mean-edged voices, but neither the lights nor the medley had any effect. Faces bathed in glare, the Mexicans kept coming, running toward the dollars that lay beyond the neat tract houses of San Ysidro.

Harry was hoping some would pass through the line of cars so he could catch the contrasting desires in their faces and those of the protesters when it started raining. The fine mist quickly became a downpour. Lightning illuminated the Tijuana hills. He heard thunder in the distance. Quinn's people took shelter. He wanted Quinn's reaction but he was nowhere in sight and Harry didn't feel like going from car to car, peering into fogged windows like a cop on Lover's Lane. He couldn't risk getting his camera wet so he started back to the Bavaria, stopping twice to let people run by.

He was crossing an open space behind Quinn's line when he heard the wet slap of shoes behind him, then felt the jolt as the strap of his camera bag dug into his shoulder. The force spun him around so that he was looking at the man who'd tried to rob him running toward the chaparral.

"¡Cabron!" Harry shouted.

No sooner had the word come out than the man stopped and walked back, stopping ten feet away. He was tall and thin and his angular face looked mean and unafraid. "¿Que dice?" he asked. A silver crown on his front tooth glowed briefly in the headlights' glare.

"You heard me," Harry answered in Spanish. He imagined the Mexican running away into the rain with his cameras and added, "You asshole. Keep your goddamn hands off my equipment."

The man stuck his free hand into his pocket and pulled out a knife. Light glistened on the blade which snapped out as he swung his hand sideways. The Mexican jerked his head back quickly, inviting Harry to get it on. Harry backed up, keeping his eyes on the blade. He remembered the zipper scar on Wilson's arm. The BMW was close enough to run for but he didn't need to because the man suddenly stopped, made a slicing gesture then folded the switchblade.

A second later he turned around and headed north.

Harry waited until the Mexican was far enough away so he couldn't sneak up on him while he was getting in the car. He quickly opened the door, slid in, and pushed down the lock, dumbfounded by his stupidity. The cameras were his livelihood, essential to his well-being, but they weren't worth being knifed. That he'd been lucky only made him feel more disgusted with himself. As he drove away from the river, the moment of violence took the edge off the satisfaction of the work, giving the evening a whole new cast. Overtones of the danger resonated through his body on the way into the city. But a few blocks from the hotel he regreted the missed opportunity. He had to laugh at himself when he thought of pulling out a camera while the Mexican stood there waving his knife. It would have made one hell of a picture.

Since the weather had cut the demonstration short and it was still fairly early, he decided to check out of the hotel, eat at a nearby restaurant and drive back to Los Angeles where he could develop the film first thing in the morning. He was fairly certain which ones he'd use: Quinn pointing across the river; the wide-angle of the levee with people streaming down; men and women going over the fence. There were some of children too, looking wide-eyed and scared as they ran beside their mothers. Kids in situations like this had bothered him ever since his first day in Vietnam. He had gone for a walk with an old China hand named Morgan when they came upon a group of street children. Their filthy clothes hung loose on their skinny bodies and their eyes were skeptical and old. The youngest couldn't have been more than seven or eight, the oldest in their early teens. They all talked at once, begging for food and money. Harry was reaching for his loose change when Morgan put his hand on his wrist, saying he knew how he felt but it didn't make sense. "Start like this and pretty soon you'll want to pick up the babies. Take the pictures and write what happened, period. You can't afford sympathy. It'll get into your pictures, infect your prose. You'll become sentimental and that'll be all she wrote. You'll be washed up. Nobody will take you seriously." Morgan had tried to make him feel better by adding that after a few months he'd be numb to the things he had to look at. Lousy as it made him feel at the time, it had been good advice, survivor's lore, and he'd followed it wherever he went afterward, repeating it like a mantra to neophytes wearing new bush jackets and unscuffed Timberline shoes.

Before dinner he rewarded himself with a Beefeater martini, drank half a bottle of Chianti with an indifferent veal parmigiano, and finished with Amaretto and coffee.

Thunder crashed as he went out to the parking lot. Sheet lightening whitened the downtown high-rises before it started raining again. Harry switched on the radio while he waited at a stop light, holding down the search button until he found a weather report. The announcer said things were bad on Highway 5 from Oceanside to Laguna Beach. "You might as well kick back and enjoy it, folks. It's gonna be a long night."

Feeling loose from the drinks and in no mood to deal with snarled traffic on 5, he decided to double back to I-15, the inland route he'd taken on the way down. He listened to a country-western station, then a Mexican one playing Mariachi music before picking up a Rachmaninoff concerto. The pianist was reaching the end of the final movement as Harry took the curving loop of the access road onto the freeway and accelerated into the fast lane, freeing himself from the spray of a semi truck and trailer. He brought the BMW up to seventy, fast enough to make good time and still leave a margin of error. Even at that speed an Alfa Spyder passed on the right, its taillights disappearing quickly in the rain.

He thought about his return to London. If everything went according to schedule, there would be time for a little sightseeing before he had to catch the plane to Berlin and start working on a story about Neo-Nazis. He was debating whether to go down to Cornwall or north to York when the announcer said, "And now a little music for the night." There was a pause, then a kettle drum sounded and the first words of the Carmina Burana filled in the car.

O Fortuna

The drum again.

velut luna

And again.

statu variabilis

Chanting voices rose, crescendoing, demanding. "*Nunc obdurat*," they sang, "*et tunc curat / ludo mentis aciem*."

Harry remembered enough college Latin to understand. Unruly, eerie, strangely plaintive, the music held him with its rhythm. Keeping time with his left foot, he turned up the volume until the radio drowned out the wipers' slap. Nothing could suit him better than this continuum of speed, rain, the wild celebration.

As the highway crested a hill the glare of the headlights on the opposite side of the road almost blinded him. He looked straight ahead, blinked, waiting for the spots dancing on his retina to go away while a baritone sang about the glories of spring. Ahead, flashing yellow lights marked the Border Patrol checkpoint. Half a mile separated him from the backed-up cars whose taillights glowed like party streamers on the glistening road. He eased off the accelerator. While the speedometer needle fell to sixty, a male chorus burst into a drinking song just as a heavy gust of wind side-swiped the car. Harry reached over and turned the wipers up to high; even then rain filmed the windshield.

He was lifting his foot to the brake when four men materialized in the cones of his headlights, one in the lead, the others lagging a few paces behind, the quartet running through space measured by drum beats and clashing cymbals. He jammed the brake pedal down, felt the rear tires lose their grip, then the weirdly smooth sensation of the aquaplaning car. The men reappeared while he pumped the brakes and spun the steering wheel clockwise, away from the direction of the slide. He was jerked back in his seat as the tires regained traction. A sensation of relief flickered through his mind as the car fishtailed away from the runners, its momentum rebelling against the angle. He was about to ease the pressure on the steering wheel when the rear end broke loose again. The raised foot of the man in the lead revealed a white sock before he disappeared in the darkness. Another appeared in front of the car, his head rising like a balloon in the window on Harry's side before he vanished behind shattered glass. The third, struck by the left fender, came over the hood, arms and legs gyrating as his back struck the windshield. Through the wet air blasting his face Harry saw the last man raise his hands just before there was a heavy thud and the car skidded off the road.

There was a rushing sound, as of a great wind, then a single note struck from a triangle. The soprano, whose voice he'd admired, sang above the roaring in his ears. His head spun. Images came, disappeared, returned. As the chorus implored, "*Veni, veni, venias, ne me mori facias,*" he looked stupidly through the gaping hole where the windshield was supposed to be, just conscious enough to know he was upside down. A long time seemed to pass before he connected the pressure against his left shoulder and across his chest to the fact that he was hanging from his seat belt. There was an odd sensation of weight, pressure in his head, intense but devious pain sliding liquidly from one part of his body to another.

It seemed that the woman crying was in the music until he saw upside-down bare legs and stiletto heels. A man's inverted face appeared, telling the woman to get hold of herself, pleading with her in a disembodied voice. Harry couldn't hear the rest because the music surged and then the roaring. Their feet walked into the darkness as the voices gave way to sirens. The rotten-fruit smell of leaking gas scared him. He imagined an explosion, a ball of fire as the sirens peaked, then faded in long slow whines.

The samaritan tried to comfort the woman, who was still crying. He heard other voices, saw a flashlight beam searching the ground, a hand, a badge on the peak of a hat, a large round face framed by a yellow slicker. His left side hurt when he tried to shield his eyes from the light.

"Take it easy," the patrolman said.

Two men crawled through the space where the windshield had been. One put his hand on Harry's shoulder while the other quickly traced the belt up to its catch by the seat.

"It's okay," one of them said. "We're going to pull you out."

The kettle drum sounded as they eased him through the opening into the rain. He heard the chorus singing the refrain as he looked around. A man in a suit was staring at something on the other side of the BMW. Suddenly his face contracted and Harry heard him mutter, "Jesus Christ!" before he turned away. The paramedics kneeling beside Harry reminded him of the men crossing the pool of red light. He was about to tell them that the men had been running in slow-motion when they lifted him onto a gurney and he saw two white shapes in the distance. When the chorus began chanting again someone shouted, "Turn that fucking radio off!" but nobody crawled into the car and the music followed Harry all the way up the median to the highway. Ambulances were lit up like carnival booths; a photographer's flash exploded. Cars were coming through a corridor of pink flares, waved on by a Highway Patrolman whose flashlight made half-moons against the night. Disoriented, in pain, he was aware of a terrible feeling of loneliness spreading in the hollow of his chest. He was acutely aware of people gazing at him as they drove through the pink corridor and vanished in the night.

Revolving lights painted everything the soft chalky down of pastels. He heard the hum of car engines, the business-like voices of patrolmen and paramedics. He was looking at them, trying to identify the ones who'd saved him, when he noticed half a dozen Mexicans standing in a semi-circle. One covered his head with his jacket and suddenly took a step backwards, revealing a man on the ground, knees drawn up, head resting on crossed arms. When he looked up, Harry realized he was crying; all along there had been a slight, irregular tremor in his folded body. White socks showed in the gap between his shoes and cuffs. Without taking his eyes off the man Harry said, "I couldn't stop."

"Just relax," one of the paramedics said. "We'll be at the hospital in ten minutes."

The man on the ground raised his head as his companion pointed in the direction of the ambulance. The man stared dumbly for a moment before his face contracted in agony. He began to shout as the paramedics lifted Harry inside, pushing the gurney all the way to the back of the bright tube-like interior. The taller paramedic got out and closed the doors. The one who stayed in back leaned over Harry and ratcheted up the end of the gurney. Harry looked out the windows. The one on the left framed the man with white socks, the one on the right two pale shapes tenting the darkness. Muffled shouts penetrated the steel box and Harry was glad when the siren came on.

When the ambulance moved off the shoulder onto the highway he looked through the windows at the strobe-like flicker of emergency lights. Scored by the colored rain, the man and the shapes were soon obliterated, but Harry kept watching as the ambulance picked up speed and the paramedic's head floated above him, a strange disembodied shape.

JOHN STEPPLING

The Chinese Girl's Blindness

Blanchard listened to Lorraine recite the point spreads. He could see himself in the mirror from where he stood at the pay phone. He turned to face the opposite direction and saw himself in another mirror. Gyms are full of mirrors. Lorraine asked if he wanted the college games. Blanchard said no. He said he'd call her back in a minute. He hung up and stepped away from the phone. He looked at the folded sports page in his hand. He'd scribbled the point spreads and the over/under totals in the margin next to each game. Blanchard had to hold the paper at arms length and squint in order to read it. The pose made him feel like his father. How he remembered his father reading a menu, or the racing form. Blanchard had reading glasses but he didn't like wearing them at the gym. Once someone had passed Blanchard while he was writing down the lines and jokingly commented, "Talking to your bookie huh?" Blanchard had just smiled. He didn't tell him, "Yeah, in fact I am." This wasn't the kind of gym where people called their bookies, or even talked sports for that matter. It was a young clientele and was really a fitness center and not a gym as Blanchard thought of gyms. Just now it was four-twenty, leaving ten minutes until most of the East Coast games tipped off.

A young man with twenty inch arms began a warm up set of curls next to the phone. He acknowledged Blanchard with a nod which Blanchard returned. He was tall and Nordic looking, with crew cut blond hair and a wide mouth that conveyed little humor. Blanchard watched him perform his set, easy and graceful. Blanchard made him for about twenty three, twenty four. His upper body was overly vascular and his face flushed deep red as he pushed through his set. Probably doing Deca, Winstrol, a stack of that sort. Trying to get cut, to get harder. He wasn't holding much water so Blanchard figured he wasn't doing anything too severe. Blanchard had been thinking of another cycle himself. Something mild, some Primabolin maybe, Anavar, whatever steroids he still had left. The Nordic blond put down the Olympic bar and massaged his bicep. Blanchard marvelled at the complete narcissism of the young man.

"Feel tight today," he said. He had an accent. Danish. He enjoyed the admiring gaze of a couple of older queens. He stretched and pulled his Spandex shorts up higher. Fucking Europeans, thought Blanchard, always wearing their pants too high. Over the loudspeakers a Janet Jackson tape began. At least Blanchard thought it was Janet Jackson. Blanchard turned and faced the mirror. Still had guns, still had his deep grooved triceps. His biceps lacked peak, but that was genetic, nothing to be done about it. He was thicker in the waist, and his skin was loose in places like the elbow, a sign of inching toward fifty.

The first sound was a scream of tires. It sliced through the room with evangelical command. The collision followed and all human movement came to a stop. From the street you could feel the air that had been so violently displaced, begin to repair itself in that mystical non-time in which such things occur. Blanchard felt his stomach reach upward. He saw through the smokey glass at the front of the gym that the cars had impacted head on. He ran toward the crash. Already people were in the street, moving in unclear ways. Then he heard the woman. Her car was maroon, a sedan, a Nissan, or Toyota. It was new, spotless, except for the now caved in front end, and for the lacy pattern of blood thrown across the inside of the windshield. Blanchard found himself moving alongside another man, moving toward the maroon sedan. Like Blanchard the other man wore gym shorts and tank top. Blanchard didn't think he knew him. The man was yelling.

"Call nine one one, she has a baby." The woman was out of the car and had reached the passenger side door. She was trying to pull it open but it was stuck. The other man was pulling on the door now too. Blanchard looked down into the front seat. The child was crying silent cries, bits of glass spilling from its mouth. The child was bleeding, and the blood seemed to grow out of the child with uncontrolled insistence. The child was a girl, and she was struggling to get free of her car seat. The tiny Asian face howled without sound, like a freakish recording artist in its own private studio. The door jerked open and Blanchard reached down to pull the young girl out of her harness. The other man was restraining the mother, who flailed her arms and called out her

Cantonese prayers, or oaths, or curses. Blanchard carried the girl across the street. Carried her past the traffic that wasn't moving and toward a bench just inside the gym. The mother was helped inside, and to the bench too, where she sat, shaking. She was speaking her language, looking frantically at these strangers, and knowing nobody understood. Her bone colored cable knit absorbing so much blood that it appeared almost red by design. Blanchard kneeled next to the stretched out child. There were faces and voices and movement behind him but he didn't turn around. Someone brought moist paper towels and Blanchard took them and wiped around the child's eyes. The other man sat, holding the mother, telling her to calm down, that it would be all right. Blanchard did not think anything would again be all right. He picked pieces of glass from inside the child's cut mouth. The child was crying loudly now and reaching out her arms. Blanchard told someone to get ice. He didn't know much about what to do, but the child's eyes were swelling and it seemed that trying to keep the swelling down couldn't be wrong. The mother continued trying to grab for the child.

"Keep her away," Blanchard said. "She's got to let the little girl lie still." Blanchard didn't say this to anyone in particular. He wasn't sure if he actually said it at all. He knew that it was right, though. Keep her still. He pressed the moist towels against a deep puncture wound between the girl's eyes while keeping the ice on the bruised swollen eyes themselves. Blanchard could not imagine how these injuries occurred, how the child had been thrown forward against something while strapped in her car seat. That such events seemed to always defy logical reconstruction caused Blanchard, at that moment to feel small. He pressed a little more firmly against the puncture wound and his thoughts returned, despite resistance, to the endlessness of space. He knew paramedics were on their way, yet he felt, also, that what he was doing would not ever end. It occurred to Blanchard that he might be hallucinating. Someone had gone and brought the Korean man who owned a nearby liquor store, to try and talk to the mother. He was a gray haired surly little man, and he seemed surly even now, and Blanchard wanted to hit him. Blanchard clenched his teeth, and concentrated harder on the child's eyes. The liquor store owner was making gestures of frustration, his Chinese was not good he said, his Chinese was very limited. Blanchard cursed the man silently. Other voices were discussing how the accident had occurred. Blanchard didn't care, he felt it pointless to blame anyone. He looked over at the mother. She was bouncing up and down and still talking, but her voice was very soft now, it had gone far away inside her. Blanchard lifted the ice up and looked closely at the eyes. There was still blood, but Blanchard could not tell where it was coming from. The swelling had closed both eyes and Blanchard could sense, in the child, the tiny formation of inarticulate panic that would soon grow much larger. The child was quieter, and her movements slower. Blanchard was suddenly terrified as he considered what would happen if she fell unconscious. The mother held her daughter's hand now, speaking to her in that soft distant voice. She was leading her daughter into a cool storeroom, a place of stored root vegetables and fertile odors. Blanchard noticed blood on his shorts and on his legs. Who is this who bleeds on me? He didn't know them. He really hardly knew anyone who surrounded him at this moment. The mother had her face close to the little girl's face. The flesh around the eyes was purple and blood kept seeping. As though ground water after an earthquake was rising through a process of liquefaction to form pools like quicksand. Blanchard knew nothing he ever touched again would not be sticky. It was a universe of blood and damage. The sound of a siren from outside. People shuffled out of the way, leaning back, making room. Blanchard stood up, his mouth was dry and hot. The first paramedic was a tall black man. He wore a yellow jacket that looked like a child's rain slicker. He saw the little girl.

"Oh no," he said very quietly, to himself. The second paramedic was short, with greasy brown hair. As they worked they started asking questions of the mother until someone explained that she only spoke Cantonese. First thing, they began trying to stabilize the child's head. Blanchard backed further away. He tossed the paper towels and melting ice he held into the trash receptacle. He walked back into the free weight area of the gym. Someone had turned off the Janet Jackson tape. It was twilight now. A young man with a shaved head and earring was doing squats. He was squatting with around three hundred pounds. Sweat poured off him and he grimaced with the effort of every rep. He finished his set and placed the bar back on the rack. He saw Blanchard watching him. He had an expression of wantonness on his face. Blanchard imagined the expression was there permanently. Blanchard returned to where the paramedics worked on the child. They had placed the child on a gurney. Her head was wrapped with bandages and braced with a styrofoam collar of some sort. That's what it looked like. Blanchard couldn't really see very well. There was a fireman there too, in a black uniform. He spoke into a walkie-talkie but Blanchard couldn't hear what he was saying. The mother was next to the gurney and was speaking very rapidly to the black paramedic. He wasn't listening, his gaze was on the child. The other paramedic began pushing the gurney. Blanchard could see flashing red lights outside, and the back of the paramedic's van. Blanchard walked over to the men's room. He stepped inside and stood at the sink. He washed his hands. On the wall was a framed photo of Franco Columbo striking a double bicep pose during the Mr. Olympia competition. It was an old photo. Blanchard was reminded of how many bodybuilders had been sick as children. Had taken up the pursuit of weight training as way to overcome perceived deficiencies. Lots of short guys, immigrants, abused and wayward young men; body building was a means toward self-confidence. Blanchard dried his hands. He felt a little dizzy. He would skip his workout today.

Blanchard came to the gym earlier than usual the next day. Bob, who managed the gym, was behind the counter. He was reading a muscle magazine.

"Exercising your mind as well as your body, huh?" said Blanchard. Bob laughed. He put down the magazine.

"They've been publishing variations on the same articles for forty years," Bob said. Blanchard nodded and signed in. He headed for the men's locker room. He sat on a stool in front of the mirror and began changing into his workout clothes. He thought how he had gone home last evening and immediately taken a shower. He'd thrown out the blood stained shorts and tank top. He took the box containing what steroids he had left off his shelf and planned out his cycle. He decided on about fifteen weeks. Nothing drastic, just enough for a little size, a little more density. Standing naked in the bathroom he'd injected two c.c.'s of Equipoise and fifty milligrams of Deca-Durabolin. He'd used his buttocks, the upper-outside quadrant. It was still a touch sore today. Blanchard finished changing and stuffed his gym bag into one of the small lockers and headed for the leg room. Legs were the foundation of a good physique Blanchard believed. A lot of people neglected their legs but Blanchard had learned years before that serious leg training was the basis from which the rest of your routine was built.

Blanchard was alone in the leg room. He started with a light set of hack squats. He concentrated, careful not to stress the lower back as can happen with this exercise. The best legs he'd ever seen belonged to Tom Platz. Even with this new generation of guys, Platz stood alone, in Blanchard's opinion. After the set Blanchard walked back up to the front desk. Bob was reading the magazine again.

Blanchard asked him for a carb drink. Bob took one from out of the small glass front refrigerator behind the desk. He handed it to Blanchard knowing Blanchard would pay for it on the way out. Blanchard stood at the counter sipping the overly sweet carb drink. He picked up a body building magazine, a different one from the one Bob was reading. He turned the pages, looking at the photos of various new body builders as they worked out or posed. He read a paragraph from one of the articles. The copy was laughable, geared toward inarticulate young men resentful of a world they found confusing and scary. The message was always the same, become big and powerful, overcome your fears through physical development. Blanchard closed the magazine.

"You know that little girl in the accident yesterday?" Bob asked. Blanchard turned and nodded.

"Her grandparents came by this morning. Wanted to thank everyone I guess," Bob said. "The girl has some serious eye damage."

"What do you mean?" Blanchard asked. Bob shrugged.

"What's that mean?" Blanchard asked. Bob shook his head. "For the most part what that means is, she's blind. That's what it means." Blanchard looked out toward the street. Traffic was light, nothing was going on. Blanchard turned and walked toward the leg room. When he got there he was still the only one in the room. From the parking lot outside came the mechanical voice of a car security system. It said something about now being armed and it made a beep. Blanchard added two forty five pound plates to each side of the hack machine. He realized he'd left his carb drink back on the counter. He didn't want to go back and get the drink. He didn't want to look at Bob. The hell with it. Three more sets of hacks then he'd go right to the leg press. He'd work low reps with heavy poundage. Big Ron had once said to him, a leg workout wasn't any good unless you felt like throwing up afterward. Big Ron had some powerful legs. Blanchard rested, leaning both forearms on the hack squat machine. He wasn't sure why he felt so pissed at Bob. He thought of his ex-wife. How she had never wanted to have kids. As they were breaking up he remembered, she came to his hotel room one day to tell him that she was pregnant. She stood in the doorway and told him she would get the abortion and within a week she did. A few days after that at a follow-up examination it was discovered that she had a tubal pregnancy. They rushed her to the hospital and operated, tying off one of her ovarian tubes. Something like that. Blanchard pictured the squished little creature in the tube. At that time it had made him cry but the memory no longer had that effect on him. Blanchard noticed the odor of disinfectant. Someone was mopping out the shower room. He didn't mind the smell. He was relieved the gym was so empty. Nobody was going to interrupt his workout. He settled into the machine, the pads resting on his shoulders. He released the lock and began to squat.

DISASTERS IN THE 'HOOD

High mountains are a feeling,
but the hum of cities torture.
—Lord Byron

JERVEY TERVALON

All Along the Watch Tower

We knew the neighborhood was changing. We, being the knuckleheads, Gumbo, Onla and me but the fellas had no idea. They didn't seem to notice how much fear was on the streets. Somehow their age blinded them to all the teenagers with vicious sneers in bright blue or green bomber jackets, wearing jeans starched and ironed at home, shiny with dirt. That ass kicking I received trying to visit the wrong number girl woke me up to what was happening around the avenues and all through black L.A. Suddenly, our neighborhoods were divided up into territories with hard and fast boundaries which if you crossed them could result in a serious beating, even get you killed. But it didn't effect the fellas. As though sitting under the big tree, with their nice cars and dope to be smoked, excluded them from our world. Even in '72 when the drive-bys started and we took to squatting behind whatever was solid if a car slowed as it passed down the street, the fellas just didn't seem to notice how jumpy and unhappy we were with the turn of events. Then a rash of shootings swept through the neighborhood. Dinky got shot at a party, a glancing blow which broke his arm and gave him something to brag about. But it was one of those events which shaped the future. Not that I liked going to house parties, dark living rooms filled with teenagers and booming music, and spiked punch and off-brand potato chips. Half of us hugging the walls to get up the courage to ask someone to dance, and the other half on the dance floor working up a sweat. But then some guys couldn't afford new tailor-made knit shirts, or shiny, blunt biscuits, those ugly, thick shoes. Or they had short hair, couldn't grow a huge afro like the Jacksons. Maybe they couldn't accept the humiliation most of us knuckleheads had to go through at those parties. The girls were not interested in dancing with junior high school freshmen. They didn't want to dance with geeks wearing thousand eyes shoes. So we were ignored, and that was fine with me. I was willing to hold up a wall until I understood the intricacies of the Texas hop/cha-cha, but I never got a chance, parties lost all interest for most of us knuckleheads. Up at the Mack family house, at their weekly party, I stood next to Onla, both of us in our stiff church clothes looking proper and dumb, instead of cool and dangerous. Carol, a girl in our class who liked us, but that we tried to avoid because she was fat like a sumo, was eyeing us. Tonight, she had on a flouncy dress which made her look like a huge, roving sunflower, trying to find someone to dance with to the "Psychedelic Shack." She grabbed Onla's skinny arm, and said, "Let's dance," and he threw himself in reverse, went down to the ground and dug in his heels, leverage to break her hold, then he latched onto me.

"Dance with him," he said.

She nodded, put her arm around my waist and with that grip pulled me from the wall. She had me but I wasn't going to dance. I didn't have to. All our attention turned to the ruckus at the door. Somebody didn't want to pay the 25 cents.

"Turning this shit out!" I heard someone shout.

BOOM!!

I have never heard something so loud, shattered plaster rained down on us. The record player fell over and exploded onto the floor. It was totally dark because the red light got blown away with the ceiling. We were down on all fours, as was everyone, feeling our way forward — but which way was out?

"See, ya'll got your shit turned out!"

The room was strangely quiet as though we were at church. Finally, when it seemed as if the party crashers had gone, crying started. People were standing up, rushing out onto the porch and the lawn. The room had emptied out except for me and a few other people. Carol was there in a corner, blubbering. Onla was gone, just like him to make a getaway. I went outside, dodging the angry knots of Mack relatives. A gang unto themselves, planning revenge. Nobody seemed hurt. Those who weren't related to the Macks or tied to them out of friendship had moved down the street, making themselves smaller targets.

I walked the block home passing people, nobody noticed me as if the shooting blinded everyone to everything else. Most of my part of the block were on Kay Kay and Trice's porch; Onla and Kay Kay, Trice and her new boyfriend, Roachie, and retarded Sally. Usually, when Sally was around Onla and me and most of us under 16 and shorter than 5'8 kept our distance. She was hell on us young guys, tossing us around and stealing our money if she felt like it, and she often felt like it.

"Garvy looks scared! Bet you peed on yourself."

I didn't say anything, that was the smart thing.

Though she was our age Sally had quickly matured into a rock hard, deep voiced, cartoon like bully, who would have provoked a lot of nightmares if she were a guy but being a girl...a girl with lots of desires, she made us sweat in a number of complex ways.

"You was inside?" Trice asked.

Trice and Roachie didn't go to the party because Roachie's family didn't get along with the Macks.

"Yeah, I was inside, me and Onla."

"Bet you was scared," Roachie said.

It was amazing how big his afro was, so huge it flopped down to his shoulders.

"Yeah, I was scared but Onla beat me out by a long shot."

"Yeah?" Roachie said, and everybody turned to look at Onla. Onla smiled nervously and folded his arms around himself.

"Onla's always been scary. He probably pooted on himself," Sally said.

"It was them William boys from Hillcrest, that was what they were saying," Onla said.

Roachie laughed.

"It wasn't nobody from Hillcrest. It was them Harlem Cribs. They turned it out."

Roachie nodded as if to affirm his statement and everybody nodded along with them.

That name again, Cribs. The name was circling through the neighborhood faster and faster. The Mack family and the William family were bad enough; they got into serious stuff and if that wasn't enough, we had the Brotherhood, a motorcycle club with big weightlifting men, but they were peaceable, at least to the neighborhood. The Cribs were different. They were us, regular brothers transformed into gangsters. Even their name implied they were homeboys — they were from the crib. Suddenly, out of nowhere came organization. Not any kind of organization, not one built on mutually shared goals and a leadership hierarchy. It wasn't like on TV and those old gangs from New York where members had titles such as Minister of Information or the Sergeant of Arms. No, the Cribs were a home grown Barbarian Horde which appeared on the block one hot summer day in their sporty outfits of Bomber jackets with thick fur collars, and Levi's shiny with starched dirt, and black croaker sac shoes and a black or red handkerchief, starched rigid. They came, sprung up from the concrete, the lawns, the backyards and especially the schools and they ruled. At first nobody belonged to the Cribs, (Mysteriously the b became a p and they became known as the Crips.) but many kids had a big brother in their ranks. The ultimate threat started to circulate: "Fool, let me drop a dime and I'll get your house knee deep in lowriders."

Something to really fear, the idea of your enemy having your house surrounded with Crips in lowriders, hydraulics bouncing the Impalas like rubber balls. Then like in "Night of the Body Snatchers" kids started converting; some big head pootbutt with bad teeth and breath got the "look," and the attitude, that whole sullen maniac trip, slit-eyed, laconic, barely even a nod and then on a bad day, "What fool?! Yeah niggah, this is Crip here."

Of course every now and then they would have to rat pack someone just to show the world how it was done but that escalated quickly into its more deadly variant, the stomp. That's how Lamar died, stomped flat at a house party. Cool, handsome Lamar. It wasn't a mystery why he was stomped, all over the city, throughout black L.A., it was happening, a kind of teenage arms race. While in our part of the world it was the Crips, a mile south it was the Brims, east the Pirus, and all of them with as much of a intolerant view of outsiders as the Crips. So Lamar, the handsome young ladies' man with no intention of beating on anyone, was killed by a bunch of fools who kicked him in the head till he stopped breathing because he was too good looking and he might have stolen one of the girls they didn't have in the first place. His stomping made it obvious what everybody knew was happening: our blocks, which were like small, self-contained towns, were now territory to be defended as though the avenues and streets had natural resources or religious significance. Notions of self defense, of preemptive strikes, the need to never be caught slipping, became a way of life. It was inevitable or so it seemed that sooner or later we all were going to die some stupid, embarrassing death.

All those outdoor gatherings, something one would expect in Southern California, an afternoon with family and friends in one of the many neighborhood parks, became a big gamble. At the Festival in Black, where some good-hearted community people who believed in black pride and the need for black businesses and who gave crafts-people and t-shirt vendors and incense sellers an opportunity to make some money, those kinds of events were dying out fast. But then it was exciting to see all the families having picnic lunches or barbecuing and all those the fine girls who would never talk to us and the hip people, the people who put the festival on. It was easy to tell them because they wore cool black t-shirts with "Festival In Black," in flowing cursive script and a line drawing of a black man and woman in a sort of heroic style, huge afros and big muscles on the guy, big breasts on the girl. But these events that brought the community together became unpopular. Who wanted to be out in the open, exposed to whatever might jump off, now that teenagers ruled the streets, unafraid of dying and unafraid of killing somebody.

For some reason Sidney, Winnie and Jude let me and Onla trip with them to the festival. They were sitting down under a tree near the bandstand where the music groups were playing, smoking joints and drinking beers, cooling out. Onla and I went on another hot dog run; it was boring watching them get loaded, because we didn't. We wandered around counting our change, spying on the girls, looking at all the cool African stuff in the booths, not paying attention to, but hearing the music, drums and horns, saxophones...something happening in the distance up where it was most crowded by the bandstand. We could see the drummers in their African outfits moving around on the stage and people in front of the stage struggling, rolling on the grass and then other picnickers chain reacting, grabbing their stuff and running for high ground. Me and Onla did what we had grown accustomed to do. Instead of the habit we had for years, of running towards trouble, to see what we could see, what tales we could carry back to our neighborhood, now we high-tailed it, wise enough to know we couldn't stand at the edge of trouble and expect to avoid it. Nowadays the fists and bullets flew in all directions.

We ran back to Jude and Winnie ready to get to the car and get the hell out of there, but they weren't on the knoll near the trees and basketball courts.

"Where are they?" I asked, but Onla didn't bother to answer.

From the knoll we could see the trouble spreading, the knot of fighting had swelled to a mob and more and more people were running from it in various directions, some had even caught up to us, and passed us on their way to the parking lot.

Then the hollow, dumb sounds of gunshots, and the screams and even more people running. And Onla, cool calm Onla, started to panic.

"Fuck! We gotta get out of here."

"Yeah," I said. "Where are we gonna go? We got to be ten miles from the Aves."

"So?" he said, and started pogoing up down.

"What you doing?"

"Seeing which way to go."

Things were getting scary. If Onla did something dumb and tried to run home I'd have to try to hang with him. He knew the way and I had no idea of what direction home was in. More shots in the distance, more people rushing up, a big woman shoved Onla aside so hard he almost fell.

"They wouldn't just drive off and leave us."

I was sure they wouldn't do anything that dumb.

Mama would probably throw high and inside on Winston with the frying pan this time, instead of low and out. I was sure even if Onla wasn't, that they had to be somewhere near. I trotted away to the parking lot as it was starting to clear out. There was a big jam-up at the exit. There, near a tree was Winston's Jag. We just hadn't seen it but there they were. We ran for it. Right ahead of the biggest wave of people. Jude was in the back seat, Sidney and Winston were in the front with the windows rolled up to keep the contact in. Jude had his window down. Onla dived right in; feet barely clearing Jude's head.

"What the fuck is wrong with you?" Jude shouted.

Onla unlocked the door for me and I tried to get in but Onla slipped around me. He didn't want to sit next to Jude and maybe get thrown out.

"You guys should go," I said, trying to be cool cause I knew if I sounded pushy they'd ignore me.

"Man, don't ya'll see! Look!" Onla said.

The gangbangers had arrived, running for the cars and whatever weapons they had stashed in them. Four bloodied and bruised guys got to a lowrider and the trunk opened, out came a shotgun and a handgun. The armed ones led the way back to the park. Onla had scrunched down to the floor in a little heaving ball. I wanted to join him but I was too big to fit. Jude continued sipping his beer and the joint continued circulating between the three of them.

Boom Boom! Pop Pop!

The gangbangers had unloaded at a distance and were running back for the car to reload. They were more than a dozen yards away and their enemies were coming after them.

"Getting pretty wild around here," Sidney said.

"Young knuckleheads," Jude said.

"Let's get out of here!" I said, cause one of the rival gangbangers had stopped on a knoll and let off at the gangbangers near us.

"Go!" Onla shouted.

Jude reached across me and hit Onla in the shoulder so hard his head ricocheted off of the car window.

"You guys shut up. Nobody's worried about us. Running away might get 'em thinking."

"What?" I said.

Winnie was good and buzzed, pointing to four squad cars coming down on Manchester.

"Man, fucking pigs!" Sidney said.

"Yeah," Winnie said, "We gotta go!"

Winston stepped into action, gone was his beer and weed-induced stupor.

He wheeled the car around and ignored the congested exit. He drove the Jag across the parking lot, across the sidewalk and over the edge of the curb. The heavy front end of the sedan boomed down onto the street, then the rear wheels landed, and we bounced about again.

"Damn," Winnie said, "I gotta replace those shocks."

He cut across two lanes and turned along with the police. At first I had no idea what he was trying to do, maybe get us all arrested. But then I saw more police cars coming down the street we just turned off. We arrived there just as the police were getting ready to block the intersections with squad cars.

Winston waved to them as though he knew them. For a moment it seemed as
though the policemen was going to pull us over and get a whiff of Winston's
weed and beer-scented breath. Winston though, had risen to the occasion. He
gave that million dollar, matchbook smile, and his straight teeth, and green
eyes and his white skin, reassured the cop, convinced him that Jag with the
longhaired white guy and his black friends and not even that black, weren't
really worth stopping. We drove away, back to the quieter Westside.

It continued on like that, us knuckleheads seeing our world undergoing
blurring change and the fellas seemingly missing out on the whole thing as if
they were walking on different sidewalks, breathing another kind of air.

Maybe it was because they had money, enough income so they weren't
forced to hang out in the neighborhood. They didn't hang out at the Baldwin
Theater every weekend cause it was the neighborhood theater. They had cars
to drive to the Marina or Westwood.

A few years back the Baldwin theater was hip to hang out at, check out the
double feature, "Hang 'em High" and "Where Eagles Dare." Maybe some of
them cool Hammer horror films — then the black exploitation flicks were
really live, "Coffee T.N.T.," "Foxy Brown," "Nigger Charlie," "Abbey the
Black Exorcist." And young love was there too, couples huddled up while the
nons like me and Gumbo who couldn't pull females, had to content ourselves
with hot dogs and popcorn. Man, you couldn't keep us out of there. About
the only thing which could was rest rooms.

It got to be a dicey thing wanting to go to the Baldwin, and getting home
became another worry altogether. Of course it was the boys in gang-bang blue
packing the rest rooms. That was another manifestation of the new
neighborhood order. I wouldn't drink sodas no matter how thirsty I got from
salty popcorn. No way I wanted to go in the rest room and be surrounded by
gangbangers, and if you didn't know a few of them, it could get serious.
Somebody might ask, "Hey, homes, loan me a dollar," and that was the worst
thing about it, it wasn't a standard kind of jack where you could come out
with a quarter and give it up and you could slip away. But these chumps were
raising the rate to a point where the average pootbutt couldn't stand it. There
would go the hot dog, the bus ride, even the phone call home. You'd have to
get bold and say, "Sorry, man, I ain't got it," then there would be that long

moment where everyone is looking at you, encircled by his partners and your accuser ups the ante.

"Stand for a search?"

Me, I'd try pulling my pockets inside out, "See," I'd say, and walk my ass out of the rest room. Sometimes though, we'd see some knucklehead standing there on that nasty rest room floor, socks in hand, barefoot. He had to undergo a full search.

The bus ride home got to be crazy too, buses seemed to make gangsters nuts. Once after the movie theater closed and everybody hit the bus stop at the same time, the bus pulled up and stopped like a rookie bus driver would, not like those bus drivers who knew the ropes, who would speed by, and avoid what he knew would be nothing but trouble. Gumbo and me got on because Gumbo hated walking. We were towards the front of the crush of passengers, and got to board first. We sat close to the bus driver in our silent hope that we would be safe. And like clock work the first paying gangbanger slipped to the rear door, and forced it open. Then the flood gates opened. The mob by the back door flowed in filling the rear of the bus first. Once a old man and woman sat frightened behind the rear door well. There wasn't anything for them to do but huddle together, faces tight with worry and shock and hope to weather the wave of teenagers.

That day we both knew this bus driver had lost control of the bus. We needed to get off before it got really insane. I waited for Gumbo to make the first move. He was wider than me, it would be easier to follow in his substantial wake. But he wasn't having any of that. I was older and taller, a fifteen year old with some facial hair, it was expected of me to lead. I stood up, and immediately my seat was taken by a guy in a Bomber jacket with a fake fur collar, fur so white I knew he had just gotten it, same with his blue beanie, right off the rack, here he was exulting in his new uniform.

I put my head down and got by the panicked bus driver who knew he had lost it. Control was in the hands of a teenage mob and they wanted his transfers.

"Get off!" he shouted.

Nobody but me and Gumbo heard or paid attention to him, we shoved our way down the stair well and through the crowd still trying to board. Finally, free of people pushing against us, we turned to see the bus driver fleeing the bus, broken field running down La Brea.

We started walking because we had no choice. Even as kids it seemed weird, to have to walk somewhere. It used to be easier to just beg parents for a ride but now as a teenager, that was no longer a possibility. How would that look going over to some girl's house in my Daddy's beat up Galaxie 500. So we walked home from the Baldwin because it was safer than taking the bus, but also because it was an adventure slipping by the Jungle, walking on the edge of the street, listening for voices and if hearing them, retreating down another block, or even diving behind hedges to wait for the hoodlums to troop by. Sometimes though, it would be so quiet and empty walking down Coliseum in that affluent area that we walked in the center of the street like it was our own personal road.

Once we got away from the sprawling clusters of apartments in the Jungle where we had to be quiet and watchful, we could talk loudly in the neighborhoods which were still mostly Japanese with their clover lawns and their decorative pagodas, and then the black affluent neighborhood near Audubon Junior High. The homes were beautiful, nicer than what we would see on TV. Beautiful two story Spanish homes, with large windows and ornate wrought iron fences to keep the riffraff out.

★★★

Then I got a job, not another half-assed, washing the neighbor's car or cutting lawns and having to try to sneak out our lawn mower without Mama finding out but she usually did and she'd yell at me for using things I can't replace.

No, it was a real job tutoring little kids in a science program out of the community center at USC, $1.95 an hour, more than $10.00 a day, great money for a fifteen year old.

The guy who hired me was a serious black man who just graduated with a degree in biology from Berkeley. His name was Ron and right off I knew he was different from the fellas on the Ave. Sure some of the fellas were serious; Walter was as serious as a walking heart-attack about money as was Sidney but skinny, dark skinned, well spoken Ron wasn't in it for the cash. Ron was really smart but that didn't set him apart. Jude was smart too, if you got him to talk about missiles and tanks and warfare. Winnie was a gifted mechanic and was great with numbers but neither he nor Jude seemed interested in anything beyond smoking weed, playing basketball and going to work. Ron was a different kind of bird.

He received a grant to run a science program for minority kids out of USC's community center. I knew Ron from Foshay where he volunteered for and ran the science after school program. He heard that I won a science fair with a model rocket I built.

"The job's yours," he said, "Just get your work permit. Fill out this form and I'll submit it for you."

I guess he saw some leadership potential in me but I think he was probably asking everybody and whoever turned in the application first would get the job. I filled out mine and forged my Mama's signature and returned it in minutes.

"You must really want this job. You'll like the work helping little brothers and sisters learn the importance of science."

I nodded, but I wonder if he knew I knew more about science fiction than actual science. We started the program soon as summer break began, me and a dozen other black and brown kids stepping onto the grounds of USC for the first time, a spot of color of that very white campus.

Most of the kids I was supposed to tutor were seventh grade scrubs from Foshay. Professors would invite us into the labs inside an old ivy covered building with gargoyles above the entrance to give us tours and a little lecture. "Water is made up of one molecule of hydrogen, two of oxygen," I was told on more than one tour.

Afterward, we'd head back to the community center with kids asking me questions I couldn't answer.

"Why can't you see them molecules?" Some big headed kid asked me afterward.

"Cause they're too small don't you remember what the professor said."

"But you can see them. I see water all the time."

The kid pointed to the water faucet and I wondered why this kid was asking me.

"We don't fall off the earth because gravity is pulling us down!"

"I don't see nothing holding me down," another kid said.

"Cause it's like a magnet."

"I don't see no magnet holding me down."

That's when I just would shrug and walk away, more aware of how I didn't know much more than the scrubs I looked down on.

Ron was very excited about the program. He'd give us little speeches about the importance of what we were doing.

"We can't make it as a people if we don't have the engineers or the scientists. Not all of us are going to be athletes or entertainers. You all have a much better chance being a brain surgeon than a quarterback for the Rams."

The kids seemed shocked as if they thought if they stayed out of trouble and stayed in school a professional career in sports was a lock. Billy, one of the tough seventh graders was sure going to make it at football even though he was the runt of the group.

Ron did get most of us to learn how to solve a simple problem with a slide rule and how to use a microscope and even how to do some math but I think what everybody really liked about the program were the weekly field trips.

"Where to this week?" a kid would ask.

"Griffith Park Observatory," Ron would say dryly because he knew what was coming next, the plea for thrills.

"Man, what about Disneyland? They got robots and Tomorrow Land."

"Ya'll shut up and learn to work that slide rules. Then we'll go."

We never went because we couldn't work the slide rules as well as Ron wanted us to. That was okay. Most of us had been to Disneyland. Where Ron took us we never heard of but it was usually interesting. Once we went to a naval base in San Diego and got to see docked submarines. We actually were there to check out the tide pools near the vase but Ron got interested in the subs and we couldn't get near enough to make him happy because of the fifteen foot high fence with concerti wire at the top and posted warnings, "No Trespassers!"

We hiked up the sand dunes to the highway where we could see the submarines more clearly; giant black tubes with crossed wings.

"One of those things cost half a billion dollars," Ron said, angrily.

"How much is that?"

"More than a million?" someone else asked.

"No, it ain't," the first kid replied.

"One of those subs could blow the whole world up," Ron said as though it really depressed him. I didn't believe him.

"Not the whole world," I said.

"Maybe L.A.?" A kid asked.

Ron's sisters, Penny and Terry, two girls around our age looked pained as Ron explained about nuclear missiles.

"He oughta be a preacher," Penny, the older of the two said.

"I knew I should have stayed home, but Mama said I had to go with you," Terry said.

"I didn't want to go. Ron said I had to go," Penny replied.

Both of them fixed on me, finally noticing that I wasn't paying attention to the seventh graders as I was supposed to do, "Don't you hate having to go to all these boring places?" Penny asked, in a clear, correct voice that most of us at Foshay thought of as being white. I tried to conceal my happiness at having one of these pretty middle class girls talking to me but I liked going to labs and tide pools and museums. It was like being in a science fiction movie.

"Yeah, it's boring," I said, looking disgusted.

"Stop lying," Terry said, "you know you like all this science stuff."

"You leave him alone. You know you like him," Penny said.

"He's too young for me. He's your speed."

Ron had finished explaining the perils of nuclear warfare to the captive band of seventh graders.

"I should see if we could go on a tour of one of these bad boys. Let ya'll get close to the missiles that could end the world as we know it," Ron said.

The seventh graders began to peel off one by one, slipping away to the school bus. But nuclear war scared me even if no one else seemed interested. I hated the first Friday of each month because the air raid sirens would sound and sometimes I'd think it was the last Friday or another day and that the world was gonna blow up before I grew pubic hair.

"Shadows, after they dropped the bomb on Hiroshima all that was left of some people was a shadow outline, just ashes on the ground, they were fried so fast," Ron said shaking his head.

"Man," I said, knowing that I had another image of the bomb along with hugh mushroom clouds and gigantic ants.

"Only twenty minutes away from a missile fired in Siberia and we're all dead before we know it."

I stood there thinking about how I'd go, on the toilet, cutting the lawn, picking up the dog mess in the backyard. I wished the bombs would wait until I had a girlfriend.

"Come on, Garv," he said shaking me out of my morbid funk. "We've got to go. I've scared you enough. That's enough fun for today."

I knew Ron kind of got a kick out of telling us of these end of the world nightmares because I think he knew how dangerous life was in the here and now. Science fiction violence and death was almost a relief from what could happen walking to the liquor store or working at the community center with guys who didn't care for science or science fiction death.

First, it was the little things; all the supplies in Ron's office disappeared. He suspected that someone from the staff of the community center was up to it. How else would they have keys? That was the problem about the community center, the science program, not even two dozen kids plus Ron and me and his sisters had to share a small building with people who didn't seem to do anything but argue and play basketball and be paid for it. We were instructed by Ron to avoid them, "USC got them here on salary so they don't set the school on fire. They know they sold out so they make trouble," Ron said.

The rumors were that Crow, this muscle bound, tight pants wearing guy who was the assistant supervisor of the sports program, thought Ron carried himself too highly, and he might have to knock him out, but as disturbing as this rumor was at that moment I didn't have time to worry about him because the community center became a tensely-armed camp. Crips from my neighborhood were driving through the parking lot flashing hand signs. I was afraid of the Crips but I knew they wouldn't bother to shoot at me and waste a bullet. I wasn't worth it. But I didn't want the community center rabble to know I lived in a Crip neighborhood. That could be serious as a heart-attack. Being from somewhere had gotten to be a big point of contention with gangsters, and we were all from someplace if we liked it or not. Being from the

Thirties implied that I knew those gangsters on those particular streets and were on reasonably good terms with them. So, it was good to be vague, or even to lie about your address because it was too complicated and dangerous to be honest.

After the flashing of the signs I knew something was going to happen. These guys had to shoot at those guys and those guys would be back at the community center to shoot at these guys and maybe even me.

"Shouldn't brought his ass up here if he didn't want it kicked," one of the Gladiators said, the gang that most of the community center workers seemed to belong to.

"I don't care if he don't gang-bang. His brother do. Think cause he's some punk ass lover he won't get beat down."

"Shoulda thought about who runs things up here," another gangster said.

So it was going to happen, a time bomb ticking that could take any of us out. Wayne, another undercover avenue guy I went to Foshay with, had a job coaching baseball. He was worried too.

"We're straight in the middle of this shit."

"Think something's gonna happen?" I asked.

"Oh, hell yeah. And I'm damn sure gonna lock myself in that bathroom and let these fools kill each other," Wayne said.

That sounded like a good plan so when I wasn't working with the kids I started hanging near to Wayne, looking for that clue to break for the bathrooms. I knew the score from Foshay, run somewhere and lock yourself in till the shooting or the ass kicking stops.

Most of the Gladiators and their sympathizers were ready for whatever might jump off. Enough of them were deep into the martial arts, practicing kicks and punches and coming up with odd weapons I'd never seen before, chains hooked to sickles, short sticks with handles, and one guy even had a samurai sword. I heard they were training with this Korean master but I wondered if the Korean master guy knew he was dealing with gangsters?

Wayne and I glanced at them as we did our grunt work, sweeping the large main floor of the center.

"Those fools better have something more in their trunks other than that Bruce Lee shit or they gonna get blasted," Wayne said, and I agreed.

Guns ruled the land and they didn't seem to have any. Maybe they knew magic along with the marital arts and could make guns useless, the kind of thing we saw in those Kung Fu movies.

When it happened, it was straight out of the "Wild Bunch. I was sweeping when I saw shadows stretching across the hard wooden floors of the community center and one of those shadows had something long and pointed, extending from an arm. I should have run but I didn't. I was stuck there in that moment, seeing more gangsters with guns drawn backing up the lead guy.

The Gladiators vanished like ghosts somehow leaving the center without making a sound or being seen. I would have done the same thing if I saw the Crips coming. Only Crow and Ron were left between the Crips and the community center. Then Crow gave up on trying to look hard enough to stare down six armed men and he broke, zig zagging for the kitchen. After hesitating for a minute the Crips flowed through the double doors calling out the Gladiators, "Fuck all you punk ass Gladiators!" one of them said.

"We better raise," Wayne said, and we hurriedly walked to the bathrooms but we knew better than to run. The bathroom doors were all locked. We heard voices, girls crying and guys telling them to shut up. So that's where the gladiators hid. I bet Crow was in there too. Then we heard Ron's voice. First it seemed like he was trying to block their way but then his voice rose. What was he going to do, preach to them?

"Hey, brothers! Calm yourselves. There is no reason for this kind of ugliness."

"What the fuck you know!" the one with the long gun, said. He looked familiar, then I realized that it was Dennis, the wannabe gangster who took my bus money a number of times at Foshay. Some people said he had moved up, now supposedly he was the godfather of the Harlem Crips.

"The guys you're looking for took off when they saw you coming. The rest of the people here are in the science program and none of them gang-bang."

"Stop lying!" Dennis shouted.

"Black man to black man I'm telling you the truth. All the people you want ran off!"

A long pause and then Dennis and his boys started backing off.

I started sweeping again glad to have something to do. Wayne had managed to slip away so it was just Ron and me in the big bare hall and a half dozen Crips with their guns drawn. But now they were no longer faceless thugs. I Could see beyond the bomber jackets and croaker sac shoes and the guns; if I didn't know their names I knew their faces. Then Dennis and his boys backed out of the community center, "Tell them Gladiators we're gonna be back!"

It wasn't over. I can hear them on the outside of the double doors arguing.

"Fuck em! They're hiding. Let's shoot it up."

"Man, let's go," I heard Dennis say.

The arguing continued and poor Ron sagged against a wall as if he knew he had more convincing to do. But Ron didn't wait for them to rush in again, guns blasting. He stepped outside.

"Brothers, I understand that you're angry that somebody did you wrong but they're kids here, that's all."

"Let me check it out," Dennis asked, and before Ron could reply the first guy with the gun craned his head around the door. Giving Ron a little respect by not coming back inside. Dennis looked dead at me. I nodded agreeably.

"See any of them gladiator fools?"

"They ran," is all I managed to say.

"Your pootbutt ass better not be lying."

"I ain't lying," I said, shrugging.

He waved me off and I saw them head out for the parking lot.

Ron quickly pulled the doors but not before we heard a few quick shots causing us all to flatten. Afterward, after five minutes of quiet, the doors to the bathrooms opened and most kids took off but the Gladiators were talking about payback. Ron watched looking bone tired. Then he gestured for me to follow him into his office.

"Why do I have to deal with these god damn idiots!" he said, sitting heavily at his desk and putting his head down into his hands. Even long after the girls and kids and the gladiators ventured from the rest rooms, Ron sat with his head on the desk. Finally, he looked up at me.

"Go home, and tell all the kids to go before those idiots come back."

I didn't have to tell anybody because we were all cutting out. As I crossed the parking lot making sure to walk between cars in case I needed cover, Wayne appeared, smiling sheepishly.

"Man, we lucked out. We coulda got blasted."

"Yeah, I was scared. I don't know about coming to work tomorrow."

Wayne laughed, "I'm quitting. It's gonna get wicked. The money ain't enough."

Wayne quitting got me to thinking. I decided to take a day off.

The next morning I called Ron and told him I was sick. He said he understood and I'd still get paid.

The following morning day I caught the bus to USC and I noticed that the front of the community center was pockmarked with bullet holes. It was an interesting thing to see, just like in the movies. The holes made ribbon like patterns across the face of the building, even smashing a few of the raised letters of the University of Southern California. The Crips had returned and left serious graffiti to let everybody know.

Ron was in the office looking tired and pissed off.

"The police are coming to talk to us about what happened here last night."

"I guess it didn't stop after we went home."

"No, it didn't. I'm sure they all came back here to prove their manhood," Ron said, smirking. "Watch, USC is going to shut the center down because of this."

"Think there's gonna be more trouble?"

"These brothers have a disease that's spreading. They're robots programmed to kill each other."

"You mean like robots with diseases?" I asked, Ron made everything sound like science fiction but he ignored my question.

"Yeah, Garvy. You might want to quit. I can't guarantee your safety. I don't feel safe. I don't want my sisters coming up here."

"I don't mind, I mean it's crazy around here but it's crazy everywhere."

Ron frowned as though whatever he was thinking filled him with disgust.

"You'd think USC would cut us some slack. They know this center is a pit. They just want this nonsense to continue so they can run all the programs off. They act like teaching science is just the same as shooting baskets."

The police showed at noon. Two somber, red-faced cops who looked ready to leave the moment they entered. The whole center came out to hear what they had to say. Even the little kids were quiet because they like everybody else wanted to know if it was safe to come to the center.

The cops began before everybody arrived and found a seat in the hastily arranged folding chairs of the main hall. The policemen sat on the edge of the stage and didn't bother to introduce themselves.

One cop did all the talking, "Listen up, people. I think it's important for you to understand what the situation up here is."

Ron watched from the far corner of the room with his arms folded across his chest.

"There's a gang war going on some of these guys have machine guns."

Finally, the other cop found the energy to speak.

"If we get a call from security here and we hear that somebody is shooting up the place with a machine gun don't expect us to arrive till it's all over."

"Yeah, that's right. You're on your own. We're not rushing here knowing the bad guys have automatics," the other cop said.

That was that. The cops got up to leave but Ron stopped them with a question.

"So what are we paying you for?"

"What?" One cop bothered to ask, checking his watch.

"We pay taxes like everybody else."

"We're being honest. The's the deal. We don't have the training or the manpower to deal with a gang war."

"Why'd you come? You're not here to help or protect us. You just want us to go away."

The cops didn't even glance at Ron as they left.

After that the center was just dead anyway. We couldn't pretend anymore that we were safe even from ourselves.

I wanted to work for the last check and have that much more money to start the school year but that was a dead issue after seeing Ron beat like a dog in front of his sisters and all the rest of us.

Crow was crazy and he was vicious even more so than Walter or anybody I knew. I was signing my time card to go home for the day when I heard Ron's sisters shouting for help. I ran through the double doors to the parking lot and saw Ron on all fours crawling away from Crow who had a pool stick and was beating Ron so hard in the head that I thought it was going to burst like a cantaloupe.

"Stop him!" Tracy said to me. "He's going to kill him!"

But I stood there frozen, doing nothing while the buffed Crow, in skin tight tank top pounded Ron with the fat end of the stick. Penny found another supervisor who ran over and gingerly guided Crow away. Crow talked as though he was right for beating Ron.

"Wouldn't let me use his car. Talking all that shit like he's really somebody. He ain't shit. I broke his ass down."

Crow was breathing hard but he wasn't drunk or loaded, excited was all I could see. Crow held up the pool stick as if he wanted us all to witness what he did Ron in with. The sisters had sense enough to leave Crow alone and tend to Ron. I think if they had, Crow would have clubbed them too.

We stood there in the parking lot waiting for help as Ron floated in and out of consciousness. Campus security arrived with the paramedics. Crow was at the edge of the scene watching so none of us said a word about how Ron got thrashed. Tracy gave me a ride home crying so hard she could barely find the road between having to drive and calming Penny who was crying harder than she was. Finally, Tracy pulled over in front of my house.

"Don't you go back there. Somebody is going to get killed."

"Yeah, you're right," I said, but it wouldn't be Crow, that worthless piece of shit. Crow would live, the rest of us, Ron or Tracy or some goofy kid or even me would be the one to die.

JUDITH FREEMAN

Wertheimer in the City

It had been many months since Wertheimer had been in the city. During his absence his apartment had stood empty, as it always did when he was away. The apartment was small but adequate for his needs. He kept it more out of habit than necessity, for he had increasingly fewer occasions to use it now that Lothar was gone and his life had undergone a great change.

Usually his visits to the city last only a few days but he expected to stay longer this time. He hoped to see a few friends, and there was also a family matter requiring his attention. Before leaving the country he had called Mrs. Cochran, his neighbor in the city with whom he had a long-standing arrangement. He had asked her to air out his apartment and tidy up in preparation for his arrival, and to watch for a package from his doctor which might arrive before he did.

He drove into Los Angeles at dusk on a clear and beautiful evening after a long trip across the desert. The aria from Wagner's *Tristan and Isolde* was playing on the car radio as he pulled up in front of his apartment. It seemed to Wertheimer a perfect moment—the exquisite music, the sight of the old building, the evening light raking the garden. He climbed the steps slowly and put his key in the lock and opened his front door. Immediately his eyes went to a vase of tulips sitting on the table at the end of the living room. Once again Mrs. Cochran had carried out his instructions perfectly: a dozen white tulips had been arranged in his favorite blue vase. And arranged very nicely, he thought. He must remember to compliment her.

Only when he'd unpacked and finished his first drink did he call Nadia.

"Who is it?" she said instead of offering a hello. He was used to her abruptness, and said simply,

"It's me."

"Oh, it's you. When did you get in?"

"Just now."

"How was the drive?"

"Very pleasant." He started to describe his trip across the desert, how beautiful the saguaro had looked and the ocotillo in bloom, but she cut him off in mid-sentence.

"The question is, what are we going to do about Arthur?"

"Did you tell him I was coming?"

"Of course. He's expecting you to have lunch with him tomorrow. He plans on bringing her to meet you."

"Her? . . . ah, yes. What is her name again?"

"Bea. Didn't you get their Christmas card? It was on the card."

Wertheimer had gotten the card from his son. And of course he did remember it. He hadn't ever gotten a Christmas card quite like it. It showed a picture of partially-naked blonde with the words, *I'll be your perfect fantasy*. The image was still quite vivid. And now he did recall that the card had been signed, *Bea and Arthur*.

"She's a hippie," Nadia said. "A hippie who makes pornography."

"I was under the impression she was an artist."

"An artist who makes pornography is no artist, just another purveyor of smut." This last word, colored by her thick German accent, came out as *schmut*.

"Well I don't think . . , " Wertheimer began. And then he stopped himself because he didn't want to get into an argument with Nadia over someone he hadn't even met.

"You'll see when you meet her. Arthur has lost it this time."

"Lost what?" Wertheimer asked. He had become momentarily distracted by the dogs barking next door and thought he had missed some part of the conversation.

"His head—he's lost his head completely. He's decided to marry her. That's why I insisted you come here and talk to him. He listens to you. He doesn't listen to me."

"But Arthur's an adult now, Nadia. He's thirty-five—"

"Thirty-seven," Nadia said, correcting him. "You never remember your son's age."

"Anyway, he's certainly old enough to make his own decision."

"I'm not asking you to work miracles here," Nadia said. "I just want you to convince him to get the prenuptial agreement. He doesn't think he needs to do this."

"Maybe he doesn't." Wertheimer thought such agreements were silly.

"He's sunk if he doesn't get an agreement. I know a gold-digger when I see one, and this Bea is only looking for a rich ore to mine."

For a moment Wertheimer thought Nadia had said a *rich whore to mine* and he felt shocked, thinking she was somehow making a reference to herself since it was her money Arthur had lived on for years, although recently he'd come into control of his own trust. Then he understood what she'd really said was *rich ore* and he laughed.

"This is funny to you?" she snapped.

"No, no," he mumbled.

"It shouldn't be. It won't be so funny when she dumps him and takes him for all he's worth."

"It's his money now." He did feel he should point this out to Nadia.

"The problem is she's not serious about him."

Wertheimer suddenly felt a deep weariness come over him. "Look, Nadia, I'm rather tired after the long drive. I think I'll go to bed early. Why don't I call you tomorrow?"

"Don't bother to call. Just come and see me after you have lunch with them. Arthur's expecting you at 12:30." She named a restaurant where he was to meet his son, the one restaurant he himself would have picked if anybody had bothered to consult him on the matter.

2.

Wertheimer awoke early on his first morning back in the city and went out for a walk just as the sun was rising. He strolled down Alvarado and made a right on Sixth, heading west toward the congregational church which rose up in the mist, looming before him like a massive granite tomb.

He was struck by certain changes in the neighborhood, most of them unpleasant. As he approached Lafayette Park, he was sorry to see that the local branch of the public library had finally closed. For years the little library had been in a state of decline, used less and less, until it seemed most of the patrons were old men who sat snoozing at the long wooden tables. Still, he was sad to see it boarded up, surrounded now by a chain-link fence. Also, the little park next to the library had undergone such a change he hardly recognized it anymore. The grass had disappeared, and the only people he saw as he picked his way along a muddy path was a group of pitiful looking homeless men who gave him blank looks as he passed by.

He crossed Commonwealth, heading for the Sheraton Townhouse where he intended to buy the morning paper and have a cup of coffee. He was especially fond of the old hotel and its beautiful gardens. But instead of the gardens, or the familiar face of the doorman standing under the portico, he saw a boarded-up building. The hotel, too, had closed.

It had been such a lovely little hotel. Wertheimer looked at the boarded-up windows in disbelief. The flowers had been left to dry up, and the garden walls were topped with razor wire. The place where he'd enjoyed eating lunch and entertaining friends had simply gone out of business.

He walked away from the hotel, shaking his head, wondering how so much could have changed in such a short time. That was the dispiriting part. Ugly things managed to survive while the old and the beautiful—the carefully made, Wertheimer thought—simply disappeared.

He started for home, aware of a certain pain in his legs which came frequently now and made it difficult to walk. He wished he had thought to take a pain pill before he left the apartment. He felt a little disoriented and had to stop for a moment to get his bearings at an intersection. Sound came at him from all directions. Somewhere far down the street a siren wailed. He hesitated before crossing the street and then set out, stepping carefully off the curb, but the light changed suddenly and he had to hurry back.

As he stood waiting for the light to turn green, he gazed around him. Everywhere he looked he could see trash laying on the sidewalk. He had to hold his breath against the smell of ripe garbage that came from an over-filled dumpster. Had the city really become so much harsher in his absence? Or had he simply been away too long and forgotten what it was really like?

He felt dispirited as he headed for home. He did not see how civilization could endure such decay. Libraries closing, parks in ruin, people without a place to live, and garbage everywhere. What sort of life was this, he wondered? Then, as he rounded a corner near the Casa de Cleaners, he was stopped by the sight of something that lifted his spirits. Something extraordinary. At least he found it extraordinary to see a cluster of golden mushrooms growing beneath a large oak tree.

He stopped and bent down to examine the mushrooms. Moving aside the layer of dead leaves, he touched one gently. They were morels, just as he thought. Morels growing right in the city! The beautiful crenulated caps, so distinctive in their appearance, like the folds of a brain or a desiccated apple, were a rich golden-brown. He had never seen larger or more beautiful morels—more than a dozen beautiful caps. And they were at the perfect stage for harvesting.

Wertheimer grew excited. He began thinking of the meal he could make out of such beautiful mushrooms. But soon he was confronting the problem of how to carry them back to his apartment. He didn't want to bruise them, to spoil them in any way by handling them roughly. What he needed was a basket or a paper bag, but he had neither. At last he decided the thing to do was to return later and gather them. Surely no one else would spot the mushrooms and pick them before he could. But just for safety, he piled a few handfuls of leaves around the mushrooms, and hurried away, excited by his find.

3.

Wertheimer arrived at the restaurant a little early. He killed time by browsing in a bookstore next door.

Only a few minutes passed before he saw his son arrive in the company of a young woman. They came down the sidewalk hand-in-hand and stopped in front of a magazine rack placed outside. Arthur was wearing a suit and he looked as if he'd lost weight. The woman with him did not look like the woman on the card that said *I'll be your perfect fantasy.* She wasn't wearing sexy clothes, nor did she have long blonde hair. She had dark hair and she was wearing a simple outfit. She seemed very young—much younger than his son. Wertheimer thought she was very pretty.

He didn't rush out to greet them but instead stood watching them through the window for a moment. He wanted to observe them while remaining hidden himself, even if this did amount to a kind of spying. They stood out on the sidewalk chatting, their shoulders touching as they leaned towards each other. They were almost exactly the same height. Wertheimer noticed how relaxed and happy his son looked. He couldn't remember the last time he'd seen his son looking so happy. Wertheimer thought they made a very striking couple.

"There you are," his son said when Wertheimer approached him. "I was about to look for you in the restaurant."

"I arrived early," Wertheimer said.

Wertheimer embraced his son, and then stepped back and extended his hand to the young woman with him.

"How do you do—Bea, I believe, isn't it?"

"Nice to meet you," she said, and gazed at him with a serious expression. The hand she extended was cold and very thin. He clasped it lightly, touching it only for the briefest moment before letting it go.

"Shall we go inside?" Arthur said, and taking the initiative, he led the way into the restaurant.

Wertheimer followed his son, who even at that moment didn't feel like a son so much as a fond acquaintance he hadn't seen for a while. To his regret Wertheimer had never felt much like a father. He hadn't exactly taken his duties lightly: he thought in many respects he had carried out his responsibilities admirably. He had tried to see that the right decisions had been made in regard to Arthur's life. Yet he had lacked something—not love exactly, for he had always been very fond of Arthur. He simply felt none of the requisite authority he associated with parenthood, that instinct to dominate he had so often observed in other parents. He'd certainly been supportive of Arthur in all the crucial ways. He'd intervened with Nadia on Arthur's behalf on many occasions—when Arthur had decided to go to art school, for instance, instead of studying law as Nadia had wished. "You don't know what it means to be a father," Nadia had said to him at the time, in a voice full of emotion, and he'd found that comic, coming from her. He'd done his best, that was all he could say, but he knew his role had been limited. Mostly he had acted as Arthur's intercessor over the years. But later he had wondered if Nadia wasn't right—he didn't know what it meant to be a father. It wasn't only the fact that Wertheimer, after the divorce from Nadia, had lived apart from his son for much of his life. He had also lived most of that time with Lothar. He had always been grateful that Arthur had accepted this arrangement without noticeable difficulty.

"Well, Arthur," Wertheimer said to his son when they were seated across from one another at a table. "What have you been up to since I saw you last?"

"I've been falling in love," Arthur said and gazed fondly at Bea.

"Always an admirable undertaking," Wertheimer said.

"You know we're going to be married?"

"Yes. Nadia told me. Congratulations to you both."

"I'm afraid mother is against it," Arthur said.

Wertheimer glanced at Bea to judge her reaction to this comment. But her expression didn't change. She gazed calmly at him with large dark eyes, which had been heavily outlined in black.

"I know mother asked you to come here to try and talk us out of it," Arthur said.

Wertheimer cleared his throat, feeling suddenly uncomfortable.

"I'm sorry you came into the city just for this because nothing could change our minds."

"Yes, yes, of course," Wertheimer said. "Nor should it."

"It's the money," Arthur said. "With mother, it's always money I'm afraid."

Bea said, "She thinks I want Arthur only for his money."

"I'm sure she doesn't mean anything against you personally," Wertheimer said.

"Of course she does," Bea replied. "She hasn't liked me from the very beginning, from the moment Arthur and I met."

Wertheimer sensed an opportunity to take the conversation in a different direction and seized upon it.

"How *did* you and Arthur meet?" he asked. "I'm just curious…"

Bea laughed and looked at Arthur. "Shall I tell him?"

"Of course," Arthur said. "He might find it amusing."

"We met in a porno shop. I was buying something—"

"A dildo," Arthur said, rather too loudly judging from the way the couple at the next table suddenly looked over at him.

"Let me talk, darling. Yes, I was buying a dildo for a piece I was doing." She was interrupted by the waiter, who approached the table suddenly and asked if they were ready to order yet. Wertheimer briefly consulted the menu, and then they all ordered quickly. When the waiter left, Bea continued eagerly, as if she'd been waiting anxiously to get on with her story.

"I'm an artist, maybe you already know this. I make videos of myself acting out roles. You might say my work is an investigation of women and power and desire. I needed some things for a new work. So I went to a porno shop where I met Arthur. He was looking at a rack of porno movies, trying to decide what to get. But instead of a video, he got me!"

"Interesting." Wertheimer laughed. He could not quite picture the whole thing—Bea's videos of herself, the sort of art she was describing. And he was also thinking of Arthur, whom he would not have previously suspected of being interested in pornographic movies.

"When—and where—do you plan on being married?" he asked, thinking it wise to focus on specific details.

Arthur said, "We thought we'd go to Las Vegas. We haven't set a date."

"I see." He did not actually see the thing at all. The idea of getting married in Las Vegas was appalling to Wertheimer. He wondered if Nadia knew of their plans. If so, it could only have fueled her objections.

"Bea likes the idea of getting married in Vegas, don't you darling?"

"I *love* the idea. I'm going to rent a dress at one of those Mexican bridal stores. Something red, low-cut, sexy. We'll get married by an Elvis-impersonator. No witnesses, no family, no reception—no bullshit in other words. It should all be over in five minutes." Bea looked flushed with happiness as she described their plans.

Wertheimer wanted to say, why bother? Marriage was enough of an anathema to someone like himself, let alone a marriage that sounded like a charade.

"I can tell you don't think getting married in Vegas is such a good idea," Bea said. She looked disappointed, and he realized too late he'd let his disapproval show.

"No, no," Wertheimer protested. "It's just . . . it's just that I often don't see the point of marriage at all. I mean, in our day and age, when it's perfectly acceptable to live together as a couple—"

"Like you and Lothar did?" she said, interrupting him.

He was surprised to hear his deceased lover's name come from her lips. Surprised, and a little annoyed. It seemed presumptuous of her to speak about Lothar, someone she'd never met, and he realized his life must have been fully discussed by the two of them.

"Forgive me," he said, unable to prevent a slight chilliness coming into his voice, "but I wouldn't think Lothar and I would have provided a model for anything, least of all a relationship between you two."

"I've upset you, haven't I?"

"On the contrary, I'm just . . . surprised."

"You must still be mourning him, aren't you?"

This was too much. Wertheimer felt dismayed by the impropriety of it all.

"Look, Dad, we've never really discussed Lothar's death," Arthur said, trying to intercede. But it only made matters worse as far as Wertheimer was concerned.

"Nor do I think it's the time to do so now," he responded stiffly. "I think the subject at hand is marriage."

"Why do I always say the wrong thing?" Bea stood up suddenly.

"Where are you going?" Arthur asked with a look of alarm.

"Home," she said. "Don't worry, I'll take a taxi. I think you and your father have things to discuss and you don't need me around to do it. Only . . ." And here she stopped and bit her lip and Wertheimer saw that she was about to cry.

"My dear," Wertheimer said, extending his hand to her, "Please don't—"

She stopped him, holding up her hand to indicate he shouldn't go on. She looked so young, and so distraught; her mouth began trembling, and this disturbed him. It was with considerable difficulty that she managed to finished her sentence: "Only I don't think . . . I mean, you should know . . . I meant to say *something good*." At that point, she turned and hurried out of the restaurant.

For a few moments Wertheimer and Arthur said nothing. They stared at the doorway long after Bea had disappeared from sight, as if hoping she'd suddenly return.

"Oh dear," Wertheimer finally said. "That was a bit of botched business, wasn't it?"

"Botched business? *Botched . . . business?*" Arthur gave his father a disgusted look. "You didn't give her a chance. Not a chance. You're worse than mother!" He was seething with anger.

Wertheimer had never experienced this sort of anger directed at him, at least not from his son. It was alarming. He couldn't think of anything to say. And it only made matters worse when the waiter arrived bearing three plates. Noticing Bea's absence, the waiter said,

"Shall I ask the kitchen to keep the young lady's food warm until she returns?"

"NO," Arthur snarled. "Take it away."

"Are you sure—"

"Very sure," Arthur snapped. He flicked the back of his hand toward the waiter. "She's gone. Take it away please."

"Very well," the waiter said. When he had gone, Wertheimer said, "Look Arthur, I'm terribly sorry."

"You would be," Arthur answered in a dull voice. He lifted his wine glass and drained it, then filled it again.

Wertheimer looked down at his plate. He lifted his knife and fork and cut into his fish. He put all his attention toward the food in front of him, trying to ignore his son who was staring baldly at him while Wertheimer focused on his meal, trying to make himself oblivious to everything except the large plump trout sitting on his plate, its eyes milky, its head grilled to a crisp dark color and resting on a festive bed of spinach and carrots. He inserted the tip of his knife at the base of the head and made a careful slit down the trout's back. He lifted the top half of the fish with his knife and fork, cautiously separating it from the bottom half. Then he grasped the tail and removed the spine and bones and placed the skeleton to one side. Throughout, Arthur continued to regard him with an unhappy look.

Wertheimer began eating slowly and deliberately. His son did not eat. His son lit a cigarette and stared at him across the table. This went on for some time. And then he spoke up.

"Why did you and mother get married? I've never asked you before. I'm just curious."

Wertheimer set his utensils down and looked up at his son.

"Is this actually important to you?"

"I'd just like to know. It's something I've always wanted to know and never felt I could ask."

"I suppose we were in love. Isn't that why most people get married? Because they think they're in love?" Wertheimer responded hastily, not bothering to give much thought to his reply.

"So you didn't marry her for her money?"

Wertheimer almost choked on the sip of wine he'd just taken.

"You didn't marry her because it would make you seem . . . " Arthur faltered for a moment, but quickly rallied. "I mean . . . you weren't just trying to cover up what you really were?"

"And what do you think I really was?" Wertheimer responded icily, although he knew very well what his son meant.

"Well," Arthur said, "didn't you know you were gay? And if you did, why else would you marry her unless it was for money, or because you were trying to appear normal?"

Wertheimer felt deeply humiliated.

"What a quaintly reductive picture you have of human nature," he said quietly. He lifted his napkin to his mouth and gently stroked first one corner of his lips, and then the other. As he did so, he felt a compression in his throat, as if a piece of fish had become lodged there. He coughed, trying to clear his throat, but the thing wouldn't go away.

"It's just that I have a hard time even picturing you and mother together. I can see mother. I can see you. I just can't see you *together*."

"Perhaps a visual aid might help you. . . *picture* us, as you say. I believe there are photographs of us at that time. When we were young. Just after we were married. The time, in fact, when you were conceived. I'm sure I could locate them for you."

"I've seen the photographs. And you know that's not what I mean."

"I'm afraid I only know too well what you mean. I suppose I'm just trying to avoid facing the ugliness of your remarks. The implication that I used your mother for some unsavory purpose. To gain an economic advantage, or to conceal something I was afraid of admitting. I believe that's what you're insinuating, isn't it?"

"Well—"

"And the damnable part of it is—the worst part—" He found he could not finish his sentence and actually say what the worst part was. But the thought continued to run through his head: *the worst part is I came here to help you and I find myself accused of the very thing you and Bea resent. . . marrying for money*! He realized at that moment the tables had been turned: it was his life now being questioned. How had this happened?

Wertheimer said very little else during the rest of their lunch. Arthur made no attempt to undo the damage he'd done with his remarks and Wertheimer, after recovering his composure, had assured his son that he, himself, had no objection to his marriage to Bea and he would do whatever might be required of him to see that things went smoothly. He promised to speak to Nadia on his behalf. He encouraged his son to get a prenuptial agreement only if it was something he and Bea wished to do. He spoke precisely and in a voice devoid of emotion, and added that he himself didn't think such a thing would be necessary, not if Arthur was sure of his feelings. He said he regretted getting off on the wrong foot with Bea and he hoped there would be a chance in the very near future of seeing her again and putting things right. She seemed a very (here he hesitated a moment, searching for the right word), she seemed a very *interesting* person. And then, calling for the check, he said he was feeling rather tired and thought he ought to go home.

Out on the sidewalk, Wertheimer turned to his son and said, "Well, then." He meant to add something, but couldn't think what that was.

"You know," Arthur said, "Bea's had a very hard life. She's had none of the advantages I have. And yet she seems to know things I don't. She has a better feeling for people. I trust her completely. And she makes me happy—very happy."

"Then I bless your happiness," Wertheimer said. He patted his son's shoulder, and then he turned and walked slowly away.

4.

It was not until Wertheimer was preparing for bed later that evening—not until he had changed into his robe and slippers—that he remembered the mushrooms. He had an urge to dress again and go out and collect them but of course this wasn't a reasonable thought. It was dark. It was late. He could hear what he thought was the sound of rain falling softly on the leaves outside the window.

He abandoned the idea of mushrooms and instead put on a tape of Verdi's *Aida* and settled himself on the sofa with a drink.

No sooner had he begun to relax into the music, allowing it to transport him into another realm, than the phone rang, as it had done regularly throughout the afternoon. He didn't answer it. He knew it was Nadia calling. She'd want to know why he hadn't come by as he said he would. He had no desire to explain this or anything else and so he simply ignored the phone.

The events at lunch had left him exhausted, and more than that, they had brought on a bout of deep self-examination. Wertheimer had spent the whole afternoon thinking about his life.

He'd found himself going back over the years, in particular to those first years with Nadia. What Arthur did not understand—what Wertheimer thought he could never have possibly explained to his son—was how deeply in love he had actually been with Nadia. But as he thought about this word love, Wertheimer had to admit that perhaps he wasn't being fully honest. Perhaps what he had felt at the time was actually something quite different, more accurately called lust. And this had led him to wonder whether he had been capable of feeling love, of really understanding the difference between the two words at such a young age. It had led him to question whether he even understood the difference now.

He had been so young when he met Nadia. She was older, an heiress whose father had made a fortune in munitions, a strong-willed and supremely confident sort of person. They met shortly after she arrived in Los Angeles, on an extended visit from her native Berlin. He had only recently graduated from university with a degree in Medieval history. Wertheimer knew nothing of sex or women when he met Nadia. He was an awkward and shy young man who had not yet conquered his habit of stuttering. The real question was, what could Nadia have possibly seen in him?

Nadia had been his first real affair. She was so high-spirited and beautiful. He had never known anyone quite like her. Someone so confident, so bold, whose accent and European manners had seemed so attractive to him. The night of their first meeting she had worn a blouse made of transparent material and the dark rings of her breasts pressing against the fabric had thrilled him as few sights ever had. This is what struck Wertheimer most about her. She didn't seem to care about what people thought, and this had made him feel reckless himself, as if anything might be possible.

He remembered how in those early days together they would be at a party and Nadia would begin to excite him, intentionally attempting to arouse him. She would let her nipples graze the back of his knuckles until they stood up and felt like hard little fruits. She would whisper things to him, words meant to excite him. Then she would draw him away by making some excuse and they would find a darkened room or a spot outside in a corner of a garden and she would proceed to touch him: they would have rapid, furtive sex that left him breathless and flushed. She had taught him to love the illicitness of these couplings, the spontaneousness of quick sex in public places. She especially liked to watch him masturbate. *I love watching a man get off for me*, she would whisper in his ear. Later, he had begun developing a taste for the same thing. And gradually he had found his interest in Nadia waning.

Still, for reasons not terribly clear to him now, he and Nadia had married and produced a son—perhaps because Wertheimer had felt this was what was expected of him. Lothar, whom he'd first noticed at a concert (he played the cello, Wertheimer's favorite instrument, so of course he'd noticed him), had come into his life around this time. It had been a mutual seduction, one which took place in a hotel room in Pasadena, though he could no longer remember the name of the hotel, only its muted elegance and his feeling of initial, almost paralyzing, nervousness. For a long while he'd led a double life, conducting his affair with Lothar in secret, until the strain of such an existence had finally led him to ask Nadia for a divorce.

Perhaps it was neither love nor lust that had drawn him to Nadia in the first place but rather a deep sense of gratitude. Maybe what he'd really felt was something as simple as this, an immeasurable sense of relief that someone so sure and skilled, someone so sensuous, had introduced him to love, and then rather graciously agreed to set him free, so that he might follow his true feelings.

5.

He went out early the next morning, carrying a basket and a small paring knife. It had rained during the night. The city was damp and smelled of clay. He headed directly for the spot where he had seen the mushrooms and was delighted to find them still there. He picked them carefully, checking to see that each one was free of mold or insects. When the last morel had been gathered, he headed back to the apartment.

She was sitting on the porch steps when he returned. He didn't spot her immediately because he had been walking with his head down, thinking of Lothar. He missed him terribly. It seemed to him all prospects of any future happiness had died along with Lothar. When he lifted his eyes and saw her sitting there, she took him by surprise. She stood up as he approached.

"Hi," she said. "I wanted to talk to you. I hope you don't mind but Arthur told me where you lived and I decided to just come over."

"No, of course I don't mind." He wanted to add, *I'm glad you came.* He found he was actually happy to see her.

She followed him into the apartment, into the kitchen, which was filled with a warm light. The room seemed a little stuffy to him—there was a faint odor that wasn't exactly pleasant. He only noticed it now as he came in from outside.

If Bea noticed the smell, she didn't mention it. "What a nice apartment," she said. "How long have you had it?"

"Forever," Wertheimer said, setting his basket down on the kitchen table. "How old are you?" he asked suddenly.

"Twenty-four."

"I moved to this apartment before you were born then."

"The neighborhood must have changed a lot in that time."

"Oh my yes," Wertheimer said, removing his coat and hanging it over the back of a chair. "All downhill, I'm afraid."

"I used to buy drugs around here," she said.

"Really?" Wertheimer was surprised by the casualness of this admission. "What sort of drugs?"

"Oh, the usual stuff. Pot, mostly."

"I went through a period when I enjoyed cocaine quite a bit," Wertheimer said, feeling emboldened by her honesty into making his own little confession.

"I never did cocaine," Bea said, wandering over to a shelf. She picked up a little figurine of a cat and looked at it closely, then replaced it. "I couldn't afford cocaine."

"Lothar used to like psychedelics. We did LSD together a few times. But that was when we were considerably younger. When everyone was trying psychedelics. Here, sit down, you look rather uncomfortable standing there like that. May I take your coat?"

"No, it's fine. What's in the basket?"

"Mushrooms," Wertheimer said. "Morels. I found them right here in the city! I thought I'd cook them for breakfast. Can you stay for breakfast?"

"Well—"

"Please do."

She peered into the basket. "Are you sure they're edible?"

"Of course. I *do* know my mushrooms. I won't poison you, my dear, if that's what you're thinking. I may have left you with a rather bad impression yesterday but I'm not that sinister—"

"It was really my fault," she said and sighed, looking up at him sadly. "I've been pretty depressed lately."

"Really? I'm sorry. What's troubling you?"

"My nerves are shot. Mind if I smoke? What's this stuff?"

He turned to face her and saw she was looking at the rows of pills lined up on the counter next to the table. Before he could answer, she said,

"You're sick, aren't you?"

"Just a little trouble with my heart."

"I knew you were sick, I could tell, but Arthur said you were fine. He said that when Lothar died you assured him you were okay. But with AIDS you never know. My friend Steve just died of AIDS. You don't have AIDS, do you?"

"No, I don't." Wertheimer didn't know whether to be offended by her bluntness or to admire it. It certainly cleared the air. He had to admit that. Yet he wondered if he had managed to sound convincing. Did she believe him? He couldn't be sure. "I guess you wouldn't lie to me. I mean what would be the point?"

"There wouldn't be one," he said solemnly.

He began cleaning the mushrooms with a little brush. When he looked over at her, she gazed back him with a blank look. She held her chin in the palm of her hand. Her fingernails had been painted a dark purple and it gave her hands a bruised—a *damaged* quality. It didn't seem to Wertheimer that she'd bothered to comb her hair that morning. It stood up in tuffs from her head and made her look disheveled.

"I'm so thin-skinned," she said, drawing her coat around her and holding it closed at her throat. It was an old coat, frayed at the collar and cuffs. "I get upset so easily. My shrink says that's the way artists are. We feel things more than other people do and if we didn't we couldn't be artists. Do you think that's true?"

"Quite possibly."

"Anyway, I shouldn't have gotten so upset yesterday and left like I did. I acted like a baby, didn't I?"

"And I acted like a silly old man, which is what I am much of the time now."

He put a little oil in a pan with some garlic and soon the room was filled with a rich aroma. Then he began slicing the mushrooms, cutting them into even segments. Bea stood up. She wandered over to a cupboard and opened it.

"What's this? Man, this stuff in here is a million years old. You ought to throw out this flour, it's full of bugs. Do you know there's a cockroach in here?"

"Oh, dear no." Wertheimer stopped what he was doing and rushed over to see. The cockroach was partially hidden by a can of mushroom soup. It suddenly stirred and scuttled toward a bottle of olive oil, then grew very still. It disgusted Wertheimer. He felt his stomach turn.

"I'm terribly sorry—I've been away—my cleaning woman, Mrs. Cochran, I had expected her to . . . oh this is awful—"

"Don't worry, I'll take care of him." She got a paper towel from the dispenser and very nonchalantly picked up the cockroach and dropped it on the floor. Then she stepped on it, crunching it beneath her shoe, and picked it up with the paper towel and put it in the garbage. Wertheimer felt deeply embarrassed as he watched her do this.

"'Don't worry. Cockroaches don't bother me, I grew up with them. Happens in the best of families, as they say. Do you have anything to drink? A beer maybe?"

"I'm afraid not. But there's a little sherry in the liquor cabinet, I believe."

She helped herself to a glass of sherry and sat down at the table again.

"I just got out of a treatment program and I'm not supposed to drink, but . . . " she lifted her glass and took a sip. Wertheimer glanced over at her. She smiled and brushed a wisp of hair out of her eyes.

"Do you think I'll be any happier when Arthur and I are married? Or do you think I'll just make him as unhappy as I am?"

Wertheimer didn't know how he could possibly be expected to answer such a question—such a *troubling* question.

"You're probably wondering whether I'm right for Arthur, aren't you,"

"Well—"

"I wonder about that too sometimes. We're so different. But they say opposites attract. So maybe it'll be okay. Maybe we're just made for each other—two halves of something that will make a whole."

She refilled her glass with sherry while Wertheimer dished up the mushrooms, dividing them carefully between two plates. He was thinking about her, about what she'd just said, and he felt deeply troubled. He found himself alternately repulsed and drawn to Bea. What drew him to her were feelings of sympathy, the sort of sympathy he might feel for a wounded animal. What repulsed him was a certain rawness about her that seemed somehow dangerous. Perhaps Nadia was right. This marriage was a bad idea—a bad idea for Arthur, anyway.

As they ate Bea began talking about her work, and she mentioned that she was working on a piece called "Three Stories About Men," a video about a woman who is incapable of feeling anything for the men she seduces. She had been depressed lately because she'd had a fight with someone who had been helping her with her film. Someone she thought was her best friend who had turned out not to be her best friend at all. This person's name was Sylvia and she'd done something quite terrible, quite unforgivable. Wertheimer could not resist asking what had happened, what terrible thing Sylvia had done.

It turned out that Bea and Sylvia had gone on vacation together, along with Sylvia's boyfriend, Richard. They had rented a place on an island in the Caribbean for two weeks. It was supposed to be a working vacation: Sylvia and Bea were collaborating on the script for the film, which Richard was going to direct, and in which Bea would play the main role. They planned on shooting the film during their vacation, using the island as a backdrop for their story. It was to be pure cinema verité: Richard was going to shoot Bea having encounters with men who were total strangers. Only Bea's parts were scripted: the rest would be left to chance.

At first everything had gone well, they had settled into a bungalow on the beach and spent a few days scouting locations, and they'd even managed to shoot some footage of an encounter Bea had with a black man in a bar. Things had begun to go wrong when they picked up a hitchhiker one afternoon and Bea had told him he could spend the night with them.

"I didn't see anything wrong with that," Bea said. "I thought he could just be part of the film. But Richard went bonkers when I told the hitchhiker he could stay with us. I guess it was a bad idea because the hitchhiker started acting pretty weird. So we told him to go away. There was a big argument, but finally the hitchhiker left. We thought he had gone away for good. But we were wrong."

It turned out that the hitchhiker came back to their bungalow the next day while they were out and stole some things. When they returned, Richard's leather jacket was missing, as well as Sylvia's suitcase. Worst of all the video camera was gone. They were sure it was the hitchhiker who'd taken these things. So they went to the police and made a report.

Now everything began to go from bad to worse. Sylvia and Richard blamed Bea for the thefts and they no longer wanted to work with her on her film. They said they were going home and the next morning they left without paying their part of the hotel bill.

A day later the police found some of the missing items—they didn't find the hitchhiker but they found the suitcase, discarded alongside a road with some clothes and books. When Bea went to the station to identify these things, she was arrested. The police had found some marijuana in the suitcase. When Bea tried to explain she hadn't known anything about the marijuana (it was true, she hadn't, it was Sylvia's pot which she'd brought along even though they had all agreed there would be no drugs on this trip), the police didn't believe her. She had to spend a few days in jail before Arthur arrived and bailed her out. He'd managed to pay some people off and Bea had eventually been allowed to leave the island.

At this point in her story, Bea sighed and took another bite of mushrooms. Wertheimer didn't know quite what to say. It seemed the more he learned about Bea, the more worried he felt for his son. Here, he thought, is a deeply troubled person—a person not quite in control. Drugs, depression, a treatment center—encounters with the police—what sort of situation was Arthur getting himself into here? If it was true that he had acted primarily as an intercessor in his son's life over the years, should he not intercede now to protect Arthur from someone who might prove disastrous to his life? And yet he could not forget the way Arthur had looked at him yesterday and said, *she makes me very happy*, how he'd seemed to be pleading with him to understand how essential this happiness was to him.

"Anyway," Bea said, taking the last bite of the mushrooms remaining on her plate, "I shouldn't have told you all that. I'm sure it doesn't make you think good of me. You're probably feeling right now that you should discourage Arthur from marrying me, aren't you? Just tell me the truth. That's what you're thinking, isn't it?"

Wertheimer took a few moments to answer. He wanted to meet honesty with honesty, but it frightened him to think of doing so. In truth he just didn't know what to say.

Finally he said, "Yes, I guess I am worried. It would be dishonest of me to say otherwise. But I've never been one to rush to judgment and I'm trying not to do so now. I want nothing more than for Arthur to be happy. He seems to love you deeply and to think you'll make him happy. I suppose the question is, do you also love him?"

She looked down at her hands and didn't speak. Tears began running down her cheeks. It distressed him greatly to see the tears. He felt sad just looking at her, at her old coat, her stubby fingers with the dark nails, her matted hair. He had a great urge to give her a pep talk, to tell her to pull herself together, to forget about Sylvia and Richard and making videos about desire and power and encounters with strangers. Above all he wanted to say, don't even think about marriage until you're older, until you have a better grip on life. Instead, he got her some Kleenex and waited for her crying to stop.

Which it did after a while. And once she had gotten control of herself, she looked up at him with her large, brown eyes—so sad! So full of the anguish of life!—and said, "I do love Arthur. He knows I do. And I'm going to marry him because I think this is my best chance at happiness. So that's all I have to say."

She stood up and cleared the dishes from the table. She began washing up even though Wertheimer protested, insisting she should just leave the dishes for him to take care of. When she'd finished this task, she prepared to leave.

At the door she said, "You know, I didn't have to tell you any of this stuff, about my problems and all. For some reason I always want people to see the worst side of me first so they won't feel deceived later. I guess it's a sort of test I put people through. If they can look at the worst side of me and still accept me, then maybe when they see the best side they'll even learn to like me. I know this is crazy but that's just the way I am. Maybe later you'll see that I'm not as bad as you think. Maybe later we'll even be friends." She drew her coat around her and stepped out onto the porch.

"By the way," she said, turning back to him, "thanks for the breakfast. The mushrooms were delicious. I've never had mushrooms like that before."

And then she was gone.

6.

Wertheimer began to feel ill at about four o'clock that afternoon. He felt his stomach seize up and he was overcome with nausea. He began vomiting, and then broke out in chills. At first he thought it was a case of bad nerves combined with the new medication which his doctor had prescribed and which had arrived that day. Only when he felt himself becoming violently ill did he suspect it might be the mushrooms.

Mrs. Cochran had taken him to the emergency room. Before leaving the apartment he had managed to reach Arthur by phone and explain the situation. He asked if Bea had also taken sick and discovered Arthur had not heard from her that day, nor did he know her whereabouts. He had not been able to stay on the phone long with Arthur, who in any case had begun shouting at him.

The last thing he remembered before blanking out in the emergency room was the doctor calling for a stomach pump.

He awoke the next morning in a hospital room. Nadia was sitting in a chair next to him. His throat hurt terribly and he felt so weak he could hardly lift his head. A horrible feeling of anxiety came over him as he looked over at Nadia and remembered what had happened.

"You're lucky to be alive," Nadia said. Those were her first words to him. He did not feel lucky. He felt miserable.

"What about Bea?" he asked weakly. "How. . . is . . . "

"She's down the hall, recovering in the privacy of her own over-priced room," Nadia said. "How could you have been so foolish? Poisonous mushrooms, my God! Were you trying to kill yourself—and her, too?"

"No, no," Wertheimer muttered, feeling absolutely wretched. "I thought they . . . were morels—"

"They were morels—the poisonous kind! If Mrs. Cochran hadn't gotten you to the emergency room, you'd be a goner. Are things so bad you have to go grubbing around in the city for something to eat? What is this, Henry? You can't just go to the grocery store like everybody else and *buy* some mushrooms?"

He looked over at Nadia—really looked at her for the first time since opening his eyes. She had grown heavy with age though she had not given up the battle for youthfulness. Her face was made-up in the same way she had made it up for years, only now the rouge lay too heavily on her cheeks and her lipstick bled into the lines that creased her upper lip. The heavy kohl around her eyes gave her an odd, startled appearance. Still, he felt comforted by the sight of her. He felt grateful she was there, sitting beside him, wearing a vivid blue dress and thick strands of ancient yellowed pearls, and now smiling at him as if all the distance of the years had suddenly melted away. It seemed to him then that he could almost remember how they had been with each other all those years ago. He could almost feel again what he had felt for her then—so much gratefulness. Or was it simply affection?

"Henry," she said, "you look like hell." Somehow this comment sounded extraordinarily sweet to him, as if she were telling him how much she truly cared. And he closed his eyes and felt a welcome drowsiness overtake him.

7.

Wertheimer lived to see his grandson born, just a little over a year later. This seemed to him a miracle, that a boy, bearing his name, had come into the world and arrived amidst so much love. It also seemed something of a miracle to Wertheimer that he was still alive—that he had manage to survive his illness as long as he had, and still get around as well as he did.

Many things had turned out in ways that he wouldn't have necessarily expected. It surprised him to watch the way in which Arthur and Bea greeted the birth of their child. They cherished the boy, just as they seemed to cherish each other. To enter their world was to enter a realm of happiness, so completely did their joy spill over and infuse the lives of those near them.

Shortly before the baby was born, they bought a house near the ocean, high on a cliff with a view of the Santa Monica Bay. Wertheimer was often invited to visit them here, invitations which he was only too happy to accept. He found himself spending more and more time in the city, mainly because of Bea and Arthur, but also because of the child. Above all, he wished to be near his grandson.

For some unknown reason, little Henry had taken a particular liking to Wertheimer. Sometimes he was left to care for the baby for hours on end—immensely pleasurable hours filled with games of peek-a-boo and this-little-piggy-went-to-market—while Bea worked in her studio in the rear of the garden. She had given up making videos and turned instead to painting, a medium in which she showed a remarkable talent. Her canvases were filled with a serene beauty—little seascapes flooded with light that evoked all the splendor of the natural world. He often felt humbled by her kindness to him, for the way in which she entrusted the baby to him, leaving him for hours on end to enjoy the boy he had come to love so much.

Only once, not long after little Henry was born, had Bea mentioned the incident with the mushrooms. She said, "You know, I had a vision during that time in the hospital: I could suddenly see how much time there was in the universe—so much time, millions and billions of years, and then I saw how little there really was, I mean for us—hardly any time at all. I realized I couldn't waste it anymore." They had been sitting in the garden when she said this. He had been looking out toward the ocean, at the glassy waves, undulations that ceaselessly rolled toward the shore. She had reached over and taken his hand and held it for a long time.

Strange gifts in strange packages, Wertheimer sometimes thought to himself. He came to realize that he had been wrong about his happiness deserting him in the last days of his life. It had come to him, in all its fullness, like a gift he had never expected.

ROBERT CRAIS

The Man Who Knew Dick Bong

The woman came in first, taking hard fast steps that made her spike heels dig into the linoleum out in the little reception office. She had bright red lips and penciled eyebrows and orange hair that was pinned back on one side and waved forward on the other. She was in a cheap camel suit with big shoulders that looked like it had seen a lot of wear. So did she.

When she saw me she stopped with her hand still on the knob and said, "Are you Deets Boedecker?"

I would've taken my feet down from where they were napping the desk, but she had been too fast for me. I let them snooze. "If the price is right."

She gave me a hard grin. "A smart guy. I like that." Knock'm dead, Boedecker.

She said something into the hall and a little boy came in. He had a chubby face and a chubby body and pencil-thin arms and legs. She had him dressed in a plaid short-sleeved shirt and short pants that were too big for his skinny legs and black wingtips that looked like they had never been polished. He was slurping at a grape-flavored Tootsie-Roll pop and hanging onto a little tin model of a P-38 Lightning twin-engined fighter plane. You could smell the grape all the way across the office.

She pointed him at the couch beneath the window and said, "Sit over there till I'm finished." He sat. She took the hard chair across from my desk and made a big deal out of looking at my feet. "Are you interested in a little job or is your dance card full?"

I shook my head. "I don't do divorce work."

"What makes you think that's what I want?"

"You've got the look."

She gave a single sharp laugh that I didn't like very much. The boy was sitting quietly on the couch, playing with the little airplane and sneaking peeks at me. She said, "The divorce I got twenty months ago. What I need is someone to collect the alimony and child support that the sonofabitch I was married to owes me."

I glanced at the boy. "Are we talking about the boy's father?"

"You don't think I'd make this mistake more than once, do you?"

When she said it, the boy turned and looked down at Hollywood Boulevard. His right shoe was on the couch, but I didn't say anything. Worse than that had been there.

Her name was Louise Barris and her boy's name was Robby. She'd met and married an aeronautical engineer named Frank Barris who'd worked in Burbank near the end of the war, but the marriage hadn't amounted to much. Frank boozed, Frank whined about everything, Frank couldn't make the grade as a man, and finally they'd split. Robby was their only child. Louise said, "The sonofabitch hasn't been able to hold a job since the start of Korea, but now he's managed to scrape up some kind of measly little irrigation engineer thing out in Tarzana or Woodland Hills or one of those places. I figure I can't wait. I figure I better get mine before the no-good lush finds another way to get shitcanned."

I looked at the boy again. He was holding the airplane out the window, lost flying in the hot summer sky three stories above Hollywood. I said, "If your ex isn't paying alimony and child support, you don't need me. Go back to court."

She made a face, like I should've been sharper than that. "Going to court costs money."

"So do I. Thirty bucks a day."

She shook her head. "Jesus, things have gone up since the war."

I nodded. Thirty was a backbreaker, all right. "If he's been out of work, maybe he doesn't have it."

"He has it, all right. Don't you worry about that." She dug around in her purse until she came out with a photograph and a yellow piece of paper and put them on my desk. I had to move my feet to get them. "That's a picture of Frank. I wrote down how to get to where he lives and where he's working. There's a little map."

I didn't bother with the map. Frank had a blocky head and a high brow and a pencil mustache under a zucchini nose. The picture looked like a college yearbook picture. Cal State, maybe. Or City College. The boy looked just like him.

She said, "It's not even lunch time, now. I figure you could get over there just after lunch, lean on him, then get back to my place by early afternoon with the money."

"I'm not a hired thug."

"So we're not even talking a full day here, are we? Shouldn't cost more than, what, fifteen dollars?"

I looked at the boy again. "How much does your ex owe you?"

"Nine months at fifty a month. Four hundred fifty. But don't start thinking you can screw me out of a percentage. I need that money." She frowned at the boy. "I got expenses."

I nodded. Fifteen bucks.

She said, "He knows I want it, and he knows he's got to get it to me. We talked about it and he said he would, only now he's double-crossing me. Don't let the no-good piece of shit kid you on that."

The boy turned away from the window, both hands holding the little airplane as if it were in a long gentle turn. His lips moved as if he were talking to himself. Pilot to pilot. If I had a son, I wondered, would he look like me the way this boy looked like Frank Barris? I stood. "I'll see what I can do."

She opened her purse, took out two fives and five singles and put them on my desk. I didn't touch them. "My address is on the little map, too. We'll be expecting you."

I watched her seal up her purse. I said, "Tell me something, you always shit all over your ex-husband in front of the boy?"

She nodded. "Every chance I get."

Louise Barris stood, put her hand for the boy, and they left.

Frank Barris worked at a county irrigation station in the San Fernando Valley, in Tarzana. I drove up through the Cahuenga Pass, then went west along Ventura Boulevard for about a million miles. The further I went, the drier the air became, until my skin felt tight and raw and gritty. It was cooler than I had expected, though. Only about a hundred and fifteen.

After a while, the number of buildings along the boulevard grew spotty and the orange groves began. They stretched up into the valley across desiccated ground, row after row of short, dark-trunked trees, each heavy with bright orange balls. Tarzana. Edgar Rice Burroughs had lived in Tarzana, but Tarzan never had. Everything was flat and dry and empty except for the endless rows of orange trees. No rivers. No alligators. No elephants or lions or friendly chimpanzees. Orange trees would be hell to swing through.

I followed the directions that Louise Barris had drawn on the yellow sheet of paper until I came to the irrigation station. It was a single-story industrial building made out of cement blocks and corrugated tin, with three county trucks and a couple of sedans out front. I went through a big sliding door into a warehouse where the county stored pipes and fittings and valves and pumps and the other equipment they used to fight the desert. A couple of Mexicans were carrying a pump that was too heavy for them, and a bald man was sitting at a dark wood table, smoking and reading the news. The bald man didn't look up. I walked past him and went through the door into a little hall that joined a couple of glass-walled offices. One of the offices was empty, but Frank Barris was in the other.

Barris was lighting a cigarette with a big Zippo lighter and laughing at something that a goof named Tip Wilson was saying when I went in. There were large flat tables in each office with official-looking county irrigation plans spread over them and the sort of T-squares and angles engineers use for drawing, only Barris's looked like they hadn't been used in a while.

Barris saw me first and then Tip Wilson saw me. Tip was holding a short glass with something brown in it. There was another short glass on the desk in front of Barris and a pint bottle of Old Crow. Wilson stared at me until he put a name to the face, then raised his glass. "Deets Boedecker. My, my."

Tip and I went back. His older brother had been a pretty good peeler, splitting twenty-dollar bills for a living until a couple of psychos tortured him to death with an electric iron. Tip had wanted to take up his older brother's trade, only he didn't have the steady hand. His criminal career had topped out at two-bit burglary and making out he was better with safes and locks than he really was and telling lies. Some guys are born small time. "Hiya doing, Tipper. Haven't seen you in a while."

Tip took more of the Crow. Just a couple of guys meeting in a bar. "Korea."

Frank Barris looked nervous. "Who is this guy?"

Tip smiled. "He's a shamus. Forget him."

"I didn't think engineers were your style, Tip." I grinned at Frank Barris. "Usually it's pimps and horse dopers and nose coolers."

Barris said, "What's he doing here?" He didn't look any less nervous.

I said, "Tip doesn't have anything to do with this, Frank. This is between me and you."

Frank stared at me and so did Tipper Wilson and I wondered what the staring was about. I also wondered what a guy like Wilson was doing in a county engineer's office. Frank said, "I don't have business with you."

"Your ex-wife."

"Louise?"

I nodded. "She needs the alimony and the child support and sent me around to see about it." I showed him the private buzzer. "How about it?"

Tip Wilson laughed suddenly and put down the glass. "These dames." He went to the door. "I'll see you later, Frankie. You, too, Boedecker." He went out. There was a slight limp that I hadn't seen before. Korea, maybe.

Frank Barris waited until Wilson was gone, then opened the desk drawer and flipped a maroon checkbook onto his desk. There was a framed diploma on the wall behind him. University of Southern California, College of Engineering. Not bad. Better than I had thought. He said, "You're just here for the check?"

"Sure. Why else would I be here?"

Barris crossed his arms and leaned back in the chair, away from the checkbook. You could see the boy in him, all right. Same round face, same wide nose, same high forehead. "Don't worry about it," he said. "How much she paying you to arm-twist?"

"Fifteen dollars."

"Man, you must be big-time." Barris put on a smirk. "She'll haul you in the sack if you like'm that way."

I didn't answer. There was a small photograph of a P-38 Lightning fighter thumbtacked to the wall over one of Barris's drafting tables, the same plane that the boy had played with in my office. The photograph was seven or eight years old, and looked as if it had been handled a lot. When Barris saw what I was looking at, the smirk went away. He uncrossed his arms, dug out a pen, and wrote the check. "I owe her nine months. That's four hundred fifty. Tell her she would've gotten the damn money without spending any of it on you."

"The kid will appreciate it." It came out harder than I liked.

Barris tore the check out of the book, blew on it, then slid it across the desk. "I've been out of work."

"Sure." I picked it up.

He looked as if there were more to say and he was deciding whether or not to say it. There was something soft in his eyes then, and it made me wonder if he ever called his boy or took him to the park to play ball. It made me think he wanted to. Barris looked at the Old Crow bottle, then lifted his glass and sipped some of it. "Don't ever marry a whore, Boedecker," he said. "You end up doing the damnedest things."

"Sure." I folded the check once, put it in my coat pocket, and went back out into the heat.

Louise Barris lived in a beige stucco bungalow on Whipple Street in North Hollywood, just off Lankershim Boulevard. There was a '38 Ford coupe and a red Columbia bike lying on the ground by the little front porch. The lawn was brown and ratty because no one watered it and no one mowed it, and the house and the car and the bike and the lawn looked dusty.

I parked behind the Ford and went up to the front door and knocked. Boedecker earning his fifteen dollars.

The boy opened the door. The plaid dress-up-to-visit-the-detective shirt was gone. He was wearing a dirt-stained white tee-shirt with a vee-neck collar, cutoff dungarees and scruffy black sneakers. He was eating a Mars bar. I said, "Is your Mom home?"

He nodded.

"You think I could see her?"

He said, "My daddy knew Major Richard Bong, America's Ace of Aces." He blurted it out, the way he'd heard it on the newsreels. Richard Bong was America's top fighter ace in World War Two. The last couple of years of the war, a week didn't go by when Dick Bong wasn't in the headlines.

I said, "Yeah?"

"My daddy built fighter planes. He went all over making sure that the planes worked right, and Dick Bong gave him a ride from Brisbane, Australia, all the way to Port Moresby, New Guinea. My daddy had to scrunch down in the back because there's only one seat in a P-38." P-38. The little twin-engined airplane the kid had carried into my office.

"Man," I said. "That must've been something."

The kid finished his Mars bar. "She's in the kitchen. I'll get her."

I went in as he ran back through the tiny living room into the house. The living room wasn't much cleaner than the front yard. There was a tattered davenport opposite a round-screen RCA television with a pecan coffee table keeping them apart. Empty Coca-Cola bottles and plates and dirty napkins were on the coffee table and on the TV. An ashtray with about fifteen thousand butts in it sat on the couch's arm, and old cigarette burns on the arm looked like furry black caterpillars. There was a copy of *Life* magazine on the floor with Marlon Brando on the cover. I walked over to the coffee table and looked at what was left in the plates. Lunch had been jelly sandwiches.

Louise Barris came out wearing a slip. "Buddy, you work fast. Did Frankie come across?"

I gave her the check. "He said you'll get what's yours. Every nickel."

She looked at the check as if she thought he'd written it in disappearing ink. "If he knows what's good for him, I will. You wait right here. I wanna call the bank and check on this sonofabitch."

She went back into the kitchen. I heard ice in a glass before I heard her dial. Maybe I would ask for overtime.

The boy came in and stood with one foot atop the other and watched me the way you watch something that's on television. I gave him a smile and he smiled back. I said, "You're a pretty big kid. You like to play football?"

He crossed his arms and looked embarrassed. I wondered how long it had been since he'd talked with a man who wasn't over here just to jump his mother.

He said, "Did you see my daddy?"

"Uh-huh. He said to tell you hello."

He looked pleased. "Were you in the war like my daddy?"

"Nothing as classy as building fighter planes. I was in the infantry. In the

Philippines."

"Did you know Dick Bong?"

"No."

"How about Tommy McGuire or Pappy Boyington?" Other fighter aces.

I shook my head. "Guys like me watched guys like Bong and McGuire fly by overhead and wished we were up there."

He rubbed at the side of his face with the back of his forearm, smearing what was left of the Mars bar. "You wanta see what I got in my room?"

"Sure."

We went back past a small turquoise bathroom into the boy's bedroom. There was a single bed with a painted iron frame and a chest of drawers and a very old wicker trunk and an oval throw rug on the floor. A small stack of Human Torch comics was on the floor near the head of the bed and a G-Man Big Little Book was on the windowsill and four immaculately painted balsa wood P-38 Lightning model airplanes were on top of the chest. There were pictures of more P-38s pinned to walls and three or four clippings from the *Los Angeles Times* showing Dick Bong, America's Ace of Aces. The papers were yellowed but the edges had been neatly trimmed and the clippings had been pinned in place with great care. The models were free from dust and the floor free from litter. There were no dirty clothes scattered about and no clutter. The bedroom was spotless. It was as if this room were not part of the house, as if stepping in here were stepping into someplace special and preserved and private.

The boy said, "My daddy built these models for me. That's Dick Bong's plane. That's Dick Bong right there." He pointed at one of the browned clippings on the wall. A smiling young guy with blond hair and a baby face was standing beside the wicked round nose of a P-38. A girl's portrait had been painted there. Beneath the painting was her name. Margie.

I said, "Dick Bong was something, all right."

"He got forty Japs and the Medal of Honor, see?" Robby ran to another spot on another wall and showed me another clipping. Douglas MacArthur was placing a ribbon around Bong's neck. The headline said <u>Bravest of the Brave</u>. "I'm gonna be a fighter pilot just like Dick Bong," he said. "I'm gonna be just like Dick Bong and Tommy McGuire and Pappy Boyington and those other guys my daddy knew. Lookit this."

He ran to the chest, pulled out the bottom drawer, and took a flat package from under some clothes. There were two pieces of cardboard, tied together with yellow cord. The cardboard was old and smudged, but strong and stiff. He untied the cord and lifted back the top piece of cardboard like he was lifting the lid on a treasure chest. "My daddy gave me this last year. Dick Bong signed it himself."

It was a simple black-and-white photograph of three men sitting together in a tent, very likely somewhere in the South Pacific. The man in the middle was Frank Barris, ten years younger. The man on his right was Tommy McGuire. The man on his left was Richard Bong. The three of them were smiling, and Tommy McGuire was kidding around by pulling out Frank Barris's ears so he looked like Dumbo. An inscription across the right corner of the picture said *Keep'm flying, Frankie! Your pal, Dick Bong.*

Robby Barris tapped the picture and looked at me with wide, bright eyes. He said, "You see. I'm gonna be just like Dick Bong. Just like him. You wait and see." He kept tapping. He wanted to be like Dick Bong, all right. Pals with his dad.

Out in the kitchen, Louise Barris yelled, "That sonofabitch!"

She came crashing through the house, first into the living room where she screamed where in hell had I gone, then slapping barefoot back along the hall toward the kid's room. Robby sandwiched the cardboard around the picture, then put it back under the clothes and shut the drawer. When I turned away from him I was in the door and she couldn't get into the room. She expected me to move so that she could come in, but I didn't. Her face was red and her eyes bulged and there was a dribble of spit down her chin. She held up the check and shook it. "The goddamned check's no good! The sonifabitch is trying to screw me."

I spoke quietly. "Not in front of the boy."

"What in hell do you mean, not in front of the boy? He's my boy." She tried to look past me at the boy, and shouted louder. "He's cheating us, Robby! You see how that no-good bastard father of yours cheats us? You see?"

The muscles in my neck and jaws went tight and I moved so that I filled the doorway as much as possible. She took a step back, and you could tell she was thinking that I was a no—good bastard, too, just like every other man she had ever known. I said, "Not in front of the boy."

She leaned close to me and hissed, "You tell Frank his ass is mine. Tell him I'm going to get him for this."

I looked back at their son. Robby had climbed up onto his bed and was sitting cross-legged, face stuck in one of his comic books, eating a Tootsie-Roll that had appeared from God knows where. One cheek was puffed out with candy and his jaw worked furiously and he looked the way he'd look if the guy who drew the comic book had drawn him. Only tears were dripping down from his cheeks onto the pages.

I turned back to Louise and took the check. "I'll go straighten it out."

I left without saying anything.

I drove around for a while and stopped at the Studio City park and watched some kids playing softball. There was a guy selllng ice cream out of a little white cart, so I stood in line and bought a bar. I was twice as tall as anyone else in the line. You wonder why people have kids. You think maybe people ought to have to get special licenses or take classes. How to be a good parent. How to love. How to beat up each other without damaging your child. You think maybe there ought be a special goon squad that goes around checking up on parents and beating the shit out of those who don't measure up. Ah, Boedecker. You crab.

I watched the kids playing softball and ate my ice cream and after a while I drove to a little market on Moorpark at Coldwater and called the Tarzana irrigation station and asked for Frank Barris. The guy who answered the phone told me Barris had taken off for the day. I asked if Barris usually called it quits after lunch. The guy said a couple of Barris's buddies had stopped by in a maroon Caddie and if Barris wanted to go with them that was Barris's business, Barris being the station's chief engineer, though maybe not for long, heh-heh. I asked if the guy knew who the buddies might be. The guy said no, but they looked like a couple of high rollers, maybe I should try Santa Anita.

I hung up and shook my head. Frank Barris, check bouncer and all-American father.

I went into the little market, bought a strawberry soda then drove over to

Frank Barris's apartment. Deets Boedecker, Captain of the Goon Squad.

Barris lived in a ground-floor apartment on Valley Spring Lane in Toluca Lake, a couple blocks up from Universal Studios. It was a small building, just six units, home for secretaries who worked at film studios and apprentice film editors and people who like things quiet. On a Sunday there would be radios playing and a couple of the secretaries sunning themselves and the smell of suntan oil. Midweek it was empty.

I parked by the hydrant out front, walked back to Barris's apartment, and knocked. After enough knocking I went around to the side of the place and let myself in through his bathroom window.

Frank had two rooms and a bath and not much else. There was a bed and a round wooden dining room table and two wooden chairs and a fridge in the kitchen and a lot of empty beer and Gilbey's bottles. His underwear and socks and things were in a suitcase on the floor by the bed. Two wrinkled suits hung in the closet, and there were dozens of rolls of county blueprints leaning against the walls. Someone had dumped an ashtray of cigarette butts into the toilet and forgotten to flush it, and the heat made the whole place stink sour with booze and cigarettes and sweat. Nice. Just the sort of place for a guy who had known Dick Bong.

On a high closet shelf in the bedroom, there was a kit with a half-completed balsa wood model of a P-38 Lightning. The main body fuselage had been finished, and the right wing along with the right engine nacelle and tail boom had been assembled and sanded and cemented into place. The left engine and tail boom were sanded, but hadn't been put together. When it was finished and painted, it would look just like the models in Robby Barris's room. Only there was dust on the kit. No one had touched it in a while.

I put the little airplane back on the high shelf and went out to the dining table and sat and lit a cigarette and looked around and got ready to wait. There must have been a hundred rolls of blueprints around the little apartment. Most looked like stamped county plans for pumping stations or irrigation site maps or topographic studies. Not aeronautical engineering, but not particularly complicated, either. Maybe just right for a guy with a booze problem and trouble keeping a steady job. I was trying to spell my name with smoke rings when I saw that one of the plans was a little different. It had fallen over and uncurled so you could see the job description. It wasn't a pumping station or an aqueduct. It was a private home, and it belonged to a guy named Leo Pinella. Well, well. Leo Pinella ran a party house in the hills above Glendale. You could gamble, you could have girls, you could watch the kinds of movies they don't show at Grauman's Chinese Theater. You could get or do just about anything that money would allow you to get or do.

I unrolled the plans and looked at them. They were county file plans showing the plot map, the floor plan of Leo's house, his electrical and plumbing layouts, the front and side elevations, and the grading and footing specifications. I rolled them up and put them against the wall where I had found them and wondered why a guy like Frank Barris would have Leo Pinella's house plans. A guy like Barris was just the kind of guy who'd find his way up to Pinella's as a customer and dump what little money he had into Pinella's pockets, but he and Pinella wouldn't be friends. Pinella wouldn't lower himself.

I thought about it some more, then I got up and unfurled the plans again and stared at them. Plans show you how to get in and how to get out. Take a guy like Barris who was hurting for money and mix in a heist artist like Tip Wilson who talked a good game as long as you were buying and one thing leads to another and maybe they start thinking they can take down Leo Pinella. Sprinkle in Barris telling his ex-wife he was going to pay her off and a couple of guys in a maroon Caddie taking him for a ride in the middle of the day and it didn't look good. Of course, maybe it didn't look bad, either. Maybe everything was fine and Barris was out at the track with a couple of his old buddies from the Dick Bong days.

Sure.

I turned to the first page of the plans, tore off Leo Pinella's address, then let myself out through Frank Barris's bathroom window.

Just before the war, Leo Pinella had bought six hundred acres of orange groves north of Los Angeles at the far edge of Glendale where the Verdugo Mountains push up from the valley floor. With mountains and desert behind him and a plain of orange groves in front of him, it was as far as he could get from cops and preachers and parent-teacher associations and anyone else who might object if he built a big place and ran people up there and let them do whatever they had a taste for doing. Leo Pinella had made a fortune.

I drove through Toluca Lake into Burbank where the Santa Monica foothills petered out by Griffith Park, then went north on Olive Boulevard toward Glendale. Up against the Santa Monicas there were little tract houses and movie studios, but further north along Olive the houses and studios gave way to factories and industrial facilities and finally the groves.

I turned off Olive and followed state roads into the trees and drove for a long time. There was an Eagle filling station and a Simms Feed & Hardware and still more orange trees. The trees swallowed everything and pretty soon there was nothing else, just orange trees and crows and a hot, dry wind rippling the leaves. Out here, you could scream as deep and as loud and as long as you wanted and the trees would swallow it and give nothing back.

Pinella's house was easy to see from the valley floor. It was a sprawling white hacienda, bright against a mountainside that had not been irrigated. Everything was stone and dust and rock lizards just as the valley had been before the knuckleballers like Mulholland brought the water. I was at the edge of the groves and wondering how best to approach the house when the maroon Caddie nosed its way down the hill.

I reversed off the road and backed into the groves and hoped that the shade and the trunks and the heavy green boughs would hide me. There was a guy with a pushed-in face driving and Leo Pinella sitting in back, but no Frank Barris. Maybe Leo had run out of mixers and Frank was waiting up at the house while Leo and his trusted bartender sped into town to repair their embarrassingly bare larder. That Leo. He had a fleshy face and long sideburns and what hair he had left was oiled straight back. He kept a cigar as long as a cop's baton in his mouth but he never lit it. I guessed he just sucked on them til they fell apart.

When the Caddie passed I eased back out to the road and continued on to the house. The road climbed quickly and pretty soon I was above the grove and could see forever. You could see the county roads that cut through the orange groves. You could see the Eagle station and Simms hardware. You could see across the valley to Burbank, crawling up the Santa Monica mountains. You could see through the Glendale pass into Pasadena and the Los Angeles basin beyond. You could even see that the maroon Cadillac wasn't going into town. I stopped and got out on the side of the road and watched.

The Caddie had turned off the county road a couple of miles back and was kicking up a rooster tail of dust along an unpaved service road. It turned onto another service road and then another and pretty soon it stopped at a small adobe-brick shed that was the only building around for miles. Not a place to go for mixers or to repair embarrassing social situations. Not a place a guy like Leo Pinella would ever go except for something very important or very secret. When the dust settled, all was still.

I got back into my car and turned around and pushed down the mountain as hard as I could, counting service roads and turnoffs and praying I had the right one when I slewed into the groves. I tried to remember how far the Caddie had gone and which irrigation road it had turned onto and how it had gotten to the little shed. I drove as hard as I could and I didn't give a damn if anyone saw my dust trail. When the little hut and the Caddie were a hundred yards in front of me, I jerked the car into the trees, yanked off my coat and tie, got the .38 out of the glove box, and ran toward the old building.

It was hot in the grove, and earth that had been watered that morning was already seared crusty and brittle. Tiny flying things swarmed in the trees, clouding around fruit that had gone bad, and the smell of the bad fruit was thick and bitter. I worked my way to the Cadillac, and then across to the shed. It was a small single-story box of adobe brick with a door in the front and a couple of windows on the north side. It might have been built a hundred years ago by some Spanish don who owned all of Verdugo as his rancho. Once a roof for vaqueros, it was now a place to store replacement pipe and harvesting tools, and where itinerant day laborers recovered from the heat before being pushed back to the trees. When I got closer I could smell the chemical fertllizers and bug sprays and the oil they used in the smudge pots. Within the shed there was a radio, Julius La Rosa singing Eh, Cumpari.

I looked in the nearest window and saw Frank Barris. He was sitting in a wooden chair with his hands tied behind his back to the chair's rear legs. Leo Pinella and the pug with the pushed-in face were standing in front of him,

Pinella gesturing with the mile-long cigar. There was a black guy standing behind Frank. The black guy was short and shirtless and slicked with sweat from the work he had been doing.

Leo lifted Frank's head and jiggled his chin and said, "Where's my fuckin' money?"

Barris mumbled something. His eyes were puffy and rolling around in different directions and his lips were split.

Leo looked disgusted and let Barris's head drop. He said something to the pug that I couldn't hear and the pug took out a Nazi Luger and put the muzzle in Frank Barris's mouth. Leo grabbed a handful of hair on the top of Frank's head and shook him. "That ain't no lollipop in your mouth, bubbe. I wanna know where my goddamn money is."

Frank mumbled something around the Luger.

"What?"

More mumbles.

The black guy said, "Tip Wilson."

Leo smiled like that was a real kick. "What a dumb shit you are, a guy like Tip Wilson." He put the cigar back in his mouth and made a little gesture to the pug. "Blow this bastard's head off."

I leaned through the window with the .38. "Forget it."

The pug with the Luger jumped, but the black guy didn't and neither did Leo Pinella. He rolled lizard eyes toward me and took the cigar out of his mouth. Frank Barris saw me and strained against the ropes. Pinella said, "Who in hell are you?"

"Arthur Godfrey's talent scout. We're looking for people to enter the greasy hair contest." I pointed the gun at the black guy. "Cut him loose."

Pinella said, "Like hell. This fuckin' weasel stole twenty-two thousand bucks from me."

"He got in a tight place, Leo. He got desperate and he did something dumb. You'll get it back." I cocked the gun. "Untie him and we'll get out of here and he'll get the money back to you."

Leo Pinella said, "My ass," took the Luger from the pug, and shot Frank Barris once in the chest.

I shot Leo Pinella in the body as I went through the window. He dropped the gun and tumbled back into the pug, and the black guy came for me, throwing a handful of something gritty in my face and swinging a piece of pipe. I fired blind, pumping out shots until the black man fell, then dragging Frank Barris and his chair behind some crates. The pug pulled Leo Pinella out the front door, Leo screaming, "You fuck! You fuck!" while his pants grew dark with blood. Then the Cadillac ground to life and sprayed gravel and Frank Barris and I were alone, the only two left alive in the grove. .

I untied his hands and packed a burlap shipping bag tight into his chest and told him he was an asshole. I said, "You've got a kid, you dumb shit. You've got a kid, and you go and get mixed up in something like this."

Frank Barris looked at his chest and tried to see the hole and opened and closed his mouth like a fish. I got him up and went out of the little house and down the long straight dusty road to my car. I ran with him in my arms. I ran as fast as a man can run like that, but by the time we got to the car he was gone.

I drove back to the little adobe house and put Frank Barris in the spot where Leo Pinella had shot him. While I was doing that I found some papers in Barris's outside coat pocket. Deposit slips to his checking account in the amount of four hundred and fifty dollars. I kept them. I brought the Luger that Leo Pinella had used to kill Frank Barris outside and hung it safely within the tight branches of a Valencia orange tree. If Pinella's people came, they wouldn't be able to find it. The cops would, though, because I was going to tell them. They would find Frank and the black man and the Luger and it would be hard as hell for Leo Pinella to beat the charge.

When I finished with all of that I put on my jacket to cover the blood on my shirt and I drove to the Eagle station. I washed my face and hands with water from the little hose the attendant uses to fill your radiator and brushed off as much of the dust as I could. Then I made a couple of calls and got a line on Tip Wilson and that's where I went.

Wilson was sitting in the bar at Musso's Grill in Hollywood, sipping neat scotch and craning his head around to watch Donna Reed across the room, smiling at a couple of studio executives. He was wearing a brand-new dark blue herringbone suit and a pair of black loafers shinier than a set of chrome hubcaps and an immaculate snow white brushed felt fedora with a brim like a broken back. Ah, sudden wealth.

When I climbed onto the stool beside him, Wilson said, "Well, well. Look what the cat dragged in." Always the sharp line.

I said, "You know something, Tipper? Your brother was a small-time chiseler, but I liked him okay. He had some heart. But you, you're just act two, and act two ain't never as good as act one."

The bartender came over but I waved him away.

Wilson gave me what he thought was a hard sneer. "We can go out in the parking lot and see just how good I am, you want."

"You're scaring me to death. Here's a guy, knocked over Leo Pinella, and he's sitting in the middle of Musso's wearing the evidence."

Tip Wilson's right eye began to twitch and he looked at me like he thought I was kidding him. "What the hell are you talking about?"

I unbuttoned my jacket and opened it enough so that he could see what was on my shirt. "I just left your partner Barris in an orange grove up by Pinella's party house, Tip. Pinella and a couple of his thugs were working on him and he told them you were involved."

Tip Wilson went as white as his hat. He said, "He's lyin'. It wasn't me."

I shook my head. "Tip, I can see you nine years old saying that. You've been saying that every day of your life. You gotta think of something new."

He picked up the scotch, then put it down. Donna Reed got up with the two executives and the three of them left. Wilson didn't look at her now.

I said, "Pinella put a bullet in Frank Barris and killed him. I shot Pinella, but it looked pretty low in the gut. He might not die. He'll be with a doctor now and if he makes it, he'll send a couple of his boys to pay you a visit."

Tip Wilson began to sweat. There was a film of droplets above his lip and across his forehead. He picked up the scotch again and this time he drained it. He took his hat off and then he put it back on. He shook his head to himself like he couldn't believe this was happening. Guys like Tip Wilson never could. "We had that job aced. We got in and out of there on a charm. There must've been a couple of hundred other people up there. How'd he put the finger on us?"

I put my hand on his arm and squeezed, settling him down. "You got twenty-two thousand."

He nodded.

"I want Barris's split."

He looked at me sharply and frowned, still thinking to chisel. "What are you talking about?"

I shifted my stool closer and put one foot on the floor and leaned into him. The .38 was in my belt and he could see it now. "I've been through Frank's apartment and it isn't there. Barris didn't put his cut in the bank yet. I'm thinking you were trying to work a way to weasel all of it, and you have the whole nut."

Wilson's mouth got small and his eyes got wide and he blinked a lot, maybe telling himself he had enough to worry about without me, but not yet able to convince himself. "I spent it already."

"You spent your side, Tip. Frank's side is still there."

"I had expenses." A whine.

I reached under my coat and put my hand on the .38 and I spoke very slowly. "Leo's on his way, Tip. Frank had some things to take care of, and now I'm going to take care of them for him, so I need his split."

He looked down at the gun and he lifted his glass again but the glass was empty. He gave a little shrug and put down the glass and said, "Sure."

He paid his bar tab and we went out to his car and there it was. What was left of the twenty-two thousand dollars in hundreds and twenties and tens and fives and ones, sitting in an army knapsack in the trunk of a gleaming new 1953 Lincoln Continental Cabriolet. He counted out eleven thousand, all the while shaking his head as if he still couldn't believe that this was happening. He lost count twice.

The small bills filled my pants and my jacket and made each pocket bulge. When I had Barris's split, Wilson looked at what he had left after the clothes and the car and the looking good. It wasn't much to have a guy like Leo Pinella after you. I said, "You still got a little time. There's New York. There's Mexico."

He shook his head. The sky was falling. "We had that job aced. We knew when to go in and when to come out and where Pinella kept the money. We got away clean."

"Sure. For guys like you it's always clean."

Wilson shook head again. "This wasn't my baby. It was Frankie's. Frankie was a regular at Pinella's since the war. We were talking about all the money Pinella pulled in and what he did with it and where he must keep it and Frankie said he could find out and he did. Then he got the plans from the county and it was a piece of cake. In and out, man. In and out."

"Sure." I had it, then. I could see the whole thing.

Wilson kept shaking his head. "It was supposed to be a snap. Now I'm fucked. I'm fucked."

I left Tip Wilson in Musso's parking lot and drove back to my apartment. I counted the money again and arranged it by denominations and then put it in a shoe box behind the refrigerator. I pulled off my clothes, took a long shower, and dressed. I drank half a tumbler of Tennessee bourbon, and then I drove to Louise Barris's house.

The little boy answered the door. He was wearing the same shorts and the same dirt-smudged tee-shirt as yesterday. He was eating another Mars bar. He smiled when he saw me. It was a good smile, and made me smile back. I wanted to tell him that with all the damn candy he'd better be sure to brush his teeth.

He went into the kitchen and came back with his mother. Her radio was going back there, Tony Bennett singing *Rags to Riches*. When Tony Bennett was on the radio, you couldn't worry about what your boy ate. She said, "Did the sonofabitch cough up what he owes me?"

I made my right hand into a gun and shot the boy with a wink. "Tell you what, Robby. Head outside and give me and your mom a minute to talk."

He left without saying a word or looking at his mother. Come to think of it, I had never heard him say a word in her presence. Maybe he never spoke to her and she never spoke to him. Maybe she ignored him. *I'll never make that mistake again.* I waited until I heard the front door slam, and then I looked at Louise. She didn't look happy. "I don't need any lectures on how to raise my boy from some two-bit peeper."

I said, "Frank's dead. Leo Pinella killed him because he stole twenty-two thousand dollars of Pinella's money."

She stared at me for a solid ten-count, then raised her hands to her head and

went into the kitchen. I heard water run, then the pipe-hammer you get when
you turn the water off too quickly, and then she came back. She said, "I guess
I'll have to take care of his affairs. I guess I'll finally get what's coming to me
from the sonofabitch." She looked around the seedy little room when she said
it, as if everything were suddenly going to change. "What about the twenty-
two thousand?"

"I have Frank's split."

She wet her lips. "Well, I guess that should belong to me now."

I shook my head.

Her mouth stretched and the skin around her eyes tightened. "Goddamn it,
he was my husband. The bastard had obligations." She shouted it.

"You put the finger on him to Leo Pinella."

She turned the color of steamed clams.

"Frank told me he married a whore and he meant it. He met you when you
were working up at Pinella's party house. He took you out of there and
married you but he could never get what you had been out of his head."

She looked at the door as if she expected the boy to come back.

"So Frank hit the bottle and fell apart. Maybe he wasn't all that together to
begin with. He was broke and he owed plenty and maybe the scumbags he had
for friends helped him get the idea of taking down Pinella's. Only he needed
to find out how Pinella ran his operation, and only someone who had worked
there would know. That's you. You knew where Pinella had his money room
and you went along because if Frank had some money he could pay you what
he owed you, and maybe a little extra. Only Frank was still a lush and lushes
have a hard time doing what they're supposed to do. When it looked like he
was stiffing you with the bad check, you called Pinella. You tipped him that
Frank had been the guy who'd taken him down."

"He owed me." Her voice was shrill.

I took out the bank papers that I had taken off Frank Barris's body and
threw them at her. "Deposit papers," I said. "Frank was going to cover the
check, he just didn't get around to it."

Her mouth worked, and when her voice came out it was hoarse. "I should
still get the money. It's mine. I need it."

"You get nothing. I'm going to put the eleven grand into an account for the boy."

She came at me with her hands balled into fists, flailing at me and spitting and telling me I couldn't do that, that the money was hers, that I was a no good sonofabitch just like Frank. I grabbed her wrists and shook her and slapped her hard one time. Her hair was wild and she was breathing deep and if she could've gotten to a butcher knife she would have used it.

I said, "I'm going to put the money into an account for the boy. When he needs it for school or for clothes or for things like that, I'll draw some out and use it. When he's twenty-one, if there's any left, I'll give half to you and half to him. His father's dead and he's going to need you more than ever. You're going to be here for him. If you aren't, or if you try to create a problem for me, I will go to Leo Pinella and tell him that you were the person who fingered his money room. Do you understand that?"

She nodded. She looked scared, but she would get used to it.

"I'm going to go now and call the cops. They'll find Frank's body and they'll be by to tell you that he's dead. Play stupid. You're going to have to sit down with the boy and tell him. That's going to be hard, but that's part of being his mother."

She said, "I know what being a mother is."

"All right." I wanted to say something more. I didn't want to just leave. "Maybe you got a raw deal in all of this, too. If Frank was willing to marry you, maybe he should've been willing to accept what you were, and maybe you had a right to expect that he would. If he had, maybe you would've gotten what you wanted and he would've gotten what he wanted and everything would've been just great. He didn't. I can't help you with that."

She crossed her arms and looked small and pinched and alone. She was not looking at me. "No one ever could," she said. "Go to hell."

I nodded and left then, and drove to Frank Barris's apartment. I went in through the bathroom window again and took a beer out of Frank's icebox and sat at the little dining room table and drank some of it. I called the cops and told them that Leo Pinella had killed a guy named Frank Barris and left the body in an orange grove up in Glendale. I gave them directions to the little adobe shed. I told them where I had put the Luger, and that they would find Leo Pinella's prints on it and that the bullet in Barris had come from that gun.

Then I hung up. I sat a little while longer and finished the beer. I felt old and I didn't really want to go home. There was nothing there to go back to.

After a while I got up and went into Frank's bedroom and took the unfinished model of the P-38 out of his closet. I put the pieces carefully in the box, making sure I had the instructions and all of the parts. Then I closed the box and left.

If I took my time, I might be able to do a pretty good job on the little airplane. It would give me something to do in the evenings, and at the end of the week it would be fun to show the boy .

DISASTERS IN SPIRIT, IMAGINATION, AND THINKING

One by one, like leaves from a tree,
All my faiths have forsaken me.
—Sara Teasdale

AMY GERSTLER

Dinosaurs

I've always felt at ease here in my hometown Natural History Museum, among these familiar fossils of giant Cretaceous fish and stuffed birds. Nothing calms my nerves like looking at dinosaur bones. Peering up at this plaster mount of a duck billed dinosaur, his skeleton blackened as though he'd been the guest of honor at some Mesozoic barbecue, I sigh with relief. For a minute, my jitters subside. I've stood looking into these glass cases for what must add up to several years. In the glorious Natural History Museum in New York City, visitors can stare at the last Great Auk who lived on earth. That's a singular and moving experience, despite the fact that he's suffered the indignities of taxidermy and has glass eyes now. The Great Auk is surprisingly small. He resembles a penguin. I get a little choked up each time I see him. But otherwise everything contained in any Natural History Museum I've visited makes me feel temporarily as jubilant as my mother Felice appears to be every waking minute.

Right now Felice is watching the giant pendulum swing at the other end of the large room that constitutes this museum's first floor, keeping her eyes fixed on it so she won't miss the second when it knocks over the next little wooden block in its path. It knocks over a block every fifteen minutes. Of course the Natural History Museum in Manhattan makes this local two-floor museum look like a closet, but this was my very first Natural History Museum, so I'm sentimental about it. As a child, I came here as often as I could wheedle Felice into making the trip. I've got it memorized. I could give tours in my sleep.

It's a comfort to find my Museum never changes, and comfort's what I seek on this visit home. Yesterday I drove the pleasant two and a half hours south down the Pacific coast, from my office in Los Angeles to San Diego where I was born, and where my parents still live; past beaches and salt marshes, old Spanish missions and the Navy base in Oceanside. Surfers dotted the ocean, black as seals in their wetsuits. At night you can see the blinking red lights atop the twin domes of the San Onofre nuclear power plant as you drive past.

Sam's my other comfort. One I don't have to come all the way to San Diego to partake of. His office is on the floor directly below mine. The first time he and I went out for a drink I told him I liked the idea of walking back and forth on top of his head all day long. He gave me a quizzical glance, then laughed. My remark was sort of a test and he passed. Few people think I'm amusing. Sam seemed to. That made me feel like I had something to offer him. My friend Miles thinks I'm a laugh riot, but we've known each other since we were kids. My father thought I was funny, but he'd chuckle and then say "Mimi, let's face it. You and I got our senses of humor from Pluto."

In the rocks and minerals section of the museum, I sneak up behind Felice to see what she's giggling about. She's peering at a black and white photo of a quartet of grizzled miners assembled in front of a dilapidated shack. Such historic photos always make the world of the past seem claustrophobically dingy, as if no brightness or cleanliness was possible then. The shack sports a cockeyed hand-lettered sign: THIS HERE'S THE DON'T BOTHER ME GOLDMINE. How easily amused Felice is. One of the miners is small and slight, like Sam. I guess it was an advantage to be short in a low-ceilinged mine. Sam's small enough that we could probably wear each other's clothes. Except he dresses like he plays lead guitar (he's a partner in a small independent record company) and since I'm a speech pathologist, specializing in preschool children, I dress so my clients' mothers will trust me. A wardrobe swap would never work. Sam looks a lot younger than he is. He's got reddish hair that sticks up, nice and punkish, but not too way out. Sometimes he slicks it down with brilliantine. Half his record collection is new wave stuff he plays so loud my ears buzz: The Dickies, XTC, the Ramones. Exotic names I didn't used to know. But I'm happy as a peach to have Sam educate me. The other half of Sam's record collection, and I like this clash in him, is German lieder music. In his college days, Sam informed me, he sang. Sacred songs. Early English madrigals about the buds in spring, and lying down with your love under green trees. Beautiful Irish ballads in which someone's horse comes galloping home with a wild eye and an empty saddle. I didn't actuallly believe Sam's claim, until one night, via a combination of begging and tequila, I got him to sing for me. The minute he opened his mouth he looked like a choirboy, even with his hair spiked in all directions the way I used to draw the sun's rays in crayon when I was a child. To be precise, he looked like a goddamn angel. His voice was so sweet I wanted to lick the air. His face had a serene expression I've never seen on Sam while he's awake. He sang with his eyes downcast. Sam's attractive, but he does look a bit like a cartoon character, and his zippy clothes and quick, nervous movements don't help. What would you do if late at night in a tiny fourth floor apartment a young man with a frowsy haircut who looks like he might have escaped from the next morning's Sunday comics sang you Bach's "Vergiss Mein Nicht" in perfect German, his voice so pure it knocked the wind out of you? I did what any red-blooded thirty year old doctor's daughter would do: I let my long hair fall into my face and wept quietly, and when he was done I applauded, poured him another shot of tequila and whined for more.

The sad fact is Sam's ashamed of his beautiful voice. It embarrasses him. He wishes he was a foot taller and fifty pounds heavier, with a bass like Paul Robeson's—so low it sounds like first tremors of an earthquake. Sam's tenor floats up among the tallest eucalyptus trees' leaves, tickling the clouds' bellies. He's not effeminate, but after a long hard day of dealing with some of his leather and spike laden clientele, I think Sam feels like a ninety-seven pound weakling. I wish I didn't have to get him so drunk to coax him to sing. I'm afraid it might not be worth the brain cells we both have to sacrifice.

Sam and I aren't in love, but I like to think there's genuine affection between us and that we'll continue to find each other interesting for awhile, till one of us meets a better match. My soberest diagnosis is that Sam sees me for sex and for conversational variety—since I differ, at least superficially, from the girls he meets at music industry parties, with their hollow cheeks, topiary haircuts and the torn black slips they wear as eighties versions of evening gowns. I look like a kindergarten teacher and never bug Sam for drugs. Once when I refused his generosity by saying "No thanks, I'm not crazy about cocaine" he stared at me like I was a species of animal he'd never seen before. I take Sam to Sunday afternoon readings by contemporary novelists where quiche, white wine and smoked salmon are served. I'm his uptown girl. As for what drew me to Sam, some of the same motives apply. His milieu provides such a contrast to mine. Sitting on his sofa, I can turn my head one way and look down on the street in front of the liquor store below, or I can turn back and look at the poster over his stereo of a British girl group I've forgotten the name of, whose three members are naked and smeared with mud from the waist up. Being with Sam is a cultural vacation for me, and that's a godsend. I need diverting right now, as well as at least one night a week of life-affirming physical love to strengthen my emotional immune system. I could get by just on his singing, but he's stingy with it. He's a lot freer with the gifts of his libido, much prouder of what he can do in bed than of his beautiful tenor.

Now Felice is using a magnifying glass on a chain to examine the cross section of a giant redwood tree the sign says was alive during Mohammed's time. Some of its many concentric rings are labeled. She hangs the magnifying glass back on its hook and traces a ring with her finger. A tiny arrow by this ring has a typed, laminated caption which reads THE BEGINNING OF THE FIRST WORLD WAR. While Europe was coming apart at the seams, this tree, in the "New World," was quietly forming this ring.

My closest friend is in the hospital. Miles' sudden illness is the reason I wanted to visit the dinosaurs of my childhood this afternoon, to steady myself. We met in high school when poor Miles was assigned to hoist me into the air during a dance number in our senior musical. Miles was never athletic, and he had a growth spurt still a year in his future. I had already attained full height, so we had an awkward time with the lift. He was a sport about it, though. Miles was my first real intellectual and looked the part. He cracked gentle self-deprecating jokes during rehearsals about how I was no heavier than the two volumes of the Oxford English Dictionary, which he also had trouble throwing into the air and catching again. "But you're much more fun to juggle," he added. Miles spared my feelings, and I ended up liking him so enormously that I lived on Diet Pepsi for a week before the show so he wouldn't get a hernia. During the performance he gasped, "Light as a feather," in my ear as he set me back down on the stage. He looked dizzy, and we were both sweating profusely, but he gave me a terrific grin.

People often think Miles and I are lovers. We slept together only once, an awful night when we were both home from our respective colleges one summer. We talked about it too much beforehand and not at all afterwards. I was convinced our friendship was ruined. The next morning, Miles took me out to a very glum breakfast at a restaurant in an old trolley car. He ate his ham and cheese omelette in silence. I couldn't swallow, and forked holes in my white paper placemat. Finally he wiped his mouth thoughtfully, cleared his throat and said "Did we commit incest last night? Shall we swear on this stack of pancakes never to sin again?" I was so relieved and grateful that I knocked over a water glass in an attempt to hug him across the table, and the ice cubes flew into his lap.

When I lose something I want to hang onto, I start bargaining. "Let me lose this watch I hate, and not the necklace my father gave me." "Let me misplace some of this junk mail and not that form I need to do my taxes." Even with something as serious as Miles being sick, I find myself thinking the same childish way. Take something I don't treasure. Grab my appendix. But don't take smart, skinny Miles, whose absence will surely push me farther out of the world.

Miles has a rare form of bone cancer. He could recover. After two surgeries they might have "gotten it all." I remember my father talking about patients while carving turkey. Gray and I sat facinated by the latest installment on his pet case, our dinner getting cold on our plates. I know all too well how human physicians are, how hard the good ones try and how little they know. I can figure out the right questions to ask Miles' doctors when they get evasive, and how to react so they won't keep everything important from me. I don't worry about how to act with Miles because I've known from the moment we met. I love him and that colors even the way I yell at him when he pisses me off. What I'm unsure of is how to handle the answers his physicians give me, and how to make myself believe what they say really applies to Miles, whose overly erudite vocabulary, grin and wit are so dear to me. Miles who did pushups for a month so he could lift me up in front of a small audience of our parents and peers.

Felice walks slightly ahead of me into the DENIZENS OF THE DESERT corridor. A giant model of the skull of a folding-fanged rattlesnake gleams behind glass. The viewer can press a small black button and a tape recording, in English, then Spanish, will begin imparting facts about rattlesnakes, while the snake skull opens and closes its jaws with a soft mechanical whirr. The fang dutifully unfolds and then folds in again. This was my brother Gray's favorite exhibit. I have a mental picture of him as a kindergartener, standing here patiently pressing this button again and again, watching the model go through its motions over and over, smiling faintly. Felice, too, has seen these jaws gape thousands of times. "Look at that!" she sighs.

One of the best things about Felice is her ability to be amazed. The amazement is stored in her, and from it she manufactures a joy she feeds on, similar to the way bees gather pollen and make honey, as was explained to us in an earlier exhibit. I'm proud of Felice. She has an adventurous and curious spirit. She leans over a glass case containing a display which would make most women her age squeamish, entitled FRIGHTENING BUT HARMLESS. The display includes a preserved tarantula and a trapdoor spider complete with his silk-lined nest, which Felice loves so much she calls me over. But my mother has no stomach for inhumanity or pessimism. That's where her curiosity comes to an abrupt halt. She won't see war films, or read any book that contains information about the Nazi concentration camps or the Spanish inquisition. She avoids darkness. If she could, she would lobby the powers that be to legislate against it.

I've never known how to answer her vigilent optimism. She does an admirable job with her determined lightheartedness keeping grief, disappointment and self-pity at bay. But sometimes I'm allergic to cheerfullness, especially hers. I was born to brood, and there are times when that's what I must do for awhile before I can move on. Felice was born heartening. She sweats like a racehorse even in winter. I can barely keep warm in August. Obviously our ideological differences have metabolic origins.

We proceed up the cool stone steps to the second floor. The railings are thin metal, painted a soothing pale green. Two eager little girls race by us, ponytails flying. Felice smiles. A jade boulder from China is the first thing one sees on reaching the second floor. We follow signs into the HALL OF SHORE ECOLOGY. Five stuffed sea lions adorn a pile of fake rocks. A tolerable oil seascape dotted with hundreds of their relatives is painted behind them. Another display contains a heap of white sand stuck full of scrubby shrubs...a beach, upon which the bones of a small pilot whale lie. A few stuffed coyotes and lizards are stationed by the skeleton, which looks weathered, stark and dignified, not unlike the frame of a small building. Further on, a display about the breeding cycle of grunion poses the question "Why Would Fish Come Ashore?" Here's a favorite display: fake tide pools, with hardened, semi-transparent resin for water, inhabited by plastic anenomes, crabs, starfish and graceful seaweeds frozen in midundulation; all of which resemble the model foods sushi restaurants display in their front windows to whet potential patrons' appetites. The next window in the display wall reveals a glob of sand dollars, followed by a series of window dioramas explaining how fossils are formed.

So far, Miles has remained surprisingly good natured during this crisis. The hospital staff likes him. He's funny, intelligent, articulate and he complains more to me than them. He doesn't like being drugged. That's the only thing he argues with his doctors about. Since I have the luxury of being able to lighten my caseload when necessary, I made arrangements. I go to the hospital once or twice a day. My cooking has improved because I've been concocting portable meals for Miles so he doesn't have to subsist on the depressing "vegetable medley," "savory baked lasagne" and other inedible creations the hospital kitchen dishes up.

Miles has terrible parents. They're not monsters, they're just not very warm. On birthdays and Christmas they give checks or fifty dollar bills. Never presents. Not even cards. The minute Miles went away to college, they divorced, as though they'd been holding their breaths till he moved out. His father immediately remarried and his mother moved to Oregon where her family lives. They're polite, well-educated, disinterested people. Money has never been a problem. I've been fuming at them all this month while Miles has been hospitalized. He's had surgery twice, and though they phone and send large amounts of money, they haven't been to see him once. When Miles and I first became friends they seemed so pleased. I was flattered. Now I think they were relieved when they saw the kind of bond Miles and I were forming because emotionally, it took him off their hands. Miles says he doesn't want to see them anyway but I hate them for not coming. What are they doing that's so important they can't take a few days off and visit him?

I catch up with Felice again in front of a display on the excavation of a late Pliocene bone bed. A bone bed sounds lumpy. Not so restful. The clock says four p.m. Past my nap time. It's so difficult for a slug like me to wake up.

Posessed of a snake's metabolism, I have to wait for the sun to heat my blood. All winter I'm only half conscious. It's a good thing I live in Southern California, which is practically the tropics. A good self-respecting rain with thunder and stuff borders on mystical experience here, it's so rare. Even for us, it's been a warm dry winter.

If I ever truly awake, I won't know myself. I'm so used to living behind a veil of sighs and yawns. I speak slowly and deliberately, which is helpful since I work with kids who have language aqusition dysfunctions. Low blood pressure is partly to blame for everything about me running in slow motion. That's what doctors, most of whom I trust about as far as I can spit, have proclaimed when asked why my hands and feet are always so icy. It was a family joke during my childhood. My father, a hand surgeon, used to call me "Polar Paws." If I wanted to get back at my brother Gray for something, I'd just sneak up behind him and lay my frigid fingers on the back of his nice warm neck, while he bent unsuspecting over some model of an air craft carrier, using tweezers to place the tiny plastic jets on the dots of glue he'd applied to the deck with a Q-Tip. Gray would yell "CUT IT OUT MIMI!" without even turning around, and he never dropped the tweezers or the model. Now that he's a surgeon too I'm sure his steadiness of hand serves him well.

I've always tried to lead my boyfriends to believe that my chilly extremities cloak a passionate heart. This was Miles' idea. Specifically, he suggested I hint that I was a secret sex volcano. "You know, cold hands, but hot where it counts." Perhaps I could be accused of false advertising there. Perhaps not. I've never had any bad reviews. But it's difficult, in or out of bed, to get an accurate sense of oneself—how one is seen as one passes through the world. There's such a gap between the way one impresses other people and what one feels like inside. When I was younger, I was dying to know what I was like: as a pal, dance partner, patient, lover, raquetball opponent, sister or stranger met for the first time. I was nervously facinated by my potential effects on any audience. Lately, that strikes me as a young person's vanity. Now that I'm thirty, shading my eyes for a hard look at the second half of what I hope will be a reasonably long life, I'd rather worry about how to remain sane and keep my mind pryed open during the unknown span of time I have left. So when an aquaintance aims a sentence at me beginning "You're so..." or "You remind me of..." I quit listening. Or I switch topics quickly, which I'm quite good at. At my age, I want to be spared casual assessments. Other than that, I'll listen to just about anything. Hard luck stories, love drool, even money whining. I guess I've given up trying to find out what I give off or reconcile the conflicting pictures: self image versus how I'm typecast. No way do I want to know what I'm like at this late date. Better to spend my time defrosting the freezer or scrubbing out the bathtub—doing something useful—than to waste time wondering what my fellow creatures think of me.

Now here are some worthy fellow creatures. In a glass specimen case next to the one containing the scenes of "Bee Swarm" and "Bee Hive" (how odd a bee swarm looks all silent and still) are examples of insects which are "not a boon to man." The coddling moth (destructive to apples), the oriental fruit moth (sad news for peaches), the blackheaded fireworm (death to cranberries), and the grape berry moth, pea moth and strawberry leaf roller, named for crops they enrage farmers by devouring. Impaled on pins like merry go round horses skewered by their poles, "it's hard to believe such tiny insects are so ravenous." I don't really have trouble believing it, but that's what the text says.'

Felice pretty much sticks with me. I'll wander off or linger in front of one exhibit for ages and she doesn't complain, but left to her own devices she seems to adjust her viewing speed to mine. She prefers having someone to comment on the exhibits to. Normally, her constant hovering might make me tense. Not today. Maybe I'm softening up toward my parents. After I finished graduate school and began making some kind of post-adolescent peace with my folks, I constructed a little religion out of trying to spare Felice's feelings at all costs. After all, I'd spent from the ages of twelve to twenty trying, sometimes intentionally, sometimes unconsciously, to hurt her. I wouldn't let Felice touch or hug me. I told her it made me feel suffocated. I'd act as devoid of emotion as possible in all my dealings with family. Then I'd make sure she could hear me laughing on the front porch with my friends. Eight years of variations on the themes of uncommunicative sullen rudeness left me ready for an about-face, and when I surfaced as an adult I thought I'd have a stab at trying to make it up to her. Now I don't want to break Felice's heart by telling her about Miles.

Protecting my mother from bad news. Aren't I kind? I thought coming here might make it easier for me to say something heartfelt to Felice. Now waiting for that to happen feels like waiting to fall asleep when it's been out of the question for hours. My heart pounds, my mouth goes dry. No dice.

The air throughout the museum is sweet with swirling dust. I'm sure somewhere in this place there are photomagnifications of dust motes, accompanied by a rectangle of text explaining that dust is x percent dead skin flakes, x percent hair, x percent bedbug larvae and x percent extraterrestrial fallout. There must be a curator of dust up on the third floor where the offices are located, between comparative anatomy and ecology. I imagine the curator of dust to be meticulous, thoughtful and hopelessly obese. A wearer of pince-nez who's sensitive to loud noises. He's also a waterlover, as he can move more easily in the lapping ocean. He looks funny in his bathing suit, but so what. Maybe he's the sort of man I'll set my sights for. We could be married in the swimming pool at the club my father belongs to.

As we walk back towards the stairs along the other side of the room, Felice notices that CREATURES OF THE MANGROVE is screening in the museum's little theatre, so we enter the dimmed room and seat ourselves in folding chairs. We have walked in on the middle of the film. The audience is composed of elderly couples, several junior high school lovers, and a handful of weary mothers with toddlers. One little boy sleeps quietly and his pregnant mother, her feet up on the chair in front of her, looks grateful. The place is three-quarters empty. The narrator speaks like a well-educated cowboy. He refers to one species of rodent that inhabits the mangrove as "these little critters." "Where does this take place? What's a mangrove?" I whisper to Felice. She smiles and shrugs. We watch it rain on screen. Wherever they may be, mangroves are decidedly swampy environments.

Within a few seconds, we're both entranced. It's a beautiful film. I can feel my scalp prickling the way it does when I really love something. Felice looks rapt, watching the huge machine-like face of a catepillar as it devours a leaf. The crunching's so loud in the film it sounds like an army hacking its way through dense jungle with machetes. The creatures of the mangrove live two lives. Dry lives, when the tide is out; and then lives of retreat when the tide rushes in once a month and completely covers the mangrove, leaving it partially submerged. The thoughtful looking monkeys take to the treetops, and various insects, crabs, and lobsters et al build themselves airtight mud retreats, or live miraculously inside air bubbles for twenty four hours, till the tide recedes.

Felice sighs several times during the film and repeats what I've come to regard as her mantra: "Goodness gracious, look at that!"

As the film ends, the narrator describes how all over Borneo (aha! home of the mangrove) these delicate wetlands are being destroyed in the name of civilisation. The concerned cowpoke pleads for the protection of all such wildernesses. Then the lights go on. The sleepers wake up.

I let Felice know I'm going back down to the first floor to use the ladies room. Except for the height of the towel dispensers, mirrors and sinks, it could be an elementary school bathroom. Before returning to the second floor, I wander into the DINOSAUR GIFT SHOP. A Poindexterish-looking lad is perched on a high stool behind the cash register, reading Bullfinch's GREEK MYTHOLOGY. The dinosaur gift shop is an annex to the regular museum gift shop. The regular shop sells microscopes, fossils, science kits, shark's teeth earrings, etc. The dinosaur gift shop sells only dinosaur related items. They're having a half-off sale. I buy five glow in the dark plastic stegosauruses and five pens with a tiny tyranasaurus rex trapped in the transparent barrel. The dinosaur slides from one end of a tiny primeval jungle scene to the other when the pen is tipped. A delightful writing instrument.

All of a sudden, I'm so tired. I close my eyes for a few seconds, after checking to see that Poindexter is still engrossed in his myths, so he won't think I'm going into a trance. When I open them again, the first thing I see is the back of the hand that's holding the pen, with greenish veins in it. It looks like an old lady's hand, but it's mine. Here I am, still safe among toy dinosaurs. I use the hand to pay for my dinosaurs and my feet take the stairs back up to the second floor. Minute to minute we conquer things and continue. Felice is standing in front of a life-size model of a saber-toothed cat. She's talking to a uniformed guard, who's smiling and nodding at her. As I start toward them I see him throw back his head, bare his teeth at my mother and laugh.

RACHEL M. RESNICK

Entertainment Tonight And Forever

How is it we learn to lick boots, and love it; the oily leather on our tongues.
How do we know to welcome barked commands as excuses to sway this way
and that, the tree the dog and our fever. And what of the desire to bend
toward screams and frowns. The finality of manacles and locked hours,
employment and love one steady nightmare feed.

★

My first Hollywood job: slave to ET's celebrity reporter, Darlene Fox.

★

It was summertime in Pasadena. Smog, string bikinis, Ray-Bans, cars with
the tops down, the rush of heat-squeezed chatter, skin. So much bare skin, I
was exultant. Even breathed the thick poison, liked the way it filled the throat.
The sun hung there like a curved copper button, stitched into a thin blue
cotton sky, burning up the clouds. Me, it was my body that burned,
demanding immolation.

Isaac and I fucked all day in the deserted Caltech dorm. I scored a
waitressing gig in the school's restaurant. We were broke, the dorm was hot,
the few students around were suspicious of our presence, but I was going to
get a job in ENTERTAINMENT. Soon. And Isaac and I, well, I wanted us to
always be together. I figured the more he wanted me, the harder it would be
for him to leave. Sort of like my desirability was a choke chain, or a type of
collar. And Isaac was my dog.

There was the white button-down shirt tucked into a short black cotton
skirt, nude drugstore pantyhose, cheap black flats, and the swinging double
doors leading to and from the kitchen in the Caltech restaurant. Isaac got a job
working there too. When we worked the same time and passed each other at
the kitchen, we would kiss quickly before the doors swung shut.

*

Doors closed, the constant thrum of lowgrade pain, these are the telltale signs of slavish love. When girls would proffer themselves on platters recently shined, and wiped, and generally made ready for the crowning delicacy of their own served up head — severed, groomed and perfectly dressed with candied eyes of adoration, boiled lips wincing at the ardent cut of head from neck. They are eager. They are volunteers. Have no pity.

*

After graduation I developed papillary conjunctivitis (tiny bumps on the underside of my eyelids) from contact lenses that prevented me from wearing them for a year. So it was back to glasses. I hadn't worn them since seventh grade, a time of oily hair, gawky limbs, braces, sexual unease.

"Still love me?" I said to Isaac, pointing at the offending frame resting on my face. I was also conscious of my breasts, the way they swelled in the lilac Warner's Sizzler Isaac liked because it was so flimsy. Slowly, imperceptibly, I jutted them forward. I was my own subliminal message. So I fancied.

"Sure, babe. You're like one of those secretaries in the commercials, y'know. Hair in a bun, glasses, uptight suit. Then they shake out their hair, whip off the glasses, throw off the jacket and, voilá."

Isaac gazed at the full-length mirror in the dorm room, arched his eyebrows, then tilted his jaw slightly upward. I did, followed his every move, though the trajectory did not always please me.

"What're you..." I said, vaguely disappointed.

"Nothing." Isaac stuck his tongue out like a gargoyle and wagged it at his reflection. He looked in the mirror more than any woman I knew. "Maybe, though, you could lose some weight."

"Lose," I whispered, freezing my body in its present position.

"What?"

"Nothing." I quickly sat down on the mattress, pulled my knees to my chest. I watched damp spots appear on the hose. Saw amoebas fattening, mini-maps expand and blur. I imagined Isaac's arms hugging me close, skin on skin, body pressed to body as it had been in the beginning, but he didn't move.

Something had altered.

"You'll be late," he said.

★

The watch was hand-me-down, a fake Rolex. In the heat, the gold scabbed off. The face was scratched. The second hand dragged, then flew forward. As if it had a tic. Toc. I shook it off my wrist into a softly puddling Japanese fountain and left it there.

★

"An educated girl," Darlene Fox said, glancing at my resumé. I noticed her feet only touched the floor because she was wearing heels. I didn't like short legs, never had. The higher the height from which to fall on bended knees, chastised and shamed, this was the unarguable advantage of long legs. The better to embrace one's wretchedness.

"Degrees don't matter," she said, speaking rapidly. I nodded, taking in the stiffly sprayed hair, the pancake foundation and thick mascara. Would I have to dress like that? The phone rang and she answered it, putting up her index finger to let me know just a minute. I wanted to bite it, sever its authority. Pack it in my handbag for future use. Instead I focused on this woman's appearance. Her fingernails were long and coral pink and matched the shirt she wore under a tweed Chanel jacket and skirt. On her breast was pinned a shiny gold star. Though in her late forties, early fifties, Darlene had a girlish quality. She seemed to be the complete opposite of the woman I knew best. My mother. The one with the sepulchral voice.

"Hello, darling. Mm hmm." The reporters' den was crowded with desks, papers, file cabinets, posters, pencils, bags of take-out, typewriters. In the corner a stout older man in a tweed sportscoat and turtleneck was smoking a pipe and tapping on a heavy duty Smith-Corona. He winked at me. The nose was telltale red. I smiled, roughed up my hair, and wondered idly if he wanted to fuck me, the same way I had wondered with all my mother's come-and-go boyfriends. I liked the look of chaos, the sensation that business never stopped. I wanted people to want me. I wanted chaos.

"The stupid, he didn't."

I studied Darlene's work area — scribbled notes and snapshots of Darlene posing with celebrities tacked to the bulletin board along with an array of cocktail napkins, Hallmark cards, a sachet of candy bound by a satin ribbon, and a big yellow smiley sticker with dead black eyes. I smiled idiotically to mask the discomfort of waiting. Forced into limbo, a temporary invisibility.

"No, Joan Collins was divine."

Joan Collins. Who knew who I'd meet? I was already thinking about introducing these people to Isaac, the glamorous part of the couple. The stars would recognize him as one of their own, give him a film part, and we would both be on our way. He'd see what I meant about L.A. being wide open. He'd change his mind. He'd change his mind, and I would eat the sugar-spun humility Darlene Fox offered with a deep throat.

"Kiss, kiss."

Darlene turned back to me.

"There's not much money, you'll have to work hard, seven days a week, hours are whenever I need you, but there's movies, TV, parties, celebrities, the whole shebang." The phone rang again. "What do you think?"

I didn't have to.

★

In the bathroom. Behind a metal door, I touched myself. Imagined Isaac wanting me, needing what I had, what I was. More than anything. Anything. Anything. Anyone. Flushed. My hands supplicating beneath an empty spigot, then, the miracle of spat water. Too brief. My fingers, they smelled of sex, and something irreversible.

★

A hundred-and-twenty-five bucks a week is what I got as Darlene Fox's personal assistant, with a chance of getting raises. Less than half what I needed to live on. But with our savings and money from the restaurant, it was enough to make a deposit on an apartment closer to Paramount. We gave notice at the restaurant and began looking for places to rent.

★

There was no air-conditioning in the car, no radio. Isaac had his blaster playing. We had the windows rolled down and the Beastie Boys whining. Isaac held the Thomas Guide, a map of the city that was thick as a dictionary.

"Hollywood first?" I said. Isaac shrugged. The sweat was already fanning over my back, sticking me to the seat upholstery. Instead of getting irritable at the weather and at Isaac, I luxuriated in the perfect press of heat that came equally from every side, and let it hold me.

Isaac was singing along to "It's Time To Get Ill," drumming on the dash. He hadn't spoken since we left Pasadena.

As I downshifted to get off the freeway at Highland, I remembered when we drove cross-country, Isaac said to me, "You'd rather grab that stickshift than me." He was right. Much as I desired him, the sense of power and freedom I got from being behind the wheel was, if not more basic than sex, then more self-contained. It didn't matter if Isaac was beside me once I was in the car, except that he was a distraction, whereas on still ground my need for him bordered on fanatic. Driving required no partner, no passenger, only a sense of purpose, a destination, a tank of gas and concentration. I never tried to explain this to Isaac because I was afraid the secret would be diluted, or worse, disappear. I had never told anyone what driving meant to me. It was too important. I was never more alive, more fluid, more present in my world than when I drove distances.

Every day I discovered new streets, new shortcuts, forgotten cul-de-sacs. One day we passed a weird little house with a rippled roof that looked like dripped sand, and another made out like a Buddhist temple with a red wooden pagoda frame over the porch and a shiny black Buddha on the stoop. Another day I saw a yard of carefully swept dirt and right next to it a yard thick as a jungle with vines choking the telephone lines and covering the door. There were mini-malls featuring three or four different nationalities — Jewish, Indian, Thai, or, Chinese, El Salvadorean and Armenian — in the middle of busy intersections. Things were for sale everywhere — in yards, on lawns, on sidewalks at freeway ramps. On some streets, vendors sat on milk crates with their wares spread on card tables or leaned against brick walls — I spotted cheap china swans, hard plastic flowers, heaps of brown-spotted bananas, chestnuts, shiny tin rings and bracelets, huaraches, stuffed animals sealed in cellophane pouches, fat plastic-wrapped pillows, and aluminum-framed mirrors decorated with paintings of Jesus, Jimi Hendrix, lowriders, Our Lady Of Guadalupe, palm trees. Over one "barata" bargain store, I saw the sign: NEW BORN BIKINI PANTYHOSE BRASSIERE SWEAT SUIT. A new born bikini — a little-bitsy teeny-weeny yellow polkadot wet bundle popping out the snap crotch of a padded lycra one-piece. Wadded and tossed so it wet-slapped the wall. Only then did the bikini let out a lusty wail, clarion call of the born. Forward motion a birthright.

I learned new, bolder maneuvers: how to slip through orange lights flickering to red to make left turns before oncoming traffic came surging in from the front and side, how to move into the right hand lane at a stoplight, then instead of turning right shoot forward in front of slow drivers when the light turned green — in these ways I began to achieve a communion with traffic, congested streets, bad drivers. The skill surface street driving required was tight, precise, more poetic than the epic quality of freeway trips. I found my sense of exaltation and peace rose to new heights of satisfaction, and grittier states of grace.

"Hollywood's a dump," Isaac said the first day after we left yet another noisy overpriced miniature courtyard apartment with low ceilings, soiled off-white carpeting, dripping faucets and peeling paint. I didn't bother to tell him the elegant faces I saw in the mottled striped wallpaper, or the way the paint peeled outward like flower petals radiating from a stained core.

We were driving west on Fountain when Isaac spotted a "For Rent" sign. Cochran Avenue. The manager, a five foot tall woman with a nasal voice wearing a Japanese kimono, showed us around. She wore no shoes and she had hammer toes. It was a two-story white stucco building. The apartment was two-bedroom, with wood floors, sunlight, high ceilings. It was old, but cheery. At five hundred a month, it was more expensive than we could afford, but it was Saturday, my job started Monday, and I was tired of looking.

★

"Name's bad," I told Isaac at Fatburger's which was around the corner from the apartment. I watched him eat a burger with chili fries while I sipped a seltzer water.

"Fry?" he said, pushing a cardboard carton filled with fries glopped with suspiciously orange chili.

"Cochran is just, you know..."

He licked chili off his fingers.

"I have a weird feeling about the name. Maybe it means we're making a big mistake."

Isaac said nothing, wiped his mouth.

★

On Monday I started my job. As instructed, I parked on a dingy side street so I could enter the studio's B gate. Because I was hired by Darlene Fox personally and not by Paramount, I could not park on the studio's lot.

★

Friday night after my first week at ET, we went to the Formosa Cafe for dinner and drinks. I ordered egg rolls, a vodka-tonic, and Isaac ordered Chinese spareribs and a Rolling Rock. The egg rolls were soggy and shiny with grease, the filling tasted like day-old coleslaw, the tonic was flat and the amount of vodka was slight, but neither food nor drink was why anyone came. We'd been to The Formosa a few times and loved it from the start. The place was low rent, dimly lit, crammed full of rickety brown tables, cozy round red leather booths, a dark bar with rows of bottles lit up behind the shadowed bartender, signed photos of celebrity customers tacked everywhere along the ceiling (a custom that extended in L.A. from restaurants to drycleaners to gas stations), wobbly Chinese lanterns, and lit-up glass case displays of Elvis dolls, statuettes and memorabilia. And it was cheap.

"So?" said Isaac, gnawing on a rib. "The crazy hours worth it?" Isaac was wearing his baggy jean overalls and a tank top underneath. I sighed at the sight of his torso and smiled at him. He looked better than any bust of a Greek god I'd seen.

"Excuse me," I said to the waitress, pointing at a tiny white cup of red sauce that sat on a saucer, "could I have some more of this red stuff?" She nodded without answering and bustled away. "You have to drench these rolls."

"That was fast. Going Hollywood."

I frowned. The hard glint in his eyes ruined the Greek god effect. "I asked for more sauce? Big deal."

"Don't frown," Isaac said, pointing at my forehead where I had grown a small furrow.

I drank half my vodka-tonic. They were small glasses. I still loved him, I repeated to myself. "You want to hear or not?"

"Shoot."

"I sit at a big fat typewriter, headphones stuck to my ears, listen to a tape on a Dictaphone and type out the whole fucking interview. Every 'uh huh,' pause, 'hmm,' cough...takes hours."

"Huh." Isaac took my hand and kneaded the fingers. I glanced at a ceramic Old Elvis with white bell bottom jumpsuit striped with emerald green. The cock of his hip was right, but his eyes were flat and phony and the Chinese red paint around his trademark snarling lips was so sloppily applied it made him look like a transvestitic Kewpie doll.

"I answer phones and file, y'know, shit like that, but not every day." I took a bite of egg roll with a big smear of hot yellow mustard. The mustard stung.

"Sounds boring as hell. To your new job," Isaac clinked his beer bottle against my glass.

"Thanks. I didn't even get to Darlene..."

Isaac sighed.

"...every day, does herself up like Dolly Parton. I think she cakes the makeup on to compete with younger anchors, y'know, try and fool the camera. They still use extra filters."

Isaac tossed the last rib onto the plate and grabbed one of my egg rolls.

"We stay late, there's this high heel up on the file cabinet, and in the toe, get this, she's got a pint bottle of Chivas Regal. Takes nips or spikes her soda while she's writing."

"I could use some good weed," said Isaac, peeling the label off the Rolling Rock. Shreds of white fell to the tabletop.

"She's got a white Jag, leather interior, car phone — and I drive. I figure out the directions to the interviews while she talks on the phone..."

"...a chauffeur?" Isaac coughed. "You, Miss Ambition?"

"I'm paying my dues."

"For no bucks."

I sucked down the rest of my vodka-tonic and nodded when the waitress pointed at it to see if I wanted another. "I met Bob Hope. We went out to his private house in the valley somewhere, this rambling ranch monstrosity. I was carrying Darlene's bags, and I saw the camera crew set up and Darlene chatting to this dried-up old man, I thought he was the gardener — it was him. He looked like a walking corpse. They sat him in a big wicker chair, the sun was beating down, and I thought he was going to die right there or was already dead. Then they turned on the camera."

Isaac leaned forward, stroked my arm.

"The lights fell on Hope's face and he came to life. Soon as the camera started whirring, his face got animated, his nose sharper, he started talking and didn't stop until they turned the camera off. Then he slumped back down and didn't say another word. Someone had to lead him away."

Isaac said nothing. I fished the lime out from the bottom of my empty vodka-tonic and sucked the fruit off. The tartness calmed me.

"Sounds pretty damn lightweight to me." Isaac leaned back against the booth, stretched his arm along the top. His muscles rippled there.

"I'm learning. Jesus. It's the first fucking week."

"I gotta go to the john," Isaac said, getting up. I turned to watch, saw him glance at a woman in a booth by the bathroom door. She was sitting with another woman and a man. When he walked by, she waved, then covered her mouth with her hand. The woman was probably a model or an actress with high cheekbones, porcelain skin and revolting cascade of red Botticelli curls. She was wearing a filmy white lace midriff shirt and an armful of silver bangles. I turned back to the table and ran my fingers down the glass, streaking the wetness. Pushed my glasses up. Maybe Isaac was right and the job was bullshit. Isaac sat back down.

"There's something else I did this week."

The waitress brought over another Rolling Rock for Isaac. "I didn't order this," he said. The waitress winked.

"Gift from the lady back there," she said.

"Don't let me interrupt," I said, exhaling. "Go talk to her, go ahead."

"Don't start," Isaac said.

"I saw you looking at her."

"Rebecca."

"I sit in this cubicle, watch videos of movies to find clips for stories. This week we interviewed Claude Lanzmann."

"New hearthrob on 'Days Of Our Lives'?'

"No. Directed a ten-hour documentary on the Holocaust from the point of view of present-day survivors. Darlene said pick out five juicy seconds." Isaac was gazing over my shoulder.

'I can't believe you," I said.

"I should at least say thank you. Someone's friendly, what's the problem?'

"Please. With blessings."

"Be right back." Isaac got up and went back to the booth. I didn't turn around. I took my glasses off and everything looked better. All the Elvises were blobs of white, silver, green and red, the lanterns spilled warm light, the Formosa was a watercolor painting, a wacky Matisse, peoples' faces blurred and fuzzed, bottles shone. Behind me I heard voices. Laughter. Isaac said, "Hey, Brotherman," and slapped someone's hand. Then he was sitting down again.

"An actress," he said, his voice scornful. "Wanted to know if I was an actor. Guy was nice. Works carpentry down by the beach. Said he might be able to swing me some work. Other girl's a costume designer. They might join us."

"You didn't."

"Don't you want me to work? Pay you back?"

"I want to finish telling you. I chose this scene with the barber." Isaac waved at the table, at the redhead. I kept talking. I needed him to hear the story, though I wasn't sure why.

"He's cutting a customer's hair and remembering how he survived the camps by cutting prisoners' hair before they were gassed to death. There's a closeup on his hands trembling as he shears away this guy's hair, hunks of it float down onto the floor behind him, slow, and the barber just breaks down." I paused. "I kept replaying the hair floating through his hands, through the scissors and onto the floor. Over and over. I couldn't stop. Are you listening? All Darlene said when I showed her the clip was did I think the director was sexy."

The waitress walked out from the kitchen with a slice of apple pie and a single candle burning in the crust. She brought it to the booth where the redhead sat.

"HAPPY BIRTHDAY TO YOU, HAPPY BIRTHDAY TO YOU..." sang the man and woman.

"It's Katrina's birthday," Isaac said. "The actress."

"Katrina. Like I give a shit."

"HAPPY BIRTHDAY DEAR KATRINAAAAAAA..."

"You are too fucking much," I said.

"HAPPY BIRTHDAY TO YOU!"

"What?" Isaac said sharply, leaning forward. "I heard your story. You want me to pat you on the back? Tell you how incredible you are? How smart? How you'll be driving a white Jag? I'm sure you'll be successful," Isaac said bitterly.

"HOW OLD ARE YOU NOW, HOW OLD ARE YOU...."

"Shhhhhhhhhhhhh..." the redhead said to her companions. A burst of laughter came from the booth. Tears slid down my face. I thought it was impossible, but the Formosa got even blurrier — reds merging with yellows and shadows and glinting ice cubes. Flesh blending with 8" x 10" glossies and smiling gold buddhas.

"Fuck," said Isaac. "Rebecca."

"Hey, Isaac!" yelled a female voice. "Come join us. Katrina wants you." More laughter. "Bring your friend!"

"Isaac," I whispered. "Isaac, I love you, I love you so much." Isaac kept his head down, toyed with one of the picked clean bones on his plate. I reached out to grab his hand, but I must have misjudged the distance without my glasses on, because I only got my sleeve wet on the table and didn't manage to touch him.

★

There's this. The way the sky would rinse clean after a rainstorm. See the rooftops sharpen in the newborn air, edges poised to razor the blue? Their intent: spill celestial guts on the hoods of cars.

★

One morning I came to work with a buzz cut.

Darlene raised her eyebrows but didn't say anything, just gave me a tape to transcribe. At night, when the reporters' den was empty except for us, Darlene tapped me on the shoulder. I took off the headphones.

"We need to talk," she said. Darlene never spoke to me that way. Nobody else had either when I was growing up. If anyone scolded, it was me. "Why don't you get a job? Pull yourself together." "Fuck off," is what my mother said.

Darlene sat down on the desk next to me with her styrofoam container of Thai food. We were eating invisible noodles, silver yum-yum and mee krob from Chan Dara on Cahuenga. Try as I might, the noodles would not obey my chopsticks.

"You're only hurting yourself," she said, pointing a wooden chopstick at my hair.

"Don't you ever feel like, I'm a woman, screw me?"

"I'm a woman, I do all right. Call me shallow." She flashed a brilliant, manic smile. "You'll never get anywhere dressed like that," she said, pointing at my green Converse All-Star hightops, magenta ankle-zip jeans, untucked shirt with a singed brown patch around the lowest button where I'd brushed against a lit gas burner and then sported the damage. "Gotta show some leg," she said. "Didn't your mother teach you anything?"

She didn't really want to hear the answer to her question. She didn't want to hear about the Marlboro Mom, a woman who never wore high heels, who couldn't even keep a lousy job waitressing at IHOP or delivering newspapers. I kept the image of my mother in her daily uniform of Levi's, ragged t-shirts, jean jacket and heel-cracked cowboy boots to myself. I hated that jacket — a blue jean canvas for Jackson Pollack-style visual violence in cigarette burns, wine stains like woozy flowers, holes fringed with white cotton threads, rips and faded strips like washed-out shorelines, etched creases from her elbows bent around the steering wheel, her elbows bent on the bar, her elbows bent on the pillow where she lay sleeplessly — but after she died, I kept the jacket in my closet.

"I'll tell you a secret, Rebecca. I'd rather have beauty than brains," Darlene said, taking a large plastic forkful of invisible noodles. I watched her add a shot of Chivas to the Thai iced tea before I left.

★

On the way home, winding through darkened streets with melancholic Brazilian music on the radio, I thought maybe getting a buzz cut, dying a forelock purple or green, wearing baggy long johns under ripped jeans didn't mean rebellion. Maybe it meant something else. With one hand deftly guiding the wheel and the other stretched around the passenger head rest, I thought about my mother. I saw her stumbling down the stairs in a cheap rayon K Mart baby doll nightie, handing eleven-year-old me a book of food stamps, "Get me a six of Miller's and a pack of Salems," while I avoided the scary ice-floe blue of her eyes. How did that square with the earlier vision I had of her — the lively brunette, hair bound back with a turquoise scarf, full lips laughing as men come up to her on the street and whispered what nice legs she had, and how pretty she was, me at age four or five trailing alongside, enraptured too and proud, as we walked through Central Park with hotdogs and I climbed the metal statue of Alice In Wonderland, perched on her shoulder with one hand grasping Alice's rippled cold metal hair and the other waving at my mother, the whole show all for her.

I sped through the last milliseconds of an orange light and turned smoothly onto Fountain, executing a perfect, tight arc to the right. Revenge. That was my motive for wanting to make films. I stayed in the narrow right lane, squeezed boldly past parked cars, just missing their side view mirrors. Everyone thought my mother was a failure. Driving through the streets of West Hollywood, past shadowed palms and dimly lit bungalows, I reaffirmed I was on earth to vindicate my mother's memory.

I glanced at my reflection in the rear view mirror and wondered how long it would take for my hair to grow out.

★

Hands grabbing, lifting, replacing hanger on rack, shoved far inside to the left. The jacket, hide it, no, revere it, just, give it a special place, a sacred spot deep inside the closet. Yes, sacred. Never mind the dustballs rising. Never mind the jacket still smells of her. Feels of her. Against the wall, place the jacket, note the emptiness of sleeves, the way the shoulders poke in soldierly fashion. Remember, wipe your hands on your pants when you step back out and shut the door.

★

Back at home, Isaac wasn't taking off anywhere except to the bookstore — either Samuel French Theatre Bookshop on Sunset or Book Circus on Santa Monica where all the male hustlers hung out. Even though we were trying to save money for rent and other essentials and Isaac didn't have a job yet, he bought books and didn't read them. Philosophy, acting theory, anti-apartheid tracts, plays, literary criticism, poetry. He bought books when we had nothing in the apartment but a futon on the floor and all our belongings piled in the closets. The place was empty. Still, he couldn't stop buying them. And I didn't stop him.

★

Stack the cars. Thread the cars. Glue their bumpers together. Paint them all red, one long red line of cars cars cars. Doesn't matter. Traffic is unavoidable. You are one car among many, indistinguishable.

★

"Damn carphone. I didn't see him turning."

"Where are you?" I said. Darlene's voice was low and shaky. "I think Ivar," she said, pausing to look out the window. "Yes...north of Sunset. Transfer the phones up front. Hurry."

When Darlene climbed into my beat-up used Toyota Corolla, I was embarrassed. There were cracks in the dash, paper scraps and dirt clods on the floor mats, stains on the cheap vinyl seat covers, dirt on the windshield.

"Sorry about..."

"Just drive." The aroma of Giorgio perfume filled the tiny car along with another smell almost as sweet. I realized, as I pulled onto Sunset Boulevard, that the other scent was whiskey.

Darlene didn't talk, except to give directions. She held herself stiffly in the seat, as if she didn't want to get dirty by moving around too much, or maybe that was my paranoia. I liked the sight of her Gucci heels perched on the wrinkled floor mat. Rare reversal. The joy of seesawing, watching them with split legs bouncing wide apart, flailing in the air. Crushed back to earth. Shattered knees and feet. Excuses for devotion.

As we drove along Sunset and the houses and shops got fancier and cleaner the further west we went, I thought about all the accidents I'd been in with my mother. Thought about them with the same powerlessness as a common housefly watches its own wiry legs disappear one after the other in the spider's mouth. I remember the first accident — her hand bracing my body when the VW bug impacted a guardrail, or a curb, or something, was it another car? The song playing on the radio was "Echoes Of My Mind," it kept playing even after the crash, there were orange and yellow, green and blue stickers of daisies on the hood, so it must have been late in the sixties. There was a long wait in the police station. I sat on a large, uncomfortable polished dark wood bench sucking on Luden's cherry cough drops while my mother came in and out from different tests — breathalyzers, lie detectors, alcohol level testing.

I glanced up at the Marlboro Man billboard rising above Sunset, his cowboy hat peaking against the hills, and remembered how people walked by where I sat in the cop station and looked at me sadly, how I furrowed my brow and stared them down. Every time my mother came out from another test, I pretended not to know her, instead studying a *Guns & Ammo* magazine I found on a table nearby while she chainsmoked and I coughed loudly.

When we turned north on Sunset Plaza, Darlene perked up. "I can just hear Paul. 'Again?' Married thirty years," she said to me, smiling too brightly, "I was twenty. Oops," she giggled. "Don't tell anyone."

"Twenty?"

"Had four children, and kept my career going too. My kids, they're, special. They don't say that about me," she giggled again. "I was a bad bad mother."

"Four, huh," I said, winding up Sunset Plaza through narrow, lushly green streets bordered by spacious houses.

I was disappointed. Success was fine. I admired that in a woman. Craved it for myself. Family, though, was a big blotto in my mind. Family was the missing jigsaw piece that ruined the interlocked picture of a daisy-dotted Swiss Alp and showed you the knife-gouged cardtable underneath. Family was fragments of busted beer bottles left jagged and piss-sticky on the kitchen floor.

"Not so fast," Darlene said, gripping the arm rest. Enjoying her fear, I pressed the accelerator, pulled into Darlene's driveway and raced to the top. There was her house. It was perched at the edge of the hill and commanded a panoramic view of the city. I had never seen anything like it.

I wasn't invited in. Before she got out of the car, Darlene kissed me briefly on the cheek. "Bring your boyfriend by sometime." Then she was gone. I stayed for a few minutes in the driveway looking out at the tiny diamond lights of L.A. popping up before I wound back down into the lowlands.

✦

I introduced Isaac to Darlene. The only thing she had to say about him later was, "Loser."

At that time, I thought she meant me.

★

We were in the Crystal Room of The Beverly Hills Hotel, it was five-thirty, and we were waiting for the celebrities to arrive for the Contessa Foundation Fashion Show. All the proceeds would go to an animal rescue shelter. Before anyone with a *TV Guide* name showed, I raided the buffet table. I wrapped sandwich triangles, truffles, monster strawberries and paté in napkins, then placed the moist packages in my shoulder bag. Isaac and I would eat them later.

I picked up a glass of champagne and went to look for someone to help me spot stars. I decided I didn't want to be a loser. I began to enjoy spotting celebrities with the help of tipsy Foundation patrons, even let myself fantasize about being invited to such an evening instead of infiltrating with the ET crew, wasn't that what Darlene called positive thinking? A little more champagne, and I was imagining what it would be like to don a clingy silver sheath and strut down the lit-up runway, knowing that every twitch of my ass and flex of my calf was contributing toward a dog house for some poor homeless canine. My idols Antonioni, Scorsese, Wertmuller, Fellini tried to wave me back to them in a corner of the Crystal Room where they stood badmouthing the crowd and pooh-poohing Hollywood, but I was gone, up there on the stage cocking my hip for the sake of some outcast canary, fully inhabiting the shimmering skin of a star.

★

Every four and a half months they come around to shave the palm trees. The city that is. Special vehicles. Motorized pulpits lifting bodies up toward the shaggy bark. Oversized razors in hand, they shear the dead brown skin. Great buzzing noises and roaring gears. It falls in heaps on the street. Along with yellow, sickly fronds. All gets piled and shoved to the curb. Scooped up and discarded in metal bins. Ritual sacrifice for the skyline. Thing is, the fresh shave makes them look so goddamned vulnerable.

★

One morning near the end of my stint at ET, I arrived at Darlene's house to drop off some dubbed tapes half an hour early.

She opened the door in a terry robe and bare-faced. It was the first time I'd ever seen her without makeup. I was stunned. I never knew she had such enormous hazel-green eyes underneath all the shadow and concealer and liner and mascara. Her skin minus heavy foundation was the biggest surprise. Smooth and supple and dotted with thousands and thousands of floating freckles shaping and unshaping like free-form constellations as I watched those eyes widen.

When she saw me, Darlene got flustered and fled back to the bathroom. I left the tapes on the front door mat and wound down Sunset Plaza onto the Sunset Strip, thinking of my first Hollywood boss. In that moment when she came to the door, Darlene looked like a little girl lost, but more beautiful than I'd ever seen her. A little girl lost who wanted more than anything to be adored.

Drunk, she reminded me of my mother.

With her naked face, she reminded me of me.

JAY GUMMERMAN

That Whole Ever-After Number

My name is Bill Harris and I have no imagination. I am one of that sullen breed of customer service representatives who continually wear a tired expression on their faces, tired from listening to people like you whine about their problems via their cappuccino makers and electric tortilla warmers. I am essentially joyless, which is why the personnel manager here at the large department store where I work keeps me at my position. I have dreams of gridlock, but they are not nightmares. They are, instead, sunny depictions of that moment when consumers are forced to consume themselves, and it's not very pretty except to someone like me, who has been waiting for this day of reckoning forever.

Which is not to say I am a religious fanatic or have a great loathing of the human race; this would imply I still hold claim to that body of emotions known colloquially as passion, which have long ago faded from my being. By my own choosing, I lead an inconsequential life, a life that has steadily been losing consequence over the seven years I have worked here. According to plan, nothing of a very dramatic nature has ever happened to me. No life-threatening injuries, no childhood traumas, no time in jail or the military service. The occasional death in the family, but always the predictable eighty-five-year-old-with-heart-failure sort of thing. I don't believe in Heaven or Hell, God, or particularly, Science. I haven't voted in the last several elections, presidential or otherwise, and I have no belief in the institutions of either holy or unholy matrimony.

What I do believe in is the undying force of mediocrity, which I have allowed with the appropriate ennui to rise to my swelling, approaching-middle-age midsection. At my mother's insistence, a battery of physicians at my HMO has tested me for any number of modern diseases — Epstein-Barr, chronic-fatigue syndrome, etc. — which of course misses the point entirely: even if I were diagnosed with the deadliest of maladies I would resist treatment. I want to be the way I am.

There is, however, one part of me that's in need of minor adjustment, a little glitch the doctors uncovered in their search for something deeper — it seems I was born with a defective heart, a heart that on occasion beats irregularly. This news came as a pleasant surprise to my mother, only because she feared I might have been ailing from an incurable sickness. But in two weeks' time these very same doctors will be installing a pacemaker in my chest, and my mother is convinced I will be a new person afterward, a man capable of rising above his peers to perform great things. Sadly, what she fails to realize, especially given that I have authorized such an operation, is that I will be instead joining the ranks of the one-hundred-percent normal. A lifelong ambition of averageness will have been fulfilled.

It is one minute before opening, and I am perched on my metal stool looking out over the catalogs of product information that sit before me on the counter, out into the department store at large where its forty or so employees pace among the waving fields of candy-colored merchandise like edgy circus animals. If Van Gogh were alive today he could paint this scene and be called a realist.

Like clockwork, the music of perpetual orgasm, otherwise known as rock-and-roll, bursts into the climate-controlled air from Home Electronics. Sang the Magnificent is already at it, moaning and flailing to the sounds of rockstar-of-the-month, whose haggard image, like rockstar-of-the-previous-month's, flies in synchrony across the hundred screens Sang has been given charge of. Sang, who can't sing, has been warned many times by Aziz, our supervisor, that he is scary to the customers when he's performing and that scared people rarely buy televisions or personal stereos. But Sang, either through malice or the chronic form of optimism he suffers from, chooses to ignore such advice. He will continue these sorry exhibitions of his without being fired, however, because there is no one to replace him — not because who else would work so cheaply but Sang or his equivalent, i.e. some other poor unfortunate from southeast Asia with little or no experience?

As a matter of fact, I am the one remaining white male to clerk in this store, my caucasian peers having either failed the drug test or donned a white collar to pursue highly-paid careers in a myriad of service occupations. I was such a person myself at one time (I programmed militaristic video games for a living), but I made enough money to purchase free and clear the American dream of a single family tract home, and my needs are no longer extravagant, particularly considering as a native Southern Californian, I am worth hundreds of thousands of dollars in equity simply by staying put an extended period of time. And for those among you who rhetorically state, "You can't go home again," I have a rhetorical question: "What happens if you never leave home to begin with?" The answer, at least here on the Pacific Rim, is that everyone else will abandon theirs to come live with you in yours.

Now Sang has caught me staring at him, and in my moment of regret, he twists around in his studied version of cool to see if Aziz is nearby, or there are, God forbid, any prospective customers in the vicinity. But with six more shopping months until Christmas, the store is filled with everything but the warm bodies it is meant to attract, and Sang begins his studied version of a cool walk into my department, his thumbs, like a latter-day Sal Mineo, hooked on the waistband of his industrially-faded jeans.

When Sang first started working here, I was often tempted to explain to him, without ever actually succumbing, that there isn't much demand in the entertainment industry for balding, tone deaf Laotians with stumpy bodies, that the long tufts of hair practically dripping with mousse above his ears and below his bald spot make him look like a down-on-his-luck Elvis impersonator moonlighting as Bozo the Clown, and that this image would appear truly aberrant to the viewing public, unlike the finely-crafted aberration it so wantonly craves.

Nor did I intercede when the reticulated salesman at Howard's World of Music, which is just down the mall from us, sold Sang a synthesizer on thirty-six easy payments, a keyboard that can emulate the sounds of every known instrument, including the Jew's harp, and can play salsa-cum-bossa-nova rhythms without even once missing a beat in its entire factory-guaranteed lifetime. The salesman is clearly playing Sang for a fool, but I won't say anything. I am like on of those rangers at Yellowstone Park who, when a bison falls through a hole in the ice, refuses to rescue the thing from drowning. To do so would be tampering with some perverse form of nature, which certainly this mall, and countless malls like it, embodies. In the last two years what in my youth was known simply as a shopping center has been incorporated into a full-fledged Galleria, complete with huge cathedrals of natural light that bathe the inhabitants and the nursery-grown palms, making for a kind of hermetically-sealed Eden. I'm certain if given the chance the Galleria would survive intact, like one of those glass-enclosed ecosystems composed of brine shrimp and plankton that go on rejuvenating themselves indefinitely. On those rare days of self-reflection, which I briefly transcend my role as Suburban-American, I wonder where exactly I fit into the food chain.

Sang has at last arrived and he leans what little I can see of his upper body against the counter, his face, like mine, turned outward into the imaginary living rooms of Home Furnishings. "Harris," he says, in as flat a voice as he's capable of, which is quite flat considering his great musical deficiencies. It's as though he expects I will be driven to extraordinary speech by the mere sound of my own name.

"Sang," I tell him and avert my eyes from the glare of his bald spot, migraine headaches being a more prosaic affliction of mine. Sang has no immediate reply, which is the way all my conversations with Sang start out. He seems to think that as a person born in the shadow of Hollywood I have a natural predisposition for coolness, and that cool people are men of few, carefully-spaced words. In my own case he mistakes cool with resignation, but I won't ever explain this to him either.

"You have a good weekend?" Sang asks, and when I don't answer immediately, he picks a piece of lint off the inseam of his pants as though to mitigate the directness of his question.

"Nothing out of the ordinary. I washed my car; weeded my lawn; watched a little television — not necessarily in that order."

"I have TV myself," he says and looks thoughtfully toward the bank of screens fluttering now with palsied fingers on a fretboard. Like a pretty waitress, Sang has that way of never looking you in the eye but somehow never letting your attention waiver either. "At night I watch late movies: Lisabeth Scott, Van Johnson. You know these?"

"Not personally."

"Last night I watch *Singing in the Rain* with Gene Kelly and Miss Debbie

Reynold. They are very good these two. I enjoy very much the dancing. There is scene near start when Gene Kelly, who play movie star in movie, lie about his life to big crowd fans. He say he go to dancing school, but movie show him, as boy, dancing on street. He say he go to Shakespeare while young, but movie show boy dancing outside movie theatre. I know this face of boy! I think and think, but I can not place. Many good scene pass by. There is scene when Miss Reynold throw cake at Gene Kelly. There is scene when Gene Kelly first sing to Miss Reynold. Then I know face of boy. This is Harris, I say out loud, this is Harris while young! I am up and down, this excitement is so much. I wish to phone you, Harris, but I do not have number. So I wait and wait for names, but no names at end of movie. I phone station but nobody answer."

Sang is looking right into my face now and there is genuine desperation in his eyes, an urgency I have never seen in him, even when Aziz is doling out one of his lectures on the importance of temperate behavior; this is the most I've ever heard him speak at one time.

"You play in this movie?" Sang asks. "You know Miss Debbie Reynold?"

For a moment I consider telling Sang I was a child star, and the best scene in the movie had me sitting in the lap of Miss Debbie Reynold, though in the end the footage wound up on the cutting room floor due to a contract dispute between my agent and Sam Goldwyn. But in truth I was born a year or so after the premiere of *Singin' in the Rain* and to lie to Sang now would set a dangerous precedent.

"No, Sang, I have never been in a movie. I was however a do-bee on Romper Room at one point, but that was the end of my career in media. Miss Betty saw to it that I never worked again."

For a moment Sang is unable to gauge the veracity of my statement, which must prove especially difficult since I doubt he has any idea of who Miss Betty is. But then the corners of his mouth start to bulge and he looks away to conceal his smile, and I'm sure what he's telling himself is that we Americans are such good kidders.

In the same moment an actual customer, a woman of indeterminate age from this distance, is stepping off the escalator to begin the hazardous walk through various marketing booby traps on her way to Customer Service. She bears the telltale body language of someone returning something: the head held almost too erect; the steps chose a little too carefully; the same god-awful aura of an avenging angel they all manage to shroud themselves in. No doubt she belongs in one of both of the two broad categories our customers fall into — she is either a shopper from a bygone era, when there was still some shred of dignity left in shopping, or, she is wealthy enough to help finance all the glitzy atmosphere in this place, unlike the rest of the unregenerate masses, who are doomed to walk the drafty aisles of some pay-to-shop consumer warehouse. Everything in this store can be had cheaper elsewhere, even our marked-down items, which explains our precipitous decline in sales in recent years. If it weren't for the employee discount, I would never buy anything here myself.

Vivi, setting out a new line of comforters in Domestics, make the requisite eye contact, but this is the proverbial tough customer, brushing by Vivi without letting her gaze stray from her destination. Sang tries to nudge me, but he misses, and I see now that this woman is someone I would have found quite attractive in my hormonal period — curvaceous, long red hair, a look of wary confidence set in translucent green eyes — though she's a bit old to be wearing the kind of loose-fitting prairie dress I associate with hippies, a person a former colleague of mine would call a "sunny fairy girl," and not in a flattering light. She hesitates just short of where we stand, I suppose to determine which one of us she should be addressing, then smirks at Sang before hefting her shopping bag up on the counter.

"You have several levels in this store," she says smiling a little too pleasantly. "But no matter how many times I travel up and down your escalator, I can never tell them apart. I know this is probably at the root of your campaign to disorient the shopper, so that she'll stagger around until her wallet falls open near a cash register, but, honestly, don't you think you could clearly mark the floors in this place?"

Of course I have a snappy answer for this, and, of course, I don't verbalize it. My job is to channel the conversation to the task at hand. The trick as always will be to explain to the customer, without expressly doing so, that she is the one who's defective, not the merchandise she is returning, while at the same time agreeing with everything she says, and in the end making good on our money-back guarantee. The customer, braced for argument, will at first feel a vague satisfaction, though by the time she arrives home she will once again experience the feeling that her life is missing something, without being able to identify what it is. In a few days, she will return here to fill the void by purchasing more superfluous items, thus completing the cycle.

"I'm sorry you had a hard time finding us," I say, laying out just the right amount of smarm. "I'll make your suggestion to the floor manager and perhaps he can work something out with the home office. Here is always the bureaucracy to contend with."

"Cha cha cha," she says and glances over at Sang before returning her eyes to me. "Who's the leprechaun?"

"Pardon me?"

She turns to Sang. "I guess you're around in case Cheez Whiz here strikes out and I have to be dragged from the store kicking and screaming. A head case for the head cases. What a novel idea."

Sang looks at me as though I might have insight into this woman's personality. When I offer him no expression, he nods goodbye and begins his deliberate walk through the obstacle course on his way back to the land of video ejaculation.

"Some bouncer," the woman says winking at me. I still have no idea yet if she's being serious. I guess you and I might just as well get down to business."

She reaches into her bag and lifts out of it a Hamilton Beach blender, our top-of-the-line model, and sets it on the counter. It looks as though she's used the thing to make guacamole dip or pesto sauce and didn't bother scraping it out when she was done — chunks of brown-green organic matter cling to the sides of the glass, and a pungent odor like cat food rapidly permeates the air.

"Okay, so it's a little dirty," she says. "But it works great. Plug it in if you want."

"That won't be necessary."

"Go ahead. I didn't make a bomb out of it."

"No really, that's fine. I'll take your word on it."

There is a brief lull in the conversation as I perform my hesitation routine, followed by my scratching-of-the-head voice: "I'm just wondering. I mean, if it works so well —"

"Then why am I bringing it back?" She slowly shakes her head. "You're good, Bill," she says, without noticeably reading my name tag. "You, my friend, are the right man for the job." She presses the button marked "Liquefy" and seems disappointed when nothing happens. "There really isn't *anything* the matter with it. The little blade spins around at the twelve different speeds. I tried all the buttons and they all cause variations on the same violent theme."

Again she reaches into her bag and this time produces a toaster oven, complete with charred crumbs, and then a coffee grinder brimming with pulverized French Roast. "I left the rabbit at home," she says and winks at me again. "No, really, there's more in the car, but right now you'll have to use your imagination. What you're trying to picture is this: I've got all these appliances set up in the kitchen of the town house that Mario and I spent weeks picking out together. I've been working all morning filling up little slots and bowls and compartments with all the proper ingredients and I've got the devices plugged into one of those power strips — you know, with a surge protector? — and then I set there with my thumb on the switch waiting for the phone to ring, because I figure the more the merrier, right? Plus the telephone is a very Zen starter's pistol. I mean, who knows when the phone is going to ring? So ten, fifteen minutes go by, and I'm starting to zone a little bit, I'm starting to watch myself levitate in the old cranial lounge, and then all of a sudden the phone starts ringing and my thumb throws the switch without me even realizing it, and, presto, they're off: seven or eight little patented marvels doing this whole metaphysical number right before my very eyes. I have to admit I was really thrilled. I mean it's like the March of the Wooden Soldiers. It's Babes in Toyland right in my own kitchen.

"When I get over the initial buzz, I pick up the phone and it's Mario, and he has to say what he's saying at least three times before I can understand him: 'How's your first day of married life?' he says, which isn't actually the case if you count the honeymoon, but I get his drift — he means how's the first day of *real* married life, not room service and gondola rides, but how's life with the machines there? And you know what I tell him? I don't tell him anything. I let the contraptions do my talking. I just set the receiver on the stove island and split, take a walk around the compound, say hello to some fat ladies out by the pool. And when I get back, you know what? Those machines are still going at it."

She pauses here looking rather pleased with herself, as though she's just managed to communicate something of Richter-scale magnitude, when in fact I have no idea what she's talking about.

"*Tabula rasa*," she says and nods her head soberly. "I get it now, Bill. You need the straight skinny for your records, don't you? In that little blank that says 'other explanation?' This is what the customer must supply before she gets her refund." She gives a snort for a laugh. "OK, here it is: The machines are still going, right? Doing their little riff until the next cataclysm or brownout, whichever comes first. But the question remains, will they produce anything anybody can really use? Practically speaking, no. It's pretty much a primordial soup is what it is, and I don't have a million years to let it take shape. I've got thirty, forty years tops. That's when it hits me this whole thing with Mario isn't going to work out — he needs Queen Merlin, not me. He needs somebody who can transform things behind a little screen, then sit down on the couch with him and watch 'Unsolved Mysteries.' Mario's been nothing but sweet through the whole deal, I want you to know that. This has nothing to do with Mario. What I'm telling you is I successfully altered my personality for six months, through rehearsal dinners and registering and various in-law marathons and then the day we get back to L.A., it's like total meltdown and I revert right back to my old self. What I'm saying here, Bill, is I'm cashing out. I don't want dime one of alimony from Mario, either. I just want what's coming to me for the machines. That should be enough to get me to the state line, and from there, who knows? But then that's another story, isn't it?

The total comes to over four hundred dollars and because she literally wants cash instead of the refund check customary in such large-sum cases, I have to verify with Aziz, and he dials her up on the computer and sure enough, there she is in the registry, a Mrs. Mario Andretti — the race car driver? — and not the crack-hungry appliance burglar I had her pegged as.

At lunch I see her in Howard's, and for once the salesman looks like he's in over his head. She's got three or four synthesizers going simultaneously, each of them spewing forth a competing drum and bass line that spills out into the Galleria and melds with the carousel music wafting up from the floor below, her hips all the while shaking madly, yet amazingly in synch with the convoluted racket, and the salesman tries feebly to quash her instinct for dance.

There is a moment when I have the overwhelming sensation the building is trembling, and it occurs to me this woman has single-handedly managed to create the one resonant vibration the engineers hadn't anticipated in all their computer-driven studies, a frequency that will shortly cause the Galleria to collapse on itself and the likes of Chuck Heston will have to be summoned to rescue the few, self-serving survivors.

But, of course, nothing of such a fanciful nature is in the cards this day, and I spend the rest of it humoring the usual assortment of hapless underwear exchangers and discombobulated barbecue assemblers, with a few sessions of Sanskrit sandwiched in between.

At home, I check my messages — a call from my mother inviting me to a mixer at the Unitarian church she drags my father to on a weekly basis; yet another offer to refinance my house, this time from a heavily-accented, middle-eastern-sounding salesperson named Wally; then several hang-ups, no doubt from other telephone solicitors, of both the mechanical and human genders.

On TV I watch an interview with a man who kept a woman hitchhiker his sexual hostage for three years, with the full knowledge of his wife, a crime he freely admits but in his damaged way he is unable to acknowledge. The interviewer is a sprayed blond reporter with a stern demeanor and a good tan, perhaps a reformed surfer, who periodically takes the moral high ground with his subject in the form of admonishing stares and smug asides to the camera, probably all of which have been spliced in later. For the most part, though, the reporter coaxes the prisoner into lurid descriptions of his illegal activities, much to the delighted terror of his home audience.

The telephone rings and instead of my usual call screening, I answer it directly — how soon I have forgotten what contact with the outside world can bring.

"Hello?"

"I'm a woman, I'm aggressive, and nothing can stop me," a woman's voice — naturally — announces, and as I wordlessly lay the receiver back in its cradle, I hear a witch's cackling, faint but unmistakable, rattling through the little paper diaphragm in the earpiece.

The phone rings again but this time I let the machine handle it. "Billy, pick up," the same voice instructs me, followed by a long pause, presumably to allow me to answer. "Bill-ee," the voice says in a hands-on-her-hips tone, "I know you're in there. I can see your TV blazing through your ecru drapes. It's quite a garish image, if you must know, not the sort of thing you mean to proje—"

The endtone sounds and she is cut off. Immediately the phone rings again, and again her voice is broadcast through the speaker on the machine: "Bill, I've invested a lot of time on you. I dialed twenty or so William Harrises before I recognized your nondescript voice, which is no mean feat on a cellular telephone in heavy traffic. That by itself took me forty-five minutes, and before that it took me an hour just driving around in Mario's Buick before I figured out who I know outside of Mario and his family that's normal, and it turns out you're it, Bill, and I can't very well go to Mario or his family for advice, when Mario's the one that's upset about what I told you earlier — you know, annulment city and all its little suburbs — so will you please pick up the goddamn phone, please, before I have to drive Mario's fine Buick through your fine goddamn living roo—"

Endtone.

When she calls back, she seems at first distracted, the way my mother sometimes sounds when prompted by my recorded voice to speak, as though I was the one who called her: "Well look Bill, you know there won't be any wreckage or mayhem because this isn't L.A. proper, which is I know the unencumbered living death you've designed for yourself out here where the housing tracts roam. Violence isn't necessary in this situation — I realize that, Bill — even if it is more than called for. The real deal is this: I don't need your permission to speak to you, and there certainly won't be any huffing and puffing on my end. I'm just making this as a courtesy call, in case you need to zip up, or make your bed, or perform some other piece of superficial social etiquette, which is the closest thing to instinct you have anymore." She clears her throat, and I can hear her take an long drag on a cigarette. "Synchronize your watch on this, Bill. It's time for *me*."

The thought does cross my mind to call the police, but I'm not sure how I would describe what's happening, and even if I could, there probably wouldn't be a law against it. In hindsight it seems I made a glaring error in having my number listed, except that I felt a certain pride and comfort in the large number of my namesakes in the directory. In the face of such a lengthy roster, the average person would never have tried finding me. But I realize now, in a kind of Custerian catharsis, that one should always factor the boundless energies of the psychotic mind into any home security efforts.

I go to my front door and open it wide, in a blatant concession at humoring this woman. Contrary to her earlier statement to Sang, no one outside of the occasional shoplifter has ever been forcefully removed from the store in my tenure there, and I like to think this has much to do with my skills at conciliation. I freely admit, however, which my perspiring body is communicating in that most universal of languages, I am swimming at this moment in untested waters.

In another minute or so Mrs. Andretti appears in the doorway, in the same, now quite wrinkled, dress, only this time empty-handed; I have often considered it a blessing we don't sell firearms at our store. She strides across the living room without acknowledging my presence and sets herself on the sofa, directly atop the remote control that's resting there on one of the cushions. Immediately the channels start flitting by on the screen, which she watches for a moment before lighting a cigarette. I don't keep any ashtrays in the house, probably because I would never willfully invite a smoker here.

"Something's the matter with your TV," she says and inhales intently, her gaze firmly planted on the screen. "It can't seem to make up its mind."

With her free hand she reached underneath herself, extracting the remote, and the TV comes to rest on a group of Asian youngsters playing baseball. A subtitle informs the English-speaking world it is watching the National Taiwanese little league championship game: over and over we see a Taiwanese outfielder making a spectacular catch against a fence draped with a Taiwanese ad for Kentucky Fried Chicken. "They really should expand the range on these babies," Mrs. Andretti says. "Wouldn't it be slick if we could all control each other's televisions? We'd all have to watch potluck every night of the week."

When I don't say anything, she holds the remote above her head and aims it backward in my direction, her thumb pushing several buttons at once. "These things won't even go twelve feet. I'm not getting any volume."

"You're the one who interrupted my life," I'm surprised to hear myself tell her. "Perhaps you should be the one doing the talking."

"What do you think I've been doing, Bill? A lip-synch contest?" She shakes her head. "Mario would die if he knew I was here, singing to a stranger in our identical floor plan. It's hard enough being heartsick about your wife leaving you without knowing some guy in the next block is laughing his head off at something that's not even close to funny, and he's doing it in your house, or a reasonable facsimile of your house, in the same goddamn spot where you're bawling you're goddamn eyes out." She sets her burning cigarette on the glass surface of my coffee table, then swivels around to face me. "Got any liquor?"

"I wish you would please just get to the point."

Her eyes seem to lose their focus and she turns around again, sliding down the couch until I can just see the top of her head. "Gin is the opposite of tranquility," she says. "I'm not picky about my alcohols, except where it comes to gin. You can look it up in Webster's. It's right there in the antonyms under Peace and Quiet: chaos; meanness; Tanqueray."

The TV starts changing channels anew, at the same furious pace, only this time it would seem to be a deliberate act. "Well, there is no point, of course," she begins, in what I have by now determined is her lecturing voice. "There's just matter and antimatter. Einstein, or whoever came up with that theory never said anything about there being a point. Your problem is you don't know what I'm going to say or do next and it's got your pores opened up like the spillways on Aswan High Dam and here I am wondering if this masterpiece of twentieth-century engineering is going to save me or drown me. It's Mario, baby, I already told you. Mario needs your help, Bill. He's deep into causality, just like you are. He wants the explanation, man, and all I can do is pop the flipper one more time, smack the pinball where the bells start going off. I don't got time to know what it fucking means. I'm just trying to get my quarter's worth without the whole fucking thing going tilt on me."

She relaxes her grip on the remote and we are presented with the image of a Taiwanese manager pacing in a Taiwanese dugout. By now it's impossible for me to take my mind off her errant cigarette. I go to the kitchen for a coffee mug, and there, above the saucers, I see the Chivas Regal my mother keeps stocked at each of her various haunts. When next I see her, I will calmly explain I fed her scotch to a madwoman and leave it at that. She has leaned by now to curb her curiosity when she's around me; it produces the opposite of its intended effect.

"Here," I tell Mrs. Andretti when I return to the living room. "The cup's for your cigarette. I'm sure you'll want to drink the scotch directly from the bottle, that being consistent with your style."

"Oh, Christ," she says, standing up and taking hold of her cigarette. "I can ash in Mario's Buick. Put the goddamn Chivas in your holster and let's blow this taco stand."

"What if I told you I had a previous engagement?"

Mrs. Andretti laughs and picks up the remote, firing it back over her shoulder, and I watch as the face of a Taiwanese Vin Scully devolves into a million random pixels.

According to the clock in Mario's Buick, we've been driving now for over thirty minutes and we still don't seem to be any closer to our destination, wherever that is. Mrs. Andretti keeps pushing the seek button on the radio, then sampling the station content for a millisecond or two before pressing on to the next frequency. This behavior might be explained as the nervous habit of someone who's lost, except that Mrs. Andretti is also making high-pitched skidding noises around every turn and rumbling acceleration noises after every stop, all with the manic enthusiasm of a small child. Clearly this is the stuff of one's biggest mistake in life.

At the moment we are stopped at a busy intersection — we've passed by here three times already — waiting for the light to change. To our left, in a top-down, blood red Cabriolet, a young woman of perhaps Nordic descent is deftly applying her makeup even as she bobs her blonde head to a music whose salient characteristic is a throbbing subwoofered bass that practically lifts her car off the pavement with every reproduced note. Ahead of us, a Waspy older gentleman encased in an air-conditioned Mercedes is talking to someone on his cellular phone while he somberly peruses the funny papers. To our right, a teenaged melancholiac has tilted his runneled face to the late afternoon sun as though actively courting melanoma.

When my eyes return to Mrs. Andretti she is staring at *me*, as if I were the most exotic species in this menagerie. "I really thought you got it by now," she says, shaking her head. "Everybody's driving around L.A. in these superimposed states waiting to be observed; otherwise they'll never come to life, like sea monkeys that never make it to the aquarium — you know, suspended animation. But the question Schrodinger never got into, the real biggie, if you ask me, comes down to what I like to call experiential economics: If you throw a goddamn circus, you'd better make sure there are people willing to show up for it."

The left turn arrow shifts to green, and we watch Miss Cabriolet finish her makeup on the very next beat, driving in perfect rhythm with her fellow turners, so as not to break the chain. Mrs. Andretti steps on the gas herself, while at the same time merging dueling sitars on the radio with a hoarse-voiced woman belting out her recipe for ketchup.

"I used to run a head shop in San Francisco," Mrs. Andretti states, almost sadly, and turns the car, without sound effects, into a newer residential neighborhood. "I couldn't afford to live there back then, so I'd take the bus in from Oakland, which was where I was crashing at the time. Sometimes I'd get picked up at my stop by commuters needing an extra rider for the car pool lane, and there was this chick driving an Alpha once — actually, she was about the same age I am right now, which is thirty-something — and she asks me if I'm going to the City and I say, you bet, and the whole way over the bridge she can't keep her fingers off the buttons on her radio, jumping stations like her time is a whole lot faster than everybody else's, like she can hear whole tunes in the space of one note.

"Well, I knew a lot of methers and cokers in those days, sniffers of just about every denomination — I'd even seen the Thorazine dance by then — but this chick wasn't none of those — she was something else entirely — and when she left me off I thought she wasn't long for this world, and that maybe

I would be the last person to see her alive. At least on earth."

She turns up the volume on a pair of gray whales groaning into an underwater microphone. "I may not've known where she was headed," Mrs. Andretti nearly shouts above the radio, then cranks the wheel hard as we are propelled at too high a speed into somebody's driveway, "but right now I sure as hell know where she was coming from."

The car stops just short of a garage door, and when Mrs. Andretti cuts the engine, the car shimmies a good while before we are actually at rest. The house looming before us does bear a resemblance to my own, at least superficially, though the robin egg blue it and its counterparts have been painted would never pass muster with my homeowner's association, a cabal fiercely dedicated to the earth tones.

"End of the line," Mrs. Andretti says and reaches for the bottle of scotch sitting on the floor between my legs. She unscrews the cap, discarding it over her shoulder, and takes a good slug before offering the bottle to me.

"I never drink when I'm on duty," I tell her. "Especially when I have no idea what my duty is."

"What if I told you it was getting shitfaced with me in a stolen Buick?"

"Stolen?"

"OK, borrowed."

"I'd say that wasn't in my job description."

She nods and takes another slug, then opens her door and sets the Chivas on the ground outside. "Just act natural," she says. "Or, I mean, the way you always act."

She stands up, gathering her dress and the scotch, and then comes around to my side of the car and opens my door, ordering me out with a throw of her head. For a moment I consider fleeing, but then I remind myself I haven't been forced into any of this, that in fact I'm here because I've chosen to be here, albeit subconsciously, and that running at this point in my life from an aging female hophead with small-appliance-phobia is one of the more ludicrous scenes I can think of.

Mrs. Andretti starts walking toward what I assume is the realm of Mario, and I follow in the practiced nonchalance I have developed over my years of suffering fools. At the front door she pauses and looks through one of the windows in the upper half and, apparently satisfied with what she has seen within, swings the door open, and together we cross the border into a frontier of certain weirdness.

At first nothing seems out of the ordinary — the standard cottage cheese ceiling with smoke detector, the neutrally-tiled entryway leading to the neutrally-carpeted living room — but then as we round the corner, a player piano, sans bench, and on the floor next to the sustain pedal, a piece of wedding cake, at one time thoughtfully frozen as a memento, now as haphazardly thawed, with a little plastic groom lying face down in the frosting, at the feet of his little plastic bride. The soundtrack for all of this is an intermittent chirping whose source and timbre are impossible to locate, due to its random interval. What's most disconcerting, though, is that I've heard this noise somewhere else, and I still can't figure out what it is.

Mrs. Andretti waits here a moment, as though interpreting the spoor of some rare and dangerous animal, then moves into a thicket of Scotch-guarded furniture, where a fair-skinned, small-featured man in a three-piece suit lies face up on an unmade sofa bed, a pair of plastic forks clutched in one of his smooth white hands, the other placed reverently over his heart as if pledging allegiance, to what I cannot say. He turns his head, mantis-like, and regards us a moment before assuming his original position — a swarthy international Grand Prix veteran, obviously this man is not.

"Mario," Mrs. Andretti says and leaves it at that, seemingly without effect. Her voice, which was so penetrating in other settings, now sounds muted, perhaps by the drapes and the wall-to-wall carpeting, or, more probably, by the oppressive amount of neurosis in the room. "Mario, honey," she says, "listen to me. I've brought along a disinterested party. In case you wanted to get a few things off your chest."

For quite a while each of us holds his own peculiar ground, and then Mario's face, which up to now has been a virtual blank slate, suddenly reddens and distorts, a face on the verge of crying, except that it just as quickly normalizes and we are back to status quo. In the next moment a voice, cloaked in a Midwestern rather than Italian accent, comes up out of him: "I wanted to share our cake together."

"Honey," Mrs. Andretti says and shoots me a look as though I should be the one responding, "don't you think scotch would be more appropriate, I mean under the circumstances?"

"I'm sorry," Mario says, in as pained a voice as I remember hearing. "I dropped our cake, Patricia. I don't want you to think I did it on purpose."

"For godsakes, Mario, everything you've ever done in your life has been on purpose."

Again Mario's face ruptures momentarily and Mrs. Andretti sits down on the sofa bed at his feet, propping herself up with her elbows. "Besides," she says, in a much gentler tone, "that cake has freezer burn, Honey. You might as well eat Play Doh, for all the flavor it has left in it."

"It's our cake," Mario says. "Our cake could never taste like Play Doh."

Mrs. Andretti motions for me to get a glass out of the kitchen, and when I return she's sitting by Mario's side, having worried the plastic forks out of his hand. "This here is Bill Harris," she tells Mario as she pours at least five fingers of scotch into the glass. "He does this sort of thing for a living — talks people down out of their trees, I mean."

Mario waves off the scotch and slowly tilts his head up to look at me a moment before laying it carefully back down again. "I'm not in a tree," he says flatly. "I'm in our home. I'm with my wife. This is where we live. You call this Harris a cab, Patricia. It'll take him back where he came from."

He withdraws from his pants a black billfold and presents it on his outstretched palm. "There's money in my wallet," he says, and, as though to corroborate this testimony, the mysterious bird produced its one, grating note.

Mrs. Andretti downs two-digits worth of the Chivas. "Goddamn it, Bill, if you're not going to roll out the B.S., at least you could put a new battery in that fucking smoke detector."

I glance at Mrs. Andretti, who looks at this instant like someone waiting in a laundromat for her underwear to dry, and then pitch my voice, softly, to Mario: "I have no intention of meddling in your personal affairs, Mr. Andretti. I am in fact an ambassador of sorts, but I have no experience in the field of marital counseling. Your offer is very generous, but I can pick up my own cab fare, thank you. Which doesn't mean I don't appreciate the pickle you're in — I really do — but I don't see how I can have any material bearing on your situa—"

"You two are so full of it," Mrs. Andretti says matter-of-factly. "That's why I wanted you to meet each other, I though you might just cancel each other out. Instead I'm getting this amplified signal, this blaring white noise that makes me think I'm sitting in a waterfall. In case you haven't noticed, Mario, I took everything back today, the whole goddamn museum. Edison will have to raise the rates, they'll be losing so much business. Bill, here, is the guy who receives the merchandise. He's the one who takes down the story that goes with it and then puts everything back on the shelves so the next chump can have at it. He wouldn't take *you* back though, Mario. That's why I had to bring him here. It's the first time he's ever had to make a house call, so I hope you'll forgive his retardedness. I frankly thought he'd have better material than this."

Mario is sitting up now, staring at his wife, like a child engrossed in one of Disney's animated features.

"You think he's all bummed out," she says, standing up, and I swear she's talking to the both of us, "just like you thought you were all jazzed when we got married, when we did crepes at that joint on the Seine, like everything was set for life. That whole-ever-after number. Man, this is my Declaration of Independence, so listen up. It has a lot in common with that forefather version, the one all those cats in wigs and wooden teeth put together over drinks, only mine bears just one signature. They didn't say nothin' about happiness and neither do I. It's that whole pursuit of happiness gig, that's what I'm talking about here. Freedom, OK? That's another one of their big goddamn codewords."

She puts her hands on her hips and stares at us a moment with her unyielding green eyes. "I guess I'll have to spell it out for you then. The D of I ain't nothing but walking papers, man. D-I-V-O-R-C-E. Everybody agrees to remain apart from each other forever, that's pretty much it in a nutshell. Somewhere along the line people got the idea it was a marriage license, the same way they bought into all this salt-of-the-earth Pilgrim crap. You know, about people coming to America to flee persecution. What never gets explained is that they totally fucking deserved it. That for every Tom Jefferson, there were fifty Charlie Mansons, smokin drugs and branchin out to lay their weird trips on all sorts of native peoples. It's no different now:

people run away so they won't have to listen to anybody but themselves, which is basically the story of all criminals. What I'm saying is ninety nine point nine percent of the people who ever landed in the U.S. of A. are these antisocial, egomaniacal deadbeats, and they've been pouring nonstop into this country for over two hundred years. By now we've just about got the market cornered on flakes, and there ain't a whole lot of export on those. The world's supply of denial genes is right here on native soil, mixing together into one big denial gene pool. It's time to face facts: we're living in a big goddamn vineyard of freaks!

"Now I'm not saying I'm any different. I've spent my whole life perfecting not being like anybody else which is the only thing we Americans have in common. That's where the new science comes in, to try to map this whole goddamn thing out. The Second Goddamn Law of Thermodynamics. Chaos. String Theory. The Nth Dimension. They say it all makes sense if they take it out to twenty-seven parallel universes, which is pretty goddamn strung out, if you ask me. You do acid enough times, you'll be just as strung out. The Theory of Everything. Try to hold that one in your buffer for more than a second or two."

She pauses here a moment, as though to grant us the opportunity to do this. "We've hit rock bottom here, guys. It's time to bail, it really is. But where in hell will we go this time? We've been kicked out of everywhere else and goddamn Mars doesn't have any goddamn atmosphere."

She sits down on the bed again, looking spent, almost as spent as I feel having listened to her over the past few hours. Mario seems invigorated, though, like a man newly risen from a calm and efficient sleep.

"Shopping," he says and looks at me, as though I, of all people, should understand perfectly well. "That's where I met Patricia," he says. "At the mall. People go shopping when they're sad. It helps take the edge off things."

Mrs. Andretti sighs and lets her torso fall back on the mattress, then balances the glass of scotch on her expansive forehead. "You want to go shopping?"

"I'll drive," Mario says.

"No," she says, her head still weighed down by my mother's Chivas. "Let Bill drive. He'll make a dandy chauffeur."

They both look at me expecting a reply, while in my head I search for another situation I might have encountered in my life that roughly approximates this one. What becomes quickly evident is that even if such an unlikely scenario existed, I'm certain, for survival's sake, it would never have been allowed into my long-term memory. "I hope you're well insured," is all I manage to come up with.

Mrs. Andretti comes up smirking, a ring on her forehead where the glass made an impression, and hands me the keys to Mario's Buick.

"You've got to be kidding," she says.

It's a little past eight, nearly an hour left before the Galleria closes, but still the traffic is copious. In recent years rush hour has become unpredictable, though slowly the gaps are being filled in — soon we will have entire rush days, rush weeks, rush years.

Ahead of us lies a compendium of taillights that stretches on for miles, finally wending its way, out of view, into the hills separating one population center from the next. The effect is like one of those shots you see of molten lava on TV documentaries, only it's running uphill instead of down, as though the film were being shown in reverse, or the earth itself somehow gained the ability to repair itself.

The stop-and-go affords me the chance to watch the Andrettis in the rearview mirror — I have no idea if they are moving toward reunion, or dissolution, or some way station in between. At the moment they are sitting apart and there is nothing in their body language to suggest they might soon be joined, though there is nothing to suggest they won't be either. They resemble strangers on a bus leading separate lives in close proximity, who by chance must endure a comradeship, at least to the end of the ride.

As for me, like any good chauffeur, I remain a dispassionate observer. Oh, I know what Mrs. Andretti would say, in her sensational mix of modern science and new-age pyschobabble — that there is no seeing without effecting, that the notion of the innocent bystander is just another excuse put forth by the vast majority of dishonorable Americans.

But I am university-trained and well aware of Heidegger's — or is it Heisenberg's — principle of uncertainty: it applied not to the broad strokes of human reality, but to the inner workings of the modeled atom, where the blink of an eye puts quarks and muons in a dither. We mortals, on the other hand, live in the calculated world of Newton, where a chosen few in funny suits are precisely catapulted to the moon, where this same elite is doomed to fall to earth again at the appointed hour, while the rest of us watch on television.

Still, I can hear Mrs. Andretti's rebuttal, delivered in one of her colorful and timely spasms; surely, she would argue, the human soul is made up of such tiny and precarious debris that to take hold of it at one end is to let it slide through one's fingers at the other. And who am I to quarrel with this? Fortunately, there is no place for such abstract notions in my routine: I am the driver, after all, and like my peers, I must keep one eye on the road at all times. To attempt anything more would be flirting with disaster.

I feel the eyes of someone staring at me from the adjoining lane, and when I swivel my head to look, the gargoyle face of a rottweiler bares its teeth and scrabbles against the passenger window of the next car over, apparently trying to get at me. I'm so startled that I practically hit the car ahead of us, slamming on the brakes, and I watch in the rearview as the line of cars behind our own all lurch, one after another, against their reins.

We are close enough now to reach the Galleria by side streets, and in one swift motion, a la Mrs. Andretti, I leave the boulevard and speed off into the neighborhood I grew up in, an early housing development of modest homes and tree-lined streets that has slowly given way to ostentatious pseudo-mansions featuring the accoutrement of self-imposed royalty: ionic columns and balustrades, tile roofs and multi-car garages. The streets as usual are empty; it would seem half the homes stand vacant, waiting to be sold, with the rest owned by people who never seem to occupy them, or perhaps, always do, as if they've reached the ultimate goal of leading their lives entirely from within. For a moment I slow down as we pass the site of my boyhood home, a typical three bedroom bungalow, but my heart staggers when I see a monument of glass brick and palm trees in its place, and when I glance in the rearview and see that the Andrettis haven't noticed, that they remain in the same state as they were before, my foot, as though acting independently, lays heavy on the accelerator, and we are delivered once more to the blaring signage of commercialdom.

The Galleria, with the sun just setting now behind it, is pressed against the sky-like mountains. There are only a few cars remaining in the lot, which is only logical so near to closing, so far away from Christmas. Still, I can't remember ever parking this close to the entrance, which I might take as a good omen if I only held a belief in such things. The Andrettis exit their respective doors without command, and abreast we walk the twenty or so feet through the unfiltered air, through the huge glass membrane into Paradise. I realize now I am lightheaded — in fact I am lightbodied — and we travel as creatures beyond the material world, or perhaps buoyed by it, on a cushion of earthly attempts to reach Heaven. Like wildfire, a birthday party from my youth, a gathering of six-year-old crewcut boys and their pretty young mothers, and the guest of honor, Charles Lennox, a smaller-than-average boy with frail sight, his glasses sliding off his face into the cake beneath him — later he would turn to drugs, then to Jesus; the sandy voice of Lorna LaMott, coaxing me into trouble in the fourth grade — in the fifth grade I would spurn her friendship with a shower of ice plant, and later, years after our paths had diverged, she would take her own life in a motel room near Phoenix; then Twonbley, the pigeon-toed somnambulist, and Eugene Gershwitz, the first person I ever knew to own his own car; there is Kenny, the Korean man who gave me my first job; there is a man called Labrador who my mother caught stealing my father's new golf clubs on the day after Christmas. All of these spirits are synaptic misgivings, like caricatures from an imaginary past — except they are real — they belong to my life. Someone is crying, huge exaggerated sobs — what else? — and watching my hand on the rail of the escalator, I swear I can see my pulse. When our eyes meet, the baby's and mine, she stops crying, gaping at me with cloudless orbs, and they hold their gaze as she descends to some other place, bound securely in her mother's arms. Meanwhile, we are being transported — up, up — there is no more sound — and I see myself — in brief reflection, a figurine — in the lens of the surveillance camera that records us. Sang is waiting in Home Electronics, with my grandfather, circa 1960, who holds by the scruff of its neck an expressionless albino rabbit. Together we watch as the dozen odd screens fill up with images of musicals and dancing: Fred and Ginger, Frank and Bing, Cyd Charisse, and Jane Powell. Gene Kelly, the movie star, is telling his life story to a crowd of adoring fans, but the whole thing's a lie, and when I see the truth, that the boy dancing for the sheer joy of it, is, in face, me, I know, as my heart folds in on itself, that I've become, by necessity, by all known laws of physics, someone different that myself.

I wish I could say I was wakened in Kansas, by Aunty Em, or Ray Bolger, or even Bert Lahr, but instead, it's Francine, from Optical, who, I suppose because of her white uniform, was the closest thing to a doctor they could find. At first I don't hear anything — I can just see — Francine mouthing "Are you all right?" and looming above her, the grotesque faces of late-night shoppers who have gathered around the spectacle, which is me, of a man collapsed on a marked-down Persian rug.

But then I recognize the voice of Mrs. Andretti, whom I'm certain even God would have trouble censoring: "The thing about being dead," she says, staring down at me, her arms folded across her chest, "you have to be alive to begin with." Mario, who is standing next to her, nods his head solemnly, and as though I've been given a clean bill of health, the crowd quickly disperses, leaving me alone with the Andrettis — and Sang, who, for some unknown reason, is still here at this late hour.

But I suppose the most peculiar thing about that night is that no one ever asked about my condition. The paramedics were never summoned, or if they were, they never arrived, though, in hindsight, I don't believe it was for lack of concern. It was more that some brand of intimacy had been established between us, however temporal, and that each understood intuitively that problems of my health would shortly be resolved. Sang wheeled in a television, and like friends gathered in someone's real-life living room, we watched movies long into the night, slumped in our respective sofas. And I remember distinctly — this was not a dream, mind you, though it might be characterized as the invention of a wayward heart — that moment at daybreak when the sun's light supersedes any created by man, and, seeing it fall on the Andrettis, who lay together like children in slumber, and on Sang, who was smiling in a dream of untold proportions. I thought, these human beings truly are blessed, as though they'd risen, in that one shining moment, above our diluted race.

MICHELLE LATIOLAIS

The Legal Case

The young woman knows of a legal case in which on a winding mountain road an ex-husband intercepts his former wife. They have been divorced by some type of official decree and the woman resides now with another man. She is carrying this new man's child; the ex-husband says something to the effect, "I've heard you're pregnant. You sure are. I'm going to stomp it out of you." He rams his knee into her belly; the baby is born with a crushed skull— is born dead.

The ex-husband is let off the charge of murder because the law, or the way the penal code was written in 1872, didn't expressly state that killing a fetus in this manner was criminal behavior, feticide being distinguished from abortion, being an entirely different thing and not illegal in 1872. Why?

Because there is the more important issue, the dispositive question of whether or not the fetus was a human being on February 23rd, 1969? Murder is the unlawful killing of a human being and in the Legislature of 1850 "human being" had the settled common law meaning of a person who had been born alive.

Advances in medical science have redefined what a live or viable human being is, but not before February 23rd, 1969, when a man kneed the fetus out of his ex-wife's belly, had the law managed to redefine its terms. The ex-husband could not be convicted of murder by a law that would not convict him of murder, let alone convict him of feticide, which wasn't a crime.

The young woman understood that the judge, the counsel, the court could call "stomping" a fetus out of a woman's belly a crime, but that because it was not enumerated in the statute, it could not be punished under that statute. We could all agree a crime had taken place, but if the law didn't enumerate it, the law as it existed could not be used to convict.

The young woman wonders if she could sit here now in this cafe with pencil and paper and come up with every possible example of criminal

behavior surrounding women and men and unborn fetuses, wonders if even
the most brilliantly generative minds could ever possibly meet with law what
the real world serves up? She decides she must try though, because every
horrible scenario she can come up with would then be covered by the law.
Wouldn't—if her mind were particularly generative—the law have broader
and broader scope, wouldn't there be fewer and fewer crimes that the law
didn't cover? If she could make her mind so utterly contemptible, so hatefully
imaginative, wouldn't she have done the world a great service? Wouldn't
there be fewer crimes the law didn't cover, fewer crimes for the world to
surprise us with?

Before she even begins to move her pencil along the page she is reminded
of Zeno's paradox, her mind implying she will never actually achieve
comprehensive law, will never actually quite get there; and she is reminded
also of Occam's razor, that "entities are not to be multiplied beyond
necessity," and she sees a pregnant belly sliced so methodically, so finely, so
many times from breasts to mons veneris the fetus is born through gills—her
imagination is a tremendous lack of consolation in the face of the world's vast
store of unimaginable events which happen every day. Just then she is
distracted by a couple at the front of the cafe:

The man props his foot on the spindle of the cafe chair and thus his knee
comes to just below his chin because he is leaning forward toward a woman he
finds enthralling. The young woman watching can read this from every
momentary tableau the man folds into, folds out of, his foot finding its way
back to the floor, his back even more tilted toward his wife, he is animate with
love of her, his arms now laid across the table, both palms resting open right
beneath her face, his head lifted to her, smiling, talking through the smile, his
words continuous, his body is draped across the table to her, but now instantly
rampant, he is talking to the waiter, ordering something, the young woman
watching cannot tell as yet what, the waiter vanishes, and the man, his
shoulders swoop down again toward the table and he rests his head on his arm,
but then he raises his head and brings the hand of that arm and tucks it beneath
his ear so that he's now resting on an elbow, talking the entire time, his eyes
cast out toward the street then at her, a finger stiffening from his other hand,
pointing, she is laughing, accused, and the finger waggles a bit in the air and his

foot is once again propped on the chair rung, his knee up close to his chin, close to her belly, they are seated so near to each other, they are both laughing and his body straightens slowly, quickly, like time-lapse photography, a flower stalk emerging up out of the ground, sword-shaped leaves flaring away from the stalk, shooting outward, the flower bud forming furled now unfurling, blossoming, his body is so completely in thrall to hers, the fine camber of pregnancy beneath her white trapeze dress a pearl within the bivalve which is both their bodies, a desire so physically realized he can barely keep himself from the appetite which is his life with her, now, in these days, a hunger so happily hunger, an oh god yes in every conjugation of his body again and again and again,

it is, it is becoming, it will be,

he is in her body, he has not touched her once though all his body is of one verb, the young woman watching can see this, one verb.

The young woman watching cannot take her eyes from this scene in the cafe. Battering at it from every angle is the legal case:

Keeler v. Superior Court
Supreme Court of California
2 Cal. 3d 619, 470 P.2d 617 (1970)

[Five months after obtaining an interlocutory decree of divorce, a husband intercepted his wife on a mountain road. She was in an advanced state of pregnancy by another man; fetal movements had already been observed by her and her obstetrician. Her husband said to her, "I hear you're pregnant," glanced at her body and added, "You sure are. I'm going to stomp it out of you." He shoved his knee into her abdomen and struck her. The fetus was delivered stillborn, its head fractured.]

That is the actual wording of the case. The young woman thinks of the mountain road, of what it means or does not mean, of how evocative it is of isolation, or perhaps of something else? Is it legal coding for a certain class of people? Or a certain area where there is a certain class of people? And there are other curiosities. There is the first decree, the interlocutory decree of divorce, which, if you read the grammar of the sentence, the husband has asked for and received, and then the second decree: "I'm going to stomp it out of you." You see, you see, all the verbs are wrong, he got his divorce, he can't also stamp out his ex-wife's future children. He can and he does and even more strangely he uses his knee as a foot, the knee remade into foot, or was it the verb remade?

And what of these last words, "its head fractured"? This peculiar wording, do heads fracture or get fractured? Don't we say a fractured skull? A broken head having almost a cartoonish benignity, like "hey, you're busting my chops," said in a Bugs Bunny voice? So many words all wrong — and most cruelly the law worded in such a way that neither the word crime nor the act to which it is referent mean anything at all—

DISASTERS OF EARTH AND MAN

*The fate of finite beings
leaves them at the edge of themselves.
And this edge is torn.*
—Georges Bataille

JIM KRUSOE

A Distant View Of Hills

I think it was a gloomy Tuesday evening when I first lay down to stroke a strand of Marsha's long, dark hair and thought of how she'd cut it off just a few weeks earlier, following that incident involving an overhead fan in a not-so-good-but-still-expensive French restaurant located in one of the farther suburbs of Los Angeles, where I was living.

"Here," Marsha had said, "you take it. You're the one who always liked it so much," and with those words she walked out of my life.

But why was she so angry at me, I asked myself. I wasn't the one who picked that particular restaurant, or even chose that particular table beneath the ceiling fan, though come to think of it, I was the one who spooned the extra sauce onto her *lapin roti* spilling just a bit down the front of her generously cut dress, causing her to leap from her chair straight into the whirling blades above her head. Even so, later, on our mostly silent drive back home, Marsha had to admit that it wasn't so much the actual heat as the idea of heat in general that had bothered her.

As a result, now I was alone, just another Mr. Lonely Guy like so many other Mr. Lonely Guys, in my black and white wing-tips, my pleated midnight blue pants and white conga shirt, ready to roam the streets and byways of our city in search of romance and perhaps a friend.

The night was overcast. I could feel the beginnings of a light drizzle as I found myself near the center of the city at a private club I knew of called "The Peaceable Kingdom." What was unusual about "The Peaceable Kingdom" was that, once accepted as a member, each patron, after entering, was expected to choose the mask of an animal he or she would wear, and then keep it on for the entire evening. Indeed, to remove it, even for something as awkward as a sneeze, was to risk expulsion by the bouncer, a large man (I'm assuming it was the same person each time) wearing the mask of a rare black rhino. The club offered a variety of species to choose from, but I found that most of the regulars, like me, after a few times of experimentation, soon settled on one favorite mask for every visit. I had begun as a horned owl, for example, then tried out a panther, then a tiger, but finally settled for a jackal. And the same pattern was evident in others as well, so that far from being, as one might expect, a place of majestic beasts and exotic creatures, most evenings the place was inhabited by a group of happy squirrels, a few rabbits, and maybe even a rat or two. Elephants, lions, bears and so on, were usually the mark of a newcomer.

The cuisine of "The Peaceable Kingdom" was both simple and ingenious: For those wearing the heads of rodents or herbivores, the club offered a variety of vegetarian dishes — wilted greens spiced with a touch of garlic, a tray of fresh alfalfa sprouts sprayed with a mist of lemon, nuts in a light cream sauce, even peeled avocados on a stick, with each football-shaped treat studded with crystals of rock salt. As a jackal, my own favorite dish was tiny frankfurters done up as field mice, with wisps of dill for whiskers, little wedges of bacon for the ears, and for a tail a single chive that was thick enough to allow a diner to pick it up and drop it down his throat.

That night the club was quiet. A herd of Guernseys were grazing in a corner, and several rabbits were whispering into one another's ears at the bar. I sat at a booth in front of a reproduction of the club's namesake, the famous Quaker ideal depicting lions and lambs curled up together. In this version, however the artist had also included giant carrots, tomatoes, and tree-like stalks of celery, so the question of who got what to eat was even more of a puzzle. In my booth, overcome by a sudden wave of loneliness, I wept quietly into my mask and then, pulling myself together, ordered several field mice and a half dozen chicken hearts.

I had finished all but one of the delicious mice and was poking at the hearts when I saw her — by whom I mean a female jackal looking around as if this were her first time in the club. I invited her to join me, and suggested she try the remaining mouse. She did, and responded by ordering a half dozen more, and whether there was magic in the air, or just some mysterious toxic chemical leaking from the freshly laid carpeting that caused two strangers to become more than friends, I'll never know. Her name was Belinda ("It means 'Be

Beautiful' in Spanish," she said), and later that night, we watched from her comfortable queen-sized bed a rerun of an episode from one of my favorite television shows, "The Swamp of Time," in which Uncle Jed, his pirogue crushed by the charge of a bull alligator so that he is unable to perform his daily routine of helping maimed and dying wild animals, learns, by way of compensation, the pleasures of settling down in his cabin with a good book.

Belinda said that she enjoyed the show, but, she confessed she couldn't get all those animals dying without Uncle Jed out of her mind. Probably, she ventured, it was because she herself was a travel agent who specialized in tours for the terminally ill. She had, she said, "a great deal of sympathy for their situation," and explained that her agency, Sunset Travel, had made quite a name for itself by arranging nurses, medical support, and even "relocation experts," her name for those whose job it was to silently and swiftly dispose of any fatalities along the way ("we call them 'sidetrips,'" she said), with minimum disturbance to the others on the tour.

"They like to see ruins," she told me. "Also the biggest and the tallest and the oldest — that kind of stuff. I guess if they think they've seen the best, or whatever, they feel like they can skip everything that led up to it." Belinda paused as she rearranged a false eyelash which had crazily plunged into one eye. "Tell me about *your* last vacation," she said.

I thought for a moment. Before my last vacation I had written letters to several parts of the country asking the owners of various resorts to describe a typical view that might be seen from one of their rooms. I had been, I wrote, "in the city too long," and had decided that what I needed was a change of scenery. Most of the replies were cursory — the usual illustrated brochure, a list of rates, and an occasional wistful scrawl "Hope to see you," in the same broad, purple ink favored by PTA committee members and doctors' receptionists. The note that caught my attention however, was none of these. It was simply a few lines, penciled in a sort of painful, sixth-grade hand on lined paper apparently torn from a pad with spirals along the topmost edge, and, misunderstanding my request, described the view not from a guest's room, but from the place where the person was writing. "There is a sort of farmyard here," it said, "and I'm looking at a wheelbarrow, which has a kind of glazed or frosted look because we've just had a little rain. And next to it are some leghorns, and in the back there is a distant view of hills."

The Bar-H Dude Ranch consisted of the main ranch house, three small cabins, a stable with two horses (Blacky and Whitey), and of course a farmyard, complete with chickens. (The wheelbarrow had been moved or perhaps stolen.) "Howdy," said the grey-haired peculiarly-featured woman who greeted me on my first day. "I'm the widow Harkens, and this" (she pointed to an aged man in faded denims) "is Gramps. There's no other guest right now but you."

That night, after a roast chicken dinner I fell asleep. I was exhausted, so it wasn't until well after midnight that I was awakened by the sounds of what seemed to be large animals moving just outside the walls of my cabin, which, unfortunately, had no windows at all, so I was unable to sneak up and see what sort of creatures they were. I say "animals," but in truth they made a curious shuffling sound, almost as if they were walking on two feet instead of four. I lay there in the dark, not knowing what to expect, and then, as suddenly as they had come they shuffled off, leaving me alone.

The next morning, over scrambled eggs, when I mentioned the events of the night before to the widow, she explained that the noises had been made by rats, which found the foliage at the edge of my cabin to be a favorite hiding place. "Don't worry," she said. "Everything sounds bigger at night." Still, after breakfast, curious to inspect the spot where the mysterious noises had occurred, when I looked outside my cabin, not only was I surprised to find that there was no foliage to speak of, but the dirt itself had been swept clean.

The rest of the day was glorious. I sat in an aluminum lawn chair, much as Uncle Jed himself when he found himself pirogue-less, passing the time reading and occasionally looking up at the distant view of hills. Oddly enough, Gramps informed me with a sort of swaggering manner I found inexplicably offensive, the hills were not so distant after all, but because of a combination of factors, both vegetal and atmospheric, they only appeared to be. They were, in fact, no more that a few miles away, a ride of a couple hours at most. I decided that the following day I would pack a lunch, saddle either Blacky or Whitey, and make the trip to see the hills myself. That night after dinner I turned in early, and if there were any sounds outside my cabin I have to say I didn't hear them.

And so the next morning, after a breakfast of three eggs over easy, a bowl of Frosted Flakes, a slice of melon and several homemade biscuits, I saddled up one of the horses and set off toward the hills. It was another perfect day — sunny, with the temperature in the low sixties and a slight breeze from the north. As Gramps, who had looked unusually fatigued over breakfast, had predicted, it didn't take long before I reached the hills. Leaving my horse tied to a stunted tree, I climbed up a couple hundred yards to where there appeared to be an entrance to a long-abandoned mine, and I suppose from that point on you can guess the rest: The mine turned out to be a secret laboratory; Gramps, far from being the senile old codger I had initially supposed, turned out to be an internationally-known scientist, notorious for his experiments that involved splicing together the genes of humans and animals (his most perfect creation so far the widow Harkens). I managed to stumble over a pile of loose rock, there was a shout, a cry, a discovery, and then a struggle between us in which a lantern got knocked over, some smoke, f ire, the cries of Gramps as he saw a lifetime's work go up in f lames, the screams of his helpless creations, my own hoarse coughs as I crawled slowly toward the entrance, clutching the stirrups, pulling myself up into Whitey's saddle, and then, back at The Bar-H, putting the widow, who had reverted into inconsolable howling, out of her pain with a couple quick blasts from the shotgun kept around for chicken hawks.

"Wow, that sounds *so* interesting," Belinda said, and told me how, coincidentally, on her last tour, she had taken a group to an obscure natural wonder in the southwestern United States called "The Bat Cave," believed to hold the largest concentration of little brown bats in the entire world. "Once inside the cave," she continued, "the stench of the guano was overwhelming. The acridity of the droppings (this being the greatest unmined concentration of such nitrates on earth) made it impossible to breathe except by clasping handkerchiefs over our mouths and nostrils, and even so, one middle-aged tourist, Mr. Kessler, who had been suffering from acute kidney failure, fainted dead away and we had to leave him for the relocation experts, who were already complaining bitterly and demanding time-and-a-half pay.

"We pressed ahead," she continued, "to where, thanks to a draft of air from an underground river, the smell abated. Moving forward, often on our knees and hands, at times having to drag some of the weaker members of our party by means of ropes tied under their arms, working in total darkness except for what was illuminated by our special miner's lamps, at last we reached our main destination, an immense cavern that had apparently been the center of some ancient Indian rituals, its walls decorated with strange pictures of half-human and half-animal forms — coyote men and bird women, elk and snakes with human heads, and at times the figures of people who, instead of a hand might have an antelope's hoof, or a crow's wing for an arm. The entire ceiling was smooth, like the inside of a skull, and we wondered aloud how those artists whose work was displayed at or near the very top of this gigantic cavern could have drawn it there without the evidence of great ladders or platforms. Mr. Shanberg, a retired geologist with hardening of the arteries, speculated that at one time the cave may have been filled with water, and the artists had sat in boats as they completed the topmost, and therefore oldest work.

"So there we were, staring awestruck at the still-fresh power of those ancient drawings, when suddenly all three carbide lamps, none of which had never even once failed in any circumstance, sputtered and went out, leaving us plunged in utter darkness. There was a moment of silence, then an awful animal moan. When at last the lamp was re-lit, I saw Mr. Le Donne, the retired host of a television science show for children, lying face-down on the ground, his body horribly mauled by I knew not what, his hand clutching a piece of reddish brownish fur, or hair. Then the light went out again. There was another scream, and when it came back on there was the body of Miss Ketterer, a former high school composition teacher who was living out the last of her days the tragic victim of 'white lung,' a condition brought about by diagramming too many sentences on chalky blackboards. She too had been mauled nearly beyond recognition, and was clutching, even as she might have held a pointer or eraser in her former occupation, a fistful of that same reddish hair.

"'We have to get out of here,' remarked a doctor from Milwaukee who had an advanced case ('self-diagnosed,' he told us proudly) of cirrhosis of the liver.

"'Yes,' replied an accountant from St. Paul who just earlier that day had repaired his malfunctioning pacemaker using only a borrowed paper clip and four feet of dental floss."

Belinda paused. "The rest is pretty much as you'd guess," she said. "We made it to the entrance without further mishaps, but by the time the relocation crew returned to the cave the bodies were gone. Not only that, when we reported our stories to the police we were slapped with a hefty fine for entering a wildlife sanctuary, and the entire case was dismissed under the category of some sort of mass hallucination, which was not surprising given the state of most of those left on the tour, one of whom, Mrs. Loach, took an unscheduled 'sidetrip' even before we could get back to the motel."

I lay back and thought about Belinda's story. Was there, I wondered, some common theme beginning to emerge? This whole strange tale, I recalled, had begun with me in my apartment, stroking what was left of Marsha's hair, and then later on those people in the cave Belinda described had also been clutching hair. Now that I thought of it, the widow Harkens seemed unusually hirsute as well, and of course I had later found out why. I turned to look at Belinda lying next to me. Her hair was short, blond, and very clean. Somehow, the puzzle had yet to be solved.

I remembered my first dog, Rusty, an Irish setter with an uncanny ability to know what was on my mind. His fur, too, and been a reddish-brown, and at times the expression on his intelligent face was almost human, and no more so than when I would come upon him unexpectedly, sitting before an open library book, staring at what doubtless to him must have been only rows of strange black marks across the page.

What other hair had figured in my life, I wondered. Certainly, when I was young, growing up in the depressive chill of Cleveland, Ohio, in winters and often into spring, my mother used to wrap me in scarves of wool from head to foot before she sent me off to elementary school, a progressive institution which was supposed to help prepare us for life by assigning each student small tasks which would make the larger ones we would have to take on as adults seem more familiar. For the youngest students, the school had a room where pupils addressed envelopes or pasted labels on bottles of shoe polish and paint remover. For the older ones, there was a small art studio, a vegetable garden, as well as a tailor shop, and a miniature abattoir, designed for animals up to the size of rabbits.

That's where I was assigned to work, stripping the skins of rabbits as they came off the assembly line at a rate of fifty an hour. If, by any chance, we fell behind in our quotas (because quotas were a major part of the adult world we would be entering) we were forced to attend long sessions during which we were required to creatively visualize, while kneeling in a corner spread with walnut shells, those emotions responsible for interfering with a smooth and efficient operation, and to banish them. After the skins were removed they went from there to the school tannery, and from the tannery to the tailor shop where they were sewn into jacket collars or made into muffs for little boys and girls. The worst part of my job came when the rabbits, as often happened, hadn't been killed properly, but only stunned, so were still twitching and making pathetic mewing sounds in front of me even as production quotas forced me to go on with the process. "Thank you," I creatively visualized them mewing as they bid a skinless farewell down the line. "Thank you very much." Still, when by the fourth grade I'd graduated to the tailor shop, despite the poor light and stifling atmosphere, I confess I was glad to have a new job.

Eventually Rusty grew old and his hair began to drop away in patches, and I would gaze at him as he lay in a spot of winter sun or thumped his tail when I walked by. Did he, I wondered, know he was going to die? Or for that matter, what were those rabbits really thinking, their round eyes wide, their little voices squealing on the way to the disemboweling room? What was Rusty's pain to mine? What was his to the rabbits? Was the recognition of pain something only a human soul was capable of? So we were told each day during the school's meditation hour, and curiously enough, once, years later, when I was asked along with the other members of my therapy group to describe my soul, I found myself agreeing with most of the others that it was approximately the size of my own body (though for some it was larger, like a loose-fitting coat, with room to grow, while for others it was slightly smaller, possibly anticipating some future loss of weight). Did this therefore mean that if the souls of rabbits were smaller that they felt less pain? If so, then what about those creatures larger than ourselves — a woolly mammoth or a dolphin or a gorilla? Did they feel more? My own theory was that perhaps it had to do with hair, that fur somehow mitigated between us and the world, and possibly the resulting fuzziness made for an easier transition from the self to some far greater other.

"How does a haircut make you feel?" I asked Belinda.

"I like it," she said. "Short hair makes me feel free, and somehow more in touch with everything. Listen, morning's here. What do you say we grab some breakfast and then spend the day at the zoo?"

Breakfast was a leisurely affair — we went out a to cozy country cottage complete with chintz curtains and china coffee cups, soft boiled eggs, fresh fruit, French rolls, and free refills of fig preserves, but the zoo that day was a disappointment. Those animals present who were not hiding in the foliage or behind the walls of their dens ("private time" the printed sign in front of each cage described it) seemed unusually somber, mostly staring off with expressions devoid of any alertness or hope what-so-ever, similar, in fact to those on the faces of my fellow citizens of Cleveland, creatures who were only killing times, and who, though they knew not what awaited them, obviously had decided that anything would be better than their present state. The zoo that day had mercifully few visitors — a few children with their distracted mothers, an occasional pair of lovers (though what sort of inspiration for a future life they hoped to find was beyond me), and one solitary man in a white coat, like a lab jacket, tossing health food muffins to the gorillas. "Health food," I thought. "Right."

The rest of what happened that day you probably have already guessed. Namely, that while heading toward the exit we were accosted by what appeared to be a giant panda. Clearly, I thought, here was a creature who had escaped from whatever compound he had been staying in and meant trouble. And was it my fault, if, as it was later explained to me, no such actual panda existed at the time of my sighting, but such a creature <u>had</u> once lived there, originally a present from a zoo in mainland China, and as a result had been chosen as the official logo of the zoo? Unfortunately, only a few months after a massive publicity blitz complete with T-shirts, posters and flags using the panda had been undertaken, the poor creature expired after eating several cartons of bamboo shoots containing lethal doses of MSG brought by the well-meaning owner of a local Chinese restaurant. And so, in order not to lose the valuable momentum already generated by the publicity, the zoo had kept the panda (Mao-Mao) as its logo, and simply replaced the actual late animal with a person whose job it was to walk around the park and, while wearing a panda suit, greet visitors.

All this however, as I have said, was unknown to me as I turned suddenly that Wednesday to see the nearly extinct, but nonetheless largish creature approaching Belinda and me. I went into my "panic mode." Running up behind the imitation-panda, I picked up a nearby 2X4 and struck the creature in its head, disregarding its pathetic cries as well as what I understand now were the well-intentioned efforts of several passers-by, who I also attacked as they attempted to explain the difference between a real panda bear, normally a docile creature in its own right, and the unfortunate human being inside the suit whose life I wound up taking.

But all that was in the past, years ago really, even though I must add it still seems like only yesterday when, following our group therapy session at the State Hospital for the Criminally Insane nestled among the golden rolling hills of Atascadero, California, my therapist, Dr. Wolf, told me he had an "interesting proposition" to present to me.

"I have noticed," Dr. Wolf continued, giving a tug to the lobe of his right ear, a nervous trait I had seen worsening in the months that I had been there, "that your responses to the entire series of psychological tests I've given you indicate a strong obsession and simultaneous fear of things underground. Caves and caverns, for example, are prominent in all the landscapes you have produced in your 'Art As Healing Workshop,' but never attics or bell towers." He smiled, barring what seemed to be an unusually large set of teeth.

"Therefore," he said, picking at one of the tiny scabs that had been forming in increasing numbers along the tops of his hands, "I'd like to try an experiment. I propose that you be taken to the basement of this very institution where you will stay, in a special cell, attended by our staff, for a full two months, at the end of which I predict you will be completely cured and able to be released once again into society."

I agreed. Who wouldn't?

"Oh, and one more thing," he added, fidgeting slightly as he tied and untied his left shoelace, "if I am correct that the source of all your antisocial behavior is simply that your biological clock has been wound too tight, you will have to spend the entire time in the dark. You will not see me or any of the attendants, nor will there be any light for anything down there. Do you agree?"

"OK," I said. "When do I start?"

"Tomorrow," he replied, and hurried out the door.

The following day I was led down the stairs to the basement where I was shown, with the last light I was supposed to see for the next eight weeks, the small room where I was to make my home. It was barely tall enough for me to stand, and if I put out my arms I could almost touch the walls, which appeared to be made of re-enforced concrete. The floor, curiously enough, had been left as dirt and smelled of urine even though it was perfectly dry. The room, I was told, had originally been built back in the early days of the institution for one special patient, some sort of an artist and a member of an old American family who, after murdering his sister in a ghastly manner, had developed an extreme sensitivity to sounds of all sorts, and thus had to be removed from the general wards above him. My attendants said good-bye, leaving behind a tuna sandwich, a jug of water, and a few utensils to contain my future bodily excretions.

It was, at the risk of repeating myself, dark, and not just any nighttime deprivation, but an atmosphere so thick, so impenetrable, so total, it had a presence all its own. This was not just darkness, I thought, but its essence. Above me I could hear the faint cries of my fellow patients, and around me hummed the pipes and ducts that were the veins and arteries of the institution. But most of all I heard my own breathing, loud and rather fast, probably from nerves. If I slept, I reasoned, then when I woke the transition from dark to dark would not be so startling and I would accept it more easily. Fortunately the bed and bedding were both comfortable enough so that almost as soon as I pulled the blanket beneath my chin and shut my eyes (a ridiculous gesture if there ever was one) I fell into a dreamless slumber.

I was awakened by someone shaking my bed with persistent and unaccustomed violence. I opened my eyes, and seeing nothing, yelled, "Hey you!" I jumped up; to my amazement the floor was shaking as well, and then I realized what was happening! As you no doubt have already guessed, we were in the midst of a major earthquake, maybe even "the big one" that had been talked about for so many years for the state of California.

Above me there was a tremendous crash, the sound, I realized, of the entire hospital collapsing, and it was only the fact that I had been put there in the basement, surrounded by these re-enforced walls that had saved my life, at least temporarily. I noticed it was impossible to stand (the ceiling of my cell had been driven down at least a foot by the impact of the collapse) and I could hear the sound of creaking beams, a few horrible human cries which gradually died out, and then a silence that was the most terrifying I had ever felt. My life had been spared, but for what? Yes, I had a little food, and more water, but it was likely I would starve to death before any rescue worker dug his way to me. In the meantime, I could do nothing. The best plan, I decided, was to go back to sleep, not only to pass the time but also to conserve energy.

How long I slept that second time and what dreams I had I cannot say, but I awoke in a sweat to the sounds of my own breath, my own heartbeat, and possibly, I thought, one other thing. In the midst of that profound darkness around me it seemed I could hear sounds, like voices. My first guess was that some still-playing radio had survived the quake, but then I noticed they appeared to be coming not from above but from the dirt beneath my feet. I put my ear to the ground. The voices, though I couldn't understand their words, were clearer. I tried to remove some of the dirt floor with my fingers, but with little effect because it was so packed. I moved to try another area, and as I did I heard my foot strike some object made of metal, a spoon as it turned out, and I used it to scrape away the hard-packed surface until I reached a layer beneath it that was softer and easier to remove.

How long I worked and how often I rested I have no idea. My guess is that I had lapsed into a time all of its own, not a human time, but one of space and distances. The dirt was surprisingly loose once past the surface of the floor, and work went easily, but on the other hand I had no idea exactly how long the tunnel I was creating would need to be. Certainly, there was no point in tunneling upward, I thought, until I was outside the perimeters of the tons of concrete above me, and because I had no idea where, in relation to the institution's walls my basement room had been located, I decided to go in the direction of the voices. The dirt, of course, was a problem, and as my basement room filled, little by little, it occurred to me that like some strange creature doomed by his own excrement, that once the room was full, because the room was the source of my oxygen, I would asphyxiate myself.

Luckily, even as my former cell was reaching its capacity, I began to notice that the wall I was scraping away on seemed to have an increasingly drum-like quality, as if beyond it there were some great hollow space from which these voices emanated, and that the voices themselves were growing louder. I would dig a little, listen, then dig a little farther. The air in the tunnel was stifling, and the heat grew more intense. Even so, once I had gotten within striking distance of my goal I began to hesitate. What, I wondered, would *my* reaction be if I were a member of some group of cave-dwelling criminals and suddenly my living room wall burst open and someone tumbled through? Moving forward by inches, I brushed away the dirt from the farthest wall with my fingers until I could see a few isolated particles of light passing through it. Then, very carefully, using the handle of my spoon, I removed just enough dirt so I could have an eye hole, a place to peer out at what was on the other side.

The space I looked into was large, and divided by a line of fire shooting out of holes from the rocky floor, like flames from an artificial fireplace log. Scattered around the floor on one side of the fire were several apparently random, but miniature objects: a table, a chair, a horse, a deer, a lion, an avocado, a pail, a man, a woman, and so on, none of them larger than about a half a foot high. I looked more closely. The chair was perfect; so were the table, the horse, the man, the woman, the avocado. Clearly these were not just random generations of these forms, but the ideal one of each. Not only that, but the voices which I had heard coming from the opposite side of the fire were speaking what was almost certainly ancient Greek. I pulled back from my vantage point, stunned. As impossible as it seemed, I could come to no other conclusion than I had somehow stumbled upon Plato's Cave.

I looked again. Around the cave were scattered at least a thousand of these perfect forms: a miniature cow, a full-sized screwdriver, a book of matches from some bar, a pencil, a set of towels and matching washcloths, an owl, etcetera, but each living thing, including the human couple mentioned earlier seemed oddly listless, as if they were under the influence of some unknown narcotic which kept them in a state of nearly suspended animation.

And then I saw behind all of them a thing so peculiar, so *indescribable* (even as I'm pretending to describe it), so absolutely indefinable that even such a detail as its size, for example, became open to debate, as it appeared simultaneously to be the size of a modest living room couch and at the same time so huge that I could scarcely believe there was room for even one other object in the cave, and yet it was both these things. And parts of it were green, the result of various plant-like appendages (I remember what looked like prairie grass, cabbage, artichokes, several pine cones, a dozen or so morels, and broad flat leaves like those of figs), while other parts were brightly colored as flowers, *were* flowers — blue and yellow and violet in spots — while still other areas seemed to glisten with scales, to shine with feathers, and to be smeared with reddish fur, long in places, short in others, merely bristles. Still other sections were just raw pink skin, which here and there dissolved into tumor-like configurations of cells spilling all around, and there were mouths and ears, and if not eyes exactly, then some things that reminded me of eyes, and some of the plants were turning brown and dying while others were in bloom or bud, and this thing was eating the whole time, though I couldn't say what, and simultaneously defecating, and sweating, while other parts were soaking up the sweat and the excrement, and there was the hiss of escaping gas, and the crunch of bones, and parts of the thing seemed to be inserting themselves into other parts and were throbbing while other parts were crawling forward and yet other ones retreated to the back of the cave (but remember this thing, whatever it was, took up the whole cave, and so had nowhere to move) and from somewhere, I can't be sure where, a high-pitched whine was emanating (which either I hadn't noticed till then or it had been there all along and I'd just missed it), and meanwhile, as this was happening there were coming from it, spewing out from various places in little arcs onto the ground all around it, more of these perfect forms — a stapler, a rabbit, a pair of dress shoes with wing-tips, a swarm of bees, a camera — because, and of course I had known this all along without knowing it, it was the source of all those things and more. And then (and I don't know how to say this either, because I've already said it had no eyes) it *saw* me, saw the tiny shining dot that was the reflection of my eye as it peered through the hole I had made in the wall of the cave, and the resulting shock of what — desire! — both it for me and me for it, was so intense I found myself thrown back from my vantage point in the dark, back into the body of my tunnel, sweating and staring once more at the tiny hole in all that darkness, gasping, knowing I no longer had a choice in the matter, and that no matter what happened, what would happen, I was about to break through the remaining barrier of dirt to confront whatever beautiful and monstrous thing that might be there waiting for me.

I felt a shudder through my body, and then another. I sat back and waited for it to subside, then realized it wasn't coming from my body at all — it must have been an aftershock from the earlier giant quake. I took a breath, and curled into a ball in the hope I might trap as much air as possible around me, and then, all at once, I lost consciousness.

There was a light, and I found myself staring at a name tag that read, "Hi, my name is BOB." I noticed that the "Hi" part had been printed earlier, and the letters B-O-B had been added later, in purple marking pen, and were followed, probably because its writer had noticed there was still room left, with the symbol of a happy face. I looked at the name tag-owner's head, and the mouth in it opened to say, complete with little puffs of breath around each word, "Hi, my name is Bob." Then it grinned at me. I had been rescued.

I brushed off the dirt, was given a plate of scrambled eggs and a cup of coffee. Except for a couple of visitors, long since gone, who had been necking in the hospital's parking lot at the time of the quake, out of all the patients and all the staff of the State Hospital, I was the sole survivor. Perhaps it was the general confusion, or perhaps having seen too many television shows depicting the criminally insane as slobbering psychopaths of hulking size and threatening demeanor, my rescuers were convinced by my calm responses that I was who I said I was: a mere custodian who, following a nasty spill of toxic glaze in the "Self Images In Clay" class, had gone down to the basement for a new supply of paper towels to mop the stuff up. So I was able to leave the State Hospital behind forever, much as Dr. Wolf had earlier predicted, although in a completely different way.

Back in Los Angeles, I now live quietly, working days for the county as an Animal Technician II, where it's my job to drag unwanted dogs and cats into the gas chambers where they are put to sleep. For enjoyment I took several creative writing classes, where I wrote the stories of my life disguised as "exercises," and every so often returned to "The Peaceable Kingdom" in the hopes of seeing Belinda again, perhaps after her harsher memories of our "date" (as she described it to the court) at the zoo had faded. Once inside the club's comfortable surroundings I put on one mask or another — a gopher or a mole — it no longer seemed particularly to matter, and sat watching the door where she would enter.

One evening a few weeks ago, after I'd nearly given up all hope, I saw a woman in the mask of a hyena walk in, and I invited her to my table. After the usual talk and an eclectic cuisine, we wound up back at her apartment, where we watched a show called "Trapper Tom," a replacement for "The Swamp of Time," which had apparently succumbed to its miserable ratings. This new show was about a modern mountain man who caught wild animals for a living, and took their skins to town to sell in order to support his favorite charity, a hospital for children, on whose board he sat. Tom divided his time between running down antiseptic corridors full of screaming children—a pelt-covered figure still sticky with the blood of badgers and raccoons — while on his way to solving another medical crisis, and then, on alternate weeks, he returned to the mountains where, covered with pelts and gore he would rescue stranded, distraught campers and help fight natural disasters. The episode we watched that evening, for example, involved a man and a woman stuck in a cave who could be rescued only after Trapper Tom first caught and uncoiled a gigantic cottonmouth, lowering it to the unhappy couple to use as a rope.

After it was over we sat back in bed and talked a while. Her name, she said was Linda ("Beauty itself," she explained). We did a little of this and some of that, then she told me the story of who she was and how she came to be at the club, and later, when she took off her clothes, to my great surprise she was nothing at all like I thought she would be.

PETER CRAIG

Appease The Natives

Bryan and Carolyn lay naked on the abandoned catamaran when a light began to flicker in his mother's kitchen window. Tinted blue by the curtains, Bryan thought it was the television. He was tired from the long, dizzying swim, and as he stood, balancing against the mast, he had trouble focusing on the house across a hundred yards of ocean. His head felt full of water. The other windows glowed faintly, enough to light the porch and the sand below.

"Carolyn, wake up. Something's wrong."

She sat up and pulled her legs to her chest, curling into a ball. Her skin was covered with goose bumps.

"What is that light?" he asked. "Straight ahead."

"I don't know. Maybe your mother's doing something."

"She's asleep," he said. "She went to sleep hours ago."

Carolyn slid forward, hanging both legs into the black water. She lowered herself down into the swells that rolled under the boat. Her jaw chattered, and she looked up at Bryan, her pale face framed in the water, and said, "We should swim back."

Bryan saw the curtains fray into streaks. A flash of orange light tore through them, and there were flames in the window.

"Let's go." He dove into the ocean. He broke the surface to find Carolyn beside him, slashing her long arms through the chop.

"Come on," he said. "Swim fast."

She stayed close, blowing out mouthfuls of water as they pushed through the chop. He felt crippled in the tide. After each stroke he craned his head upward and each time he had more trouble finding the window. They slid diagonally toward the shore.

At the breaks he timed the waves badly. They tumbled him forward until his feet touched sand. He trudged through with long, dragging strides. When he reached the shore, he stooped down in search of their clothes.

He was in front of a different cluster of houses. He could smell the fire now, the same smell as fireworks on the beach. With splashes of foam around her, Carolyn climbed out of the water behind him, a lanky silhouette. Searching the dark pocked sand, crouched down, trying to remember landmarks—the partially submerged rock, the houses on stilts, the drainage stream—Bryan forgot the urgency, and thought of everything as if it were a puzzle. He needed to wait for a moment and allow his mind to clear.

Carolyn ran toward him, her arms crossed over her breasts.

"Where are our clothes?" she said.

"Okay. Think for a second. Just take a deep breath and think. What did we do with them?"

"Bryan," she said, panicked and shrill, "is your mother still in the *house*?" She trotted in place.

"I don't know. Just wait a second."

"Oh Jesus Bryan, hurry. Hurry."

"Carolyn, relax okay. Just calm down and think. Where did we leave our clothes?"

"I don't *know*, Bryan." He looked all around the base of the stairs, beside rocks and fences. Finally Carolyn ran past him toward the house.

"Carolyn," he shouted. In the brighter lights, now strobing through the cracks in the porch overhead, he found the clothes wadded up beside one of the house's support beams, the stilts that held it above hightide. Stumbling forward, he pulled on his jeans and ran after Carolyn, into the hot air strong with a chemical-smoke like burning plastic, past the hanging plants now rocking, the wind chimes ringing in a breeze, and a high-pitched squeal—air escaping through spaces in the windows—along the stucco walls to the open front door where he heard the crumpling sound of fire. Wind gusted through the doorway and smoke bunched along the ceiling of the entry hall. Inside, the fire alarms all shrieked. He started into the hallway, his wet feet slipping on the tile. He couldn't see flames, only flashes of light in the living room at the end of the hallway.

His little brother, Luther, stumbled past him with an electric guitar, a skateboard, and an amplifier; his mother trotted close behind, covering her mouth, curlers in her hair.

Carolyn walked toward him, crouched over. He quickly draped his shirt over her, and backed with her out of the house. The shirt stuck to the sweat on her back. As they left the house into cool air, a drizzle now falling, he said, "Here. Put on your shorts."

She put them on mechanically, staring away from him. When he put his arm around her he said, "That was fantastic, Carolyn. That was really fantastic." She balanced against him. Too tall to rest her head on his shoulder, she let him support her weight, guide her across the driveway.

His mother paced the driveway. The sleepy strip of apartments along the beach was lit up now and every porch was filled with spectators in their pajamas. Neighbors stood on their winter green lawns across the boulevard, on patios, porches, and the hoods of cars, and all of the quick movement shined in the glassy puddles on the ground.

"Would somebody please call the fire department," his mother shouted at the audience.

Bryan wondered about the books inside. They were probably kindling. Of course, Bryan's and Carolyn's suitcases must have sparked up and burned at once. He had stubbornly refused to unpack, promising not to stay in his mother's house for more than a few weeks. If they unpacked, it would only have delayed them on their way to new jobs, a new apartment. But now he was angry at how compact and easy to burn all of their belongings must have been.

When the firemen went inside, smoke escaped from all the windows like the house was simply evaporating into a cloud of steam. Some firemen lingered beside the truck, taking a break, smoking and flicking cigarette butts onto the wet lawn.

Luther skateboarded in circles around the driveway, flipping his board around with his feet, until his mother ran after him in her slippers, caught him by the sleeve, and shouted at him to stay still. Bryan rarely—in all his life—had seen his mother without make-up. She was the kind of woman who would say goodnight and lock her door and not appear again until after an hour of primping in the morning. All through his childhood, he had avoided his mother's room. She had company some nights, and Bryan would hear the sound of men's voices. He was afraid of that room, and had associated it with all the secrets of adulthood.

"We're all fine," said his mother. "We're all okay."

Luther danced around the wet driveway, wearing a Chargers jacket over his bare chest, powder blue pajama bottoms. He carried his guitar now, close to his body and he strummed muted chords.

"I just grabbed my guitar and amp," he said. His jacket swung open to expose his fleshy stomach. "I didn't think, I just acted."

"Good boy," said Carolyn.

Luther eyed them both, the wet couple standing half-dressed in a crowded driveway: Carolyn's wet hair, her shivering bare legs. He laughed.

"That's it, Luther," said Carolyn. "Keep your spirits up."

"He's in shock," said Bryan.

"Man, excellent timing. What a bummer for you guys."

Bryan's mother called him from across the driveway, where she was talking to a fireman, and Luther walked through a puddle. She grabbed his guitar by the neck and wrenched it away from him.

"Don't make my life any harder than it already is, Luther."

She spoke to the fireman for a long time and then came back and spoke to Bryan and Carolyn. She had sweat beaded all around her collarbone where the robe was folded open. Her face looked different without all the make-up, somehow incomplete.

She said, "We're all okay. We got everything important. We're all fine, and Luther's even got his damn *skate*board."

Bryan imagined all the books exploding, combusting and spitting ashen pages across the room, the last bits of them swarming in sparks.

Long after the fire was out, a fireman came out with an armful of clothes, all belonging to Luther, whose room was the only one untouched by flame or water. Carolyn got into some of Luther's sweat pants and Bryan's mother took the rest.

"Do you kids have someplace to stay?" she asked Bryan.

"No," said Bryan. "Who would I know around here?"

"Christ Brian, you did live here once."

"He's a recluse," said Carolyn.

"I know that, dear." She put the clothes on the hood of her Mustang. "At least we finally found a way to get him out of the house."

She kneeled down and reached behind a tire of her car. "Look, you can come with me. This is an emergency. But everyone—especially you, Luther—everyone has to be under control." She pulled off a key attached to a magnet.

She didn't tell them where they were going. Bryan and Carolyn followed her. The top was down on her car, so her curlers twitched in the wind.

During the ride, Bryan wondered why it had taken him so long to react. He had felt no adrenaline, no call to heroics. It was simply an occurrence. Would he have run inside if he had found his clothes? He seemed to have assumed the house was impenetrable, and never considered rushing inside. Carolyn convinced him that night to skinny-dip in the ocean with her. Bryan was distressed to think—in the moment when he couldn't find his clothes—he had forgotten the house was on fire.

Carolyn drove across Orange County to a neighborhood in the hills, all the houses gray and angular with wooden fences, hedges, and rock gardens out front. His mother led them to a house with a sloped lawn, and an ornate door, carved, and made to look twelve feet tall.

They stood, the four of them covered with soot and sweat, on the doorstep of the house. His mother said, "His name is Howard. Be nice to him."

Howard answered the door, rubbing his small, mole-sized eyes. He looked up at her and said, "Laura. My God."

"This is my family, Howard. This is Bryan and his wife, and my youngest boy, Luther."

Howard was a short, stocky man, balding, with a fleshy neck and chin. He squinted at them. Then he smiled and looked anxious to please. He said, "Everybody. What happened?"

"Let us in, Howard. We're extremely tired."

She pushed past him and Luther followed, dinging his amplifier into the doorjamb. Howard dragged his slippers on the hardwood floor. He had a strange twist in his back when he walked, a limp that ran from his leg to his shoulders, his whole body lilting in one direction then straightening again with each step.

"What happened?"

"Our house got torched," said Luther.

Howard's place was meticulously decorated: white round couches in a semicircle around a glass table, two fluted decanters on top beside magazines and a Matisse book; framed reproductions of photographs over white walls, spaced far apart so that the walls appeared bare, like an art gallery; a large picture of Bryan's mother on the mantle. Carolyn stooped to look at the pictures, following them around the walls, down a few steps onto the carpet. Howard stood beside her, three steps above, and Carolyn was still a forehead taller than him. With her long skinny legs, Luther's sweats bunched at her knees, she was the most out of place here, in a room where all the pictures were hung below her line of vision.

Bryan thought it amusing that she wore Luther's sweat pants. In the few weeks they had known each other, they constantly made of fun of the other's height. Carolyn would palm his head and ask him when he was going to start growing, and Luther would tell her to put on some weight.

Standing close to six two, Carolyn towered over Bryan's mother, who was a sturdy woman, barely five three. The two women were so physically opposite that Bryan could scarcely picture them together at all, his mother with her quick, clicking walk in high heels and slacks, and Carolyn in gym shorts. She was a volleyball player in College, a middle blocker, and Bryan remembered her only appearing clumsy when she was in street clothes. She could move quickly and strongly if she knew the moves, if her adrenaline was there, if there was a clear objective.

At their wedding in Portland, some drunken uncle told Carolyn she had legs that only looked good in kneepads. He said she should've thrown a knee-pad instead of her garter. Carolyn was furious and Bryan told her it was a drunken lie, but that image stayed with him: Carolyn in kneepads, in a short-cut gown, in a wedding dress, he always thought of her two spidery legs, held together at the joint by a yellow stripe. It excited him.

Howard said, "So I'll fix everyone a drink and you can tell me what happened." He gimped into his kitchenette, brightly lit by rows of tube lighting over a counter. He poured from another decanter.

Luther plopped down onto the couch and Laura yelled at him. "Get off of there, Luther. That's a white couch. My God." He sprung back up and looked at the smear he'd put onto the pillows. Laura said, "My son, the chimney sweep."

"There's a shower upstairs," said Howard. "And one right there by the entry hall. That one doesn't have a shower curtain though. I should put on my glasses."

"Yes. Please get your glasses, Howard. My kids are wrecking your house."

Outside the sliding glass door, across a small patio, a hill of scrub sloped downward to a deserted boulevard lined with identical houses. Each plot had a small pool, lit blue.

Howard, returned to the white living room with his glasses. "Is anybody hurt?"

"We're fine," said Laura. "It's just all our stuff, Howard. All our dumb stuff."

He put his arms out slightly, to hug her, tilting his head slightly to the side.

"Don't do this to me, Howard."

"It's all right, Laura. It's terrible and I know how you feel. I do."

"Don't," she said.

He approached her slowly, scuffing his slippers on the floor. He put his arms around her.

"Do you want us to leave, Mom?" said Luther, leaning against a white wall.

"Don't hug me," she said, pushing away from him. "Please. I hate this."

"Okay," he said. "Okay. I'm just glad everybody's safe."

The rest of the night, Bryan lay awake on the floor, crammed onto the white cushions beside Carolyn, listening to the sounds of increasing traffic, watching the black sky gradually change to gray overcast filled with seagulls. He felt Carolyn's side pressing into him each time she inhaled. Her hair smelled like ash.

While Bryan was half asleep, his mind drifted. He imagined Carolyn running into the house, the flames surging up around her. He pictured her in her volleyball uniform, her hair bouncing behind her in a pony tail. She kicked through doors, splintering them off the hinges. The image aroused him wildly, and he kissed her neck and her cheek, nuzzled his face into her hair. She coughed and rolled away from him onto her side. He kissed her neck and her shoulder blade. He visualized her running up the stairs, her legs spotted with sand, number 14 on her jersey tank-top; and he was a spectator, far away from her, watching from a pocket of fans, all in curlers and mud-masks. Carolyn ran, giving high-fives to a line-up of smaller girls along the walkway to the house.

He reached down and began to play with himself, staring at the splash of her black hair around him, until—all at once—he lost the fantasy. He imagined *himself* at the door with her sandy clothes under his arm. He lay there on his back, beside his sleeping wife, holding himself, wondering what made a man a coward.

He sat with his mother on the porch, still wearing his jeans and the smoke-tainted shirt he had given Carolyn. It was hot. His mother drank coffee and stared blankly out at the houses while Bryan did a crossword puzzle.

His mother's face was made up again and he couldn't help noticing it more now that he had seen her without make-up. Her eyes looked puffier and small granules of powder showed on her cheeks. "What's a six letter word for betrayal?" he asked her.

"Ratfuck," said his mother.

"No, no. They wouldn't use that."

Carolyn and Howard were together in the small alcove of the kitchen. Howard wore orthopedic shoes this morning, one with a two inch lift, and his limp was gone. But his shoe made Bryan uncomfortable, reminding him of an old card table with one broken leg under which his mother used to shove a phone book.

"What's a three letter word for cinder-colored lava?"

"Put that thing away. It's warping your brain."

He heard Carolyn's giggle, and he went inside.

"What are you laughing at?" he asked her.

Howard said, "Do you want something else to wear Bryan?"

Bryan ignored him and sat on the couch beside Luther, who was watching a Saturday morning cartoon.

"I guess that means no," said Howard. He continued to Carolyn, "Anyway, I was shocked, yeah. A great introduction."

"Are you guys at that 3-month stage. You know, so it was an issue meeting her family."

"Sure, that's always been an issue. But it wasn't three months, Carrie. Your mother and I have been seeing each other for years."

"She's *Bryan's* mother. She's my mother-in-*law*."

"Right, I'm sorry. I know that. Sometimes we'd quit, you know, say the whole thing was just wasn't going anywhere. But your mother and I, we have something We've persevered."

"That's so sweet," said Carolyn. "She's not my mother though."

"I'm sorry. You know, it's hard to say *Laura* to you because you don't... Well, do you call her 'mom' or 'Laura'?"

"I call her Mrs. Gathers," said Carolyn.

"I'm sorry," he said.

Luther flipped through channels and said, "I wonder if our TV blew up."

Bryan thought again of the bookshelves, filled to the brim with his father's books, and thought Luther would laugh at him if he admitted to being worried about them. He remembered his father, far back in a distant childhood, a trembling, nervous man. His father spent hours at night searching for a perfect bedtime story, and always Bryan would fall asleep before he had found it. Was it possible, Bryan wondered, to know a man from his absence? He remembered his father as a space between bookshelves, paths between sofa chairs and wastebaskets. He could still picture the pillows on his father's chair, the sloughed-off shirts, his father's glasses perched on a stack of half-read books. But he couldn't picture his father. The man had left a crumb from each passing second: cigarette burns on the rug, rings on the coffee table, a thousand dog-eared pages; and Bryan wanted, more than anything, to gather all those clues in his mind.

Bryan discovered his father's old books when he was a teenager, and he read all the margin notes and underlined passages. He could see the places where the ball-points ran out of ink and his father would frantically scratch on the page. He followed the notes like a great scrapbook of his father's thoughts.

That afternoon, when they returned to the house, stepping carefully across a creaking floor, Bryan found all the books cremated.

The house felt like it was rocking on its stilts. The walls had all been scorched, a mixture of black charred areas and bubbled wallpaper. The flames had made designs on the roof, ringlets intersecting, and in places it had burned through.

The floor was soaked, bits of scorched carpet in dirty puddles. Everything was wet.

The bubbled linoleum in the kitchen looked like lava had dried while oozing toward the hall. Bryan stopped at his mother's bedroom. The water-bed was still intact, covers and all. A fern, dried to a crisp and blackened, still hung from a wire in the ceiling.

His mother lived a private life here. It was strange that in a lifetime in this house he hadn't looked at her room until now. He stood in a film of water and surveyed the damage. He hadn't simply ignored this room, he had pretended it didn't exist. It was a mere doorway through which his mother vanished. He remembered glimpses of it, always on those strange dream-like nights when she would come to him crying, take him into the room and hold him. She would cry against his face and neck and he would smell the saltiness of her, and feel that nothing in his power could ever comfort her. Always there was that strange sensation that it was another house, that this room—with its waterbed and blue tile bathroom—was separate from everything in his life.

A discolored puddle, filled with debris, sat on the bathroom floor. The tubes of hair spray and skin cream were melted and now coagulated around the counter.

Carolyn came into the bathroom and said, "Luther's fish got boiled."

In Luther's room the goldfish floated on top of his aquarium. His room was the farthest back in the house and nothing else was harmed. But somehow, the goldfish in the aquarium had been boiled.

"My fish got cooked," said Luther.

"Doesn't seem right," said Bryan. "Maybe they died of smoke inhalation."

"They don't breathe like that, stupid."

In Bryan's room, the sparse one, he found the remains of the suitcases. Safe in the back of the closet, he took the only clothes that they had hung there: his dark blue suit and her white dress, their understated wedding clothes. They stank terribly, but he took them. He folded them over his arm.

Luther had stuffed a whole bag with clothes. "So I'm the unlucky one?" said Laura.

Outside, Laura said, "It's up to some claims adjuster. We re-build the house, I guess. Howard will know how to do all this."

"It's just a hassle, Mom. That's all. It's not the end of the world," said Bryan.

"The end of the world is just a hassle," she said. "If you want to look at everything *that* way."

"They'll replace everything, Mrs. Gathers, I swear. I got everything stolen when I was in school, and I had renter's insurance."

"There were more than CDs in there, Carolyn."

"Mrs. Gathers, maybe we should try to have a good weekend. Nobody can do anything until Monday."

"Carolyn, you're a sweet girl. Thank you. But I lost everything, and it isn't that simple. I'm not going to throw a party because my house burned down. Do you understand that?"

"Of course."

"I'm not a bitch, Carolyn. I just want to stand here and I want everyone to be quiet."

★ ★ ★

In the early sixties, Laura Gathers had been one of his father's students when he was a high-school English teacher, and they used to sit in parked cars, out on the bluffs, share a joint, and he would, so she said, spin out fantastic yarns about love and a future. "He knew all about love," she said. "He knew what it was supposed to be. We both had a real, solid idea of ourselves and everything we wanted out of life. He really was a teacher. But sometimes things just get too mapped out. Like our marriage."

Maybe, Bryan thought, this man he remembered with barbs of hair around a bald crown, glasses thicker than storm windows, always pinched up into his brown suit... maybe he was a criminal of sorts. He asked once, in an embarrassing moment, and his mother said, "No, we waited until I was 18. We knew we were in love, and we counted days." But a countdown from six-hundred? He tried to imagine, 564: her braces come off, 522: she's grounded, 406: She just *has* to see the Beatles, 319: she smokes grass... and the system became so implanted in Bryan's thinking that whenever she told a story from her youth, he tried to figure out what day it might have been in her supposed countdown, from her birth to marriage to his conception. Could it be anything close to the truth? 448: a father, a blackboard, chalk on his cuffs, a windy cold day in her North Dakota town, he wanted to write on the board, "I love you, Laura. Marry me, have my son, speak well of me when I'm gone." And his mother drew little hearts on her notebook: I heart Mr. Gathers, Mr. Gathers, Mr. Gathers.

She told him those few stories to lend perspective on to the woman she'd become. Mr. Gathers was an old man by the time she grew up, reading at home in a cylinder of lamplight, while she marched, smoked pot, stayed up all night listening to jazz records with her friends. He spent all his money to pay her college tuition. She'd already had Bryan, and the old man was sick and slow, and he must have known all along that the best he could do was keep himself from standing in her way. She was twenty-seven when he died of a heart attack. She never married again.

So Bryan grew up alone with his mother. She dated often, lived with some, had Luther, a planned single parenthood. She'd lived a wild life, but had managed to keep most of it away from Bryan, behind locked doors, after hours. Many of the men she dated left her with some present, a suggested hobby: a piano, an easel and paints, a pottery wheel. They cluttered the house, and she never paid much attention to them, until her early forties after Luther was born, a quiet and lonely phase in her life in which she stayed up nights practicing: splashing paints, banging the piano, until she found some basic level of competence with each. Looking back, Bryan remembered the presents so much more strongly than her lovers, that he could only identify the

men as inanimate objects.   She used to have caterwauling fights with the
piano; the pottery wheel had a violent temper; she didn't talk for three days
after the darkroom went back to Australia.

Bryan resisted sentimentality, but he couldn't escape this sentimentality
of objects.   He mourned the loss of his father's books.

While they were away, Howard had bought groceries and he was
arranging for dinner. He was going to cook Trout A La Navarra, he said, and
Luther made a farting noise on his hand.

"You don't like fish?" Howard asked him.

"No, it's not that," said Luther, chuckling to himself.   "I'll just wait and
see what you can *whip* up."

Howard stood there in his kitchen alcove.   "What do you mean,
Luther?"

"He doesn't mean anything," said Laura.   "Don't pay any attention to
him."

Laura sat at the counter, cradling her wine glass close to her chest.
Carolyn, crammed in behind Howard and putting groceries away in the
pantry shelves, looked across to Luther and said, "Luther, don't be a little
prick."

"Did I say something? I love trout, I love Howard, I love aprons."

Carolyn put all the herbal teas in a pile, and then said, "Bryan will you
talk to Luther. He's having some kind of hormonal attack."

Laura hung over the counted and grabbed Howard by the shoulder.
"Hey," she said. He leaned forward and kissed her.

"Should I cook Luther a cheeseburger?" he said.

While the three made dinner, Bryan and Luther sat out on the patio
staring at the sun as it went down.

Luther said, "I take more shit from these people."

Bryan was thinking about Carolyn, and the thought of her cooking
beside his mother inside. It seemed improbable, even physically improbable,
with her crammed into that tiny kitchenette, putting paper towels and tea
boxes on shelves that no one else could reach. He was amazed at Howard's
ability to link two opposite women. Something about his mother and

Carolyn together was disconcerting to him.

"Hey Luther. Who woke you up last night?"

"When?"

"During the fire. Who woke you up? Mom or Carolyn?"

"The fire alarm," he said.

Bryan slid back down in his chair, nodding. Maybe that meant that Carolyn had gone straight to his mother's room.

"Did you see Carolyn while she was in the house?"

"No," he said.

"You didn't see her at all?"

"No, I didn't see her until I was outside. Why?"

"I just wanted to know if you saw her, that's all."

"What was the matter with her?" said Luther.

"Nothing. I just thought maybe you saw her in the house, when you were running out."

"Sure, we stopped and roasted marshmallows. Sang folk songs."

"I'm just asking," said Bryan.

"Well dude, it's a weird question. Did I see her when I was running through a bunch of smoke? No, I didn't."

The three were laughing at something in the kitchen, Carolyn standing between them, her head blocked from view by the low hanging blinds on the glass door, like it was a picture with her head sprouted out of the frame.

Late that evening everyone dressed for dinner. Bryan and Carolyn used the upstairs bedroom to change into their clothes. Bryan's jacket smelled like a bag of charcoal.

"Why are we doing this?" said Bryan.

"Because your mother wants to have a nice dinner. It'll make everybody feel better."

"I smell like a hibachi," he said, tucking in his white shirt, streaked gray from smoke. "Does this feel strange, Carolyn?"

"Sure."

He zipped the back of her dress, and when she turned, he saw that it was only slightly tarnished.

"I thought these were just souvenirs."

"So we wear our souvenirs."

She lowered her face to the mirror and brushed her hair.

Howard served the meal, plodding back and forth on his lift. He opened two bottles of wine, Carolyn drank red and Laura drank white, and they sat across from each other, the candle flames between them. Luther puffed, from a distance, trying to blow out the candles from his reclined position. Laura, pouring herself another glass of wine, said "This makes me feel better, Howard. A little more and I'll almost be relaxed."

"Well, we won't stop there," said Howard.

Luther blew out the candles and Laura sat up again, taking her feet off the other chair. "Thank you, Luther."

Howard walked back over and lit the candle, smiling at Laura. His smile looked more a great muscular effort to tense his lower face and jowls. He said, "I ended up stuffing this with mushrooms. So if anybody doesn't like mushrooms...."

Luther bent over to Bryan and whispered, "He got this from the Whipped-boyfriend Cook Book."

"What did you just say, Luther?"

"Nothing, Mom. Guy stuff."

Carolyn said, "A question about puberty. His body is *changing*."

"Shut up, Manute."

"Everybody, tell me this isn't great. This man has cooked a fantastic dinner. Without any notice, he's put everybody up in this place. Tell me this isn't pretty great. Look at him," Laura put her arm out, the loose-knit sleeve hanging. "Howard? *I* appreciate this."

He turned and bowed, a wooden spoon in his hand, then he went back to stirring. Mother and Carolyn applauded.

"Howard, we're going to save our applause until after dinner."

"That's fine with me," he said. "I prefer it."

They ate and Howard opened another bottle of white wine, and Laura chewed her food, eyes closed. Everyone complimented the trout, the potatoes, the salad, and then Luther said, "These potatoes are excellent, man.

Are they *whipped* or something?"

"They're fried," said his mother, chewing.

He nodded, staring at his plate, and continued eating.

When Howard flicked the napkin off his lap and offered dessert, strawberries, Luther said, "I don't know. Do you have any *whipped* cream?"

"I don't, Luther. I'm sorry."

Luther sat smirking, bobbing slightly in his chair.

As she continued to drink, Laura asked Carolyn questions about her life, about volleyball, her family, her plans.

"I really don't know what I'm going to do," said Carolyn.

"You've got a lot of choices. Just don't waste them."

"I'm not."

Howard washed the dishes and came back to the table. He said, "So you two don't really know each other that well."

Laura said, "Well, let's just say I know a little better after last night." Carolyn laughed into her drink. "This girl knows how to stage an evacuation." She slurred her words together.

Carolyn stooped, her chest to her knees, and laughed as loud as Bryan had ever heard her.

"What the hell is so funny?" said Luther.

Carolyn, still laughing, red in the face, said, "I'm sorry about that."

"Sorry? Don't be ridiculous. You have your priorities in order. I was hoping the whole fire department would show up nude."

"You were naked in there?"

"It's a good thing you didn't see her, Luther. You might have forgotten your skateboard."

"That's a very courageous thing to do, Carolyn."

Laura swallowed a mouthful of wine. "Like hell. If I was that skinny I'd be naked all the time."

"Seriously," said Bryan. "It showed a lot of balls."

Laura and Carolyn looked at each other and burst out laughing again.

"I must've missed that."

"It's an expression."

"Sounds like all the balls were on the porch," said Laura.

Brian slumped down in his chair and stabbed at his food. His mother said, "Ah, did we hurt your feelings Bryan?"

"Shut up, Mom. I'm sorry I didn't kick your door down, naked."

"Gosh, me too."

"Bryan, we're just kidding around."

"Laura," said Howard. "Bryan clearly has his thoughts about this and...."

"I'm fine, Howard. Thank you, but I'm fine."

"Dude, I wouldn't run in there naked either. I wouldn't worry about it."

"I'm not worried about it, all right? Okay? Will everyone please shut up and leave me alone. I fucked up, okay. I admit it. I'm sorry. Now just let me forget about it."

"Bryan, this is all you. We didn't say anything...."

"You've been doing this to me all night. What do I have to do? Okay. I apologize. I admit it, okay."

Carolyn asked, "You admit what?"

He was about to say, "That I was terrified," of the fire, of his own house, but he stopped. He heard loud thuds, like distant explosions.

"What is that sound?" said Laura.

"Those are the fireworks over at Disneyland," said Howard. "They go off every Saturday night when it closes."

"Can we see them from here?" said Luther.

"If it's clear enough."

Bryan went outside with them, everyone carrying their drinks. They tried to spot the fireworks through the haze in the distance. It was a mere flashing of light, followed by a few second delay and then the booming sound, cracking in quick bursts, like the foothills were being strafed.

Bryan went over and sat on the planter beside the house. He watched them stand in a cluster on the sidewalk, and then saw Luther come back out with his skateboard and begin coasting around them in circles.

Howard came over and put his hand on Bryan's shoulder.

"She's an aggressive woman," he said. "She doesn't take prisoners."

"Who?"

"Your mother."

Bryan looked at Howard's pudgy face, his eyebrows held up above the frames of his glasses. "She takes a lot of prisoners."

"You know what I mean. She didn't mean to challenge you in there. She was just being Laura."

"Okay," said Bryan. "Thank you."

"This is something that everyone has to learn to deal with. This kind of thing."

"That's true, Howard. You're absolutely right."

"Listen to me, Bryan. I'm going to tell you a secret, a huge secret, and you have to promise me you won't say anything."

Bryan put up his two fingers up like a boy scout.

"I've known your mother since you were a child, Bryan, since before your father passed away. She can make me so angry that I want to put my fist through a wall. She's left me, she's gone off with other guys, but she always comes back, and every time I kick myself and I say, get over this, why are you going through with this again. Do you know why I do?"

"I don't know, Howard. Why?"

"Because I love her," he said. He was terribly drunk and Bryan saw in his face that he was caught up in this confession. "I love her," he said. "And if you love somebody it's not *you* that's important. Ego, ego, everybody has their big ego. But I don't care when it comes to her. I've always loved her."

Bryan couldn't stand to look at the man. He thought of all the years and all the other men he'd met in his house and all the people his mother had cried over and whispered to on the phone, danced with drunken on the lawn, and he couldn't stand the thought of this little man pining for her in his badly decorated house, a man who had dedicated his life to comforting her.

"Do you understand that kind of love, Bryan," he said. "Do you love your wife like that?"

"Like what?"

"Like you would wait your whole life for her."

"I love my wife," said Bryan.

"Would you wait your whole life for her?"

Bryan thought of Carolyn now as if she moved faster than he could keep track, and he thought of his *mother* rushing through years while Howard slowly scuffed from room to room. He couldn't stand the thought of moving so slowly anymore. "I don't think *waiting* is the right idea for me."

Howard looked crestfallen, and he said, "I just love her. Maybe it's foolish. I can't help who I am."

There was a grand finale of crackling fireworks.

Carolyn hopped in the street, clapping her hands. Laura held a bottle of wine, and laughed as she watched Luther, in all his seriousness, do skateboard tricks for them. He fell a few times and they cheered for him, and Luther said, "Wait, wait." In the darkness of a suburban street, slanted downward, he cruised around them, trying handstands then trying to roll the board over with his feet and land on it.

"You're doing fine, honey," said his mother, laughing. She said to Carolyn, "I'm so proud."

Luther said, "No, I can do this."

"I know you can *do* it, Luther," said his mother. "But it's dark out for Christ's sake. You're an insane person."

Howard said to Bryan, "Your father loved her, but it was different. He was like *her* father. He used to scold her, lock her in her room. I don't know much about life, Bryan. I just know I was always there for her. I always came through."

Laura got onto the skateboard. She stood still, and then began to roll backward.

Carolyn got on, balancing on it with outstretched arms until it hit the curb and she jumped off. "I'm too drunk," she said.

Bryan felt drunk himself. He said, "Of course I love her. I would die for her. I'll go die for her right now if it makes you happy."

"Nobody has to die," said Howard. "Just be there."

"I'm here," said Bryan. He went to Carolyn took the skateboard and said, "I want to ride around on it."

She stepped back. "Be my guest," she said, and Bryan pushed his way downhill, gathering speed. He shot down the street, all the dark sleepy houses slanting diagonally alongside him, darkened and identical, fences in a zig zag downward. He sank, the wind puffing up around him. Behind him he could hear Carolyn and his brother shouting, running after him on the pavement, but he kept going, feeling the speed as the skateboard started to rattle beneath him, and he heard dogs barking at the noise of him, howling, and the whole world seemed to be opening. At the bottom of the hill was a thin film that covered the world. With enough speed he could puncture it and tumble through—however foolish, however pointless—into his own life. He sped down the street, past spotlight after spotlight from the yellow lamps overhead. The windows of the houses flickered full of televisions, and he burst through the wind with the calls of the others passing deeper behind him. He was not afraid to be pitched a mile across the darkness. He was chasing this one moment, across his long stuttering life. Racing the delay, he heard Carolyn's voice echoing all across the neighborhood, bouncing off the empty pavement. The board shook at his feet, the wheels ground. He knew then—in a gust of understanding—that he had left himself up at the house, all his thoughts and dreams, in pursuit of a fleeting rush of emergency in which he felt himself, without a margin of doubt, tripping over his own desperation.

JOHN MANDELBERG

May One

I was sleeping and I wasn't dreaming about it but my thoughts seemed dark red or burning, they were flattening back and kept turning or spiraling down. I woke up on the sofa with my hair twisted over my face, I was just remembering my sorrow and I heard a mockingbird singing two notes glassy clear and hard, repeated four times. I got up sweating in my cotton nightgown and I went across the gray carpeting to the bathroom, I saw drops from Daddy's urine bag on the floor but they were colorless and didn't smell. But I opened the window and then I was smelling the gray fog with the fragrance of the blooming privet bushes. I urinated and I was noticing the grainy blue gleam of the bathroom wall, then I was standing at the sink and heard the firetruck sirens delicately far off, and I stared at my own eyes in the mirror.

Mom was in the kitchen, which seemed dark because of the gray clouds, and I asked her, How's Daddy? and she was saying, He's sleeping now, I heard him get up in the middle of the night to do something with the urine bag, I guess he's okay. Then Deborah came in wearing blue shorts and a white T-shirt and I asked her, So what's happening? and she was saying, There's still new fires and looting but it seems like there's less, maybe it's calming down, and Mom said, Lord I hope so, it's all so horrible, it's like a nightmare.

Deborah was saying, Are you going to work? and I said, I have to call but I think all the banks are closed, I think my branch is closed, and Mom was saying, Oh I wouldn't go over the hill at all today, it's too dangerous. I said, But I have to go back to my apartment, and she said What's the rush? Stay here again tonight, where it's quiet, and Deborah said, Yeah, quiet so far.

Deborah was saying, Hey it's May Day, the First of May, go pick some flowers for our May Basket, ha ha, and I was thinking, I could pick red pelargoniums, pink impatiens, blossoming privet and star jasmine.

Deborah turned on the TV, Mom was saying, Well should I make pancakes, girls? Would you like some pancakes? and I said No, I wasn't hungry, just wanted milk. Then I was looking out the back window, a squirrel was hanging from the shaggy green branches of the ash tree and it jumped into the roof gutter, then the dry ash seeds were splashing down on the bricks.

Mom was saying, There's just so much racism in the society, they see no opportunities, they have no hope, now they see the police can do anything to them without limits, the rage just builds up.

Deborah was saying, Yeah but it doesn't matter, they shouldn't be burning down buildings and looting stores and killing people, there's just no excuse for that, it's like they don't have any values at all, like they're animals or all insane.

I was staring at the plastic yellow napkin holder, and the nubby-weave dusty gold and brown curtains, out the dirty window through the camellias.

Then we could hear Daddy shuffling out of his room in his slippers with his urine bag sloshing under his robe. We said, How are you feeling? and he was sighing, All right, and sat down slowly and Mom brought him orange juice. I said, Does it hurt much? He said, Does what hurt? I said, You know, the catheter, and he was scowling and said, No it doesn't hurt — why should it hurt?

We were listening to the far-off sirens, then the mockingbird was singing coolly and brilliantly from the telephone pole, silver trills repeated four times.

I called the bank where I was working, they were closed, I called my apartment to see if it had burned down, my own voice came on from the answering machine. I listened to my own voice, it sounded mysterious or lost and I kept listening to it carefully.

Deborah was saying, At least they don't seem to be going after Jews especially, mostly they're after Koreans. Mom was saying, Jewish people really haven't done enough, we haven't paid attention to the problems, we've gotten too comfortable. I said, Jews are just white people, we're nothing special.

Daddy was going back to bed. Then I was washing my hair in the bathroom and I could see a little chip in the old blue porcelain sink and I could smell the blooming privet from the window. I saw Mom's old hairbrushes on the little wooden shelf over the toilet. I dried and brushed my hair, I looked at the TV and I was sighing with despair. I walked barefoot across the gray carpeting to the back door and then I was standing outside on the patio with my arms folded, watching dusky-colored mourning doves coo on the telephone wires. I could smell the star jasmine from the breezeway, and distant smoke, and I was thinking, Nothing here will ever be the same again.

Then I came back into the house and I was reading the L.A. Times in the kitchen, Deborah was going to bake brownies and Mom went to lie down because she hadn't slept all night, then Deborah and I heard a noise in the breezeway, between the house and the garage, like footsteps, and Deborah was saying, What's that? and my heart was starting to pound.

Deborah went to look out her bedroom window into the breezeway, I was saying, Is it the mailman? and I was looking out the kitchen window. I could smell the dark secretive sweetness of the star jasmine, then I heard Deborah gasping, Oh my God, it's Joshua.

I said *What?* and I was rushing to Deborah's room past her yellow lace bedspread and yellow pillows and looking out her window. In the dense fragrance of the star jasmine I could see it really was our brother Joshua with his thin pale neck, standing in his tender gawky way, wearing a red and brown plaid flannel shirt and carrying something in one hand. I could see out to the driveway, I could see my car, dirtied with eucalyptus droppings, the palm trees and parked cars across the street. Then I saw Joshua was carrying a gun, and I was saying, Oh he's got a gun! I think he's holding a gun.

Mom came stumbling out of her room in her pink nightgown, her face was pale and sagging, she kept blinking desperately and she was whispering, What? What's going on? Is it Joshua? What? Is Joshua here?

We were whispering, Joshua's here, he's in the breezeway! He must've run away from the Group Home!

Sssh shh! Mom was saying, don't wake up Daddy. What should we do? Did he knock on the door? Should we let him in?

Deborah whispered, Mom, he's got a gun! I'm trying to tell you he's got a gun!

I was saying, He's holding a gun, he's holding it like this, I saw him just standing in the breezeway holding a gun like this.

Mom said, Should I talk to him through the window? I don't know, what should I do? Should I let him in? We cried out, No, no, wait, wait! He's pointing the gun! No, he put it down.

Then we could hear Joshua talking in his high voice, arguing with himself, and we could hear him saying, That's exactly it, that's exactly it, but it's different, it's different, it's different. I could smell the star jasmine through the window and I was staring at the interlocking yellow lines and coils on the yellow bedspread.

Mom said, Oh my Lord, where did he get the gun? Deborah was saying, He could've picked it up anywhere today, on a day like today, my God, he could be picking up a gun anywhere. What should we do? We better not let him in! Mom was saying, We can't just leave him out there! Oh Lord what should we do? Should we wake up Daddy? We cried out, Mom, Daddy's *sick*! What do you expect *him* to do? Mom, he just had his prostate out! Mom, he's wearing a urine bag! What do you want *him* to do? What do you expect *Daddy* to do?

Mom said, We have to call the Group Home. Call that emergency number! Oh Lord I don't know where it is, where's the number? Should we call the police? We shouted, Oh I'm sure the police are going to come all the way up here for this! I'm sure! They're all getting shot at in South Central, I'm sure they would come up here!

Mom was groaning, What if they arrest him? They might kill him! Oh Lord what should we do? Should I go out and talk to him? We cried, Mom he's got a gun! He could kill us all! Don't you understand, Mom?

I was kneeling under the bathroom window and trying to look out to the breezeway to see what Joshua was doing. I was smelling the sharp bittersweet scent of the privet and I was trembling, my heart was beating fast but exhausted, I felt a whitish spark in me was sputtering or flickering, my hands and my ears and nose felt very cold.

Mom was calling the Group Home and I heard her talking frantically on the phone, I peeked out of the window fearfully and I heard Joshua kicking at the stucco wall in the breezeway, which made the window rattle. Then I could see Joshua coming out of the breezeway and he was walking on the driveway crunching over the eucalyptus leaves and seeds. He was talking to himself, saying That's an aspect, that's an aspect, that's an aspect, and I could see his thin neck and the rumpled collar of his red and brown flannel shirt. His eyes were full of veiled trouble held or pressed back, he hadn't shaved and his thin brown whiskers were growing, he was looking toward the bathroom window but didn't see me, then he started kicking at the hubcaps of my car. The kicks sounded Bang bang bang! and when he stopped the mockingbird began singing, urgent and crystalline from the top of the ash tree.

Mom was shouting on the phone, then she gasped, They say they can't come if he has a gun! They say I have to call the police! Oh Lord—if I call the police today they'll shoot him! I saw from the bathroom window as I stood by the blue toilet my brother raise up his gun, and I saw him firing a shot high up into the ash tree, I heard the metallic crack of it and Deborah was screaming, Get away from the window, he's shooting! The echo of the shot was snapping or slapping back against the other houses and the parked cars and Deborah was screaming, Get away from the window!

We ran back to the hall and we were cowering there, Mom was blinking tears and Deborah shrieked in a whisper, I hate him! I hate him! Look what he's doing to us again! God I hate him! Then Mom was crying and saying, Oh honey, oh honey, you've got to understand, when one has suffered somehow, and one has a tremendous disturbance in one's mind—and Deborah was snarling, So one may kill one's family with a gun, *may one*? God you are so full of shit! I hate him and I'll say it out loud! She was saying to me, don't *you* hate him? God don't *you* hate him? I was thinking I couldn't speak but my voice creaked out, He's my brother, I can't really hate him.

Then we were hearing Joshua pounding on the door with the gun or with his angry kicks, going *Bam bam bam*! making the whole house shake. Then he stopped and I could hear him speaking in his high serious voice, Okay, okay, okay, the circle, the circle was moving, the circle was moving, it was moving, okay.

Then Daddy was coming slowly out of his room in his robe, we could hear the urine bag sloshing, he was blinking and pale without his glasses, and he said, What's going on? What the hell is going on?

We said, Joshua's here, Joshua's here, he's got a gun, he must've escaped from the Group Home but they won't send the van out unless the police take away the—no, Joshua's *here*! he's at the front door, he has a *gun*! We were standing in the hall on the gray carpeting, Mom in her nightgown, Deborah in her blue shorts and white T-shirt sobbing, I could hear the doves calling from the high trees.

Where the hell is he now? Daddy was demanding. We shouted, Stay away from the window! But he shuffled into the kitchen in his slippers and looked out to the driveway. He opened the window, and I could smell the star jasmine and the gray heaviness of the misty day. He was shouting out the window, Joshua! Joshua! What are you doing? His voice was tired or beaten but reaching or digging back for weak power.

Daddy was shouting, Joshua! Listen to me Joshua. Put that down, you're going to get hurt, I said put it down. Joshua! I'm speaking to you. Put it down. No, put it down by the garage door. Put it right there on the cement. No— what did I say? On the cement. That's right. Now leave it there and come up here on the porch.

Daddy was sighing and wiping his face and he muttered to Deborah, Run out there around the side of the garage and pick up that damn thing.

I was trembling as I stood by the toilet and looked out the bathroom window, over the blooming privet to the driveway, and I saw Deborah, far off now, come creeping around the corner of the garage in her blue shorts and white T-shirt to pick up the gun.

Daddy was saying sternly through the closed front door, No you can't come in. The doctor said you can't come in until you act responsibly. Stay on the porch and your sister will give you some orange juice. Then he was muttering angrily to me, Where are you? Damn it you don't have to hide now! Get your brother a glass of orange juice!

Joshua was calling out earnestly in his high defensive voice, Daddy, Daddy, I, they're mean to me, I went to the, they're mean to me, they're assholes, they're assholes, they're assholes, I mean, they're assholes.

Daddy was saying, That's okay, that's okay. Now just sit down and rest, and your sister is getting you some orange juice.

I was whispering, We're out of orange juice, Daddy, we don't *have* any orange juice! I was bringing apple juice, I carried the glass shaking, it was unfiltered so it was cloudy brown and sweet, and Daddy called through the door, Okay, here's some nice orange juice, I'm going to open the door and your sister is going to give you the glass.

I put my hand out the door with the glass of juice and Joshua looked toward me, calm and dazed without speaking, I was seeing him for the first time in more than two years but I was in the shadow of the half-open door and he didn't seem to recognize me or was seeming to not want to recognize me.

Mom was talking bitterly on the phone to the Group Home, then Joshua was saying from the front porch through the door, Daddy, Daddy, I have to go to the bathroom, I have to, like, I have to take a piss, like, I have to go, and Daddy answered, No, you can't come in, you haven't been acting responsibly.

I looked out the kitchen window to see the eucalyptus seeds dropping on my dirty car, I saw a heavy breeze was brushing the treetops and the palm trees back over the telephone wires and I heard fire sirens, far off. Then the van from the Group Home was driving up and two men were running up the driveway to catch Joshua, one in a suit and tie who was a blond Anglo man, one in khaki workclothes with keys on his belt who was an African-American man. Then the van drove away with Joshua and I could hear a jet plane flying over us, and traffic on the freeway rushing home to beat the curfew, and I heard the doves calling from the roofs.

Mom was saying, Should we still call the police and tell them? and we said, Why bother, not today. We asked Deborah what she did with the gun and she was telling us, I wrapped it up in a bunch of Daddy's urine towels and put them in the trash can. We turned on the TV and it seemed like the riots or rebellions were just about ending for now, the fires were going out, they were working on the lists of the dead.

Dad walked out of his room all dressed, he was wearing brown pants and a tan golf shirt, we were staring at him and he was saying, I want to go out for a walk before the curfew starts, I need some fresh air, do I look okay? Can you tell I've got this urine bag on, can you hear it slosh around? and we said No not at all!

I walked out into the breezeway and breathed in the night-tinted scent of the star jasmine, and then I was walking across the driveway crunching over the eucalyptus seeds and twigs to check my car, then I walked around the front of the house and smelled the keen bittersweet fragrance of the blossoming privet, then I was walking around to the back yard and stood still under the dark green canopy of the ash tree. I could hear a mockingbird singing, pointed trilled single notes repeated four times. The lukewarm air was full of thick yellow haze, it was drifting through the ash tree and spreading out along the tops of the palms and the telephone wires to the long line of rooftops and trees, far out over the city to the softly blurred hills and up into the sky. I was thinking, the birds and the trees and the sky are still the same, they are all still the same.

C.P. ROSENTHAL

Forever Burning

"How late?" Harlan said into the phone.

"Not too late," said Gala. "Ten-thirty — eleven."

"It's too late for Nena. You haven't put her to bed all week," said Harlan.

"I know," said Gala.

"Next week you're gone."

"Tomorrow I'll be home early," Gala said.

Harlan put down the phone receiver. It was attached to a FAX machine. The machine took messages, forwarded messages, paged, speed dialed. It had a speaker phone and made plain paper copies. He'd bought it for Gala.

Because under her persona of Calamity Ray, her third book of cowgirl poems was in production and she was negotiating a contract on the fourth. She was taking bids on her unfinished novel, and suing CBS for airing a TV show that lifted its pilot from her first book. Writing conferences all over the country called her daily. Representatives from the David Letterman Show gave her a phone interview, but backed off when they found out she wasn't really Calamity Ray, and that Gala was not only quicker on her feet than the wily, but homey, Calamity, she was dangerously smarter than Letterman.

In August she'd been promoted to full professor and made head of the graduate writing program at her university. All of it ironic because as recently as three years ago, when she was writing poetry, she couldn't get published, her petition for tenure was in jeopardy, and she couldn't even get into a writing conference without paying the entrance fee which, of course, qualified anyone.

"No Mama again," said Nena.

"Tomorrow night," said Harlan.

"I want Mama."

"Me too," said Harlan.

That night when Gala got home, Harlan made her a bourbon as usual.

"God," she said, "tomorrow I should just sleep."

She leaned back on the breakfast bar, her palomino hair touched her shoulders just below her exposed nape. She wore a silk scarf tied at an angle on her neck, a wrap-around, knee-length skirt, and cowboy boots. She was dressing more expensively now. Sexier. Spending more money on clothes, which she needed because she was so often in demand.

He loved to look at her. He always loved to, but at this time of the night he loved to because of the way her make-up faded, her lips pale red, the shadow of black under her blue eyes. She was a brilliant woman and in her midthirties still very young. Now, suddenly, powerful and successful. And the more of all of that, the less of him, as she came home tired, her mind in a million other places. Now, between the weekends at conferences, she spent fewer and fewer evenings at home. He did not have to spell it out. He did not want to be a cuckold, not even to a career.

"We miss you around here," he said.

"This will stop," she said, "but for now it's going to get us somewhere."

Where, he thought, divorced?

"Let's watch some TV or something," said Gala. "I've got to wind down."

"Okay," said Harlan. "Your buddy Letterman is probably on."

When they went upstairs he tried to undress her, but she stopped him. "I'm too tired, Harlan," she said, tearing her clothes off quickly, putting her hair up and slipping into a flannel nightgown and terry robe. She didn't last long in front of Letterman either, asleep on the couch before she barely started her drink.

He awoke at six. He went out into the dawn light of the living room, its windows facing the eastern cliffs of Topanga Canyon, the rising sun a red glow behind them. He sat, as he always did, for fifteen minutes. He just sat. By now the five cats knew his ritual and did not bother him until he got up, and then began their mewing and rumbling around his legs. He fed them, then started coffee and breakfast, an easy one because last night he'd prepared the fixings for fresh bread in the bread machine. He got out the bread, the butter and honey, knives, cups and plates, juice, vitamins, hot chocolate for Nena that he heated in the microwave. He ground the beans and dripped the coffee. He made Nena's lunch, a peanut butter sandwich and an apple, put thirty-five cents in her canvas lunch bag for milk. The bag was from Greenpeace and covered with black Orca whales. He fed the newts, the fish, the rabbits, then let out the cats and went up to wake his girls.

"Mama's here!" screamed Nena, and ran into the bedroom. Harlan had already finished his first cup of coffee when the two of them came out.

"We've got a half-hour till school," said Harlan.

"She can be late," Gala said.

"Here, sign her homework," said Harlan. He gave Gala a pencil and the sheet of completed additions, no combination amounting to more than six.

"Some of your sixes are backwards," said Gala to Nena.

"Those are Dad's. Mine are right," said Nena. "Let's stay home today. Let's drive to San Diego and see Shamu."

"I have work," said Gala. "But I'll be home tonight."

Gala coaxed Nena into dressing, then they got in the van and drove up to Topanga Elementary which sat in a bowl of hills and pine trees at the end of a little box canyon north of the Post Office. The public school was one of the best in Los Angeles, and much safer than the Oakwood school east of Venice Beach, where they'd lived for four years until Gala's recent success.

Gala's money had done what Harlan couldn't do, moved them up to the canyon, but he still wore scars on his forehead and chest from the knife wounds he took during a mugging, while standing between his family and their assailants. He carried them like furrows of fire, a legacy of guilt, not heroism.

They hugged and kissed Nena in front of the first grade room before she went inside.

"It still hurts me," Gala said. "It always hurts for me to leave her. My baby girl."

Back at the van, Gala stepped in front of Harlan and got in the driver's side.

"It's only a half-mile," said Harlan.

"I know," said Gala. She started the truck and drove down the hill, but when she reached the Post Office she didn't head straight home, she turned right, onto Old Canyon.

"This is a writing day for me," said Harlan, a day when he had some time while Nena was in school. He didn't have any work until the afternoon when he had to replace some fireplace tile for a woman in Pasadena, after Gala got home.

'I thought you'd stopped," said Gala. She drove down the road about two miles and took a left at Red Rock. "You run here sometimes," she said.

"Yes," said Harlan. "But I park out by the road. The residents don't like all the traffic heading in."

"They're on access to County land," said Gala.

"I know that," said Harlan.

Besides the main road, there were few other ways in and out of the canyon; this road, Old Canyon, and some fire roads through the mountains in the State Park and in Red Rock. Another road through Tuna Canyon started at the top of Fernwood and wound precariously down into Malibu. Harlan and Gala lived on the Boulevard at the foot of Fernwood.

Red Rock was a dead end, about a mile long, which followed an arroyo off Old Topanga Canyon. Harlan had discovered it on a tip from a ranger when the State Park was closed at the start of the fire season the previous fall. It was an odd place, a dirt road lined with walled mansions and tree houses, sprawling cabins and tiny trailers, wooden shacks, Job Johnnies, wandering dogs, horse corrals. A dark canopy of California sycamores, eucalyptus trees, Ponderosa pines, and live oaks grew under the shadow of the dry cliffs which rose on either side. There were KEEP OUT signs everywhere, around the mansions as well as the tree houses, trailers, and shacks.

At the end of the pavement a County fire trail wound into a narrow, red walled canyon that followed the arroyo, then opened into a huge vista of blond mountain tops and red, tilted mesas. The canyon walls erupted with overhangs, rainbow bridges, rock formations and caves. Hiking paths left the fire road and wandered up into the sky. Harlan ran here sometimes, and sometimes brought Nena here after school. They sat in the caves hooting echoes, pretending they were ancient beings.

At the fire road Gala parked the van next to a corral surrounded by signs that read NO TRESPASSING and NO PARKING. He assumed he did not have to point that out to her.

"Get out, Harlan," Gala said.

They got out and Gala went to the corral where a big silver gelding stood under the branches of a eucalyptus tree. Gala pulled a carrot out of her purse and gave it to Harlan.

"Feed him, Harlan," she said. "He's yours."

Harlan offered the carrot to the horse and the gelding nuzzled him. "You've been on him," Harlan said.

"He'll stop and he'll go," said Gala. She grabbed Harlan by the belt buckle. "Unlike you, he won't fight."

Harlan put his fingers in Gala's hair, then gently brushed it back from her shoulders. He kissed her, her lips slightly open, and soft.

"You know how hard it was to find a seventeen inch saddle for that big butt of yours?" Gala whispered to him.

"What about Nena?" said Harlan.

"She'll get her pony soon enough. We have a place to keep it now. You'll let me ride this one sometimes, won't you?"

He followed her to a nearby shed where he found fresh hay and bags of alfalfa pellets, grooming equipment, an Indian saddle blanket, a western headstall and reins, and an embossed, western saddle. He couldn't gauge how much all this cost, but he knew it was a lot, and he knew it would cost plenty for upkeep.

"You better give me a ride home before you get up on him," Gala said.

Back at the house he undressed her and they made love, sitting up at first, her softness pouring around him. Then he lifted her from his lap and lay her down as she dug in. Her passion maddened him, their pressing together like the silent pocket between a flame and its burning, it left him, always, relentless, like the fire in hot coals.

Afterwards she showered and dressed for work. He watched her place her softness into the shape of her clothes, the line of her panties under the slight bulge between her hips, the falling of her breasts into the cups of her bra, and the draping of her blouse, her skirt. He got up when she went to put on her make-up. He pulled on his Wranglers and boots and fetched his straw cowboy hat, then went downstairs to kiss her good-bye.

'Thank you," he said to her when he held her.

"I'm holdin' onto you, cowboy," said Gala Ray. "I'm gonna buy us a pick-up truck and a ranch in Malibu to drive it on. I'm gonna get rich so you can stay home and ride in the mountains, take care of your plants and animals, look at the stars. I'm gonna send my daughter to Harvard and give her enough money so she'll never have to work for anyone else."

"You won't lose me, with or without those things," said Harlan.

"Harlan," said Gala, "I'll sell my soul."

After Gala left, he drove back to Red Rock and saddled up the silver gelding. He was a big boy, over sixteen hands, and he bloated on Harlan pretty good when he cinched him up. After about a quarter mile the horse let his air out and Harlan dismounted and cinched him up again. The gelding tried to take off, but Harlan kept him to a walk. After that, the silver calmed down pretty good and took to the reins. The animal had a sweet disposition, playful but willing to please, and Harlan walked him up the fire road a mile to the ridge above Calabasas and the view across the bowl to Saddle Peak.

There on the verge of heaven he sat on the silver horse. For years now he'd stayed out of trouble, dreamed, married, worked, raised his child, and now he had a horse of his own and time for himself. But the gift made him more powerless. Before, when he had so little, he consumed more, like fire. He remembered the first time he'd taken Gala to his father's home in Lackawanna, New York. His mother seven years dead. Gala couldn't believe how they'd lived. Six children in a small house: kitchen, dining room, living room; and upstairs only two tiny bedrooms and a bath, no electricity, no closets, no carpets, no heat.

"You were poor," she'd said to him. "You had nothing."

"They never let on," he'd said.

He heard the steady clopping of another horse and turned back to the road where a woman in English gear came toward him on a bay. He recognized her, Katherine Engel, the mother of Tara, one of Nena's classmates. They'd all spent Nena's birthday together at the Santa Monica Pier, an afternoon that ended with Gala in the hospital after getting sick on the Tilt-a-whirl. Katherine's husband worked in the movie industry. He made a lot of money and spent a lot of time away.

"Well hello," she said to Harlan. "I didn't know you could get a renter up here."

"He's mine," Harlan said. "A gift from Gala."

Katherine raised her eyebrows as she pulled up the bay. "I'm impressed," she said. She shifted her reins precisely in both hands. "I see those cowgirl books everywhere." She sidled her horse up next to his, her thigh brushing him when her animal swayed. "Sorry," she said.

Katherine was a small woman, blonde, supple, with delicate hands, her skin tanned and slightly weathered. She had a gentle, yet husky voice, sexy, but with an edge that sometimes reminded him of his ex-wife.

"I didn't know the stables were so close," said Harlan.

"In the next canyon," said Katherine. "Go back down to Red Rock Trail and just follow it north over the top of the ridge. Down in Zuniga, the next canyon, there's a lake, then the trail takes you up between Calmont School and Mill Creek Stables.'

Harlan nodded. "Pretty here," he said.

"It's paradise," said Katherine. It was a common password among residents to call Topanga paradise, an implicit agreement as to why they lived here, susceptible to mudslides in the spring and wildfires in the fall. This autumn, after five years of drought, and then two years of floods and slides, the chaparral on the hills exploded into a thick dry carpet of green and brown.

"Want to ride to the top?" said Katherine.

"All right," Harlan said.

They rode side by side, quietly, as the trail made a steep rise, climbing the mountain by switchback. The gelding began to sweat and froth. Harlan hadn't wanted to push the horse so hard the first time out and he pulled the silver up when they hit the cloud layer.

"It's all right," said Katherine. "It's not much farther. It won't hurt him."

Soon the fog cooled things down and the horse calmed. The silver climbed steadily, without resisting. He was a good boy.

They rode above the clouds to the mountain top and gazed through the mist over the chaparral, the mountains rolling in infinite, silent waves. A pair of hawks spun above them in a dalliance made palpable by the panting horses, both he and Katherine bathed in sweat. Then, when the horses quieted, came the buzz of moving air under the hawks' wings.

"So," said Katherine, her voice still breathy from her exertion, "I read your novels. They weren't easy to find."

Harlan squinted over the thick, waving hills. He never wore sunglasses when he rode because the sweat made them slide down his nose. He tried to smile at Katherine.

"What would you call it?" she said. "You're not very realistic."

"It's revenge," said Harlan.

"It's difficult," she said. "Surreal. You know, bread from stones." He stared straight ahead into the chaparral. He'd given her his card at the pier. It said: Harlan Tiburon — I don't want to talk about it. "I'm a Romantic," he said to her.

"I bet," she said. She reached over and touched his arm. "Hey, it's okay. Forget it." Then her hand slipped down to his belt and rested there. She laughed. "Does Gala have a wandering eye like Calamity?" Katherine said.

After he washed and brushed the gelding he picked up Nena at school, then drove to Sassafras Nursery where he bought Gala a bouquet of lavender irises He got some Chandon at the Fernwood Market and put it on ice before Gala got home. She wore a black, silk blouse, a red and black, flared country skirt, and panty-hose, something she'd disdained before this cowgirl thing hit.

"Clink me, too," said Nena when he poured the champagne, and the three of them toasted.

"To when I can afford to buy *you* a horse," he said to Gala.

"Beware gifts from starstruck cowboys," said Gala Ray.

"Buy *me* a horse," said Nena.

"In time, cowgirl," said Calamity Ray. "In time we'll have everything."

That night a strong, hot, Santa Ana wind blew through the desert and into the canyons and by morning parts of the city were afire. One blaze swept down Laguna Canyon in less than an hour and by nightfall engulfed Laguna Beach. On television he watched the fires hop from home to home, the owners standing under walls of flame, futilely wetting their roofs with garden hoses. In Chatsworth, across the San Fernando Valley north of Topanga, a brushfire raged throughout the day. Another fire in Thousand Oaks, twenty miles northwest of the canyon, pushed by the hot winds, swept south at an acre every three seconds, a wall of flames burning through Big and Little Sycamore Canyons until it reached the ocean at the Malibu - Ventura County line.

Harlan set the alarm clock every hour to wake up and listen to the news, but at 3:30 a.m. he simply stayed awake. He kept the vigil through the next day and the next night, until after the fires were brought under control, 30,000 acres burned and 350 homes. When it was over he made Gala help him pack an evacuation box and fill it with manuscripts, floppy discs, photo albums, emergency clothes.

"Harlan," said Gala when he took her to LAX for her flight to Denver, "fear is a desert." She wore her purple boots with sterling silver boot tips, her Stetson, a black t-shirt and tight, black Guess jeans.

"There are very few ways out of the canyon," he said.

"Harlan," said Gala, "there are very few ways out of anything."

He had a new routine now. After he got Nena in school he tended to the gelding. Groomed him, fed him, took him into the hills. The morning after Gala left he took the Red Rock Trail over the ridge to Zuniga Canyon and rode down to the lake, but pulled up short when he reached the Mill Creek Stables. From the hill above he watched the English riders in the jumping ring and spotted Katherine on the big bay, taking the barriers in easy strides. He thought of the huge animal between her legs, the delicate, authoritative movement of her hands on the reins, the pressing of her thighs to make the animal jump, turn. He watched her circle, posting, the up and down movement of her soft backside in the saddle. Then he turned his gelding and headed back.

On her third night at the Boulder writing conference, Gala called.

"How is it?" he asked.

"A fuck-fest," she said. "Nothing new. I found somebody to hang out with. He runs the program in El Paso. People assume we're together and I don't get hit on as much." When Harlan didn't say anything she said, "He's been married for twenty years, Harlan. He has two grown-up kids."

"If I'm the jealous husband I tell you that his marriage doesn't matter," Harlan said. "That he's just doing the soft-sell."

"There are jobs in El Paso, Harlan. I'm a grown woman."

"That's the problem," Harlan said.

"Tomorrow's an excursion," Gala told him. "I'm not going. I'm going to stay in my room and read. I'll be back the day after."

These days without her passed in a kind of limbo. He found himself living in gaps of unmanageable time. He moved his child from school to bed. He rode his horse. He watched the movement of the stars. He lost track of when he'd fed the animals. The plants went dry. He drank tumblers of bourbon.

Because there was a planet out there of starving beings. Starved for shelter, for food, for love, and he was healthy and absurdly unhappy. He felt as if he were moving through the corridors of an old life, like someone buried in a pyramid with a pharaoh. Suddenly, he'd forgotten who he was.

He sat. If he could not stop the world, he could stop himself. But he came back to the same thing. That the world Gala offered him was preemptive of her guilt, and that he would lose her. Then he would have to give up everything to keep himself, this void that he no longer recognized.

She called him the next night. She told him she could not make it home. There'd been a snowstorm.

There are lots of them in Denver, he told her, the airport will clear, they'll defrost the plane's wings.

She couldn't get to the airport, she said. Her El Paso friend had rented a car. They drove into the mountains for lunch, to a bed and breakfast that some friends of his owned. The storm came up. Why would she tell him this if it weren't true? She could tell him something else.

He didn't give a shit about the truth, he said. She'd driven to a bed and breakfast with another man. What did she expect? He'd propositioned her. She told Harlan that she'd said, no, but now she was spending the night there. If there were only a very few ways in and out of everything, what were the ways in and out of this?

She hung up angry at him. He finished a bottle of booze. In the morning he explained to Nena that Mommie would not be home that night, then got her ready for school. His daughter cried. He promised her a toy, and that Gala would be home tomorrow. She was a good girl, an innocent child, and didn't deserve the thing he was about to do. A Santa Ana wind blew from the north in hot gusts as he drove to Red Rock and saddled up the silver. On the ridge, Katherine waits, dressed in western clothes, a straw hat, her hair down, boots and jeans. He takes the bed roll from the back of the saddle and spreads it on a ledge overlooking the world. He undresses her and places himself inside her.

When they're done she turns toward the valley, the houses and roads crawling to the edge of the earth. Like Satan, she says, "Here, all of it is yours. Here the dreams of the day are as wild and dreadful as the dreams of the night." He was a man. He could renounce everything.

He brought the gelding out of the corral and climbed Red Rock Trail to the top of the mountain. Below him, in the next canyon, the lake reflected in the sun, and beyond, the riding stables, the horses and riders circling in the ring. There, on top of everything, the wind came at him in hellish blasts. He looked down upon the small, circling riders, the rhythm of the horses. Katherine riding. And he knew. He knew as much as a man knows anything that all he need do was ride down the mountain and make a new life for all of them. The wicked, hot wind blew upon him. And finally, for an indiscernible moment, the world stood still. He pulled down on the reins and kicked the horse. Once again he turned for home. He gazed north to the next ridge, to the canyons and mountains beyond, to the relentless land stretching forever. And then he saw the fire.

It started, at first, like the tip of a match on a far mountain top, a wisp of smoke, a puff. He guessed it to be about four or five miles away. But before his eyes it doubled and spread over the top of mountain range. It came over the ridge, opened its wings, and became an army of flames.

He took the horse down the trail at a fast walk, undressed him, but did not brush him down. Already the sour scream of fire trucks filled the Boulevard. Four passed him going the opposite way as he drove home. There, his neighbor, a sculptor, pulled up in a truck and jumped out holding a large wrench.

"Do you have gas?" he yelled.

"No," said Harlan.

"Do you have gas?"

"No!'

"You don't have propane?"

"Only electricity!" He had to yell it over the roar and honking of the fire engines rushing up the road.

"Shut everything off, close up and get out! It's a big one and it's coming!" his neighbor yelled. On the other side, the woman who ran the video store locked up, ran to her car with her dog in her arms.

"Get your kid!" she yelled. "It's already on the Summit!" That was three miles away.

A woman pulled off the road and yelled to them, a plaintive, already hopeless wail. "There's fire in the canyon!" she screamed. "The canyon is on fire!" Then she sat there, her arm hanging out the window, her face running in a thousand roads of fear, while to the north a plume of black smoke rose over the canyon, eight times as high as the highest mountain and covering half the sky.

The road to the school was completely jammed, so he parked at the bottom and ran the quarter mile up to the school yard. They'd already filed the children into busses, starting with the kindergartners, and he had to go inside one of them to find the first graders and Nena.

"There's a fire!" she said.

"Yes," said Harlan."

"Are we going to get Momma?"

"Yes," he said.

Outside the bus he asked the bus driver where they were taking the kids and the man told him north, to Van Nuys.

"You wont get out," said Harlan.

"That's where I'm told to go," the man said.

"The fire's already cut off the road! You won't get out!" Harlan yelled. He'd seen the fire. He thought he knew the canyons, the winds.

They stood there, stupefied, the smoke blackening the sun. Harlan turned away. He put Nena on his hip and headed down the hill to the van.

"You're carrying me like you did in Mexico City," she said. "You said I was too big now."

When he got her in the van he told her they had to leave quickly because the firefighters would need space to come and save the house. He drove the truck at a crawl, in a confused line of cars, people heading home, others heading out, fire engines blasting their sirens and horns to make a path up the canyon.

At the house he carried Nena inside and told her to take all she could carry. He grabbed the cardboard evacuation box and ran it down to the van, and when he got back Nena had already filled two grocery bags with stuffed animals, books, and some of her own art.

"Good girl," he said.

"I'll need a cat, too," said Nena.

The fire marshals had already moved into Fernwood, their red sedans crawling into the winding roads and blasting out on their bull horns. "Evacuate your homes! We cannot guarantee the protection of this area! Evacuate your homes!"

Most of the cats were outside and he could never collect them in this havoc, but he found Garbo, the old ginger, on a chair and they put the cat and the grocery bags into the van. Then he started up and backed onto the Boulevard.

But already the road was jammed with cars, trucks, horse trailers, now three deep on the two lane road, with the far lane left open for the movement of equipment and fire trucks. He thought of the other cats, the rabbits, the newts, and for a moment it was as if something leaden had dropped from his throat to his groin.

He turned on the radio and positioned his van in the outside lane. He didn't want to be trapped between two lanes of cars and the wall of the cliff. Hours into the fire the radio was just announcing the flare up, so he rolled down his window and yelled to the woman in the car next to him, her auto filled with clothes, two dogs, and a small boy, while in his rear view mirrors the cloud of smoke advanced, blackening the sky.

"Where is it now? Do you know?" he yelled.

"The wind shifted!" she said. "It burned straight south to Malibu and it's coming east up Las Flores!"

It had to be burning at ten miles an hour. Las Flores was two parallel canyons west, then came Tuna, then Topanga, to his calculations barely more than a mile away. They were quickly becoming encircled while they sat helpless on the canyon road.

"There's too much traffic," said Nena from the back seat. She took off her seat belt. "I'm going to play, all right?" She sat down on the floor and took some of her toys out of her grocery bags. More engines screamed up the outside lane, the sirens woeful. Above them, ash began to fall from the sky.

Harlan reached back and touched his daughter's hair. "The sky is falling," she said.

They sat in the line, moving slowly, crawling. The radio announced the evacuation of Malibu. In some places, as the fire reached the Pacific Coast Highway, people fled their cars to the sea, the Coast Guard coming for them in boats. The mouth of Topanga Canyon, where it reached the ocean, must have been jammed with vehicles from the coastal evacuation. He shivered wretchedly as the air conditioning chilled his sweat. In an hour they had gone almost nowhere. Then, to his right, he spotted the fire come over the top of the western hillside.

People began to honk their horns. Still others jumped out of their cars, stood in the road and screamed. Some left their automobiles, abandoned everything, and ran down the opposite cliff toward the creek bed. Then, farther down road, an arm of the fire burned its way to the roadside, engulfed the back of a loaded pick-up truck, and leapt the canyon.

The fire ran, burning on both the eastern and western slopes, surrounding the road, advancing north over the cars. The engulfed pick-up exploded as Harlan pulled into the outside lane, backed up, and turned back in the direction of the original fire. If he'd thought, briefly, about the grief of losing his home, his things, he now thought only of saving the life of his child.

In Fernwood now, near his home, the fire trucks began their climb up the winding hill toward the top of the mountain where already he could see the smoke pouring into sky. Another line of trucks began to form on the Boulevard, facing the approaching fire that swept in from the eastern side of the canyon, threatening to encircle the town, the homes, the cars and people piled in a line on the cliff road. Across the way, on the top of the eastern slopes, already the bulldozers worked to draw up the last line between the fire and the Pallisades, the outskirts of Santa Monica.

The police stopped him near his house and asked him to turn around, but he did not point out how foolish that would be, he lied and told them he had to go back to his home to get his cats. Then he followed the line of fire engines to Old Topanga where he was stopped again, but he told the trooper he had to save his horse. At Red Rock they stopped him for good.

"You can't go in unless you walk," said the officer.

Harlan got out and put Nena on his hip.

"You're crazy," the policeman said flatly, an Angelino who had administered to hell and its inhabitants a thousand times.

Harlan ran with his daughter on his hip, into Red Rock, to the corral. The fire burned now on the hills above them, the ashes, burning orange, falling in flakes from the dark sky. But he thought with the horse he could go where roads could not, he could pick a spot to wend through the fire. What else was there to do? If they were going to die, he would not sit with his daughter, waiting to be roasted alive in his van. Around him, people were guiding their horses into trailers and driving out, onto the road which would soon be covered in flames.

"What are we doing?" said Nena.

"We're going to get away from the fire," he said.

He saddled up the silver. The gelding's nostrils flared and the big horse danced as he readied him.

"A horse ride!" Nena said. "We have to take Garbo!"

"If she gets away, that's it," said Harlan, stupidly, like they were going on a picnic.

He got a blanket and took them all over to a spigot. He soaked himself, Nena, the blanket, the horse, then he mounted with Nena in his arms. He put her in front of him, face to his chest, and wrapped the wet blanket around her and the cat, then rode into the County Park.

He saw the smoke now in the hills around him, but he could not yet see flames. He took the Red Rock Trail. He thought that maybe the fire had already burned itself out to the north, maybe he would find a way out that way, at worst they could wade into the lake. But when he got to the top of the ridge he saw that the bowl was full of fire.

A wall of flames came at the riding school where people rushed to evacuate horses as two fire trucks began soaking the buildings near the road, sacrificing the out-buildings and the barns. He couldn't tell where they would take the horses, where the people would go. Across the canyon, in the hills, the propane tanks of homes exploded into the air, mushrooming like bombs. He thought, now, that he should return to the road. He could probably convince the firefighters to put Nena inside one of the trucks, though even so he battled the image of the dozens of men caught and baked in their trucks at Laguna Beach.

"Let me see," said Nena, and brought the blanket down under her chin.

On top of the hill, they watched the flames which came upon them now from all sides in engulfing walls of advance, the fire leaping in huge arches from bush to bush, eucalyptus trees spontaneously igniting from the heat.

"It's pretty," Nena said. She peered into the blanket. "Don't worry, Garbo, you have nine lives," she told her.

Alternately now he felt both tremendous adrenalin and calm as the four of them, man, child, old cat, and horse clung to each other in the center of the fire. Down the hill he saw the flames advance on a grove of pines and live oaks near the lake. It burned beneath them, scorching the branches, and then moved on, the trees standing alone in the inferno.

He turned the silver horse and headed back down the trail. At the bottom, the fire came up over the southern ridge. He saw the smoke approaching Red Rock Road from the east. He had just come from the north. He heard the screaming engines from Red Rock Road, and thought again of taking Nena to the firefighters, but when he headed that direction he found the trail cut off by fire. He turned the horse west. Down the road he found another wall of flames. He rode the horse along it, trying to find an opening until the heat and smoke became too intense. Now the fire came over the southern ridge. He'd been a fool. He'd ridden himself and his daughter to their deaths.

He headed back again, east, thinking their only chance would be to ride through the flames to the engulfed fire engines on the other side, when he spotted the stand of oaks and pines above him, in front of the rocky cliff, and behind that, the caves. He rode the horse up the embankment and found the huge opening in the cliff and dismounted with his child.

He took them in. He brought the silver as far as he would go, then let him stand free near the mouth. He took his daughter and the cat back into the depths of the cavern until the air grew cool, and he sat.

'Hooo-wooo," said Nena. "Echoes.' She held tightly to the cat. She smiled at Harlan, but she ground her teeth. He wanted to cry.

"Hoo-wooo!" Harlan said.

"Is Mom coming here?" Nena said.

It had grown dark, but when the fire swept down the hillside the air exploded with brilliant light. The heat mounted on the rocks, and the air became orange, the fire dancing around the trees in a halo of flames. The silver came into the cave now and lay down, pushing his head toward the back and the cooler air. Harlan turned Nena's head to the very base of the cave, but he could not help but turn to watch the infernal dance of fire.

The flames came down around them, but the trees did not burn. And inside the bubble of life, they had enough air in the cave. After uncountable hours, they emerged in the black night to the black hills, the embers of the landscape burning eternally. He could see the huge flames still rising in the south, toward his home, and to the west and east, so he took the horse back over the hill to the north.

They walked beneath a sky with stars burned out from firelight, on a blackened earth, the blackened bottom of hell burned out. The embers lit the road, and when the silver came up limping, he dismounted and walked the animal, riding only Nena and the cat. He took them back over the hill and across the burned out chaparral until he came upon the road, the houses disintegrated on either side, and the abandoned fire lines cut around the ruins. He walked north until, beyond the canyon, they reached unburned land.

He got on the horse then and took the avenue through Woodland Hills. His child shivered at his stomach. The people around him slowed their cars and passed gently by, until, at the corner of Ventura and Topanga Canyon, someone stopped and told him there was a victims' center just down the road at the high school in Canoga Park.

Once there, he tied the silver with a line of other horses and took Nena to the paramedics. She would not let go of him. She clung to him, speechless, and the old cat who was dead. He procured two cots in the gymnasium and held an oxygen mask for his child until she fell asleep, sometime in the dark morning hours. Then he found a woman to watch over her for a minute while he checked on the horse. A vet working the area said the silver's leg was incurable and Harlan gave the man permission to put the animal away.

He returned to his child. They restricted the sleeping area from TV or radios, and he made no attempt to find out more than he already knew. He knelt next to his daughter who clung to the dead cat. He touched his child's hair, caressed her back. That's how Gala found them.

He stood. She came into his arms and they trembled on each other under the strange, public auditorium light. He tried to cry, but he could not. He stood with his wife while the idiocy of his life burned. He held her. He saw the fire in the mountains, fire in hell, in heaven, in his soul, his heart. He held her and felt fire. He saw nothing but fire.

CAROLYN SEE

Light Ages

Some say it was a Bad Time
But I say it was a Good Time

Here's what Franz deGeld did when things began to look iffy in California—some of this I know first hand; some I picked up from Lorna, some I read in the columns, some I heard from Golden Oaks parents, O.K. ?

He went back to his wife, really back.

The way you knew it, people joked about it—was that Scratch Cafe (that white-painted California cuisine palace that used to be the "Tumble Inn" during the sixties and God knows what else in the years before that) suddenly had its carefully architected interior despoiled by flocks of sobbing starlets, all of whom had signed up to meet Franz and, after some artichoke salad and duck pasta, were looking toward a magic afternoon in his private spa across the street in his glamourous office-studio.

Day after day Franz made dates and then stood them up. Often those girls—dressed to the nines, as we say—had *hitchhiked* or had their mothers drop them off at the far west of the city, down in the bowels of Venice. They went in the restaurant, had one Cinzano, then two, then—what?—realized they couldn't pay for what they'd already ordered, and then began to cry. Nobody knows now how they settled their bills.

Franz took out Australian visas and was on the phone to Sydney and Melbourne all day long; all night long. But he couldn't close any deals. (And also his staff overheard him saying nothing would happen.)

About that time he made a commercial for the telephone company, advising the American public to "keep in touch," just like he did. It's safe to think that all across western America and over on the eastern seaboard, shoes were flung by pretty girls and dapper young boys at Franz's petulant face, framed in luminous Renaissance black, speaking about how he couldn't *live* without calling up his old friends.

This is how Franz spent the day he went home. He woke to cottony coastal fog, so thick it drifted through the coarse-cut screens of his renovated warehouse and into the art deco studio he'd turned into an immensely profitable film factory. He woke in a cloud. Propped up by futons unfolded by minions each night to form a different pattern on the highly polished floor, he opened his eyes to see, scuttling, maybe thirty feet away, a furtive rodent, just the grey tail. Well. Old building.

Too near to him sprawled some girl, Kathleen was it? Kaitlin? A girl who worked in a nearby restaurant. Scratch? American Bar and Grill? Her sprayed hair still racked up in a tease, her eyeliner smudged, her mouth open in much the same vapid, sad smile she had when she was awake.

On a low teakwood table, a small hand mirror with "Hollywood, Here I come!" stenciled on it, and a razor, and a couple of rolled hundred-dollar bills. (He gave them to the girls afterwards; their thrills, then, were doubled.) He looked down at his body. Still firm, muscular, tan. The girl, twenty years younger than he, was the one who had aged. Lines by her mouth, lines around her eyes; little, white, round, soft, cantaloupe belly.

He reached under a flowered bolster, part of this whole futon thing, found Lorna's tour itinerary. "Whatever you do, I'll know it," she'd told him as she'd flown off for a six-week tour to make thousands of dollars on the lecture circuit and turn the rest of the country onto her particular brand of carefree Christianity. "I'll know it and I won't care, because I'll be coming back."

He'd worked so long and hard to be cool, developed such a shell, that he'd been able to smile and yet be negligent, move his beautiful hands in her shining hair, feel his prick move as she waved her hands at it, saying, "See? I can keep you hard for hours, *days* if need be . . ." And he saying, "Don't take all the credit" or, "Don't press your luck" but then surrendering to it—just as she advised on television. And truly, for hours at a time, he was able to work miracles, more than with anybody else ever before.

Before she'd left she'd given him permission: "Have your little girls, the way you always do," she'd said. "I'm not in the business of denying you pleasure. I'm in the falling-in-love business."

"I've finally met my match," he said courteously. "At last I've met my equal." Then as she gazed at him, "Someone my own age at least," and she threw back her head and laughed.

But there was someone else his own age, someone he called every day at three-thirty in the afternoon, someone he took to premieres or any charity fund-raiser having to do with Democrats, animals, or the sick. His wife: chaste as Calpurnia, and as tedious.

And it was she to whom his thoughts returned this morning, even as he checked that Lorna (staying this week at the Helmsley Palace) would get her two dozen white roses every day.

He got up. Pulled on some chinos. Walked across the long expanse of polished floor to where a corner of the vast room screened off a tiny kitchen. One of his secretaries had already been here, made coffee, squeezed orange juice, put two almond croissants in the microwave. Left out the *Times*, open to the "Calendar" section. But he looked at page one of the real part of the paper, registered the headline. Walked again, holding his coffee, past the covered, sunken, silent, hot tub, past the word processor, past the stereo equipment— mechanical ghosts in the coiling wisps of fog—out onto the small balcony, one of three or four that opened off the second floor, and looked out onto the strand.

He saw, on the beach, in the very early morning, benches already filled with old women, a couple of tall black men repeating last night's coupling in a urine-stained doorway. He saw street merchants opening their vans, setting out tee shirts on strings in the fog, the sound of the dead ocean far out, slapping against fouled grey sand. What he saw must have made up his mind for him.

Or maybe it was the headlines for that day, who knows? People got scared in increments. L. A. PREPARES FOR THE UNTHINKABLE could blare at you for days and weeks, and then just one thing, one run-over dog could turn you on to it.

Maybe it was the soft girl in his bed with her smeared makeup. Maybe it was her terror, or her decay. We do know he did it that one last time, because she became a folk heroine for a while—the very last chicklet Franz got it up for.

All we know is, after the breakfast, and a snort, and one last screw, he said, no, they couldn't go in the tub again, he had some work. He gave her the rolled hundred, walked her as far as the top of the stairs, saw her—from his window—climb into the called cab, and then went through the place pulling plugs: the phones, all of them, the answering machines, the word processor, thereby consigning all the bookwork of a multimillion-dollar business to oblivion. He unlocked the doors to this film storeroom, he unlocked files; there were no secrets to keep anymore. He finished the last of his coffee, walked down the stairs to where his two secretaries were already at work, told them to call him a cab too. They, concealing their surprise, did so, and when the second lonely checkered little sucker finally found its way through the shrouded streets where his studio maintained its unmarked, unsigned location, Franz dropped one set of car keys on one girl's desk and the other on the other girl's desk and moseyed out into the mist without saying goodbye.

It wasn't until later in the day, when one of their girlfriends who worked at Vicente Foods or Westward Ho called up to say Callie deGeld had ordered food up to the Brentwood house for three months, including fifty cases of Dom Perignon, and what the hell was going on? that they had the wit to go upstairs and discover the thawing ice, the disconnected phones, the disappeared accounts, and, underneath the handmade cedar planking that kept his hot tub free of household dust, the script he'd been developing for the past six months—a simple love story—drowned.

Lorna wouldn't find out about it for sure for another five days, when she moved to Boston, to the Ritz Carlton, and the roses stopped coming.

This is the way the dark ages looked. It was hot, and it stank. It wasn't exactly like in the movies, but it was grey and dark and smoky. You tasted the thick air. I'm talking of the years right after. People wore blankets for a long time. I think they wore blankets because the working people had memories of polyester burns, their clothes melting into their skin, or watching that happen to others. Because of the feeling of clothes on raw skin, on sores—if you could find any loose cloth, if there was any—that was the best thing to wear.

Plants grew back right away, with the first rains. It was dangerous to drink the water. It was hard to know where you were, since there were vast craters and mountains where before there had been none. When a person's skin burned away, it grew back as cracked brown hide. We became experts on the wind. The prevailing westerlies were the ones to go out in; the Santa Anas coming down from the northeast—that in the old days used to scour the city's air—were the ones now to make you take shelter. Even today, when the air darkens and the taste gets thick on the tongue, our people—without saying much—take shelter.

There was little crime. At first there was panic, looting, suffering, fire. The panic—many who live remember it. It seems funny now. People fell where they were in the streets. They prayed on their knees, they wept. (On the other hand, some didn't. In the last minutes, women turned on their husbands: "*You, you did this!*" speaking in tones, the tones they had used before only when giving birth, so that some men, even in the midst of their great fear, were blown off the planet looking sheepish. By *you*, the women meant men, males: Caspar Weinberger, Alexander Haig, Ronald Reagan, but afterwards they couldn't remember those names, only the shape of the missiles and the bragging and bullying that had preceded these times. For a while a few women went to the few intact male corpses they could find, castrated them, pinned the bloody, dried penises to walls and tree trunks, with the scrawled word *peacekeeper,* but soon it didn't seem worth the trouble. Blacks halfheartedly offed whites; and whites settled scores, but it wasn't worth the trouble; panic prevailed.

We hear that people gathered material wealth but didn't know what to gather. The price of oil in El Segundo had gone up at the very first; but then cars became useless except as dwellings and armor. Anything that plugged in was useless, but the wiring was valuable. Canned food, first thought to be valuable, often had turned into deadliest poisons. People collected things, made caves, tried to find buildings, but it was chancy.

Then fires swept through, worse than the bombs, because there was no warning, no help for them; no reason and no "cause." There was no *you* to blame but the fires. You chose to stand or run. This is when people believed that the end of the world had really come, because that's what it looked like, that's what it sounded like—the terrible roar, the walls of flames. People stood rather then knelt and cried, Jesus, Jesus! as they prepared to burn. Sometimes, arms outstretched, they ran straight in.

I'm getting ahead of myself. That's also an effect of what happened. Time changed; you never knew what day it was anymore, you couldn't remember how long ago it had started to happen, or how long it took when it did happen. (Some of the dates, even the years, I put down in this story may be wrong.) But listen to me. Some people say it was a bad time, but I say it was a good time.

There were the last few weeks "in front." We all watched TV (*TV*, how strange!). All those men had their last chance to be important, and you can't say they didn't give it their best shot. Those were the days of the two-thousand-dollar business suits, when everybody who had an opinion about anything got interviewed, and then loyal wives got cricks in their necks from looking up at them, but every once in a while, if you could tear your eyes away from whoever was talking about the grave danger we were in, you saw—sometimes—the wives falter, bring their eyes down, look into the middle distance, shudder, shiver.

Those were the days of terror, but they were short days, fourteen to forty as I remember, when we either broke away or stayed. Every day, in eight- and ten-hour special "reports" the screen showed us the riots at L.A. airport as would-be passengers brought down their wealth—their jewels, money, wristwatches, heroin and cocaine, and waved them at harried personnel behind counters, whose computers were *already* blowing up and out. Or the stupid ones, the really stupid ones, who lived in the goatish eastern suburbs of L. A.—Pomona, Covina, Alhambra, Upland—took their impulse to flee but took it *east*. Can you believe it? Besieging the rich at Palm Springs, hiking or driving with great anguish up and over the Cajon Pass, with apparently not the slightest knowledge that what they would find on the other side of the mountains was miles of desert waste, and prime military targets as well. Of course the Air Force rose to the moment and defended that desert, making occasional strafing runs just to take out a few cars and terror-stricken civilians; saying to anyone who held a microphone in front of them that these grinding General Motors vehicles, loaded to the gills with grandmothers and mattresses and Cuisinarts and sobbing shit-stained babies, were subversives, hotfooting it over the pass to prevent the imminent launching of our weapons.

Well, it was ugly to watch, but the general feeling, even then, was those people were so dumb they didn't deserve to live. And we felt the same way about the rictus-grinning housewives who bought out the stores and got themselves photographed in supermarkets, as though buying three cases of chocolate pudding powder was going to save them. We watched all that on television with disgust and dread and very strong sick feelings, but I'd be lying if I said that when it started we didn't watch it with awe. Excitement. Anticipation. A general feeling of *Wow, I'm ready and here it comes!* For one thing, if you lived in California, what was the Big Deal! Imagine the white-knuckle rides at Magic Mountain, the Simi Valley earthquake (and the floods that came later), and two or three Bel Air fires whooshing up at once; that was what it was like, and finally, of course, the relieved sense that *it was* going to happen; and we wouldn't have to spend any more time worrying about *whether* it was going to happen.

As I say, I lose chronology here, but I also say it's a miracle that I can remember the *word* chronology. The way I remember, we couldn't think of what to do. Everyone fell back on what they used to do anyway.

Thus, the housewives in the supermarkets, the frantic drivers with their frightened families stranded in the Cajon Pass or way out in the wastes of the high desert on the Palmdale Road. Please don't think I'm putting on the dog when I say that *our* friends, *our* family, spent that last couple of weeks making long-distance phone calls and making love.

And there were those of us who spent the "last" two or three weeks at La Toque, or Michael's, or the American Bar and Grill—*that* got a few laughs— or Spago or the Polo Lounge. Or we said farewell at last long elegies at tiny Mexican joints on the west side where the *mariachi UCLAtlan* sang until their voices cracked, and Mexican wives who'd spent their lives not saying or doing or (supposedly) thinking anything, finally stood up, and with tears streaking their faces, sang *La Llorona* or *Cama de Piedra* but mostly the joyous songs, and whole restaurants—I'm speaking now of the Mexican ones—would be given over to singing and dancing and drinking tequila with lemon wedges until dawn, and usually after.

Do you see why I say that even *then*, even those two or three weeks *before*, could have been a good time, depending on how you looked at it?

Over at Michael's—because there were so many who wanted a "last meal" there—they pushed the tables together and let people eat family-style. Florists all over the city had "folded their tents" and let their roses wither, so the handsome waiters at Michael's scurried out and plundered all the gardens of Santa Monica to bring back great branches of bougainvillea and entire plants of furiously blooming marguerites. And let us all remember this! Michael himself, who through the years had taken such fierce pride in owning the very finest place in town, made a last bid for the divine, for historical immortality. He laced his delicate sauces in those last days with enough old-fashioned LSD that the flowers, the trees in that garlanded patio, the desserts, began to *breathe* in that sweet way most of us hadn't seen since the sixties, and you saw, instead of bodies around you, a couple of hundred souls at the tables. During those interminable last feasts, you might look across at—well, there was the lady from the second *Invasion of the Body Snatchers* who'd gained a little weight, but it didn't matter now, and upon request she'd make her eyes dance for the people around her. And tears were shed at that exquisite sight.

While nine-tenths—my guess—of the city of eleven million were leaving, driving over that Cajon Pass to the Mojave Desert, or sneaking (oh, irony!) across the border into most unwelcoming Mexico, or driving hopefully to a midpoint between here and San Francisco, or commandeering boats in the marina to float as far out into the ocean as possible, or taking matters into their own hands with bullets, or the box of pills, or the last and final family fight— a tenth of us were staying.

This is what you often saw. Since you knew that every ride in a car was apt to be your last, and since that Pope Whatever His-Name-Was had got such good press by kissing the round of whatever country he touched down in, you saw—well, you would have seen all of us touching our cheeks and noses to the ground when we got out of cars. Or when we approached our still-intact homes. You saw little wives in front yards with their arms *embossing* tenderness, kissing the sides of their houses, for instance, or burying their faces in their children or their pets. I saw one older lady flat on her back on her front lawn looking up into a bed of birds-of-paradise.

Oh, Paradise! This is what we found.

Every minute was your minute to make a choice: It was turn on the television and watch some hated white man tell you about hell, or it was lie down on damp green grass—or the dry weeds of Topanga, or the red ants of Lancaster—and say thank you, I love you, I love this.

And as I said before, you can imagine the sack time we put in! It wasn't desperate time, or brutal. It wasn't what came afterward when it was catch-as-catch-can for a few years.

The morning after Aurora left, Skip and I drove down for a lunch at Michael's. When we began to go back up the coast, we stayed on top of the palisades—those lovely cliffs—instead of hitting the highway by the beach. We passed Felicia's luxury apartment, and—pointing it out to Skip—I saw Hal there on the balcony, beaming with joy, waving with one arm at us, hugging someone with the other. It was his own Felicia, come home to be with him.

There were other places, easy to rent now, along that short drive, and we took one for the afternoon. Would we stay here until the very end? Or would we go home? As long as Denise knew where we were, it didn't matter. We trusted the universe to let us all be together.

Never have I felt such tenderness for any man as for my own dear Skip when we lay down in some retirement hotel on the Santa Monica bluffs. Still, when you went out on your terrace, there were senior citizens taking the last clean air. They waved at us and laughed as we kissed, and I clenched my fist in a revolutionary salute.

Then we were lying side by side, looking out onto another delicious set of swaying palm fronds, the giddy ocean behind them, and *wow*, what can I *say*? We learned once and forever what it was to have the world fall away, to be one soul, to forget, to shiver and weep with happiness, to look into each other's eyes until you couldn't look anymore, because our tears came and our fingers trembled. It was love without children or future or past, not even "love" the way you'd been brought up to think of it, but just a bright pink light around our heads like those silly halos in holy cards, and you knew you were getting ready for eternity—no doubt about it now.

And there were mercy fucks and revenge fucks, and I can't die without fucking her/him fucks, but you have those everywhere and every time, even now, I'm sorry to say.

When Lorna returned from her tour it was time for her to give her "You

Can Master Fear by Going Straight Into It" talk. And she gave that one six or eight times a day—not just on TV but all around the west side for, we'll say, twenty-one days. So what would that be, maybe a hundred and fifty times? But as you might imagine there were end-of-the-world maniacs on every corner saying, I'm not even kidding, *Repent! Repent!* And people down on their knees saying, as if it would make a difference, "We do! Oh, Jesus, we do!" and Lorna wasn't popular in those last days, not nearly as popular as she might have wished.

"I am a girl from Los Angeles State College," she would begin, telling her story. "And I got my education in a quonset hut." Her dyed, curly, sun red hair hung down in flat sheets. She spoke in the homes of Jane Fonda and Norman Lear, though neither of them was present at the time. She spoke at the Amfac Hotel, a stone's throw from the airport, because she was trying desperately to leave America in those last days. She spoke wherever people asked her to, and as she spoke the sweat poured off her face and, as often as not, the tears streamed down. But, then, that was normal.

I tried to hear her at least once a day. I see now I was asking too much of her—to take away my fear, or soften it, or dent it—*are you kidding*? But it gave some of us the gist of a Christianity we could understand; that poor guy up on the cross, and before that happened to him, *he* was so scared, his face came off on a towel.

The end of our world was at hand, and nothing she or anybody else could say could change it. But, conversely, the fires hadn't started yet; there was nothing to get excited about. There was just the perfectly trimmed corner yard of Franz deGeld's exquisite Brentwood home, and he most probably locked up inside with his wife, his children, his hardwood floors.

Lorna stayed away from Franz's house itself, but she did come six or seven times to his quiet green lawn hidden by hedges to preach, and—as usual—mostly women came to hear her. The women dressed up, in everything but stockings. They were on their way to make love, or eat, or make peace with their parents or their children, and they listened with a horrible desolation and resignation, because the truth is that during that time the light sometimes left Lorna; don't ask me how, or why. Her message was about fear.

"I came from L.A. State College, do you know where that is? And I got my education in a quonset hut. My subject today is fear, and that you can go beyond that fear, on the other side of fear, by allowing yourself to go into it, experience it. Take, for example, my own fear of public speaking . . ."

But, of course, by that time, we weren't thinking of our fear of public speaking.

"I have always had the experience of coming close to success, to what I wanted, and then, as often as not, it would fall through. I have studied kinesiology; I know that very often even our muscles conspire against us. Haven't you ever stood—as I'm doing now—up in front of people and the muscles that move your tongue refuse to move, your knees shake and buckle, even as mine are doing now? I've found that if you don't express fear, it does not go away. It lodges somewhere in your body. It goes out through your arms as violence . . ."

Standing in the crowd, because she would be forever my friend, I'd try to go along with her, thinking back on all of the short history of the United States that I could remember, wondering, why didn't John Foster Dulles, why didn't that MacNamara, why didn't that Caspar, why didn't they all just let their fear stay *fear*, for God's sake?

But, of course, standing there on the grass in the hot sun, trying, trying for a grip on religion, or at least history, it was difficult. I kept thinking about the cheese enchiladas at the Hacienda, or the fresh swordfish in ginger sauce at Michael's; thought about the spirit of my father (where Carlos Casteneda had always said it should be, behind my left shoulder) where death was. Dad? It seemed like he might be smiling, but I couldn't be sure.

Lorna worked Brentwood, Santa Monica, Malibu. We usually found her every day, maybe twenty or fifty of us, at about ten-thirty in the morning. We dressed in summer clothes, some of us in hats.

"Fear will most often come out in violence, but sometimes it manifests in paralysis. You can *see* what you want, but you're unable to reach out your arms to *own* what is yours, to *decree* what is yours! *Because you deserve the very best, and now is the time for it!* There are miracles, there are miracles for all of us now, even now, if we have the strength to reach out ..."

She hadn't been eating, and her always wiry little body was shrunken now. Her silk blouses darkened and clung to her breasts, drenched with sweat. "We are in Heaven even as I speak. Believe me. That's not to say there isn't such a thing as fear. Listen. Once there was a seminar I was supposed to address. I'd never done it before. Was I frightened? You'd better believe it! I was frightened until the world looked level . . ."

"Lorna?" a voice quavered; a woman in her early forties. Tall but no more than a hundred and ten pounds. I knew from our few words together in these mornings that she spent these last days in *dance* classes, eight or ten hours a day, perfecting, I can only suppose, her perfect body in God's eyes. "Lorna, will you teach us how to pray?"

Will you believe me that the *burning* started then and there? Lorna wore plain white, medium-heel pumps. Where our heels sunk into the damp green grass of Franz deGeld's estate (if we were imprudent enough to wear them), her heels floated on the surface, as if that spongy turf were green concrete. I was staring at those immaculate, perfect pumps, because I couldn't bear to look at Lorna's face, and from out of Lorna's heels I saw—I didn't see fire, but I saw the grass parch up and shrivel in concentric circles for not far, three or four inches only.

"I can't," she cried. "You know all that better than I do. There is no *asking* for anything! There is no *getting* anything. We have it *now*. We either have it now or we *don't!*"

A few women started crying, a few men walked away. I don't know if Lorna said it or I thought it, and it doesn't matter. What had "Our Father" done for us? Who was there to pray to now but Kali, Goddess of Creation and Destruction? And what in the hell were we going to say to some Indian grudge-holding looney-tune lady goddess with twenty arms or so? What would we ask for? To survive? To die? To be saved? Saved from what? *For* what?

"We either live in Heaven or we don't live," Lorna said, and tears streaked her face. "You dumb bunnies, I don't know anymore than that and neither does anybody else."

She looked often, during these morning talks, toward the windows in Franz deGeld's mansion. Sometimes I'd follow her glance, sometimes a curtain would move, but during the last days there seemed to be nobody home. As I say, there was adequate time—*did* I say that?—for the agile, the determined, to get out. To leave the country, or the planet if they wished. And every minute you stayed inside your country, or your house, or your body, you were making the choice.

Why I didn't leave? To be perfectly frank, I never thought I'd be the one to stay. I never bought my children earrings but I didn't think, "They'll be able to take these out of the country when the time comes." On the other hand, I never drove a canyon but I didn't think of its high earth walls as shelter, and I never was so disgusted with a string of pearls as when I learned that pearls cannot survive flames, that they melt and puff into an ugly mess, and lose their value.

It turned out I couldn't leave, didn't want to leave, because of my family, and my friends, and who I was. Skip, in his courage, had shamed me.

Persistence. Surrender. Lorna's words. And if I use her words, it's because I didn't like the others. Persistence. You could get out, if you really wanted to. For the others, ice cream until the end. Surrender. I must admit I'd never known what she meant by "surrender" until those last days before the end and the beginning. All it *meant* was surrender. One afternoon or midday, Skip moved from our bed onto the balcony to look, to look. And on the next balcony, another couple. All we could do was weep and grin. We reached out our arms across that small space—our fingers touched.

Why I didn't leave was food and love and sex and palm fronds, but let's get serious. As the sun broke through the late part of the day, it was time for us to go home, to our "real life." (And there were those who went to work until the end, fought the thinning rush hour until the end.) As the sun hit four o'clock, everyone in the city went home to their families. And it was then that I learned (twenty-five years after I'd heard about it in some class) about the Great Chain of Being. My father was on my left shoulder, but my mother was still in this life and had come down from her home in the desert to be in our house, where she spent those last days of the cusp in our garden. Aurora was safe and gone. She would live and remember. Denise stayed here, with four or five friends; they moved each night from one home to the next.

Finally, it was the city that held us, the city they said had no center, that all of us had come to from all over America because this was the place to find dreams and pleasure and love. I noticed—looking at headlines—that some cities emptied and some didn't. Ours didn't, not completely. It may be argued, of course, that the hundreds of miles of desert that surrounded us had something to do with it, but I don't think so. (And if there was any rage I felt, outside of the terror that periodically seized up my body like a Porsche engine running without oil, it was a fury that "they" were finally going to have the nerve to take our defenseless little adobe houses and turn them back to blowing dust.) They said we were crazy to stay. But then someone had always said we were crazy to be here in the first place. And someone had always said Noah was crazy to build a boat in his desert, and Lot had been crazy to pack up, on an impulse, and head west.

So when it came to leaving, I found I couldn't. I couldn't even take off my pearls. They were just going to have to melt around my neck. I had to apologize in my mind for all those things I'd ever thought about the Jews. Why didn't they get out of Germany!? Because they didn't want to? Because they decided the only thing to do was "experience their fear and go through it"?

At home we played Scrabble. We stocked up on dry goods, inefficiently. We cleaned the house. We had people over for dinner. We bought the book of truly tasteless jokes and laughed our brains out. Why do girls have two holes? So you can carry them like bowling balls, wasn't that it? We all slept in the same room together; my mother and I and Skip in one bed; Denise and her friends—when they were at our house—in and around another double bed we'd pulled into the big bedroom.

And, sure, every day each of us would bring something more home; a hundred dollars' worth of Lindberg Varsity Pack vitamins, a sack of rice, some earthenware crocks for water, or raisins, or those pills that were supposed to protect your thyroid from radiation.

One morning in the first part of July, we decided not to drive down to the beach. It was a national holiday, there were supposed to be fireworks set off by the pier. It wasn't the kind of thing we wanted to see. Denise and her friends had spent the night, and a new neighbor from next door was outside busily mowing his weeds with a power-scythe. My mother wanted us to dig up a patch so she could plant some root vegetables for all. It was an ugly day, muggy and overcast; no one wanted to go anywhere anyway. When we woke up late, it was like a not-very-fun slumber party, with that crowded room on a hot, muggy summer morning, and all those kids we hardly knew. Skip got up and made us all coffee. Our last.

When it came, all we felt was a tilt in the earth, and the sky lit up but not very brightly. Then, in less than two minutes, the window jolted and fell from its casing into the room. It didn't even break. We felt the rush of thick air, and put our heads under the sheets. Skip turned on the transistor radio, but my mother said *"No!* Turn it off. What we don't know won't hurt us." And the air began to burn.

Denise, whose grammar school teacher had been predicting the end of the world since before she'd even started kindergarten, observed morosely, "This is going to make Mr. Russo very happy." Then, in the way that fatigue overwhelms you when the brush fire threatens, all eight of us dropped into sleep as if we'd been felled, as if life had served us a collective mickey finn.

The real fire came the next day. We had been ready for it for weeks, our trash cans filled with water at each corner of the house, our rags damp. Four of us stood on the roof stamping out sparks, one at each corner while the others handed up water. The fire roared down at us like a train.

And it passed us by. Our house survived. The rest of the world was ashes.

Now is where the bad part comes; I don't know how much I should tell you. How much do *you* remember? I know that whatever I'd learned of fear up until that time was only joking, a masquerade of fear. There was no question, after that, of bravery or nobility or doing the right thing, or even *fear.* Or even day or night.

Our skin had seared, and since we had wrapped up in almost everything we had to fight the fire, most of our skin sloughed off in our jackets, in our jeans and boots. We crept back to our upstairs room, knowing we should be in basements, garages, holes in the ground, but trusting the great earthen walls of the canyon to protect us. In our agony we needed beds, and to lie down, and be with each other.

Water was all we thought about. And the dying squirrels that ran squeaking in the fine ash of the canyon, leaving trails like tiny toboggan slides. You'd see them later, dead, their little paws turned up. We became fanatics about our arms, having read somewhere that you would die right away if your skin, once pinched, stayed pinched. So if some one of us was crying, we'd grab an arm— they'd grab mine, I was a great crier in those days—and say *hang on, hang on,* it won't be today! Day after day went by, and it wasn't.

If there were histories now, they'd say that plague killed the city, and thirst. But it was mostly fear that killed. Fear was the killer in those first few months. There weren't words to use for it. Remember, our house was on the crescent of a hill, in a canyon north of the city and east of the beach, and we'd go out each day, one at a time, and walk that two-hundred-foot crescent, to be sure we could still walk, to see if things had changed. We'd come upon piles of vomit, as we walked. That was the other reason we walked, to go outside and vomit. We felt that what we vomited was the "sick" part, and that what was left upon our bones would grow back healthy. When I went to walk one day, out at the far edge of the point, I saw a kid, one of ours, writhing.

He turned to look at me—I saw it was a "he," not my own beloved daughter—and I saw that his neck was swollen like a fullback's, he was black, black as a Bic, black as tar, black as coal, black as the Pit. *So, so, this is it,* is what I thought.

"Can I bring you anything?" I asked, but he looked out of his eyes with detachment, and I believe he was thinking *this is it* as well, with a sort of relief built in. And another boy went out soon after.

We let them stay there and for a week or so took our walks in another direction. When any of us felt the beginning of a stiff neck, we dosed ourselves with penicillin. When my mother died some weeks later, it could have been from a natural death. We took her out on the point; she shriveled to nothing in the sun. We found, in fact, that the dry climate of L.A. lent itself to this ancient way of taking away the dead: let them lie there and dry, seemed to be what people said later that they had done. Don't go near a tainted body, don't taint the soil by putting them underneath it. And we heard about terrible suffering later, but no more, actually less, than we had thought of it before.

The deaths by thirst we heard of later were the worst, and the discomfort from thirst was the worst. Where we lived, in the ashen, chilly canyon, there was a creek perhaps a mile away, and when the sky was cold and grey but the air was quiet enough to see through the swirling clouds of ash, two of us would take our turn to creep down to the creek or to the spring above it and bring home two pans of water. Rice would go into one pan to soak soft, and the other we would divide to sip and drink. If we vomited, we gave what was left of our water to the others.

After a few weeks, I think there were still six of us: Skip, my daughter, two of her friends, and our neighbor, Richard, who had lived a hundred yards up from us in the canyon. He was an extremely neat man and busied himself when he went outside, raking the ashes away from the house. "This is still a home," he would say when I'd give him a look. "We must keep it as nice as we can." Five out of eleven deaths, was that it? And all around us, no sign of life. For weeks and days we didn't "explore"; no one wanted to find anything. Our food supply stayed fairly even. We were very sick, of course.

Was there a miracle in this? How could we know if there was or not? Was it the miracle of the loaves and fishes—one of Lorna's very favorite stories—that two thirty-pound sacks of brown rice lasted us until the first rains came? Every morning when we woke, the six of us (I think), in two wide double beds pushed together, the dark grey stiffened sheets alive with fleas, our nightgowns covering sores and scabs, one of us would be sure to reach, cursing, into his mouth to pluck out a tooth and then carefully swallow the blood that came from that soft red hole. It's true that first, as we woke, transfixed with terror and then relief, we sat up, one by one, and touched each other to be sure we were not dead. We plucked our forearms and each other's forearms tenderly, and sometimes with an extra little pinch. Sometimes one of us might stand up and move over to the glass we had stuck back up in that upstairs bedroom window, look at the swirling ash that had persisted for weeks, darkening everything to night when the slightest breeze came up, and croak out, in the choked voices we spoke with then, "OOOO-eee! I see abundance *everywhere!*"

The neighbor, who still slept by himself, curled in a corner, looked on impassively as we . . . I supposed you'd have to say, we laughed.

Was it a miracle, then, that when the rains came and it was necessary to let the water stand for at least a week before we could drink it—and was that when we lost two of my daughter's friends whose names I forget?—that slogging out one morning we saw clustered (under the overhanging side of a broken retaining wall we'd built so long ago) maybe flfty snails, and, shivering, soaking wet, bald and raving, my ancient, neverdying, forever chivalric friend said, again, "OOOo-eee! I see abundance *everywhere!*" Then, with the exaggerated panache of a Parisian dandy, he reached over, plucked one away from the crumbling concrete, held it up against the drizzling poisoned rain to wash away the ash, and with a hideous sucking noise that I remember even now, removed it, protesting, from its shell and sent it sliding to its own Armageddon.

"You could get sick," I protested, and I saw his stomach heave in protest, but he kept it down and grinned a toothless Richie Havens grin at me, so that—what could I do? Was I less daring? Could I say no to fabled "abundance"? I picked one up (remembering how many of those mollusks I'd already consigned to oblivion by standing, in the lost days, on the crescent rim, lobbing them down, down into the dry climate, screeching *"Death to all snails!"*), put it to my lips, and sucked. It resisted, then slid on my tongue and down my throat, cool and accommodating. Our flrst food since the lost days, except rice, water, Lindberg Varsity Pack vitamins, and penicillin. What I'm saying is, Would we have seen abundance in those filthy, unattractive shells had we not been looking for it?

We were completely cut off from everyone and everything, and that was the way we liked it. My mother, in her more cantankerous days, had asked us repeatedly to turn off the hysterical messages on the radio, and one early night had taken the batteries out and hidden them. "I'll tell you where they are," she said, affecting senility, "some day. If you're good." But she passed on before she told us, and we hadn't gone over her body for them as we carried her out to the point.

From time to time now, when we went to the bottom of the canyon to get water, we'd see others, but they looked unreal and comical, stooped over and wearing grey rags, with no hair and no teeth; some of them plainly dying and all that. But I suppose that none of that seemed *real* to us. Physical suffering, if it belongs to someone else, can be easily borne.

This is how it would be.

After we woke up in the morning—not really morning that we could actually tell in those early days because, as I say, grey ash shadowed all—we would go outside and shit. Then come in and, with our right hands, scoop up a handful of soaked rice from a pot and let it lie in our mouths to suck. We had sores and holes in our mouths and the rice was soothing. It was amazing, it took an eternity, an *endless* time, to eat that softened grain. One or two of us would take an hour to pace the crescent of the hill, not keeping watch, just looking around, holding umbrellas to keep off bad air. Then two of us would begin to walk in the other direction down to the canyon floor with two dented pans, going to get water. We walked with cloth tied over our noses and mouths. To breathe in the ash was frightening and most unpleasant. It might take the better part of a day to get down to the creek and back. We'd walk without talking. I can't speak for the others, but I never thought much. When I did, it seemed the thought was absolutely new.

As when, down at the creek, on the other side there might be three women, shrouded, dipping in with pans, hunched and filthy, and you might think, Ingmar Bergman movie! And then you'd think, no more Ingmar Bergman, no more movies! But no one scurried away, and no one was afraid to send the girls down alone, because the very idea of lifting a hand against another person for any reason was absolutely out of the question.

We didn't wave at each other or say, "Are you doing OK?" We did notice the scabs and sores, and hoped they weren't too sick, but it was as though there was all the time in the world to talk. There was all the absolute time in the world. Walking home, holding the water carefully, one of us might whisper, "Ingmar Bergman." And the other one might smile.

The only time I can remember terror down on Old Topanga Canyon Road was when, as several of us were silently dunking our pans into the shallow stream (and it took all the time in the world to do it right, to hold the pan so that the clearest liquid might seep over the lid of the pan, to avoid the sometimes very hideous things that oozed on the bottom, a noise, I can't even tell you what a noise, a hideous, barking metallic vibration shook us all. And just as the aftershocks of an earthquake are far more frightening than the first jolt, I saw stark terror, heard yowls and whimpers from them all and from myself, and from a bank of ashes, faster than a snake platoon, a figure flashed past us and *out of sight,* leaving an odor of shit and fear, and the shit was right there in the spots on the pitted road.

"He tried to . . ." I couldn't think what it was he'd tried to do.

"He tried to . . ."

We thought about it. And a woman said, "Start . . . start the car?"

We talked about that at home, when we talked, for days.

No, I can't remember when our new ideas all started. And I thought so much about going to Australia in those last days before the war that I can't remember what months up here are supposed to be cold. Because even though they'd said it would be cold, I know it was a long time before things were actually cold again. But things worked out for us more exquisitely than we ever planned! Because when most people were dying, the weather was very dry. Because in our canyon we already knew how to fight the fire. Because whatever had happened all over the world, the snails loved it where we were, and we loved those snails! And by the time the rain had been around long enough for green things to come up, we'd gotten around to thinking of ourselves as alive, alive!

Because the green things made us sick as hell, and if we'd gotten that sick in the very first days we'd all have died of pure fright.

We couldn't seem to make the green stuff turn into ourselves. We'd bite down on those clear green threads that came out of the dark, wet, ashy earth, and we'd be crying, because just to say, to think, *green,* made our throats close with sadness. We'd put those green threads in our mouths, where they'd sting our raw cheeks and gums and cut across our tongues like saws or knives. We'd hold them in our mouths, until we couldn't bear it anymore, and swallow, and vomit for hours, long after the green stuff was gone.

Or walking, you'd see one of us squatting on one crescent with his butt over the side, shitting, the way we'd been doing it for months, and his head would be down between his knees and with his left hand he'd be plucking grass out of his asshole, threads just as fresh and green and painful on the edges as when they went in.

But we knew we needed the green stuff. And we kept on with the exercise. And you know how sometimes we used to wonder if Lorna was right, when she said *expect a miracle?* She used to talk about Gandhi, who looked a lot like the way we did now, and she said he used to get his nourishment out of the air, by breathing. I think, because we *knew* about it, that we did some of that. We would lay a leaf across our tongues and play at it all day. We would look for a seed, and look at it a long time, and if it didn't look back at us, we'd put it in our mouths. The snails lived for a long time around our house. We did too.

I should say that we never "built" a fire up there in the canyon. We never made one, or wanted one, because the fire that had come by gave us our fill of fire for a long time, and later there were days when people from down in the valley made the long walk up to the top of the canyon trying to get to the beach, and some of them still had burns that, well, I don't want to say anything about it.

To me the thing that seemed most clear and came in clearer every day was that—well, you know! This story proves it. We were alive, and going to be alive, and if we were, there were others, we saw them every day. Some noises were coming back. Some birds. Some lizards. The sound of rain, and mud moving. The complaints: coughing, groaning, crying in the night. The neighbor in the comer of our room saying, "Ah, shut up."

I'm sure you know it took most of that first black summer, the rainy fall and winter, the sickness of the first green spring, and the next summer—where we saw quite a few more plague-dead—and then a rain and then another whole journey of the earth around the sun before we began to think about what we were going to do. (Or maybe I'm wrong about that; it seems too long a time.) But I know that it was green when we began to think. This is not to say that we hadn't done some of that before, but walking now, on the road home from the creek, sometimes we'd wave and say, "How's your IQ?" Or I heard my daughter say when she cut herself, "Red, red, the color's dead." Or my friend Skip went out one day in the . . . *brush!* In the *brush,* that's what I mean, the words came back, with the world, and Skip came back with a handful of what looked like black sand.

"Chia seeds," he said, "maybe." He pulled at his mouth with his fingers to show me, and under his tongue, and packed into his cheek was a black wad. "Makes you feel . . ." He made his arms flail, palms up. "You know . . . lots of energy!"

My skin, by now, was halfway healed, but it itched. You know how those days were, there was nothing to do, so one afternoon I took out my old leather briefcase and opened it up. The rocks looked as good as they always had. I picked up a ruby and put it in my mouth. It hurt! Then I held it in my fingers. How red it was! I . . . do you remember how you used to drip hot wax on your arms, or pluck your eyebrows? Or pick a pimple? I took that stone and put it on the back of my left hand, and pushed. Would that stop the itching? The ruby broke through the skin and stayed. It felt like—did you ever have psoriasis and hold your hands under scalding water? It felt awful, and good. From then on, when I had nothing to do, I'd take a stone and wiggle it, teasing my itching, flaking, diseased skin, and stick that stone in there! So that after a few months, my hands were like glittering stone gloves. Very heavy, but they looked good!

One day we took our sheets out in the sun and stamped on them and poured water so they'd smell like . . . see what I mean! Laundry! Wow. We began to laugh. Laundry. (Although the dry and crusty sheets hurt our skin for a week after, and we didn't do that for a while again.)

Then we started saying "Hi!" and "Howyadoin!" as we walked down for water. Then we started saying "Howsyrold man!" Then one day one of our girls came home all flowsy and flustered. A man had been following her. OOO-eee.

The great thing is, she couldn't even remember why it was anybody would have been following her! When we told her, she said, *"You're kidding! He'd really want to do that?"* And next time she slowed down so he could catch up to her, but he got scared and hid back in the bushes.

Because by then there were bushes.

The first time I saw writing again was a sign I'd seen before up in that canyon—*I've Seen Fire and I've Seen Rain.* Yes many times before I'd seen that sign, in the old days, when there would have been a series of bad events, floods and fires, and little animals piled up in long, furry, putrid, wavery lines along the old roads. Someone would write on a plank, sometimes in paint, sometimes in charcoal, *I've Seen Fire and I've Seen Rain.* I *don't* know who wrote up this one, but he put it right by the tree trunk down on what used to be Valley Drive—a riverbed now—the way down to Old Topanga Creek.

Was it humor, irony, that made him put that sign—that we used to see on a long, unattractive, arid hill between us and the San Fernando Valley—right in the heart of nowhere where we were now, this dark deep ravine, next to the hollow tree that still bore the traces of an earlier, whitewashed warning: *This place defended by shotgun law?*

People stood and looked at that new sign: *I've Seen Fire and I've Seen Rain.* Could they read it? Were we back to reading? Were they trying to remember the song it came from? Were we back to singing?

My friend Skip, impossibly old now, his dark brown skin translucent over luminous bones, looked up one day as we walked the crescent, holding hands. "There's a bird up there," he said. "A phainopepla. They come from the south." Then tears came out of his eyes.

Let me tell you a little of what grew back. Rye grass first, wouldn't you know it? I know we should have thought of eating it, but what we thought of first *was fire,* and tried, a little each day, to pull it out of the ground. Elderberry bushes, and that first crop of elderberries made us sicker than pigs. (No more pigs!) Something with a red flower we called Indian paintbrush; those yellow daisies with the black center called—weren't they Black-Eyed Susans? I saw a snake one day and it scared the shit out of me. And that's what I mean, that's what it did.

It began to be so much fun to *talk.* "I saw a snake. It scared the shit out of me."

"So I see."

Then it isn't as if we'd laugh. But we'd get these shudders. One day, pulling at the rye grass, trying to get it away from the house, a boy, someone I didn't know, or couldn't remember his name, spoke, after weeks and months of silence. "I've been working like a . . . nigger." Then he stopped, and put up his hand to his bald skull. I could *see* his brain in there, laboring away, harder than his skinny little frame. *Nigger? Digger? Chigger? Pigger? Wigger? Siger? Cigar?*

Once, I burst out singing, "If I had a hammer." I looked around for who said it. It was me. I remembered. I'd gone to junior high school with a big . . . . *black woman* who went on to be . . . *famous.* And I knew that in the . . . *garage,* there was a . . . *hammer.*

So one thing I didn't lose was the language. But you could . . . see? that words would change. Garage. Ingmar Bergman. Chicken salad sandwich. Sometimes, when we got so we could go outside after the sun went down without being afraid, we would do a . . . game? We would do something like a game, where we would say words, to see what they meant. But sometimes it made us cry, so then we would stop. But there was another word, *sad?* When we saw tears, we'd say, *sad ?* In the first weeks we'd pinched each other, but that was different, that was medicinal. Now it got so that we could put out our arms, our hands, and put them on the others, the skin of others, and they? him? her? he? she? wouldn't . . . run, or flinch, or shriek? Squeak? Because at night we slept with the long lines of our skins together motionless, and loved that, but to be poked by a finger, in the day, as we moved, was very hard, like having your fingernails pulled out. It brought back those first black weeks. But we didn't have fingernails anymore. Finger . . . *nails?* And we might tap against something, remembering. And little, a little at a time, we might shiver and let ourselves be touched.

Here's the thing about memory. Years, years before, before the end and the beginning, we'd had a dog. Or, was it a coyote? It was . . . wild. We couldn't touch it. But a year or two after she'd come around our house, she'd finally let us touch her. And then she came into the house, if there was a door left open. Then sometimes we'd watch while she came into the living room and put her head on our knees and look into our eyes. And then it came to be that she slept all night in the house, and the minute she'd hear a voice, or one of us turning to the other, she'd gallop upstairs to the bedroom and jump on the bed with all four feet. She loved us so much. When we'd first found her wild and starving, we thought of Ishi, that last California Indian, killed with kindness by the university people up north. She was a girl dog (or coyote), and we called her Isha.

One night, then, after we'd started talking again, after the sun went down, before the moon came up, three of us sat out back—we *hunkered* down, is what we did, and out on the point, at the far end of the crescent, we saw . . . a coyote! The first we'd seen since the end and the beginning. My friend Skip said *"Isha."* That was when I felt pain, my head splitting. "My head is splitting," I said, and my eyes melted. The pain was unendurable. "I can't bear it," I said. In one awful moment I saw it all, our living room, and pink and yellow lights at night, and our skins pink and white and whole, not *hole,* and so much, wait a minute, so much, wait, wait, so much love that a wild thing, starving from the dark, could come inside and put her head on our knees and look at us for the pure pleasure of looking at us, and on the other side of me, there in the dark now, turning her head away, putting her thin, scrabbly little hands up over the holes in her skull where her ears had been was my . . . *daughter.* And I had another one, somewhere on the surface of this planet, but she was gone.

But I saw them, in that other bright world of the past forever hidden from us, on the other *couch,* pushing and jostling each other, and Skip and me wishing they'd stop!

Oh, how could we have ever wished they would stop.

"I can't bear it," I said, and put my whole self down into the dirt, let my eyes cry into the dirt.

There are people who say that a woman with fire red hair who spoke around the city before the end didn't know what she was talking about, but I say she did. I say she was a miracle. Because as I felt the unendurable pain, and I heard my own young one beginning to wail and put her hands up to her head, and my heart split because I couldn't bear it, I heard my old friend Skip say, "My past is now complete. I bless and release it."

Complete! You bet your life! You bet your ass! I thought of those men on the television set. Were they still with us? Had the breasts of their wives withered and fallen away as mine had? Had their bones splintered? Did they live on . . . did they live? Oh. What had they done. Killers. Devils. The Antichrist.

But before I could lose my soul, I heard that good man speak again: "My past is now complete. I bless and release it." I had a *memory* of clean, strong, healthy, happy people writing their sadnesses on pieces of paper, balling them up like . . . *whiffle balls* and throwing them at *Lyin' Boys,* who put on *reflector glasses* and hit at them with a *sequined* baseball bat.

"I can't. I can't. I can't bear it. My babies." But by that time I could hear myself being *corny.* And I knew I had to stop.

"My past is now complete," he said again. "I bless and release it, remember?"

What if we remembered what we wanted, and blessed and released the rest? What if we took those members of the London branch of the Royal Society in the seventeenth century who'd thought they were *on* to something when they took up science, and whiffled them and the next three hundred years, *away* into the smiling universe?

What if we tried to remember John Donne and the Rolling Stones and driving in the car with the radio on, and lying on clean sheets with perfect bodies looking out at palm fronds, and the clean blue of the biggest ocean, what if we only remember *California?* What if we . . . wait, wait, what if we took the cash and let the credit go?

"My past is now complete, I bless and release it. OOOO-eeee ! It's good to be alive, and I am alive, here in the heart of infinity!"

Was he saying it, or was I? I turned my head. Skip stood up, dancing back and forth on his long legs, his eyes rolled most of the way back in his head, because part of his lids had been burned off long ago. I could hardly hear him, but I knew what he was saying. Well, why shouldn't I? Didn't we have the same story?

Some say Lorna was a quack. Could that have been what they said? But I say she was magic, because I took all of it, the part I couldn't bear, that little lost dog, that running jump of love, my dead souls, all souls, and my beloved dearest daughter, wrapped them first in white light, then in pink, and floated them away to be a star.

I kept the words, and the present. The *present,* get it? I got up on my knees and went over to the poor sweet young woman covering her ears against my noise and said to her. The way I'd said to Isha, long ago, long ago, long ago, "Come on. I'm sorry. Just let me . . . come on. Just . . ."

It was easier with the kid, with . . . Denise. In only a few minutes, I got her to look at me. I put my hands on her arms and my lips on her cheek.

Now, I'm not saying it was easy. Not Lorna, not even Lion, could say that now and get away with it. I'm just saying it was easier than what we (those of us who had thought of it) had thought. There were days after that—after several turns of the planet, in the first recognizable spring—when we'd get the idea, and we'd say it as a joke, "So these are the dark ages!" And then we'd laugh. Because though none of us looked so hot, the hills had never been so

beautiful. The greens and reds and blues and yellows were almost more than your eyes could take.

And, of course, once we started feeling a little better we had bursts of what you'd have to call—although we didn't like the word—strength. There was a day, in the middle of a spring morning, when all of us were outside taking the sun, when we were—you know, Denise was biting on her toes, and my friend Skip rubbed the skin off his legs, and the neighbor, Richard, watched some ants. I was doing sit-ups. I planned to be a very old lady, dark brown, the kind you could pluck up off the ground with a thumb and forefinger, a dwarf, an elf. So I was doing sit-ups.

And one of us said, out of that glorious, living silence, where all you heard was the tickle of the ants on the earth and the air as it moved around birds' wings,

"Picnic?"

"Oh, yeah!"

"Summertime?"

"Really!"

The neighbor coughed and spit and said, "What a day for the beach!"

I thought my heart might split again and braced for the pain when I saw that the others were, well, they were thinking about it differently.

"Do you . . ."

"The Indians who lived up here," Skip said, "they did it. They used to go down once a year."

If any of us in this canyon knew anything, we knew that the Indians who lived here had been the last word in incompetence. No farming, no tools, no written language, no "kinship system," nothing except waterproof baskets, and that was only because they hadn't got as far as pottery. And all of us had grown up with the story of the California Indians, those dipshit Chumash, who had rowed over to Catalina Island to gather shells and left a woman over there absentmindedly and didn't get back to pick her up for over twenty years.

"To see Catalina again."

And then we all said it, almost together. "On a clear day you can see . . ." We didn't just *up and go*.

It took days of talking about it, and our first real worries about survival. But we took to mentioning it down at the creek: "Nice day for the beach!"

Others of us will tell that story of how we came down that fifth year after the world began, how we traveled the dozen miles, how we met the others who still lived down in the main part of the canyon, how we camped for a while where the two creeks met, down by the old post office, how we found to our amazement and surprise that a hundred of us still lived, just in the part we were traveling through. We heard hard tales of people in the next canyon over, too close to the city. We heard nightmare tales of the valley, where most of our city had lived; death by thirst and plague. We heard tales of defense by the canyon people at the eastern summit, wooden lances against the poor, the sick, who tried to take refuge in the highlands. But they could have never lived up here, really—or the ones who *could* were here with us now.

There were six of us, on our trip to the beach. Skip and Denise and me. Our neighbor, Richard, by now part of our family. Two of Denise's friends, Fru and—I forget the other one. We took blankets. We took chia seeds. We took the last of our rice. I had my jewels in my hands. The six of us picked our way down the cracked bits of cement, the driveway, for what we probably knew then was the last time. We turned and looked at that house, charred wood bleached out by sun and blast, a castle. But we didn't feel sad! We went on down into the slit of Old Canyon past the wide place in the creek where we'd panned water so many days, and continued, single file, picking our way along the damp creekside.

I cannot tell you with what tears and smiles we found, after three miles, among whitened bones and lush rye grass, a half-destroyed stone building that had been the old Discovery Inn and found a living skeleton—great grandmother, was it? Of the old Dear family? That woman, Marge, was it? Burnt almost black, sitting witless and toothless up against a flat rock outside the slanting building.

"M,m,m,Marge?" said I.

"Fuck," the living carcass said. "Howareya?"

It took us almost a month, from that junction of the old canyon and the new, to make our way the next few miles down to the beach. It was frightening, and we weren't good with fear. The old road that cut into the canyon ledge had been pushed out, either in the blasts or had been scooped down by the few cave dwellers who had found perfect shelters and stayed there. They threw rocks at us as we passed, thinking we were diseased or maybe just plain butt-ugly. But they were the ones who looked strange to us, with their white skin, their orange puffs of hair, their nervous dancing.

"Just goin' to the beach," we'd say. "Perfect day for it! Come on along."

But all of us had our own ways, and these people were scared of the sun. Since we couldn't take the "road," we went the simple way, right down at the narrow bottom of the canyon's crack.

My, it was strange down there! Dense and green, with large, gaudy flowers. We'd look sometimes and say, "Science fiction."

"Really!"

And we had nightmares at night. We were afraid for the first time in a long time. And we would *say* that! "Oh, I don't like this! I'm afraid." Steep stone cliffs kept the sun from us and almost blotted out the sky.

My daughter began again to call me Mom. "Wait up, Mom!" And I'd feel her fingers curling into the crook of my arm. We'd walk in step, lock-step; she right behind me.

I'm not saying we didn't see some awful things. At that curve just north of the straightaway that went directly up the middle of the steepest part of the canyon, we came upon a stack of six or seven cars loaded with passengers, who (maybe because of the dampness?) hadn't dried the way they should. You know how bad they looked, and how they smelled. And there was still the fear of the plague. We stopped for a long time and watched, trying to figure out how to get around them, wondering what had happened, wondering if this was a sign that we ought to turn back. (Wondering too what would be going on with the drinking water downstream.)

Finally Skip said, "We've lived this long, and for a reason." And Denise said, "This is about where all of them used to go off the road before, isn't it? Like, where people used to kill themselves? So maybe it's just that there isn't anybody anymore to . . . tow them out!"

That made it better, to think that it was just a collection of car accidents, but it wasn't that, we knew it. This was where someone had blown the road above us; and these cars packed with passengers had been trying to get into the canyon probably, when the road fell out from under them . . . or maybe not! Because Denise was right. This *was* the place of the accidents. The place where, so long ago, the ones who didn't make the turn at the top of the straightaway, so plainly marked, were politely committing suicide when they drove, instead, out into thin air.

To drive! To commit suicide! To get into an . . . accident. You can see that it was an amazing trip for us.

We went on down, climbing in an arc along a rough and narrow trail, past those cars, those strange dead beings, and kept at a good pace past where the straightaway turned again into curves. After a day or two, the steep slopes of the canyon softened again and we came out again into spongy foothills, with soft pink and yellow flowers, and for the first time got the smell of the sea.

We didn't say much. We kept walking, very slowly, the rest of that afternoon and evening. All of us were remembering. Our neighbor grunted as he moved and kicked rocks with his huge horny feet; *he* was remembering, but we'd never know what. He didn't talk much. And I said, as we passed a certain place, "Mark . . . *Mark* somebody died here in a crash."

Denise said, "There was a big accident I saw here once." Skip said, "I was jogging here once when we first lived together and found a workshirt and picked it up. It was from the county jail. "

You can see how it was for us. What it was doing to our brains. So that's why we took it easy. There wasn't any hurry.

This is how we slept those last couple of nights. First my friend Skip, his body a clattery, dear thing with lots of right angles, you could almost *hear* him creak against the ground. Then me, right up against him. Then Denise, dear creature. Some girls and women, I regret to say me among them, had lost their breasts in the first year. It was partly the losing of all extra flesh, partly that all soft parts tended to slough off, and partly, I'm sure, another polite way of saying *Fuck it! It was just a hobby!* But Denise, as that first puff of burning air had blown out our windows, put both baby hands over both her soft breasts, so that they remained now, with the sweet imprint of her fingers as white flower petals out from the centers which in better times . . . well. On the other side of Denise, silent and grumpy, turned away from her, making his back a wall for her, the neighbor, Richard. On the other side of him, the two other girls.

Who could be safer than my daughter and me, holding each other through the night? Our skin, so sore and sad for so long, was strong now; we could lie on stones or on burrs and *feel* them but not feel pain. We would lie down one at a time, snuffling and squirming, and maybe talk. Or sometimes issue an order, "I've got to turn over!" But when we slept we slept straight through, getting over fear, because what could happen to us, all together as we were?

So we took it slow, not seeing any more people but letting the excitement, the anticipation mount up, letting the newer sun come over us, waking up one morning in a wet fog that made us catch our breath. On that morning Denise said, only half joking, "Nuclear fallout?" But Skip said, "Think of all the water this breeze has blown over," and I felt my eyes hurt at the thought of that large and neutral blue.

"Oh, large and neutral blue," I said, and felt Denise glance me out. "Oh holy, rosy cross," she recited smartly, and I shut up.

"Remember," I said, the next morning as we ambled, oh so slowly down these well-remembered curves, past cars covered with morning glory and fragrant anise, "how the traffic some mornings used to back up all the way to here!"

"Goddamn it!" our neighbor said, out of his doltish reverie. "It takes forever here! Why don't they fix the signal! There's no excuse for this!" And thinking *that* over, we slowed down. It took us all day to make another quarter of a mile. We could hear the ocean that night, I think. We bit down on creek frogs for dinner and I was the one who said, "That woman, Marina, who lived in Topanga Gulch, a frog *ate* a wire at her place and it went . . . "

"Electrocuted?" Skip asked.

Full of sober thoughts, we lay down that night next to a bamboo grove we all remembered. I believe, trying to capture it now, that we heard voices, maybe even songs. I know we shivered and wakened and held onto each other. I think we smelled or felt fire, but safe fire. Maybe it was a dream.

The next morning when we went to the creek, besides drinking, we put water on our faces and skulls.

My daughter's lips started to quiver. I saw she was afraid, not for why you think! But because of how she thought we all might look.

I admit something of the same stirred in me; I thought my heart might crack again, but my friend said, "Courage!"

Then the six of us began to joke. "You go first," we said to our neighbor. "You're the cutest."

"Yes, I am," he said. "I'm glad you noticed."

He folded his arms against his strange chest, the way Indians in the movies used to do. "Come on," he said. "Let's get it over with."

One by one we walked down the last defile. If there had been cars here, they had been pushed away. Our feet felt . . . asphalt, the asphalt of a real road.

Then we saw the Pacific, the peaceful ocean. I heard Denise behind me, starting to cry. "Oh, Mommy. Oh, my God." Skip stopped. He had more to remember than I did, lives upon lives.

That neighbor! He grunted, then he shouted, then he started to trot. We watched him gallop down across the Pacific Coast Highway. His body disappeared from view and came up again into our sight. There was something funny about the way he moved; he slipped and fell, and fell again, and half-rolling, half-walking, he tumbled into . . .

Into the long, low, slow, soft, rolling lines of blue and white surf. Heartstruck, caught between terror and joy, we watched his head, bright brown ball, rolling and tossing in the waves. He was swimming, waving, sputtering, skidding.

The real Beginning started for me. Because all I could see was a picture with my eyes, a cosmic frame; another world. Bright green hills on either side of us, and, of course, behind us, and on my right, as I looked toward the ocean, a low wooden building which used to be the Malibu Feed Bin but looked now more like the old *center* in the canyon, with four or five . . . *guys* lounging in front of it, and I thought I saw a woman and maybe even a *child* or two just *doing business,* going about the chores of the day, as if this were the plain, the ordinary world. I saw in front of me the lush sweet thick blue ribbon of the sea, and above it the pale unscary band of sky, and even took in some *rubble* in the form of car skeletons and bleached-out two-by-fours and dying rubber tires. I heard voices in conversation, even calling out to us, but couldn't *pay attention* because the five of us were so worried, preoccupied, so locked in concern that that man who had put cobwebs on our heads when they were sore and bleeding, who had crept down his hill and crawled into our house when he thought he was going to die, but *he didn't die,* was maybe now going to (if we couldn't bring ourselves to "save" him), bite the big one, after all we'd been through.

"Richard!" Denise yelled. "Be careful, oh!"

Maybe *then* is when the Beginning started for me. Because into the frame came, you know what I'm going to say, a sail, and as its mast, a man. Well, it was wonderful to see, that wheeled board. And the brown feet that curled over it, held onto it, and the big brown body, that held out arms, that held the strong bright red cloth, and the rough voice that shouted out, "Hold on, Mate! We're coming for you!"

And as we moved closer down to the edge of the land, across the frightening highway (where there were people who drew back to look at us, and some turned away crying), the whole beach suddenly came alive with red and blue and pink sails and lifelines, and one man left his sail—which was neatly grabbed up by another—to dive into the water where he reached our Richard, whose laconic face was smitten with every kind of surprise, and with the aid of a . . . preserver, expertly thrown, pulled our neighbor out, and the six or seven competent and cheerful men pulled and hauled him over the several hundred feet of what used to be soft sand. Do you remember how hard it used to be, to walk across sand to the water? Do you remember sand between your toes, sand in buckets, on blankets, in your bathing suit? The dullness and softness of sand? The great heat of Beginning had transformed that sinking stuff, melting it into smooth jagged sheets of glittering colored glass that took the sun like rock candy, like lights in a jukebox, like jewelry in handfuls. It was that glass that Richard had slid down and was climbing back across now, helped by the lifeguards with their sturdy sails.

"Richard!" my little girl cried and dashed out onto the glacier surface to fling her arms about his neck. Her arms went about his neck and his great brown hands went to her breasts, covering her white star scars.

That night they persuaded us to come to one of their small fires. To my surprise it fell to me to tell our story—the pane of window glass as it jerked from its precarious moorings in our old home on the skyline of Topanga, the last seconds before the thick air came to sear our skins and change it forever. How Richard came down to crawl in our house. How eleven of us slept in greying stiff sheets as the ashen air swirled around us for I didn't know how long, how my mother lived and died, how we walked the crescent, how we let the time pass, how fear came with the great plague. How we learned again to eat green things. How we began to talk and sing. To make jokes.

They sat close in and listened, and the light from the fire made them so beautiful. Then I told them how my heart split, and the terrible pain of it, as I remembered things that could be no more, and how my friend Skip had saved me with his courage and his patience, how I took all of it, all of that which could be no more, wrapped it in white light, coated it with pink, and sent all of it off in a bubble to become a star.

All of their faces obediently turned up to the dark blue universe as they searched for the star I told them about, and I saw peace come over their faces, but one old woman said into the dark, and the fire that had been tamed, "Surely, these are terrible times we have come upon."

But I was filled with a terrible rage and light, and I stood up and put out my arm to quiet her. *"No!"* I said. "Some people say these are bad times, but I say they are *good* times. We have bravery! We have love! We have the future. We have the Beginning! We have the present! Listen to that word, the Present. We all know what that is!"

And without thinking about it—how could I have thought about it!—I began giving her the fairly standard Lion Boyce zap II. The first was about money and the third was short and a little dispirited, but I always loved that second one that we'd stand sometimes in front of our California yellow refrigerator and just howl it out for the hell of it, but I said it now with conviction:

"*Our universe is infinitely rich and exquisitely beautiful! We live in love, we live life fully and joyously! Our universe is dynamically aglow with Radiant Healing and Prospering Energy! We are aglow with Radiant Health!*"

That one got a laugh, I can tell you!

"*Ooooo-Eee! It's good to be alive, and we ARE alive here in the heart of Infinity, here in our . . ."*

I had never been much for talking. At least not in the past few years. But I had a vision of all I had to say to these people! How they must remember how to *cook,* how it had been so blindingly beautiful in those last weeks at Michael's. How they must never turn down love, because, outside of a wonderful meal, it was the BEST. How they should practice kindness. How they could move mountains! How beautiful they were now, how perfect in their competence.

Now I had very little hair on my head, but there was about a half-inch of it beginning to grow back, and it stood straight out. My arms crackled a bit, I could feel energy coming out of my fingers. I noticed in that second that my daughter had her face turned from me, buried in Richard's neck, and that Skip was in his own world, his eyes turned inward. But I had so much to say. This fire! This blessed fire! Some say it was a bad thing, but I say it was a good thing! I waved my arms, and I could see radiant arcs in the sky, sparks from the jewels in my fingers flashing out into the night air. I caught the sharp smell of ozone.

"It's good to be alive and we ARE alive here in the heart of infinity, here in our infinity, here in our infinitely rich, loving and beautiful universe!"

I saw it in their faces before I felt it. I loved it that they weren't afraid, that all I saw was curiosity and delight and a lovely *oooohh,* the acoustical equivalent of long low ocean waves breaking on glass. *Oooohh!* And I looked down to see the damp grass drying into a golden circle, two circles out from my thin, white-hot feet. I stood in a nest of electric smoke, clacked my hands together to see the sparks again.

I smiled, smiled so hard I thought the top half of my head might fly away. Wow.

"Wow!" I said. "Some say it was the end, but I *know* it was the Beginning! Some will call this the Dark Ages, but I know this will be the Age of Light."

And the grass crackled under me.

"Hey, listen," I said. "No Biggie. I can remember years ago, when not a quarter of a mile from where we're sitting now, a girl used to study down in the Gulch . . ."

"I told you they used to call it the Gulch," a voice said in the semidarkness.

"And she had these faulty electric plugs, and one night she heard this awful thing and looked up to see this frog dancing on the wire."

"Radiantly *aglow,* no shit!"

And they got the giggles. Laughter rocked them.

"And then," I said, "she found out this man was being unfaithful, and she went out into the creek and caught a frog. She lined a box with greens and stuck the frog in and sent it to his office marked *This Side Up,* and he opened it."

I sat down, and leaned forward a little, my arms in the air. I tried to remember what Lion used to say about creating a pyramid of light and putting everyone in it, keeping everyone safe.

"Now, *that frog,*" I said, "that frog had been waiting in the post office for at least three days for the opportunity to jump. And when that man opened up that harmless little box . . ."

"He jumped!"

"That's right. He jumped so far, he jumped over the desk and the switchboard and the word processor and the man said . . ." And they listened to the story and forgot everything else.

And that's how I knew that Lorna wasn't a quack and Lion wasn't a crook. That's how I knew the miracles they told us to expect had come. What a triumph, what a kick, what a beginning.

Not that I did that fire stuff often. I didn't want to and I didn't have to. They didn't need me. I just added to what they already had. But they did let me tell stories, in my turn. I use words that are pearls now, words, which—under heat—have melted from existence. I speak in a language no longer attached to what is real. How pretty those words were! Hoodoo. Tarmac. Triscuit. Television. I hope someday others will come to us, other people, other words, from the other side of the world. But if they don't that's OK. Jewels are beautiful before, during and after the time they are discovered. Our words, our lives, shine by themselves.

Here, in a short form, is what happened to the people along the beach.

Many people were killed south of Playa del Rey. Even now people don't go down there. And further inland, it was the charnel house that everybody had predicted. On the whole, they say, people got *what they expected.* The generals and the military were very hard hit. A certain kind of women and children were devastated. Fires destroyed the city and many died of thirst. The plague also raged for some months.

But, as in any catastrophe, there were the crackpots who hadn't paid much attention, the ones who, in a sense, went on playing poker through the quake. They were the dumb ones, the sissies, the .... hedonists who were too enchanted by their own lives to get excited by Death descending. Of course they also included, sometimes, the dedicated survivalists, with guns and dried fruit, and were rumored now to be engaged in vicious skirmishes, fighting over who earth.

But messengers have come to us, by foot and by boat, to say that people

The ones I know who lived were the ones who had been making love, or napping, or fixing dinner, when the End came, or the ones at the beach—who still talked about the great crystallization of the sand, the ones far out windsurfing who dove beneath the waves and felt the whole Pacific turn lukewarm, the ones whose boats were out on the far side of Catalina when it came and hove to, sailing back out of pure curiosity. And, of course, all of the scrabbling canyon weirdos, who saw the whole global collapse as just another brush fire.

As I say, the ones who decided to come *west* instead of heading east, were by and large the ones who made it. And the wackos, the ones who used their belief systems, were the ones who got control over the radiation. Control is a silly word. It was surrender, really. The ones who *relinquished* control, who took it as it came, who seem—out here at least—to have lived.

Now some people have questioned me. How come you get to tell stories? And why should we believe you can make fire, and why should we believe *your* version?!

In answer I say first, if a Caspar can destroy a world, why is it so strange that an Edith should preserve it? And then I say, mine aren't the only stories! Just take a walk out on the glass.

All you'll see are the new people buttonholing each other (except there are no more buttons, buttonholes), telling their stories. Because those who lived, lived. And there are no more false prophets, only real ones. We're in the desert again, the New Jerusalem. So if you don't believe me, ask anyone around here.

We hear bad stories of a planned "invasion" from the inland, and sometimes we are beset by fear. But I remember that we too once "invaded," coming down from our mountain home, and how afraid we were. I know now that when ragged newcomers come down—scarred and sad—the sweetest thing we see is on their faces, when they look oceanward and see that some things—haven't changed.

For the rest, we take it as it comes. We know there are things to worry about, but we are still in the grip of such relief and joy that we've come through—and we know death is so near to all of us—that we play the days away. We swim, and when the wind is right we lie in the sun; we weave baskets that aren't even near waterproof. When it rains we take shelter and doze. When the air is right and the stars shine we stay up all night and sing.

There's a woman about ten miles up the coast, they say, can work miracles and tell jokes. I wonder if it's Lorna. And little by little more old memories come back. I'll see a certain slumping little guy and rush up beside him to see if it's Hal, if he recognizes me, or I him. But what's to recognize? We've changed so much.

I should say that some girls have had some babies. Some babies are born angry or sad or marked, but mostly they're mellow.

When I say I tell stories, I mean, of course, I tell what it was like before, how there were maniacs abroad, and how heartbreak hurt the world, and some things were lost. But mostly I tell about affirming: "Everything always works out for us more exquisitely than we ever planned," or *Wu Wei;* practicing the wu wei shuffle—in fact we have a dance we do to that now, a very silly one. And we remember Norman somebody, and what he said about laughing, but I remember to tell that he was a man who believed in laughing, but who hardly ever laughed. That makes people laugh.

We sing. We sleep. Here's a story I tell, about the man who had ten thousand bees in a matchbox, and he was going to teach them to sing grand opera. Or have the Industrial Revolution. Or split the atom. Whatever. And so this guy tells a friend or a colleague or an enemy about his plans. (I draw this part out a lot. And they're all very good about laughing.) But then the friend says, *"Are you* kidding?!?! Ten thousand bees in a matchbox and *you're* going to teach them grand opera? Why you can't even, why, the difficulties are . . ." (and people chime in with all the difficulties). So finally—you know the end of the story—the guy tosses the matchbox and says, "Fuck it, it was just a hobby." I've seen them laugh for an hour straight at that one. Then someone will call out, "Well, it's all in the telling!" And that will set them off again.

Half a life before, on an acid trip in the canyon, young to middle-aged divorced wife, I'd looked in the mirror and saw myself old. Saw my father's lust and my mother's fury. Saw past that to my own lust, fury, grudge-holding, saw past that to a human soul, nice, with six eyes.

Half a life later, one brackish, sweaty, hazy, California winter day, I wanted to wash my face and scraped away some foamy scum from a tide pool in Topanga Gulch. There I was, when the ripples stopped, toothless, almost gumless, not a hair by now to be seen on my billiard head, my lids growing back in a kind of bright yellow, my nose looking very unessential, like one good poke might knock it off for good and all. But I saw someone who had tried to love men and wasn't ashamed of it, who had kept the memory of her best friend forever, who had a grandchild for each knee, who wasn't scared anymore—or hardly ever— who could, if she had to, start a fire by heating up her fingers; above all, someone who could, by low means, or any means, make people smile, laugh, remember.

OOOO -eee.

There will be those who say it never happened, that we squeaked through. Believe them if you can.

There will be those who say that the end came, I mean the END, with an avenging God and the whole shebang. And many more who say it came, and there was death and terror and weeping in the streets, and the last man on earth died in the Appalachians, of pancreatic cancer, all alone. I heard that story, and I don't think much of it. You can believe what you want to, of course. But I say there was a race of hardy laughers, mystics, crazies, who knew their real homes, or who had been drawn to this gold coast for years, and they lived through the destroying light, and on, into light ages.

You can believe who you want to. But I'm telling you, don't believe those other guys.

Believe me.

CONTRIBUTORS

Aimee Bender has published work in *The Threepenny Review* and *The Colorado Review*, and has work forthcoming in *The Massachusetts Review* and *Faultline*. She is currently studying in the fiction program at University of California, Irvine.

T.C. Boyle has written four collections and six novels, the most recent of which is *The Tortilla Curtain*.

Jenny Cornuelle is the poetry editor of *The Santa Monica Review*. Her most recent fiction has appeared in *13th Moon*, and she occasionally writes on photography for the *Los Angeles Times*.

Peter Craig's work has appeared in *The Crescent Review*, *The Greensboro Review*, and other publications. He is currently completing his first novel.

Robert Crais is the author of the best-selling Elvis Cole novels. His work is known for it humor and insight into the human condition, and Crais is being increasingly recognized for putting his own unique spin on the classic private eye paradigm. "The Man Who Knew Dick Bong" was originally written as an homage to Raymond Chandler, and, in a slightly modified form, first appeared in *Raymond Chandler's Philip Marlowe*, edited by Byron Preiss. Robert Crais lives in Los Angeles by choice.

Carol Muske Dukes (Carol Muske in poetry) has published five books of poems and her New and Selected Poems, *An Octave Above Thunder*, will be out in the fall of 1997 from Viking. Her most recent novel, *Saving St. Germ*, takes place in Los Angeles.

Harlan Ellison has been called "one of the greatest living American short story writers" by the *Washington Post*, and the *Los Angeles Times* said, "It's long past time for Harlan Ellison to be awarded the title: 20th century Lewis Carroll." In a career spanning more than 40 years, he has won more awards for the 64 books he has written on edited, the more than 1700 stories, essays, articles and newspaper columns, the two dozen teleplays and a dozen motion pictures he has created, than any other living fantasist.

Judith Freeman is the author of a collection of stories, *Family Attractions*, and three novels: *The Chinchilla Farm*, *Set for Life* (recipient of the Western Heritage Award for Best Novel), and *A Desert of Pure Feeling*. She lives in the

MacArthur Park district of Los Angeles with her husband, photographer Anthony Hernandez.

Amy Gerstler is a writer of fiction, poetry, and journalism. Viking Penguin will publish a collection of her poems entitled *Crown of Weeds* in early 1997.

Jay Gummerman is the author of a story collection, *We Find Ourselves in Moontown*, and a novel, *Chez Chance*.

Charlie Hauck is a comedy writer and the author of the novel *Artistic Differences*, published by William Morrow & Co. He is currently the executive producer of the television series *Home Improvement*.

Jim Krusoe is an Animal Technician II. He wrote this story for his creative writing class.

Michelle Latiolas teaches writing and contemporary prose as the University of Southern California. She is the author of the novel *Even Now*.

Sandra Tsing Loh's first novel *If You Lived Here, You'd Be Home Now* will be published by Riverhead Books in 1997. Loh's other books published by Riverhead include *Aliens in America* (Spring, 1997). The text of her one-person show she performed off-Broadway at Second Stage Theater, and *Depth Takes A Holiday: Essays From Lesser Los Angeles* (Spring, 1996). Loh won a 1995 Pushcart Prize in fiction, and currently writes a column for *Buzz* Magazine.

John Mandelberg works as a sales clerk in a hardware store in the San Fernando Valley, where he daydreams about narrative voice and symbolism among the nuts, bolts, rods, caps and plugs. He has lived in the Valley since he was five months old. His short stories have appeared in several literary magazines, including *Other Voices* and *Kansas Quarterly*.

John Peterson was born in Los Angeles. Currently, he lives with his wife, Kristen, in Seattle and teaches at the University of Washington, Tacoma.

Jerry Renek has had stories published in *Other Voices* and *Rabid Piñata*.

Rachel M. Resnick's work has appeared in *The Ohio Review*, *Chelsea*, *The Minnesota Review*, *The Crescent Review*, and *Bakunin*. She has had plays produced in Los Angeles and currently teaches at UCLA Extension. She also works as a private investigator. "Entertainment Tonight and Forever" is a chapter from her recently completed first novel, *Go West Young Fucked Up Chick*.

C.P. Rosenthal is the author of the Loop Trilogy, *Loop's Progress, Experiments with Life and Deaf,* and *Loop's End.* His current novel, *Elena of the Stars* is a paperback published by St. Martin's Press. He lives in Topanga Canyon with Gail Wronsky and their daughter, Marlena.

Carolyn See is the author of *Golden Days, Making History, Dreaming,* and a forthcoming novel entitled *The Handy Man.* "Light Ages" is excerpted from *Golden Days,* which will be out in paperback (University of California Press at Berkeley) this fall.

Judith Seltz moved to Los Angeles from Boston. "How to Marry a Republican" is her first published story.

Allyson Shaw teaches writing at Irvine Valley College and has appeared at Beyond Baroque and L.A.C.E. Her work has appeared in *White Walls, Grand Larceny,* and on the PBS series *The Works.*

John Steppling's fiction has appeared in *The Greensboro Review* and *North Dakota Quarterly.* He is the artistic director of the Empire Red-Lip theater company and has had plays produced in Los Angeles, New York, San Francisco, and London. He is the recipient of two NEA grants, a Pen-West award (for his play *Teenage Wedding*), and a Rockefeller Fellowship. A collection of his plays, *Sea of Cortez and Other Plays,* was published by Sun & Moon Press.

Jervey Tervalon is the author of *Understand This.* "All Along the Watch Tower" is excerpted from his new memoir.

Lawrence Thornton is the author of *Imagining Argentina, Under the Gypsy Moon, Short Woman, Naming the Spirits,* and the forthcoming *Tales of the Blue Archives,* the last volume in his Argentina trilogy.

Benjamin Weissman is the author of the story collection *Dear Dead Person* (High Risk Books / Serpent's Tale). He teaches writing at Art Center College of Design, where he is also a Graduate Advisor in the Department of Fine Art. His writings on art, books and music have appeared in *Artforum, L.A. Times Book Review,* and *Spin.*